Donna Alward lives _____ _____ _____
family, which includes _____ _____ _____
senior dog and two cra__ _____ _____ _____
of love, hope and homecoming have been translated into
several languages, hit bestseller lists and won awards, but
her favourite thing is hearing from readers! When she's
not writing she enjoys reading—of course!—knitting,
gardening, cooking... and she's a _Masterpiece Theatre_
addict. You can visit her on the web at DonnaAlward.com,
and join her mailing list at DonnaAlward.com/newsletter

Susan Mallery is the #1 _New York Times_ bestselling
author of novels about the relationships that define
women's lives—family, friendship and romance. _Library
Journal_ says, 'Mallery is the master of blending
emotionally believable characters in realistic situations,'
and readers seem to agree—forty million copies of her
books have been sold worldwide. Her warm, humorous
stories make the world a happier place to live. Susan grew
up in California and now lives in Seattle with her husband.
She's passionate about animal welfare, especially that of
the two Ragdoll cats and adorable poodle who think of her
as Mum. Visit Susan online at www.susanmallery.com

Discover more at millsandboon.co.uk

WEDDING REUNION WITH THE BEST MAN

DONNA ALWARD

BEFORE SUMMER ENDS

SUSAN MALLERY

MILLS & BOON

First Published in Great Britain 2021
by Mills & Boon, an imprint of HarperCollins*Publishers* Ltd
1 London Bridge Street, London, SE1 9GF

www.harpercollins.co.uk

HarperCollins*Publishers*
1st Floor, Watermarque Building,
Ringsend Road, Dublin 4, Ireland

Wedding Reunion with the Best Man © 2021 Donna Alward
Before Summer Ends © 2021 Susan Mallery, Inc.

ISBN: 978-0-263-29957-1

0421

MIX
Paper from
responsible sources
FSC™ C007454

This book is produced from independently certified FSC™ paper to ensure responsible forest management.

For more information visit: www.harpercollins.co.uk/green

Printed and bound in Spain
by CPI, Barcelona

WEDDING REUNION
WITH THE BEST MAN

DONNA ALWARD

CHAPTER ONE

ARABELLA PEMBERTON LIFTED her hair off her neck for a brief moment, fluttering it a bit to cool the skin beneath. Italy in July was nearly unbearable. Why William and Gabi had chosen to wed in the hottest month of the year escaped her. But here she was, in the Baresi villa in Umbria, preparing to be one of Gabi's bridesmaids. She was thrilled her little brother had found such happiness, and she adored Gabi. She just hated the heat, especially with her thick hair and ever-present long sleeves.

No one in the family ever questioned her hairstyles or her proclivity for garments that covered her past the elbows. They all knew it was to cover the scars she bore. As a Pemberton and a member of the Aurora Inc. dynasty, she was often photographed. The last thing she ever wanted was for the press to get wind of the dozens of cuts on her neck and arms. The worst were on her arms. The few on her face she covered with a precise makeup regimen. It was no accident that she now headed up the cosmetics division of Aurora Inc.

That one moment in time, the one night she'd been stupid and foolish, had now marked her forever. It had robbed her of so much, particularly in the friend and romance departments. Her worst fear was that she'd trust someone and they would share her closely guarded secret. In a business where image was everything, she didn't want to bring that kind of attention to Aurora, and, if she were being honest, she never wanted to relive that night and the weeks of pain and anguish that followed.

Which made this week particularly difficult.

She let her hair back down on her neck and fought the urge to scratch. For the entire week, Burke Phillips would be here, too. William's college chum and best man. Why William couldn't choose Stephen or Christophe to be best man was beyond her. Her brother and cousin were suitable choices. But oh, no. He had to ask Burke, because even though they hadn't seen each other in over a year, this was apparently a "thing."

She'd successfully managed to avoid Burke for the past twelve years. They'd both been seventeen, and Burke had been visiting Chatsworth Manor with his father, then the Viscount Downham. Even though William had been two years younger than Burke, the pair had hit it off. William had gone off to the same university as Burke and they had become fast friends. Until university ended, anyway, and Burke had gone his way and William had…well, William had had a rough few years.

Now Burke was here. And he was one of only two other people who understood what had happened the night she'd gotten those scars.

"Bella, are you coming down?" That was Gabi's voice, and Bella knew she was running late for lunch.

"I'll be right there," she called back. She turned from the window and checked her reflection in the mirror. It was so hot she'd actually wondered if her makeup had melted, but no, everything was still in place. While there was no air-conditioning at the villa, she couldn't deny that the room was lovely. Her window looked out over an olive grove, and the bed and furniture were absolutely beautiful. It was Gabi's sister's room, but Giulia had offered to stay with her boyfriend, Marco, to make room for some of William's family.

The Baresis were wonderful, generous, fun people.

She made her way down the steps to the bottom floor, where a table was set up buffet-style for lunch. Signora Baresi was a fabulous cook and knew how to put on a marvelous spread. Thankfully, it was also a little cooler downstairs. Bella grabbed a plate and began to fill it with an array of vegetables and meats. With a full house leading up to the wedding, the casual approach to breakfast and lunch made things ever so much easier.

She'd just grabbed herself a glass of iced water when William came through the front door to the villa, calling out to everyone. "Guess who's here?" he said, coming into the kitchen with a massive smile. "Burke! Finally. The last member of the wedding party has arrived."

Bella held her breath as Burke came in behind William, his entrance a bit more subdued than Will's ebullient introduction. "Everyone, this is Burke Phillips. Burke, these are Gabi's parents, Massimo and Lucia Baresi, and Gabi's sister, Giulia, and her boyfriend, Marco. And of course you've met my family before. Stephen and Maman are in Perugia today, but you know Christophe, and my sisters Charlotte and Bella."

Bella was last, and Burke's gaze lingered on her. Even that much was too much. It didn't matter that it had been over a decade. He knew. He knew what had happened and he knew the horror of it, and it showed in his eyes as they looked at each other.

"Bella," he said softly.

"Hello, Burke."

Will was oblivious to everything but his happiness, so he pulled Burke ahead and Burke shook hands with everyone and then he was given a plate. Food was truly a language of love here, she realized, standing to the side while conversation and laughter filled the room. Massimo, now through his cancer treatments and remarkably robust, was already expounding on the greatness of Umbrian meats to Burke, who had a shocking amount of food on his plate. It was their way of making him welcome, she realized. The Baresis were wonderful. No wonder Stephen and William had warmed to them so much.

She found a slightly quieter corner in which to sit, and picked at the food on her plate. It was a surprise, then, when a shadow appeared at her shoulder and Burke's voice touched her ears.

"May I join you, Bella?"

It was the only free seat in the room; how could she deny him? "Please do," she invited, not unkindly, but not enthusiastically, either.

An awkward silence fell over them, making Bella shift in her seat. "Your trip was satisfactory?" she asked, then chided herself for sounding so stilted.

"It was fine. A hop, skip and a jump to Italy, anyway. You?"

"Most of us arrived two days ago. I'm sure the Baresis will be glad when the commotion is over."

He looked over at the table, where Signora Baresi was laughing. "Maybe. But they seem to be enjoying it so far."

"They wouldn't hear of us staying at a hotel."

"I know. I'm at Marco's with William. No keeping the bride and groom together, I guess."

At least they wouldn't be under the same roof.

He picked at his food and then looked up at her, his dark eyes assessing. "You look good, Bella."

Heat crept up her already too-warm neck. "Thank you. I hear you're working in London at the moment."

"Yes, at St. Thomas's."

It had surprised her to hear that Burke had gone on to become a doctor and then pursued a cardiac specialty. It was a rather serious profession for a boy who'd been keen on partying and who had every advantage, including money and title. For he wasn't just Burke Phillips anymore, he was also Viscount Downham.

"You like it there?"

"I do. Very much."

"And do they address you as milord?" She was only half teasing, and his smile faded as his gaze held hers.

"No," he replied. "Bella, I know that—"

"I shouldn't have asked that," she interrupted. "It was rude of me. Sorry." No longer hungry, she rose and took her plate with her. "I just remembered I have a fitting this afternoon. Enjoy your lunch."

She walked away, her tummy quivering not only because it was Burke but because she'd just told a bald-faced lie about being busy. She didn't want him to be nice to her. Didn't want him to be here at all. For the rest of the week, she'd have to try to avoid him. But she could do it, because she was used to making adjustments to avoid unpleasant situations. She doubted her family even noticed anymore, she'd become so adept at it. Of all the Pembertons, she was the one most in the background, and that was just how she liked it. Let Stephen and Charlotte be the faces in the magazines and online. She was content behind the scenes, working for the company she loved. Holding things together.

It was one week. She'd built the life she wanted—well, mostly wanted—and she wouldn't let Burke mess that up for her. No matter how handsome or charming he was.

For the rest of the afternoon, Bella stayed in her unbearably hot room, laptop open, answering work emails and sending instructions to her assistant. The new cosmetics line, Naturel, had launched earlier in the year and was doing very well. It was the first line for Aurora that was completely vegan and responsibly sourced, and Bella was hugely proud of that. It was also the first real innovation she'd been in charge of at the company, and so she wanted to keep tabs on everything that was happening in the division. She tried very hard to pull her weight. All of them did, really. It still surprised her that Maman had given each child a position of great responsibility, but she always said that her children would rise to the task. It was great to have that faith, but it was also scary as heck. None of them wanted to fail and disappoint the great Aurora Germain-Pemberton.

Dinner was another lively, large affair. Huge dishes of vegetable-stuffed cannelloni filled the table, along with the ever-present bread. Everyone filled their plates and then went outside to the patio, where several tables had been put together to form one very long banquet-style table. Wine bottles punctuated the tabletop, both red and white so people could choose depending on preference. Bella found herself next to Charlotte, who passed on the wine. "Do you miss it?" Bella asked with a smile as she poured a vibrant red into her glass.

Charlotte touched her tummy, which had a small but noticeable bump. "Not really. It's worth it."

Charlotte was absolutely radiant in her pregnancy. "When does Jacob arrive?" Charlotte and Jacob were still glowing from their garden wedding only a month earlier.

"Thursday. He's working until then."

Conversation halted as Massimo made a toast, and then everyone dug in. As Bella ate, she pondered Charlotte and Jacob's relationship. It had been a whirlwind that resulted in a surprise pregnancy, but her sister was blissfully happy. So was William, with Gabi. And Bella was more than happy for them, but seeing her siblings step into marital bliss made her painfully aware that she probably never would.

And that was on her. To be in an intimate relationship meant letting someone see all the ugliness. No thanks.

The somber thought guided her gaze down the table

to where Burke sat, close to William. She could tell the
two were recounting some of their exploits as students,
and those seated around them were laughing. She took
the time to study him. He'd grown from a slightly lanky,
good-looking boy to a devastatingly handsome man. His
dark hair held a hint of curl that gave him a boyish look,
and his golden-brown eyes were more serious than she remembered. Or if not more serious… She paused. Today,
when she'd looked at him, she'd sensed depths that made
her wonder what joys and sorrows he'd experienced, because his eyes were…soulful, she realized. It was what
made him hard to resist.

Perhaps he still had his own scars from that night.

"Bella? Aren't you going to eat?"

Charlotte's voice drew her back to the present. She
hadn't even touched her food, so she dutifully cut into the
cannelloni and took a scrumptious bite. "Sorry," she said,
after she'd chewed and swallowed. "I got distracted."

"By Burke? He's very handsome."

"No, not by Burke," she replied, a little sharply. "It's just
a lot of people. That's all."

Charlotte's brows pulled together and Bella knew why.
They were almost always around a lot of people and it had
never bothered Bella before, as long as she was covered.
Now she'd lied to her sister and Charlotte had seen right
through it.

When dinner was over, Bella insisted on helping clean
up. She needed something to keep her busy and out of
Burke's sphere.

It was going to be a long week, wasn't it?

Burke watched as Bella escaped into the house with Signora
Baresi and Giulia on the premise of helping clean up after
the meal. There'd been nearly a dozen of them for dinner,

and the mess was no trifling matter. He rose from his seat and started collecting empty wine bottles.

"You don't need to help," William said, looking up at him with a smile.

Burke raised an eyebrow. "Well, Mr. Lord of the Manor, there's no staff here, is there? And I'm too enlightened to think this is something that is left to the women."

"Going to get dishpan hands, are we?"

Burke hesitated. "Probably not. I don't think your sister wants me anywhere near the kitchen right now."

William's eyes lost their teasing and he looked Burke in the eye. "I had hoped it wouldn't be this way. She's avoided you for ten years."

"Twelve, really, but who's counting?"

He gave up picking up bottles and sat beside William. He, too, had hoped that things wouldn't be awkward between him and Bella. "Will, I don't know what to say to her. We've never talked about the accident."

"I don't know, Burke," William said thoughtfully. "Part of me thinks you should come right out and deal with it together. Another part says let it alone."

"Same," Burke replied with a sigh. He waited a moment and then said what had been on his mind since arriving in Italy. "Did you ask me to be your best man so that I would have to talk to her?"

William shook his head. "Actually, I almost *didn't* ask you for that very reason. But it's my wedding. My only wedding, and I wanted you to be part of it. You've been my friend through so much."

"Not always. Not when you were in rehab."

"Not your fault I didn't tell you what a mess I was in. And you were in med school at the time. You would have been there if I'd asked. I was too ashamed, and so that's on me."

Burke looked at his friend and admired all he'd overcome to be the whole, happy human being he was now. Certainly more whole than Burke was at the moment. He couldn't fault Arabella for hanging on to the memories of the accident when he hadn't been able to escape them, either.

A boy had died. Arabella had been in hospital for weeks. And Burke and the other girl, Fiona, had sustained their own minor injuries.

He should have stopped Royce from driving that night. Should have kept Bella from getting in the car. Hell, he and Fiona shouldn't have tagged along. But they had all been young and bulletproof.

"She's never forgiven me for the accident," Burke said quietly.

William didn't answer. He looked as if he wanted to say something but was holding back. "What is it?" Burke asked.

"Nothing. Honestly, this is between you and Bella. If you two decide to talk it out this week, great. If not, I'm still thrilled you're here as my best man. Maybe you could try to not be so serious for once, as well. Take off your doctor face and have a good time. We're in Italy, man. Great food, wonderful company…a wedding. Lighten up a bit."

Irritation flared but Burke tamped it down. It wasn't that William was wrong, it was that turning off that driven part of him wasn't like flicking off a light switch. He needed time to wind down. It was hard to do that when Bella was right in front of him, a reminder of why he'd gone into medicine in the first place.

"I'll try," was all he said, and he got up again to finish collecting the bottles. "I'll take these inside."

When he entered the kitchen, he walked into a bunch of happy chatter that made him pause as a warm feeling settled over him. It reminded him of his two sisters and his mother, taking over the kitchen from the staff to bake Christmas cookies or a special birthday cake. The sound of their laughter had made him feel secure at a time when everything was chaos in his brain. First, the accident. And then, while he was in college, the aneurysm that had taken his father suddenly and brutally, shoving Burke into the role of viscount. And Lord, all the secrets in between. It was the secrets that ate at him the most.

He'd become responsible for the family at a time he was barely responsible for himself, and carried the secrets with him. Not a single person in the world knew that he'd discovered his father's affair, taking the man from hero in Burke's eyes to a cheat and a liar. It had been a heavy, heavy burden. Still was, even now.

But that happy laughter, the warm sound of female voices chatting over a menial task…it was healing in a "life goes on and everything's okay" way. It was how his mother had gotten them through those early days of grief, and something about it wrapped around his heart and squeezed.

"Burke?" Gabi appeared before him.

"Hmm?"

"Thanks for bringing the wine bottles in. Hey, Bella, can you show Burke to the pantry? We can put the empty bottles in there until later."

"Oh, uh, sure," Bella replied, and wiped her hands on a dish towel. She didn't meet his eyes, but instead led the way to a small room off the kitchen that held a shop's worth of merchandise, it seemed.

He followed her inside, and she pointed to an empty shelf. "I guess you can put them there."

He moved to put them on the shelf and bobbled one; she rushed forward and took it from his hands before placing it carefully beside the others. "Thanks," he murmured.

"You're welcome."

The close atmosphere of the pantry lent an intimacy to the moment that was unexpected. When Bella turned to leave, he reached out and caught her wrist lightly. "Bella, wait. Please."

She stilled. Not in a comfortable way, but like an animal that was trapped. Why? Was she so angry at him that the very idea of being in a room with him repulsed her?

"I should get back."

"Just give me one minute. Please, Bella. We haven't spoken since—"

"I know since when," she interrupted sharply. "We don't need to discuss it."

"Yes," he said firmly, "we do. Because ever since then you've avoided me and even now you can't meet my eyes."

She looked up at him, dark eyes sharp and defiant. So she could look at him. But with annoyance that built a shield. Nothing vulnerable. Guilt threaded through him again at the knowledge that he could have prevented what had happened if he'd been more responsible.

"I'm sorry," he said simply. "That is what I wanted to say. I'm sorry I failed everyone that night. I should never have allowed Royce to get behind the wheel. I shouldn't have gotten in that car and I should have kept you from getting into it, too."

She looked away. So much for meeting his eyes.

"Thank you for your apology," she muttered, pulling her wrist away from his fingers.

That was all he was going to get. A thank-you but no absolving him of the part he'd played. Not just the accident but the events of the evening leading up to it. Finally giving her the apology she deserved did nothing to alleviate his guilt or remorse. If anything, he felt worse.

She went to the door of the pantry, putting extra space between them. "Thank you for apologizing. But some things you just can't undo, Burke."

She left him standing there, more conflicted than ever.

CHAPTER TWO

THE FOLLOWING DAY Bella went with Gabi, Charlotte, and Giulia into Perugia to shop. It was a relief to get away from the villa for a while—and any thought of Burke. Today's excursion schedule was a final fitting for their dresses, a boutique where they planned to splurge on lingerie, lunch, and picking up the tiny organza bags that contained wedding favors—sugared almonds—for each guest.

Bella loved her dress. All three bridesmaids had similar dresses, the same pale blue chiffon, but each had chosen a favored neckline and sleeve and one of the Aurora designers had done the rest. Charlotte, with her gorgeous collarbones, slim shoulders and slightly popping belly, had picked an Empire waist style with cute cap sleeves that fluttered. Giulia, the youngest of them all and with a slightly athletic shape, went for a halter-style that tied at the nape of her neck and sent ribbons of chiffon cascading down her back. Bella had gone with a soft vee that plunged to her cleavage, and long sleeves that came to narrow cuffs at her wrist but stayed cool due to the filmy fabric. Each dress fell to the floor in delicate folds, and they'd all be wearing shoes that Charlotte had designed and had made for the occasion. Bella wouldn't be surprised if Charlotte spearheaded a footwear line at Aurora one of these days, leaving her PR title behind.

Charlotte knew Bella's reason for the long sleeves, and there were times Bella wondered if Will had told Gabi and Giulia because neither woman had asked, even though sleeves during summer was a bit odd. She didn't want to inquire, though, because if he hadn't said anything, she would then have to explain.

Once they were all dressed, they stepped out together and Gabi put her hand to her mouth.

"Oh, you all look beautiful!" She glanced at the seamstress. "What do you think? Is that a little pucker in Charlotte's bodice?"

Charlotte sighed. "Ugh. My figure changes every day, I think! If it's not my belly, it's my breasts."

Bella laughed. "And you love every minute of it."

"I do," Charlotte admitted. "Especially now that the queasiness has gone."

The seamstress had her let out a breath and then made an adjustment. "That should do it," she remarked, stepping back and nodding with approval. "You—" she pointed at Giulia "—are at that glorious age that makes a sack look wonderful. Yours is perfect." She turned her attention to Bella, and Bella's stomach twisted. She hoped there wouldn't be anything intrusive. She should have taken the dress home and let Maman do the pinning. Bella was adept enough she could do the alterations herself.

"The waist is still slightly too big."

Bella looked at the woman and said confidently, "No more than a quarter of an inch."

"*Si, si.* You are right." Thankfully the woman didn't come closer with her pins and get up close and personal.

"I don't want to take it off," Giulia admitted. "It's so beautiful."

"And you'll be able to wear it in a few days," Gabi said. "The flowers are going to look gorgeous with it."

Bella couldn't help but get swept away in the excited energy. Giulia did a swirl with her skirt, revealing the creamy white heels, and said, "And I get to be on Burke's arm. He is *molto bello*." She wiggled her eyebrows a little and laughed.

Bella's Italian wasn't great, but she came back with a dry, *"Bello è altrettanto bello."*

Handsome is as handsome does.

The women burst out laughing. Charlotte nudged Bella's arm. "Come on, Bel. You have to admit he's pretty gorgeous. And I think he likes you. Otherwise what were you doing in the pantry last night?"

Bella, having grown up with two brothers, a sister and a cousin, was no stranger to sibling teasing. Though her stomach twisted anxiously, she answered with a "wouldn't you like to know?" And then, at the increased laughter, she added, "Don't worry. Nothing happened that kept me up at night."

Nothing except that apology. He'd been so sincere, and she'd wanted to say it was okay. She didn't blame him for what happened. And yet she lived with the scars every day, and truthfully, she just didn't want to have to deal with him at all.

After the fittings they went to the lingerie boutique. While they each shopped for themselves, the three bridesmaids had agreed that they wanted to buy Gabi a nightgown for her wedding night. After several gowns had gone into the change room, Gabi finally found the one she wanted. "It's…well…" she said from behind the curtain, her voice a little hesitant.

"Come out," Giulia said. "We want to see it."

Again with a slightly nervous laugh. But Gabi pushed aside the curtain and the three women stood speechless for five full seconds.

"Dio mio!" This from Giulia. "Gabriella. That is going to knock his eyeballs out."

Bella looked at the gown with envy. It was a flowy column of sheer lace, with a narrow halter tie at the neck and a back that dipped right to Gabi's tailbone. There were no panels of solid material to cover anything, though a tiny bit of the lace pattern appeared to hide Gabi's nipples and she wore simple thong underwear. It was the sexiest thing Bella had ever seen.

She tried to imagine wearing such a thing and knew she never would. Not with the marks crisscrossing her arms. Or the one on the back of her neck. She didn't begrudge Gabi a moment of this. But she could be happy for her friend and soon-to-be sister-in-law and still harbor a little resentment toward life's circumstances.

"It's amazing, Gabi," she said. "I mean, I don't necessarily like thinking of my brother in times like this, but Giulia's right. His tongue is going to hit the floor."

Gabi blushed. "If there's any night I'd really like to surprise him, this is it."

"Then it's yours, from us," Charlotte decreed. "Our wedding gift to you."

They took their bags and stored everything in the trunk of Gabi's car, then headed to lunch at a small restaurant in Perugia's historic district where they dined on mixed salad, gnocchi with saffron and truffles, and a *semifreddo* with Perugia's signature Baci chocolates. As they finished with strong coffee, Bella found herself hoping tonight's dinner was on the lighter side. Especially if her dress was to be taken in for the wedding.

One last errand for the sugared almond wedding favors and they were on their way back to the Baresi villa.

When they arrived, the family was outside on the patio, and Stephen, William, Burke, and Marco were in the pool, cooling off. There was little swimming going on; instead, the men each had a floating chair and they were holding drinks in their hands, the picture of total relaxation.

"You're back! Come in. Water's perfect."

Charlotte shut down the challenge. "The last time I was in a pool with you two, you dunked me under water. No thanks."

"And I just had my hair colored yesterday. No pool water for me," said Gabi.

Giulia stepped up. "I will. Just let me change."

"How about you, Bella?" That was from Burke.

The patio seemed to go quiet, and Bella knew why, but she smiled and politely declined. "No thanks. Though I might dip my toes in."

"Spoilsport."

She laughed. "I've been called worse."

They took their packages inside, then returned to the patio for cool drinks in the shade. A light breeze blew over the hilltop, cooling the sheen of sweat on Bella's chest and arms. How she wished she really didn't care about her scars and could just slip on a bathing suit like Giulia and jump into the water without a care in the world. If it were just her siblings, she would. But not in front of people who weren't family. Who hadn't already seen.

When the heat was nearly unbearable, she went poolside and did indeed slip her feet into the water. The water came halfway up her calves, and she decided that later tonight she'd sneak out and go for a swim after dark. Nothing was so noticeable then, and everyone would be in bed. Maybe it would help her sleep better. Last night she'd had a fan to at least create some air movement, but she'd still slept without any covers and just her light nightgown.

Burke swam over and looked up at her, water sparkling on his lashes. "You sure you won't come in?"

"This is perfect," she replied. "And no having to mess with my hair afterward."

"I know, I have that problem, too," he quipped, running his hand over his short curls. She couldn't help it, she laughed.

Then he swam away, dipping under the water like a playful seal and emerging twenty feet away, directly beneath William's floating chair, sending William tumbling into the water.

Everyone burst out laughing at William's yell and subsequent spluttering as he surfaced, rubbing his hand over his face.

Burke looked over at her and winked, and despite the cool water on her legs, she went warm all over.

No, she told herself. *Not again.*

Twelve years ago, she'd been so taken with him. The ripe age of seventeen, a summer party, a handsome boy, both of them enjoying their last weeks before university. He'd been an incorrigible flirt but hadn't paid a whit of attention to her. He'd found a chum in William, and all the girls at the party had been curious and fawning over him. It had stung more than a little that he'd flirted with everyone *but* her.

Bella had tried twice to engage him in conversation, but he'd listened with half an ear, nodding politely and not really paying attention. She'd tossed her hair over her shoulder and sent him come-hither looks. Nothing.

So for him to wink at her now hurt, when she would have given anything for a smattering of attention from him as a teenager.

There was a huge splash as Marco picked up Giulia and threw her in the pool, and Bella got up before she ended up getting a good soaking. And just as she had yesterday, she escaped inside with the excuse of keeping tabs on work, while she felt the gazes of everyone on her back.

She went back to the pool when she was fairly sure everyone was in bed. William's car was still here, and she imagined he was stealing moments with Gabi, since they were staying in different houses until the big day. But the house was silent, and she tiptoed out dressed in her bathing suit with a light robe over top and carrying a towel. An elastic band was around her wrist; once she was at the pool she'd anchor her mass of hair into a messy bun to keep it from being cumbersome.

The lights outside were off, which suited her just fine. There was enough moonlight to guide her way, and she shrugged out of her robe, leaving it draped across a chair. She put the towel on the seat and slipped out of her sandals. Then she stepped quietly into the water, holding on to the stair railing and easing herself into the cool relief it provided.

Oh, heavenly. The cloying heat that was in the top floor of the Baresi villa disappeared from her skin as the cool water instantly soothed. She anchored her hair as best she could, though small tendrils still trailed along her neck and framed her face. With a sigh, Bella sank up to her shoulders, closing her eyes and loving the soft way the water moved over her skin.

She struck out in a gentle crawl, headed to the other end of the pool, then turned and swam back again. She changed to a breaststroke and kept swimming lengths until she was breathing hard and had had enough exertion. Then she lay on her back and floated, staring up at the stars.

"I didn't think you were the kind to indulge in midnight swims," came a voice, and she broke her float and stood in the pool, startled to be caught when she had been sure there was no one around. The water came to her chest; she quickly bent her legs so it covered her to her neck and made it look as if she were treading water.

Burke. "What are you doing here? I mean, aren't you supposed to be at Marco's?"

He went to the edge of the pool and sat, casually pulled his sandals off, and put his feet in the water just as she had earlier. "Marco left with Giulia, Christophe, and Stephen. Your mother has gone to bed, and William asked if I'd hang around so we could drive back together later. I said sure and took the opportunity to go for a late stroll in the olive groves."

She frowned. "Why would he ask you to stay?" Once it was out of her mouth, she knew it sounded rude and heat crept up her cool cheeks.

Burke merely raised an eyebrow. "Accountability, apparently. Might be a little too easy to 'fall asleep' and end up staying over. If he still has to take me back to Marco's…"

She couldn't help it, she snickered a little. "I can't believe what a stickler William is being for this kind of thing."

"I know. In uni he was always up for some trouble. Now he's on the straight and narrow." Burke leaned back on his hands and moved his feet in the water, creating little waves that purled over his feet. "But he'll do anything for Gabi, and this is what she wants, so here I am, putting in time, just like I used to when he'd end up with some girl at a pub and I'd be left—"

"With your own girl," she finished for him, a smile curving her lips. "Will's told me the stories, too, you know. If you're going to play all innocent, at least pick someone who might believe you."

She was teasing him and probably shouldn't be. After all, she was stuck in the pool until he moved on. Even in the moonlight, the ugly crisscross of scars would be visible. She didn't want him to see them. Ever.

He was laughing now, the sound warm and smooth, like the amaretto she'd sipped after dinner tonight. The sound faded away in the soft breeze, and her stomach started getting all swirly…both with nerves that he wasn't going to leave, and with anticipation of him staying.

And yet long ago, he'd been the one to turn away and barely look at her. Maybe he didn't deserve her attention now.

And maybe, just maybe, she should stop having hurt

feelings about that night. They'd been kids and he hadn't been into her. So what? What happened after he'd shunned her had been a hundred percent her decision, after all.

"Aren't you getting cold?"

She shook her head quickly. "Actually, no. My room is on the top floor and very hot. I came out to cool off and hopefully sleep a little better."

He nodded. "William said Gabi's been after her father to install air-conditioning for years."

"It's no big deal. I just thought a swim would be perfect."

"Hmm." He tapped his lips. "Maybe I should join you."

Her good humor turned to ice as her body froze. "You don't have your swimsuit on."

He pulled his feet out of the water and started to stand. "Who needs a swimsuit?"

Bella's lips dropped open in dismay. "You are not coming in here...without clothes."

"Bella. Would I do such a thing?"

That was the problem. She didn't really know, and her own mind and body betrayed her because she desperately wanted to find out. Burke pulled his T-shirt off and dropped it on the same chair as her towel and robe. He reached into his pocket and pulled out his wallet and phone, putting them on top of his T-shirt. And then he jumped in the water with a giant splash.

He was in the pool with her. In his shorts, thank God. But still. The wave from his plunge went over her shoulder and into her surprised mouth, and she coughed and spluttered. "I can't believe you did that!" she exclaimed when he surfaced about ten feet away. She coughed again.

His grin was boyish and his close-cropped curls were flat and dark against his head. "I haven't done anything impulsive in a long time. If this is the extent of my surprising behavior, I think I'm still okay."

"You're crazy."

"Probably."

She had to get out of the pool. She was actually enjoying this, but it was too risky. The last thing she needed was for Burke to get too close. To see her skin. To ask questions.

"I—I need to go," she said, backing up a few steps. But she backed up in the wrong direction and stepped onto the slope of where the deep end started. Her foot slipped and she lost her balance, sliding under the water briefly before popping back up. To her dismay, Burke was less than three feet away, reaching for her with his hand.

"I'm fine. Just slipped on the bottom."

He took another step and circled her wrist with his fingers. "That's okay. I've got you." He gave her arm a slight tug and pulled her closer. His dark eyes found hers, and a snap of attraction flashed between them. No. This wasn't okay. She shouldn't want him so much.

"Let me go, Burke."

He did. As soon as she made the request, he dropped her arm and her feet touched the bottom again. Bella knew she should move away, so why wasn't she? She was standing now, with her shoulders above the water, and his gaze dropped to her skin and his lips opened in shock.

"Arabella."

The way he said her name hit her like a brick. "No," she said firmly, starting to walk away, the resistance of the water against her legs making it slower going than she wanted. "I need to go in."

This time he followed her and when he reached for her arm, he didn't let go. "Bella. That…that's what happened to you?"

"Don't," she said. "I already hear the pity in your voice and I don't want it."

"Too bad," he said firmly. "And I'm not pitying you, not really. It doesn't mean I can't be sorry that this happened."

She met his gaze. "When we crashed, I was foolish. I

could feel us start to flip and I covered my head with my arms, like I would on a plane, you know? So when the windows shattered, all the glass went into my arms and the back of my neck. Thank God the airbag didn't deploy. I would have taken the brunt of that force right on my head."

He wasn't touching her now. The ladder was only a half dozen steps away, but she stayed where she was. Maybe it was time to not run and just say it. "The glass left me with scars that will never go away. The few on my face are smaller and I had plastic surgery, and I cover them as best I can."

"I never noticed."

"That's very deliberate."

Quiet fell between them for a few moments, and then finally he asked, his voice soft with concern, "Do they still hurt?"

She shook her head, feeling a familiar stinging behind her eyes and willing it away. "No. Actually, the scar tissue makes it so I don't have as much sensitivity there as I might otherwise. It's kind of…numb."

"And that's why you always wear the long sleeves. And your hair down."

He'd noticed. She nodded.

He turned away briefly, the water swishing along his rib cage. Bella gave him time. After all, he'd been in the car, too. He must have some memories of that night.

"I didn't see you when the ambulance came."

"You were unconscious. It…" She swallowed. "It scared me something awful. I was afraid you were dead like…like Royce." She hated when that image flashed into her head. Royce had been the one to finally take an interest in her and she'd returned the interest just to show Burke what he was missing.

"The girl I was with, Fiona. She just had minor injuries."

"Yeah. But you and I…we were on the side that took the

impact of the roll." Her heart rate was climbing as it always did if she let herself go back to that night. "And Royce... he didn't wear his seat belt."

She could see the crash site as if it were yesterday. The crumpled car. Fiona screaming in panic. Royce's body and Burke unresponsive. Her own blood. Bella started to shake. "I can't do this," she said quickly, rushing to the steps. She climbed out and ran to the chair with the towel, but Burke was close behind her.

"Bella, stop. Wait."

She grabbed the towel and tried to dry herself quickly so she could cover herself with her robe again. Her loose bun was now drooping nearly to her neck, lopsided, and she wished the blasted moon would go beneath a cloud rather than glowing down on them like a spotlight.

He retrieved her robe and gently put it over her shoulders, as if he understood her panic. The gentleness of it nearly tore her apart. Her family knew. They'd gone through the pain of recovery with her. But she had no desire to let anyone else in. It was too...ugly.

And then he did something utterly unexpected. He folded her into his arms.

His skin was cold from the water, and yet there was a heat to his body that she couldn't deny, even as the water from his skin dampened spots on her robe. She held her body stiffly, unsure of what to do with the compassionate contact, for it truly was kind and not sexual. Maybe sexual would have been easier to fight against.

"I'm sorry," he murmured close to her ear. "I'm so sorry."

"I said I don't want your pity." She attempted to pull away, but he tightened his arms.

"That's not what I mean. That night..."

And then he let out a shuddering sigh and she realized that she needed to consider he had been hurt as well. So she tentatively put her arms around his waist and let him hug her.

When he finally let her go, she looked up at him and squared her shoulders. "I don't want to talk about this again," she said firmly. "It's over and it's done. I'm fine, you see. So let's just get through this wedding and then you'll go back to your life at the hospital and I'll go back to mine in Paris and that will be that."

His eyes clouded with confusion. "Bella, I—"

"No, Burke. Please."

And then she turned and finally ran away, back into the house and upstairs to her room, where she took off her robe, stared at the white slashes of scar tissue, and cried.

CHAPTER THREE

BURKE WAS SITTING on the chair, his head in his hands, when William finally came out of the house at nearly 1:00 a.m.

"Sorry I took so long. I'm a horrible friend."

Burke looked up and tried a smile. "It's fine. It's your wedding in a few days. You're entitled."

William's smile faded. "What's wrong?"

Burke wasn't sure what to say. He put off answering by getting up and tucking the chair back under the table. William started laughing. "Your shorts are wet. Did you fall in the pool?"

"I jumped in. After your sister."

William's laugh came to an abrupt halt. "With Bella? And you survived?"

Burke finally met William's gaze, and he found himself more than a bit angry. "You should have told me, Will."

They started walking toward Will's car. "You saw, then." Will's voice was guarded.

"She didn't want me to. I had no idea. That she…" He couldn't speak for a moment.

He'd tried not to show his shock, but the scars were so angry. They slashed across her skin at random angles, from her elbows to her shoulders. When she'd turned away, he'd seen one particularly bright gash on her neck. She'd been lucky it hadn't gone deeper. Even so, even in the dark he could tell it had been big enough that it had required several stitches.

He stopped and stared at Will. "We're supposed to be best friends. I was in that accident, too, Will. For God's sake, maybe I could have helped her or something!"

Will turned on him, his eyes bright. "She's my sister and she asked that we not tell a soul. I couldn't betray that request, Burke, not even for you. Not when she'd been through so much."

His stomach churned. "How much?"

"A concussion, all the stitches, several plastic surgeries. When you were released you went home with your family. Any time I saw you after that, it was in London, never at Chatsworth."

"I was too much of a coward to go back. Not for a long time, and when I finally did, Bella was never there."

"She made sure she wasn't."

That knowledge hit Burke square in the chest. She'd been avoiding him all this time. Nothing had been coincidental. No wonder her reception had been so cool, and she'd had such trouble with his apology in the pantry. His guilt doubled.

"When you asked after Bella, I said what we always said—that she was fine. Because she was. She is."

But Burke wasn't sure he agreed. Was someone who wore long sleeves even in the hottest days, who never put their hair up because of scars, actually fine? Or just pretending?

"Bella is a grown woman who can handle things her own way," William added. "It's her body."

In that Burke was in complete agreement. "You're right," he relented, releasing the tension in his shoulders. "I just…it was a shock, Will. I barely recall the accident but I remember waking up in the hospital and being so scared, hearing that Royce had died and afraid the girls had, too. None of us should have been in the car that night."

"That's true," William said. "But you weren't driving. You didn't cause the crash."

"I got in the car," Burke argued, "instead of stopping Royce when I knew he'd been drinking." Even if at the time he'd thought he'd done it for what he thought were the right reasons, it had been a huge mistake.

They'd arrived at William's car and Will stopped and put his hand on Burke's shoulder. "Look, if any of us blamed you, we wouldn't be such close friends. It was a stupid thing that happened when kids were being stupid. People have suffered enough. And you know that because I've told you that before."

"It doesn't stop the guilt, though."

"I know that feeling."

Burke knew it to be true. Their friendship had truly faltered for a few years when Will went off the rails, drinking and doing drugs. Nothing Burke could say would make Will change. In the end, it was William's brother who got him into rehab. One of the first people William had apologized to when he got out was Burke, and their friendship had healed.

"I'm sorry, Will. I'm sorry for what happened then and I'm sorry that Bella has had to endure this ever since."

"Don't feel sorry for Bella. She's a stubborn woman, smart, successful. She doesn't let what happened slow her down or keep her from getting what she wants."

As they got into the car, Burke wondered if that were true. Sure, Bella had made her decisions, but today she'd avoided the pool because of her scars, suffering in the heat instead. She'd only gone to the pool after dark when she'd be alone. He got the feeling that Bella held herself back more than people thought.

Once back at the villa owned by Marco's family, Burke

escaped to his room and shed the damp shorts, hanging them over a chair to dry. He got into bed and stared at the ceiling, thinking about Bella and wishing they'd talked long ago. He was sure she still held on to the trauma of that night; her blatant refusal to talk about it said that loud and clear. Had she gone through therapy? People handled things in different ways. He had his mum to thank for booking him sessions with a therapist when he'd started having nightmares in the months following the accident. And going into medicine wasn't a random thing. He'd felt such a burning need to help people after he'd experienced competent, loving care from his doctors and nurses.

How had Bella handled it all? Beyond covering her scars as if they didn't exist?

The thought kept him up long into the night.

For the next two days, Burke noticed that Bella did whatever she could to avoid being near him. She either sought protection in a group, which wasn't difficult considering the number of people around, or disappeared with the excuse of keeping up with work. Oddly enough, the other Pemberton family members didn't seem half as concerned with work as she did.

On Thursday, Charlotte's husband, Jacob, arrived from London. Burke took one look at him, looked at Will, and said, "That guy looks like a Viking."

"He can kick your ass," Christophe said, moving to stand by Burke's other side.

Burke snorted, still watching as the big blond captured Charlotte in a hug. "He's the bodyguard, right?"

"Former SAS. We hired his firm to watch over Charlotte during Fashion Week last February."

Burke couldn't contain his grin. "He did that and then some, it looks like. Charlotte's beaming. Good for them."

"Come on, I'll introduce you. He's really a very nice guy."

Introductions were made, including a very firm handshake, and then Stephen said, "I guess we can have our stag night now that Jacob's finally here."

William turned his head in confusion. "Stag night? I didn't think we were doing that."

Burke grinned and clapped William on the shoulder. "Of course we are. It's my sacred duty as best man, after all. I have it all planned. Jacob, I hope you haven't put your passport away."

At William's stunned look, Burke burst out laughing. "Don't worry. We're not going to do anything that'll get you in trouble with your bride." There'd be none of that foolishness with women and last chances to sow wild oats. Those careless, selfish acts could ruin relationships.

Giulia bounced over. "And we're having what Bella has called a hen night, anyway. Marco helped us set it up at a vineyard near Siena. One of his friends."

Burke's gaze flew to where Bella was standing, wearing a pair of skinny white jeans and a flowy top that draped over her arms. She hadn't spoken to him since dashing off from the pool in the moonlight. Today she'd pulled her hair back from her face but the rest of her dark waves fell down her back, like an inky waterfall. She was so beautiful. Perhaps even more beautiful to him now that he understood all she'd endured.

As if she felt his eyes on her, she turned and their gazes met. That electrifying jolt of recognition was still between them. How inconvenient. As she looked away and spoke to Signora Baresi, he realized that being attracted to her wasn't what he wanted at all. What he wanted was absolution. But how could he ask for it when she had to live with her scars every day? It was hardly fair.

A hand clapped him on the back and he turned to find Will smiling at him. "A stag? You and your surprises."

Burke shook away the thoughts of Bella and smiled at his happy friend. "Tuxedos required," he replied. "We're headed to Monte Carlo. You'd better go pack and include a lucky charm."

Bella looked around her at the gorgeous vineyard and let out a sigh as the tension drained from her body. For the next eighteen hours, the female portion of the bridal party was going to be enjoying a wine and spa trip to get ready for the wedding. She had her own room—with air-conditioning—that overlooked the stunning Tuscan hills. Soon the Pemberton and Baresi ladies would be pampered with their choice of treatments: facials, manicures, pedicures, massages, wraps…whatever their hearts desired. There was a hot tub and a sauna as well, and a gorgeous dinner planned.

Bella knew that a typical hen night might include pub hopping and a more…unrestrained atmosphere. But when she and Charlotte had asked Giulia what Gabi would want, Giulia had known exactly what to do.

That's what sisters did, really. They knew each other. So she sought out her own.

Bella found Charlotte sitting outside on a patio, the light breeze ruffling her hair as she sipped a glass of sparking water. "I think Giulia and Gabi are still getting settled," Charlotte said. "You know it's cruel for Jacob to arrive only for us to be dragged apart again."

Bella smiled. "After the wedding you'll be together all the time. How are renovations going at the Richmond house?"

They chatted a little about Charlotte's plans for a nursery, and then Charlotte changed the subject. "So, about Burke."

Bella's body heated just at the sound of his name. "What about him?"

"He watches you a lot. I think he's interested."

She met Charlotte's gaze. They never really talked about the accident anymore. Bella had made it clear she didn't want to, but maybe that had been a mistake. It had happened. She couldn't just pretend that it didn't.

"He feels responsible for the accident, that's all. We've never talked about it."

"Not once? He's Will's best friend. How have you avoided him?"

"With great care and planning," Bella admitted.

One of the staff placed a glass of white wine in front of her and she was grateful for it. She took a fortifying sip and then put the glass down. "He..." She couldn't look at her sister right now, not as she said the words. "He found me in the pool the other night, after everyone had gone to bed. He saw my scars."

Charlotte put her hand over Bella's. "I'm sorry. I know how much care you take."

Bella turned her head to stare at her sister. "I do. And sometimes I wonder if I'm wrong to do so, but the thought—" She halted. The thought of her scars being out there for the world to see, to gawk at...she just couldn't.

"I know, sweetie. Still, it hurts to see you hide so much. You're a beautiful woman. But this is your life and your choice to live it how you want. What happened with Burke?"

"He was horrified," Bella admitted. "And why wouldn't he be? Add that on to the trauma of the accident itself and it wasn't really a fun time. I didn't know he felt responsible, though. That's ridiculous."

"Why?" Charlotte sat back, took a sip of water and sent Bella a probing glance. "All of you made the choice to get in the car with Royce that night. Maybe Burke wishes he'd found a way to stop it instead."

"That's what he said."

"Seems to me he didn't come out of it unscathed, either. Just something to think about."

Bella pondered that for a while, sipping on the wine. "You're right, you know. But I still come back to the fact that the consequences for me are far more visible. I don't want to be looked at like some freak."

Charlotte leaned forward and squeezed Bella's hand. "Bella, you are not a freak," she said firmly. "You are one of the smartest people I've ever known, and wise, too. You give excellent advice. But it seems you aren't nearly as kind to yourself as you are to others."

That tidbit of insight from her little sister hit her deep inside. Was it true? Did she sabotage herself, talk down to herself? She'd never thought of it that way, but now that Charlotte had said it, Bella knew that she was harder on herself than anyone else was. Maybe to make up for what she'd put the family through.

She was going to answer Charlotte, but Gabi and Giulia appeared, and Gabi was so radiant as the bride-to-be that Bella put all heavier thoughts aside. Tonight was to celebrate and have fun, and she wouldn't spoil it with her maudlin thoughts.

Once they were all together, the staff member in charge of their spa selections, Maria, rounded them up to get started on their itinerary. They were given plush robes to change into, and Bella watched with envy as Giulia and Charlotte went for stone massages and Gabi chose a detoxifying body wrap. But to do any of those things would mean revealing her scars, and the last thing she needed was some tabloid picking up the news and running with it. Instead she chose the sauna, with essential oils in the steam to help her relax.

An hour later, they met for facials. Bella held her breath as the aesthetician put a band around her face to hold her hair back and then began her work on Bella's skin. She rarely let anyone see her without makeup; the white scars were smaller than other places on her body and there weren't as many, but they were still very visible without the right cosmetic coverage. But the woman said nothing about it, just smiled pleasantly and treated Bella's face to a myriad of delicious-smelling treatments. Bella let out a breath and consciously relaxed her body. It had been too long since she'd treated herself to something like this.

The women were quiet during the facials, but then the happy chatter began as they were served prosecco while soaking their feet in preparation for full pedicures. The bubbly wine was excellent and so was the company. Bella's throat tightened as she realized she hadn't had this kind of girls' day out in possibly forever. Had she really closed herself off so much that she had no friends?

She'd told herself family was enough. But was it? William was being married day after tomorrow. Charlotte was married and a baby would be coming before Christmas. When they all had their own families, where would she be? Alone? Spinster Tante Bella?

"Bel, are you all right?" Charlotte asked. "You've gone quiet."

"Actually," Bella replied, shaking away the depressing thoughts, "I was just thinking what a wonderful time this is. Not just the spa, but the four of us, together. I'm so glad we decided to do it."

She reached over and touched Gabi's arm. "And I'm very glad you're finally joining the family, Gabi."

"Aw, don't make me cry!" Gabi flapped her hands in front of her face.

Giulia grinned widely and lifted an eyebrow. "Someone get my sister more prosecco." They all laughed at that, and toasted when glasses were refilled. The mood lightened even more as their feet were buffed and nails painted, and then the same treatment was given to their hands. By the time it was all over, it was after seven and time for the scrumptious dinner that had been prepared for them by a renowned chef.

Bella went to bed that night with a heart full of love and camaraderie, but as she drifted off to sleep, she found herself wondering what else she'd missed out on all these years, and if it was worth it.

CHAPTER FOUR

The weather was picture-perfect for Gabi and William's wedding, and to Bella's relief, the sweltering heat cooled slightly to a very pleasurable temperature. The wedding was taking place right at the villa, and yesterday and today had been nothing but bedlam as crews set up an arch of stunning pale pink and white roses in the courtyard, and then arranged pristine white chairs for the guests. With the forecast completely clear, caterers set up tables in the back garden, with full linens. Soon they'd add centerpieces of hydrangeas cut from Signora Baresi's own shrubs.

Inside, Bella tried to relax as the hairdresser they'd hired to come to the villa tamed her thick curls. With deft hands, the woman pulled some of the hair off Bella's face, pinning it in place with waxy gardenias, leaving the rest to trail down her back in artfully arranged curls. When she was done, she moved on to Giulia and then the bride.

Bella had offered to do everyone's makeup. After all, she managed the Aurora Cosmetics arm and she was quite adept. Her own routine was long but fairly straightforward, and the look was supposed to be summery and fresh, so she went ahead and did hers first, then went to Charlotte.

She ran into Burke in the hall.

He looked absolutely gorgeous. Dashing. Like a movie

star. Her tongue tangled in her mouth as she stared at him, already in his tux, smelling like heaven. "You're ready."

"William's a bit of a wreck. I figured if I'm ready early, it'll be one less thing for him to stress over." He patted his pocket. "I was going to make a joke about the ring, but I'm not sure his heart could take it."

She laughed a little, self-conscious because she was still in her robe. "Well, you're the right doctor, in any case."

"I suppose so. Still, better not chance it. How was your hen night in Tuscany?"

"Amazing. And yours?"

"Very James Bond. Tuxedos, martinis, casinos. But we behaved ourselves."

She laughed. His twinkling eyes said they'd had fun regardless, and she wasn't sure she needed to know any details.

"I need to go. I'm doing the makeup, you see."

"You look beautiful."

She was sure she blushed. "I'm not even dressed yet."

His dark gaze held hers. "Doesn't matter. Anyway, see you down there."

He jogged off, his shiny shoes tapping on the floors, while she stared after him. Did he realize how casually he threw out compliments? She shouldn't take them to heart or get used to it. It was all part of the Burke Phillips charm, wasn't it?

She went to Charlotte's room to do her makeup, and then on to Gabi's room, where Giulia and Gabi waited. Giulia's hair was already done, and in a similar style to Bella's, though Giulia's hair was a little lighter and shorter. Gabi was sitting patiently while the hairdresser fixed her hair in loose waves and then pinned it back, creating a romantic look that would knock William off his feet. Bella went to work with her wands and brushes and sponges and before long the sisters were contoured and polished, lips glistening and eyes popping. "All that's left is your dresses," Bella said.

All the dresses were Aurora designs, including the wedding gown. Giulia put hers on first, and Bella zipped up the back. "Oh, to be twenty-three again," she murmured, as the zip slid smoothly to the top. The dress fit perfectly on Giulia's youthful figure.

"Oh, don't be silly." Giulia spun around and tut-tutted. "You're thirty. And have a body like a goddess."

"That's a lie, but thank you." Bella grinned. "Now for the bride." Charlotte had joined them, bringing the bouquets, and it was a sweet moment where they all came together to help Gabi into her dress. The column eased over her curves and fit perfectly on her shoulders. It was absolutely stunning. A classic design suited to a garden wedding. Signora Baresi came in and started to cry when she saw her daughter ready to walk down the aisle. "The final thing," she announced, and put a white box down on the bed. From it she took the veil, holding the gossamer length over her arm as she went to Gabi. The hairdresser helped anchor it so it was firmly in place without messing up Gabi's hairdo.

"My something old," she said, blinking quickly. "I'm not going to cry, but thank you, Mama. I'm so honored to wear your veil today."

Bella stepped forward. "In keeping with that tradition, my mother has offered you something borrowed." She reached into her robe pocket and took out a box holding a pair of diamond teardrop earrings. "These belonged to my great-grandmother, given to her by my great-grandfather, the sixth Earl of Chatsworth, on their wedding day."

"I lied. I might actually cry," Gabi said as she took the earrings from Bella.

"And something blue." This from Charlotte. It was a tiny blue crystal butterfly, which she tucked in among the delicate blossoms in Gabi's bouquet of freesias, white roses, and pale pink bouvardia.

There was a bunch of sniffling in the room, and then laughter.

A knock on the door had them all turning their heads. Stephen poked his head inside and zeroed in on Bella. "Bel, could I borrow you for a moment?"

"Sure." She still had to put on her dress, but otherwise she was ready and she could dress in a few minutes.

Once outside, Stephen's relaxed face tightened. "Sorry. It's Maman. She's not feeling well, and Burke is concerned."

Something dark settled in the pit of Bella's stomach as she hurried down the corridor behind him. They went into the library, where Aurora was seated in a chair, her feet up, William hovering nearby and Burke checking her pulse.

"Maman." She went to her mother and dropped a kiss on her forehead, not caring about leaving a lipstick mark. "What's wrong?"

"Nothing, but Viscount Downham is determined I go to the hospital." Bella knew her mother was annoyed when she started using titles.

"It's not nothing." Burke looked up at Bella. "She won't listen to me."

Aurora sighed. "I'm fine now. It doesn't hurt anymore. And this is William's wedding day."

William stopped pacing and stared at his mother. "Maman. I have waited for this day for what feels like forever, but not at your expense." No one mentioned their father's sudden cardiac death, but Bella was sure it was on all their minds.

Burke let go of Aurora's wrist. "I don't have any nitroglycerin with me, and I suspect it might be angina, but without tests we can't be sure."

"Sure of…?" asked Bella.

"If she's had a small heart attack or not."

Aurora flapped her hand, moved to get up, and at a stern look from Stephen, sat back in the chair. "I get these pains sometimes, but they don't last long. Just a bit, I don't know, squeezy."

"And how often has this been happening?" Bella moved to sit on the footstool before her mother, and her alarm grew when Aurora evaded her eyes.

Bella looked at Burke. "This is your call." His eyes widened, as if surprised she'd say such a thing. "Burke, you're a cardiologist. There's no one more qualified, and I trust you with this."

His throat bobbed when he swallowed, and he looked at Aurora. "I still think you need to go to the hospital. Perugia isn't that far. I can take you—"

"I'm not missing this wedding."

He sighed. "If I let you attend the wedding, will you promise me that if the pain comes back we go?" He looked her dead in the eyes. "I don't want to scare you, but statistically heart attacks are more devastating in women. Do you understand what I'm saying? And that *would* ruin Will's wedding."

"Maman," Will said, squatting down before her. "We can't lose you, too."

She sighed. "Darlings, you won't. Yes, Burke, I promise I will tell you if the pain comes back. And I will go to the hospital for tests tomorrow first thing if that's what you want."

"I do," Burke said, his gaze serious. "Even if it is angina, you need to know and get started on a treatment plan. I'll call ahead to set everything up."

"Thank you."

"In the meantime, you can attend the wedding but you must not exert yourself. Lay off the bubbly and no dancing until we know what's happening. Okay?"

She rolled her eyes. "Do I have a choice?"

"No." That came from four voices, spoken in unison.

There was a tap at the door and Christophe looked in. "The officiant is looking for the groom. Is everything okay in here?"

Will stood and nodded. "Sort of. Stephen, you talk to Charlotte, okay?"

Stephen nodded. He and Will went to leave, which just left Burke and Bella in the room with Aurora. And Bella still had to get dressed.

"I'll stay with her," Burke said, without Bella even asking. "And when it's time I'll escort her to her seat." Burke looked at Aurora and winked. "Sorry, Lady Pemberton, but I guess you're stuck with me as your date for the evening."

Aurora laughed then, a rich sound with just a bit of grit in it, a sound that Bella loved to hear. "All the ladies will have their noses out of shape, I fear."

"They'll deal with the disappointment," he replied. Then he looked at Bella. "It's okay. Promise."

His warm assurance sent something soft and fragile into Bella's heart, something she hadn't let in there for a very long time. It was faith that what he said was true, and a level of trust that was foreign to her. She only had one parent left, but she trusted Burke to make sure everything was all right. How could that be?

"Thank you," she said, and touched his shoulder with her fingertips before leaving the room. She had to get dressed. She had to walk down the aisle as a bridesmaid. And she had to figure out what to do about these feelings that were cropping up every time Burke was around. If she wasn't careful, she'd start to hope, and she was very sure that the subsequent fall wouldn't be worth it.

Burke left Aurora in her seat as mother of the groom and went to stand with William at the bower of roses. Stephen joined him at the front, and then Marco escorted Signora

Baresi to her seat. The woman was beaming as she sat and waited for her husband to walk Gabi down the grassy aisle.

Nearly two hundred guests were in attendance, a huge crowd for the lovely but modest villa. Massimo Baresi was a successful man, and from what William had said, offered to host the wedding wherever they wanted. Massimo was also a cancer survivor, and William had told Burke that what Gabi really wanted was for her father to escort her to her groom at the villa they called home. So...the venue was brought to them. Burke had to admit it was beautiful. The sun was shining, birds were singing, and there were flowers everywhere.

Violins began playing something vaguely familiar, and Burke's attention was diverted to the arch in the courtyard where the bridesmaids waited. First came Charlotte, with her pregnant glow and a just-discernible bubble where she was starting to show. A quick glance at Jacob told Burke that the Big Viking, as he now called him, was utterly smitten.

Then Bella. Burke's breath caught as she stepped out, her powder-blue dress flowing around her ankles. The light fabric covered her arms and her hair was down, and now he knew why. It didn't make her any less beautiful. This morning, when she'd said she trusted him with her mother—that had been so unexpected. She had no reason to trust his judgment, did she? He'd made his share of mistakes. But there'd been no question in her eyes, no doubt. She'd put her faith in him to care for one of the dearest people in her life.

Of course, people did that every day in his line of work, and it wasn't something he took lightly. But for Bella to do so...was different.

She got closer, holding her bouquet and smiling, and then her gaze slid to his and her smile wobbled a little as that annoying *zing* ran between them, a current that was getting harder and harder to ignore.

Once upon a time she'd tried to get his attention and he'd ignored her. And for good reason. Now, though, he seemed unable to look away.

Giulia followed behind, and Burke noticed that Marco couldn't take his eyes off her. A smile touched his lips. They were so young and in love.

And finally, there was Gabi, on her father's arm, looking radiant in her dress with a veil that trailed behind her. Burke heard William's sharp intake of breath, and he looked over at his friend to see Will's lower lip wobbling. Who would have ever thought that his best friend would be hit so hard by love? Marriage…and probably a family, too. And here was Burke, two years older, and matrimony and babies weren't anywhere near his radar.

And then he looked and saw Bella lift a tissue to her eyes and it changed everything.

He was interested in the one woman who truly wanted nothing to do with him. Wasn't that just his luck? And even if she were interested, Bella wasn't the kind of woman he could flirt with, or have a fling with, as attractive as that idea may be. He was not his father's son. He wouldn't treat someone so special so…cavalierly. He'd kept his relationships—using that term loosely—at a surface level, charming and pleasant but never deeper. He never, ever wanted to be responsible for hurting someone the way his father had by his actions. Added to that, Bella was different. It could never be just easy and light with her because of their shared trauma. They were already bonded in a much deeper way.

His gaze shifted to Aurora, sitting in the front row with Christophe and Jacob. She smiled up at him and gave a slight nod. Good. He'd be watching her like a hawk all day. Better to put his focus there than on Bella. Easier said than done.

The ceremony commenced and when the time came for the ring, Burke reached into his pocket and took out the diamond-studded wedding band. He watched as his best friend made his vows and slid the ring over Gabi's finger, his heart catching when she said the vows back, tears hovering on her lids, and put a ring on William's finger, too. Gabi truly, truly loved him. The way Aurora had loved Cedric, he realized. Of course he wanted that for his friend. Something steadfast and loyal. Unlike his own parents' union.

No one had ever looked at him that way, though. And he wasn't sure he wanted them to. This past week was not representative of his life. He pulled long hours at the hospital, did his share of night and weekend on calls. And his career wasn't going to stagnate here. There was so much to learn, places he could go. He wasn't sure how a relationship would fit into that. He'd seen what happened when a husband was more dedicated to his work than his wife. That was not a legacy he ever wanted to continue.

The ceremony ended with Will and Gabi kissing and then beaming so brightly they nearly put the sun to shame. As they retreated down the aisle, Burke offered his arm to Giulia, while Stephen escorted Bella, and Marco, Charlotte. Soon they were in the flower garden, where the couple would receive congratulations, and Burke moved off to the side, eager to check on Aurora.

Bella came to his side. "I want to check on Maman."

"Me as well. Here she comes." He stepped forward and offered Aurora a kiss on the cheek. "Well, he's all married up now," Burke teased, checking her face for any signs of strain or pain. "Feeling all right? Any dizziness or weakness?"

"Just a little tired." Aurora smiled at him. "See? I'm being honest." Her gaze locked with his. "I promise I'm taking this seriously, Burke. The timing was just…"

He touched her elbow. "You should have had it looked at before now. You must take care of yourself, you know."

She nodded. "I know."

Bella was standing by Burke's shoulder. "Would you like something cool to drink, Maman?"

"That would be lovely, Bella, thank you."

When Bella was gone, Burke stared into Aurora's eyes. "Losing Cedric was hard on your children. I would imagine they are afraid of losing another parent. Even grown children flounder when they lose their anchor, Aurora."

Her lip quivered but only for the briefest moment. He saw it and pretended not to. His message had sunk in.

"And you would know, too. I'm sorry about your father. He and Cedric were good friends."

"Cedric was a good man. Better than I can hope to be," Burke replied.

They moved into the shade and Burke found Aurora a chair so she could rest. "Why do you say that, and not include your father?" she asked, peering up at him. "Your father was very proud of you."

"You know why."

"Ah, yes. The accident."

She was only partly right, and he wasn't about to elaborate. What good would it do now? Not one bit. If Aurora didn't know about his father's indiscretions, then maybe the previous viscount had been more discreet than Burke had given him credit for. He shifted the topic slightly. "I didn't know about Bella. Being so injured. Not until this week."

"She wanted it that way."

"So William said."

"And with you all being minors except Royce, we were able to keep your names out of it. You were foolish teenagers. And you've all paid a heavy price for that."

"Have I?" He looked down at her sharply. "My life looks pretty good, doesn't it?"

Aurora held his gaze. "What we see on the outside and what's on the inside don't often match up. I'd say you've paid more than you want to let on. Including taking on much of the guilt and responsibility."

"Because it's right. I do have responsibility."

He could see Bella returning and knew they would have to change the subject. But Aurora got in one last thought. "Maybe so. Even if you do, though, it doesn't make the burden any easier to bear."

He thought about her words as Bella handed her mother a glass of punch and they spoke for a few moments about the wedding. Oddly enough, he'd found Aurora's words comforting. She didn't try to convince him his feelings were wrong. She simply acknowledged them. Funny how that made him feel better.

They spent the next hour mingling and then posing for photos. As the afternoon waned, they joined the guests in the garden for cocktails and charcuterie, and then finally a sit-down dinner of stuffed lamb leg and seasonal vegetables that was to die for. Wine flowed and a traditional Italian wedding cake was served with more prosecco. Burke and Bella sat at the same table as the bride and groom, though not beside each other. Still, he seemed attuned to her every laugh and smile. When the dancing finally started beneath sparkling lights, Burke checked on Aurora. She danced once with William as Gabi danced with her father, and then dutifully went back to her seat, watching the festivities.

Today had scared her. He was glad of it. It would make his job tomorrow much easier.

And after he danced with Giulia, he held out his hand to Bella. "Dance?" he asked, trying to keep his voice casual.

"Oh, I…uh…"

"Can't think of a decent excuse?" He laughed. "I promise I'll behave."

She rolled her eyes. "Don't make promises you can't keep."

He left his hand in the air between them. "One dance," he said.

She relented and put her fingers in his, and they walked to the dance floor that had been installed for the occasion. He took her in his arms, one hand clasping hers, the other on the soft material of her dress. "In case I didn't tell you today," he murmured in her ear, "you look beautiful."

"You did tell me," she murmured, her feet shuffling to the music. "In the hall."

"Right. And then you put on the dress, and…just wow, Bella."

She leaned back and looked in his face. "I don't need your compliments."

"Maybe I want to give them just the same." She felt good in his arms, almost like she belonged there. "You know, I was a fool all those years ago."

She lifted an eyebrow. "We both were."

"You were flirting with me that night. And I ignored you."

Her chin came up. "Me? Flirting? You mean you were walking around as if you were God's gift to women!"

Now, wasn't that an interesting reaction. Had he perhaps hit a nerve?

"Well, I was. Acting that way," he clarified. "Not that I actually was, as you say, 'God's gift to women.' But I noticed you, Bella. I just wanted you to know that."

Her gaze locked on his, and he didn't see the anger he expected. Instead he saw confusion and what he thought might be…regret? Or was that just him projecting his own feelings on her?

"Then why?" she asked. "Why did you treat me as if I were invisible?"

CHAPTER FIVE

BELLA COULD HAVE kicked herself for asking. Burke was so handsome, so charming, and the way he'd cared for her mother today…good heavens, he was nearly perfect. It only ended up making Bella feel more flawed. And forgettable.

Oh, the irony. Because she tried to fly under the radar at the best of times. Still, when it came to wanting a guy to notice you, complete indifference was a tough pill to swallow.

He sighed, and when she met his gaze she saw nothing but honesty in the depths. "I did that because your brothers told me to keep my hands to myself. No messing around with you or Charlotte."

Her mouth dropped open. Not in a million years had she expected that sort of answer. "They did what?"

"Before the party. We're the same age, Bella, and I happened to say to Stephen that I thought you were quite beautiful. I believe his response was, 'She's my sister and she's off-limits.'" I wasn't about to argue. Have you seen your brother? He and the Big Viking make a smaller man think twice about crossing them."

Their feet kept moving to the music, but Bella's brain was awhirl. This was news that her brothers had never shared with her.

"But you…oh, never mind." What did it matter? At

least this explained a lot. But it also made her a little bit angry. If he hadn't been so cold to her, she wouldn't have sought out Royce to make Burke jealous. It had worked, too. Burke and the girl he'd latched on to, some girl that Stephen knew, had agreed to go with them to Royce's estate to raid his father's liquor cabinet. It had all seemed so daring and exciting in the moment. And remarkably irresponsible and stupid.

"Bella." The song ended and he let go of her hand. "Can we please talk about this later? Really talk about it? We both have feelings about that night that need airing. Otherwise we're still stuck there, don't you see? Don't you want to be able to let it go?"

"We'll see," she said, taking a step back. She'd gone to pains to avoid him all week, but the truth was with so many people around, it was nearly impossible to get any time alone. She was coming around to the conclusion that he was right. They did need to talk about it. He had been there. He knew. And for all Bella's assertions over the years, she hadn't moved on. She was stuck, just as he said.

"I'm going to check on Maman," she said, turning away.

He fell into step beside her. "Why don't you come with us tomorrow?"

"To the hospital, you mean?"

He nodded. "I think your mother would like to have a family member there. And that maybe a daughter might be a bit gentler than Stephen's…shall we say, autocratic tendencies?"

She laughed then. "I know you're best friends with Will, but that was very accurate."

"I can usually read people. The fact that I can't figure you out is really bothering me."

She laughed again. "Well, at least I'm not predictable." They'd reached Aurora's side and Bella took the chair next to her. "Well, Maman, what do you think?"

"I think this was a beautiful wedding, and that I'm very proud of all my children." She smiled warmly. "All of them." And she reached for Bella's hand.

"Thank you."

"I know how hard you work, Bella. I see everything." She looked up at Burke. "I'm sure you understand those workaholic tendencies, too, yes? I imagine your schedule is a full one."

"No one goes into medicine for the great hours," he replied.

"And Isabel? She's managing all right?" she inquired after his mother.

"She is." Burke sat down beside Bella. "One of my sisters got married last year. The other one is working in London so still staying in the house. Mother says that once Josey leaves, she's not sure what she'll do with all that space."

"Fill it with grandchildren?"

He laughed. "She'll have to rely on my sisters for that, I'm afraid."

A faster song came on and one of the guests came to snag Burke, who shrugged and let himself be led away. Bella leaned back in her chair and watched as Burke moved smoothly on the floor, natural rhythm taking over the movement of his body...particularly his hips. Bella jumped a little when Aurora started laughing.

"Oh, sweetheart, you are so transparent. If you want him, go get him."

"What? No. I don't...no." She dragged her gaze away from the sight of him and faced her mother. "We're barely friendly."

"You've started talking about what happened."

"A little."

"And you trust him."

She sighed. She couldn't deny that part because people

had witnessed her saying it. "I trust his judgment as a doctor," she replied carefully.

"And he's very good-looking."

"I'm not blind."

Aurora lifted her glass to her lips, then lowered it. "You could do worse, Bella. Burke Phillips is a good man."

"I have no desire to be Lady Downham." Which wasn't strictly true. Not that she wanted to marry him or anything, but the barely friendly bit had been inaccurate. They were speaking more than they ever had, but it was what they weren't saying that drew her in. And she was ridiculously attracted to him. That hadn't changed, from the time she was a teenager until now, a grown woman with her own busy life to manage.

"Keep an open mind," Aurora suggested. "You can't quite fit love into convenient little boxes."

Bella frowned. What was that supposed to mean? But before she could ask, Marco claimed her for a dance, and she went on to enjoy the rest of the wedding.

Everything was subdued the next morning. The bride and groom had driven to Perugia last night, to spend their wedding night in a hotel suite before leaving on their honeymoon the following evening. Bella was awake early, and a careful listen told her no one else in the house was up yet. She stretched, sighed, and got up to shower.

She was going to the hospital with Burke and her mother today. They'd settled it last night. Burke would be by at nine, they'd drive into the city, and hopefully be back in time for dinner.

He'd been right about her mother not being alone today. Burke was kind but he wasn't family. And Charlotte did deserve to spend the morning with her husband, whom she'd barely seen since his arrival.

She just had to figure out how to stem the uneasiness that

gripped her every time she thought about her mother being ill. It seemed like yesterday they'd lost Cedric. Aurora was now the captain of the ship. What was Aurora Inc. without her? A ship without a captain…or maybe a ship without a rudder, if she took the metaphor a little further. There simply was no Aurora Inc. without Maman at the helm.

The shower felt heavenly and she dressed quickly, in jeans and a light peasant-style shirt that would be comfortable for sitting in a waiting room. She dressed up the ensemble with a pair of melon-colored heels and a turquoise necklace, the pops of color transforming her simple outfit into something more.

Then there was her hair and makeup to consider. It took nearly an hour for her to dry and style the heavy mass, and then another twenty-five minutes for makeup. What would it be like to shove her hair in a messy topknot and go out with nothing more than a swipe of lip gloss and mascara? Sometimes she really didn't enjoy being high maintenance.

When she was finally ready, she slipped her small laptop into her bag. No reason why she couldn't distract herself with some work. Charlotte had agreed to cover William's teams while he was honeymooning, at least. But Bella knew that Charlotte was only one person. And with Maman not feeling well, keeping an eye on the company as a whole wasn't a bad idea. She paused at her doorway. Maybe what she needed to do was schedule a meeting with Stephen when they returned to Paris. Between the two of them, they should be able to carry the load so Maman could rest. Christophe, too, could be utilized in areas other than his jewelry division.

Aurora was already in the kitchen with Signora Baresi. "*Buongiorno*, Bella," said Lucia. "Would you like some breakfast?"

"I don't want you to go to any trouble. You must be exhausted after the last week."

"*Si*, but for the best reasons. Yesterday was so lovely."
She put a cup of tea at Bella's elbow. *"The alla menta, si?"*

"Grazie," Bella replied, the soothing aroma of her cus-
tomary mint tea touching her nostrils. "This is perfect."

A plate of bread and butter and jam appeared. Bella
fixed a slice and began to eat; she wasn't sure what the day
would bring and this light meal would hold her until they
had a better idea.

"Maman, you're not eating?"

"No. I don't know if I need to fast for any bloodwork,
so I'm going to wait." She said it all very calmly, but Bella
looked over and saw a tiny knit in one of her mother's
usually flawless eyebrows. She was worried. And when
Maman was particularly stressed, her appetite suffered.
She might be right about the bloodwork, but it was also a
convenient excuse.

Burke arrived and before long they were on the road to
Perugia. Forty-five minutes would get them from the villa
to the hospital. Once there, they took their time getting
Aurora registered and the paperwork sorted. Then they
sat to wait. It didn't take long. Burke had called ahead to
an old acquaintance he had in the cardiology department.
Bella went into the room with Burke and her mother during the initial exam, and sat with her while blood was
taken. She moved to the side and waited quietly while
Aurora was hooked up to an EKG machine, which made
a quiet hum as it began to print out the pattern of her
heartbeat.

Burke had a look at the tape when the nurse stepped
out, but Bella couldn't read his face at all. He was in doctor mode now, wasn't he? The way he'd greeted his friend
and then started talking…she really started to understand
that he was no longer a boy but a man, and a very successful and smart man at that. There was a gravitas to him in
this setting that she'd overlooked in the celebratory setting

of the wedding. He inspired confidence and calm. It was quite remarkable, when all was said and done.

When it was time for the chest X-ray, Bella went back to the waiting room. Despite the excellent care, it still felt as if a heavy weight were just waiting to drop on the Pemberton family again. She swallowed around the lump in her throat and dug into her bag for her laptop. The less Maman had to worry about right now, the better.

It felt like a very long time before Burke joined her again. "Bella. Your mother is nearly finished. Do you want to come back in?"

She nodded, closing the lid on the laptop. Her chest tightened and as if he sensed her nervousness, Burke reached down and took her hand. He led her down a different hallway now, to an office, where Aurora waited, her face pale.

Burke and Bella went in and sat, and were immediately followed by the doctor, who smiled and took his seat behind his desk.

"Signora Pemberton, you did not have a heart attack." He smiled at her reassuringly. "This is very good news. Your bloodwork did not show any of the enzymes we would expect to see in that case, and your chest X-ray was normal as well."

Bella let out her breath in a rush, and Aurora visibly relaxed.

"Your EKGs did show a few abnormalities," he continued. "Your resting EKG seemed very normal, but we did notice a few things on the exercise EKG that I feel require further investigation. After talking with Dr. Phillips, I'm going to recommend you see a doctor in either Paris or London for an angiogram to look for artery blockages, and treatment from there. In addition, I'm giving you a prescription for nitroglycerin in case of another event."

"An angiogram…" Aurora said, her voice a little thready. "What would happen after that?"

Burke nodded at the doctor and then turned his attention to Aurora. "Well, quite often we'll do an angioplasty right there in the cath lab if we find a blockage. That's the little balloon procedure you've probably heard about. Sometimes we put in a stent at the same time. Depending on the blockage, sometimes a bypass operation is recommended. But let's not put the cart before the horse."

"Dr. Phillips is right. Take it easy, eat well, get rest. The angiogram should tell you more. We could schedule you in here, but since you've said your time in Italy is coming to a close, and considering today's results, waiting for you to reach home would be fine, in my opinion."

Bella felt a rush of relief sweep over her. This didn't sound great, but it certainly could sound a lot worse.

The doctor wrote out two prescriptions and handed them to Aurora. "One is for the nitro. The other is for a daily medication. Your cardiologist at home may change that depending on his diagnosis. Do you have a cardiologist?"

"I have Dr. Phillips," Aurora said firmly.

"Aurora, I try not to treat friends and family. Though I appreciate your confidence immensely."

She nodded. "Well, you're my doctor until we can go back, and you can recommend someone to me."

"That I can do, and happily."

They rose and shook the doctor's hand before leaving the office and finding their way back outside to where Burke had parked.

He'd closed the door after Aurora had slipped into the back seat, and Bella looked at him over the roof of the car. "I don't know the city, but I can tell you Maman hasn't eaten all day. She was too nervous this morning. Could we find somewhere to grab a bite? It's a long time until dinner." They'd missed the lunch hour and it was now half past two.

"Of course. I can check my phone and find someplace close."

He moved to get into the car but she stopped him again, keeping her voice low so Aurora couldn't hear. "Thank you. For what you did for Maman yesterday and for taking care of this today. It means a lot, Burke."

It was hard to say that to him. It shouldn't have been, for it was simple gratitude and appreciation. But it was, just the same. Because things were not simple between them, as much as she might like them to be.

"It's what I do," he answered plainly. "I would do it for anyone."

They got in the car and Bella shut the door. She doubted he would understand, but his last statement only made her respect and like him more. Because she knew it was true. He'd take the same care with any person, and that said a lot about him as a human being.

It was getting harder and harder not to like him more than was advisable.

CHAPTER SIX

THE FOLLOWING DAY the Pemberton crew said goodbye to the Baresis, thanking them for their hospitality, and boarded a chartered jet to Paris and then London. Charlotte, Jacob, Christophe, and Stephen would be staying in Paris, and Bella was going on to London with Aurora and Burke. Aurora had an appointment with one of Burke's colleagues on Wednesday, and Burke had advised that she would be booked in for an angiogram. If she ended up having the balloon procedure, she would spend a night in hospital and then time off, recovering.

Bella had, without any formal decision, become the child to be at Aurora's side. She wasn't sure why.

Once on the plane, however, Aurora made an announcement. She held a family meeting—minus William—about what would happen with Aurora Inc. as she dealt with her illness.

She looked at Charlotte first. "Charlotte, you've already got your hands full with public relations and handling William's division while he's away. Plus you're growing another human." She smiled warmly. "I'd like your plans to remain unchanged."

"I agree," Charlotte replied, putting her hand on her tummy. "I'm trying to be very good about balancing work and rest. But if you need something, you know you must call."

"I know, darling, and I will." Aurora turned her attention to Christophe. "Christophe, I'm adding to your workload a little bit. I want you to work with Bella to take over some of her responsibilities on an interim basis. She can decide what to hand off to you and what she can delegate within her division."

"Yes, Aunt." Christophe looked at Bella. "If you're going on to London, I'll make myself available for a virtual meeting whenever you need, Bel."

"Maman, I know I'm coming with you, but I can keep up with my work." Bella frowned. Had she not kept everything going while they were in Italy? And she was fine! She wasn't overworked. It felt…punitive.

Aurora held Bella's gaze. "Of course, you can keep up with your work, but you can't do that and keep up with *my* work."

Bella's eyes widened.

"I'm going to take some time off to get my health under control. While I'm out of the office, Bella is the new me." She looked around at all the children for affirmation.

Bella's mouth dropped open. She'd planned to talk to Stephen about helping, but she hadn't counted on officially being handed the reins. "Me? Not Stephen?"

Stephen spoke up. "I'm the numbers guy, Bel. I work with acquisitions and legal and all the dry business stuff. But Maman is right. She's the heart of Aurora, and you're the next best thing. Christophe can manage cosmetics with your help."

She looked around at Charlotte and Christophe. "And you're both all right with this?"

"Why wouldn't we be?" This was from Christophe. "Bel, you're the one who is always behind the scenes, holding us together. You are *la colle*."

Hah. She would hardly consider herself anyone's glue.

She was still stunned by the announcement. "But Maman. I'm going to be in London with you."

"Only for a little while. It's the perfect way for me to debrief you on what you need to know moving forward. Then you can return to Paris and work out of my office, or yours. Whichever you're comfortable with. My assistant will be at your disposal."

Burke's voice came from behind her. "Congratulations, Bella."

Congratulations were echoed throughout the cabin.

Aurora addressed them all again. "I'm very proud of all my children. I know I've said that often lately, but it's true. You've all stepped up into your roles in the company and done a wonderful job. And covering for each other makes you versatile so you can understand the company as a whole. I'm not retiring yet, *mes petites*, but when I do, I know Aurora Inc. is in more than capable hands."

Bella blinked away a few tears, and she saw Charlotte do the same. Stephen reached over and squeezed Aurora's hand. She had the best family. Maybe they were all missing Cedric, but they still had one another and they were still strong.

When the conversation moved to other subjects, Bella got up and went to the galley to get a drink. She was pouring club soda into a glass when Burke came up behind her. "Well. I take it that was unexpected."

She put down the bottle and turned to face him. "Totally unexpected."

"You can do it, though."

"Hell yes, I can," she agreed, and was gratified when Burke burst out laughing. It did strike her, though, that she was going to be running—even on a temporary basis—a billion-dollar company. It was a huge enterprise consisting of fashion, cosmetics, jewelry. The only way to run it was to trust in the people below her. The way Maman had trusted in her.

"You're something, Bella, you know that?" They were tucked away in the little galley at the front of the plane, out of sight from the others, and he was close, so close. She looked up and saw his deep gaze probing hers, and she couldn't look away. His lips were getting closer, and then he did it…he touched his lips to hers, softly, and yet with a persuasiveness that wooed her into closing her eyes and melting against him just a little bit.

It was even better than she'd imagined.

He took his time, and Bella was in no rush, either. She couldn't remember the last time she'd been kissed, and the sensation was wonderful. Delicious. His lips were soft, and so was his beard as it brushed against her chin and cheeks. Mmm… She'd never kissed a man with a beard before, but she could get used to it.

And then she remembered that they were in a three-foot-by-three-foot section of airplane, barely hidden from her family, and she shifted back in the little room she had, breaking off the kiss and running her tongue along her lower lip, as if to savor every last taste of him. He made her feel things. Not just yearning, but a knowledge that this was a part of her life that she'd been deprived of exploring, and that brought resentment with it.

"Complicated," he said simply. He ran a finger over his bottom lip and held her gaze. "And I should probably apologize."

"No, don't," she said quickly. Perhaps too quickly. "I mean, there's nothing to apologize for. It was just a kiss. And we were both willing participants."

A slow smile crept up his cheeks, making a crease in his dimple that she could see even with the close-cropped facial hair. It would be hard for any woman to resist it. Even harder for her, because she was also starting to really admire the man inside the sexy package.

"I should get back," she added, and skirted him with her drink in hand.

Either the family hadn't noticed she and Burke had been in the galley or they were choosing to ignore it. Either way, she took her seat and then joined in the conversation, which had turned strategic. Never let it be said the Pembertons didn't know how to have a good time, she thought.

But strategy and work were her comfort zone, far more than sneaking into alcoves with sexy doctors. That was right up there with surprising midnight swims. She wasn't quite sure what to do in those situations, or how she was supposed to feel and act. Work, though, that was a familiar beast.

Maybe getting home and getting to work would help banish this restless feeling that had been plaguing her ever since she'd left for Italy. Getting back into regular habits and schedules would surely level things out.

They stopped in Paris and said goodbye to Christophe, Stephen, Jacob, and Charlotte. Then they took off again, headed to Gatwick as the drive from Gatwick to Chatsworth Manor wasn't difficult at all.

"Burke, you must come stay," Aurora said, tapping her nails on the arm rest of her seat. "It's been too long since you were at Chatsworth."

"That's kind, but I do have to be back at the hospital tomorrow morning. I'll be there on Wednesday, though. I won't be in on the procedure, but I'll be close by."

"You can keep Bella updated, then," Aurora said, looking pleased.

"Of course."

He looked over at Bella. "Where are you staying when you come to town?"

"I thought I would stay at Charlotte's," she replied. "Jacob's stayed in Paris with her and the house is empty."

"Charlotte's quite a distance from the hospital, though, isn't she? All the way over in Richmond."

Bella looked at Aurora and frowned. What was her mother getting at? If she was trying to play matchmaker, Bella wished she'd cease and desist. Especially since Aurora was wearing what her children liked to call her "innocent" face. It never worked because Aurora was always too on the ball to be oblivious to anything.

"Then I'll get a hotel," she answered, her voice firm. "Honestly, Mother. I'm pretty sure I can manage this."

"Of course you can." Burke backed her up. "And if all goes well, it'll only be for one night."

Bella was thankful that he hadn't suggested staying with him, as she was sure that was what Aurora was angling at. Not that it wasn't an alluring idea. But she and Burke had shared one stolen kiss. It was a big stretch to go from there to spending the night. At least, that was what she told herself.

They landed and it took no time at all for them to disembark. They walked through the airport together, where a car service was waiting for Aurora and Bella. Burke was going to take a taxi home. As they prepared to go their separate ways, Bella realized that even though the wedding week had been disconcerting in many ways, she was rather sorry it was over. Now it was back to real life. Or at least as real as it could be with Aurora's medical issues in the picture.

But as the driver stowed their bags, Bella turned to Burke and found that it was hard to say goodbye.

"I'll see you Wednesday," he said, his voice low. "I'll wait with you."

"You don't have to do that."

"I want to. Both for Aurora and for you, so you don't have to wait alone."

He was so caring. So considerate. Nothing at all like she'd expected or like he'd been before. "That's very kind."

Aurora had slipped into the back of the car and now was waiting for Bella, but Burke put his hand on her arm.

"The hell with kind." His voice was rough. "I want to see you again, Bella. Even if that's in a hospital waiting room. That's not kind, that's selfish."

Oh, those words were thrilling. She met his gaze and tried a saucy smile. "That's not selfish, it's efficient," she answered. "I'll see you Wednesday."

Then she slipped into the limo before she could say anything more. It was bad enough that her mother was getting ideas. If she wasn't careful she'd be getting them, too.

Flirting was one thing. But it would be folly to attempt to take this somewhere it was never meant to go. Burke was handsome and nice and she was insanely attracted. But their lives were too different for anything more.

"I got an update from Dr. Mallick. The angiogram shows a blockage, so they're going to do an angioplasty and put in a stent. It'll be a little while longer."

Bella looked up at Burke, both relief and fear making her chest tighten. "This is good, right? I mean, not that she needs it, but that they found it and can fix it."

"Yes, exactly." He smiled reassuringly. "It should only take another hour or so."

Bella nodded. They'd met Dr. Mallick earlier this morning and he'd put a lot of her fears to rest as he'd explained the catheterization procedure. Burke had been with them, and knowing he had full confidence in his colleague also helped a lot. As much as Bella wished it was Burke in there doing the procedure, she respected his ethics that kept him out of the catheterization lab. Plus, there was the bonus that he had promised to wait with her, keeping her company.

She'd brought work but couldn't concentrate, so Burke

had taken her to the café in the north wing for breakfast. After tea and hot buttered toast, she felt much better. Burke had then regaled her with stories as he gave her a tour of the hospital. One look at his animated face told her he was happy here, in his chosen field. There was passion and dedication in his voice, and she admired him for it. Despite the privilege of his birth, he'd worked very hard to get here, and her admiration for him grew.

He squeezed her hand. "Do you have something to read? A silly computer game on your phone?" They sat down in the waiting room chairs again. "You should keep your mind busy with something so you're not worrying."

"I know I shouldn't worry. She's in good hands and this is a common procedure." She looked over at him, still holding his hand. "But I worry anyway."

"Because she's your mother. And because she's the only parent you have left. I understand, Bella, more than you know."

He'd lost his father, too. She leaned against him briefly. "I know you do."

"You must miss Cedric a lot. He was such a good man. You're a lot like him."

Bella turned to look at him. "I am? How?"

"Your father never needed the spotlight. I remember seeing him and how he was so happy to let your mother shine and he stayed in the background. But he was her anchor. You could tell by the way she looked at him. He was the strength behind everything. And while Stephen has gone on to be the next earl, I think you're the one in the background making sure everything is all right. It's why Aurora chose to put you in charge while she's absent. You don't need the spotlight. You don't want it. And not just because of your scars. Because of who you are."

She stared at him in astonishment. "That's quite an assessment, Burke." But inside, she was warmed by his confidence in her. She loved the idea of being like her father. He'd been a wonderful man and she missed him more than anyone knew. What Burke had given her just now was a gift. A lovely gift she could hold inside and keep close during the days when she felt most alone.

"I've talked to William, too, you know. He said how fair you were when he and Gabi first got together and the family found out. How everyone can count on you to be the voice of reason. You're appreciated, Bella, more than you realize."

The endorsements were wonderful, but something caught at Bella, too. It was true; she tried to be fair and reasonable and see things from all sides. Because she'd deliberately tried to stay out of the limelight, she'd become very good at observing and assessing. But she wondered, too, if all that reliability made her...boring. She'd never done anything impulsive since the accident, having learned her lesson all too well. She lived a glamorous life but stayed on the sidelines. Never any whiff of scandal. What did that say about her? She didn't think it was because she was above doing anything scandalous. She had a sneaky suspicion it was because she had stopped living her life.

"What's wrong?" She'd been quiet so long that Burke had begun to frown. "Did I say something?"

"No, it's not you. I've just been thinking a lot lately." She tried a smile. "Maybe I need to get out of my own head a bit."

The creases in his brow relaxed. "We all do, from time to time."

They waited in silence for a while, and then Dr. Mallick came through the doors with a smile on his face. Burke and Bella stood.

"All done," Dr. Mallick announced. "The procedure went well with no complications. Mrs. Pemberton will be taken to her room shortly, where she'll spend the night, but barring any changes, she can go home tomorrow. She's still sedated and it'll be a little while for that to wear off completely. She's a bit groggy now."

Relief sluiced through Bella. All morning she'd told herself this was a common procedure and there was nothing to worry about, but deep down her concern had been profound. It was as if a heavy weight had been lifted from her shoulders.

"Thank you. Thank you so much," she said, letting out a breath and smiling in return.

Burke shook Dr. Mallick's hand. "Yes, thanks." Bella listened with half an ear as they discussed which medications Aurora would be prescribed. All she could truly think was that her mother was all right. Ever since the angina attack, a pall had fallen over the family.

"Excuse me a moment," she said, touching Burke's arm. "I want to call Paris."

"Of course." Burke chatted with Dr. Mallick while she stepped away to make the call.

Stephen was on a conference call, so she was put through to Charlotte, who would then relay the news to the rest of the family. "Charlotte? It's Bella. Everything went fine. She had to have a stent put in, but she's all done now and just has to stay overnight."

Charlotte's voice echoed Bella's relief. "So quickly? I thought she was just having the test this morning."

"They found the blockage and put the stent in while she was already catheterized. Dr. Mallick made it sound easy." She shook her head. "I'm just so grateful."

"Me, too, Bel. Me, too. To lose Maman…"

The silence that fell on the call spoke volumes.

"How are you feeling? Baby all right?"

"The baby's fine. And I have something I want to talk to you about, but not right now. Later this week? Personal, not business. So nothing to worry about."

"That sounds great."

"And Burke? Is he there with you?"

Heat infused Bella's cheeks. "He's been here the whole time."

"He's a good man, Bel. And he's got a thing for you."

"Don't be silly. He's a friend to the family." Not strictly true, of course.

"I know he kissed you on the plane. Why else were you in the galley for so long?"

Bella choked on a laugh. "We were discussing club soda."

"Sure you were." And Charlotte laughed back. "I'm just saying, don't turn down a great possibility because of… well, you know. I don't think Burke would care at all."

It wasn't about Burke caring. It was about her allowing herself to be so vulnerable. She didn't know if she could do it.

She looked over at him and he caught her eye and smiled. His eyes crinkled at the corners and his gaze was so warm she went melty. "I appreciate the advice," she replied.

"I doubt it, but I'm offering it anyway."

"Because you do speak your mind. Most of the time."

"When it comes to other people. Not so much when it comes to myself. But I'm getting better at it." Charlotte had tried so hard to toe the Aurora line that she'd almost lost herself in the process. Jacob had changed all that, and now Charlotte was really coming into her own. It had been good for her and for the company.

"I need to go, but you'll let everyone else know? Do you want me to text William? I know he's checking for updates, even though he and Gabi are still on their honeymoon."

"That'd be great, and I'll talk to Stephen and Christophe."

"Perfect. Love you, Charlotte."

"I love you, too, Bel."

Bella hung up with a lump in her throat. As a family their love was always assured but rarely spoken. But today, as in many days since their father's death, it felt important to articulate it. They didn't say "I love you" enough.

She took a few more moments to fire off a text to William, then looked up to find Burke waiting for her where she'd left him. Dr. Mallick was gone, and now it was just the two of them.

"All set?" he asked.

She nodded. "I've called Charlotte and texted William. Charlotte will do the rest. When do you think I can see her?"

"Soon. But she'll probably sleep for a while. Why don't we find lunch somewhere?"

"You don't have to stay," she said, tucking her phone into her bag again. "You've done so much already."

"Bella." He took her hand. "Does it look like I want to be anywhere else?"

He had to stop saying things like that. She'd soon start believing him.

"Well, I could do with lunch. Something more than tea and toast." She smiled up at him.

"How do you feel about sushi?"

"It sounds perfect."

They made their way outside. The drizzly morning had made way for a brighter afternoon, with sun and a few spots of cloud. The restaurant was situated in a hotel that was literally steps from the hospital. Burke held the door for her as they went inside. "It's so close. Do you eat here often?"

"Yes and no. If I'm grabbing lunch on shift, sometimes I don't leave the hospital. Or there's a noodle takeaway not far that's decent and fast."

"No need for five-star dining?"

He laughed. "Hardly. Some days I pack a peanut butter sandwich for myself. I can cook, you know."

She was trying to picture that as they were shown to a table. They both ordered still water to drink, and then Bella picked up her menu. She couldn't remember the last time she'd had good sushi. Deciding was going to be hard.

In the end she got miso soup to start and twelve assorted sushi rolls, choosing to stay simple with her choices. "I won't be able to eat all twelve," she said. "We can share."

He nodded. "Why don't I make a few choices and we can just share everything?"

That sounded perfect, so when the server came back Bella ordered her soup and the rolls, while Burke added his own soup, as well as edamame and sashimi. Bella's stomach growled in anticipation and Burke chuckled. "Looks like we got here just in time."

"I've been too nervous to eat much."

"You were really worried, huh?"

She nodded. "I can't thank you enough, Burke. For what you did for us in Italy and for getting Maman in to see Dr. Mallick so quickly. She'll be on the road to recovery much faster now."

"I was happy to. And blockages are nothing to play with. She's been having these attacks for a while. I don't think she wanted you to know how long."

Bella frowned. "Why would she wait to see a doctor?"

He shrugged. "Fear? Or just telling herself it was stress or whatever."

"Then I'm doubly glad you were there to bully her into going."

He lifted an eyebrow. "I don't think anyone bullies Aurora Pemberton into anything."

"You're right," she conceded. "Must be your charm."

He opened his mouth to respond but just then the server came back with their appetizers. The miso smelled heavenly, and Bella dipped her spoon in for a taste while Burke went for the edamame first.

They made more casual conversation as they ate, first the soup, and then the sushi that arrived looking fresh and colorful and scrumptious. The wasabi was delightfully hot and the spicy tuna roll was perfection. She reached for another roll with her chopsticks and clashed with Burke's.

"En garde," he joked.

"I'll fight you for the salmon avocado roll," she replied, jabbing his chopsticks with hers.

He laughed. "Maybe we can negotiate for it."

Her eyes narrowed. "Hmm. Depends on what you're offering."

His gaze settled on hers and he said, simply, "You can have it if you stay with me tonight, instead of at the hotel."

She nearly dropped her chopsticks. It was a most unexpected proposition, and one she knew she must turn down. She knew what he was asking. It wasn't a "stay at my place because it's convenient" thing. They were past that sort of platonic invitation, even though in truth they'd only shared a single, fairly chaste kiss. He wasn't offering his spare bed. He was asking her to stay…with him. Charlotte's earlier words rang in her ears. Did she really want to miss out on this kind of opportunity, with a man like him?

And yet…how well did she really know him? She knew he was kind, and that he liked helping people, and that he didn't seem to care a jot that he held any sort of title. But there was so much more beneath the surface.

How would he feel if he knew that she had never been with a man before? He'd retract his invitation, and that would be humiliating to the extreme. And yet how could she explain to him why she was saying no? He deserved for her to be honest but even being honest made her so very vulnerable. She was doomed either way.

"You can have it," she said, withdrawing her chopsticks. He didn't move, just held her gaze evenly as his lips formed a pout. "At least tell me you're tempted. My pride deserves that much."

Why did he always manage to make her want to laugh? "I'm tempted, okay? But Burke…that's… I mean…" She let out a breath and tried to gather her thoughts. "I'm not good at being casual with this sort of thing." She waited for lightning to strike her on the spot. Being casual? Being anything! She figured she was blushing and hoped it wasn't noticeable. Thirty years old and still a virgin. She figured that must be some sort of record, and not one she was going to advertise.

"Did I say anything about being casual?" He leaned closer. "What if I told you that I'm not ready for the day to end? I want to spend it with you. To have the chance to really get to know you." He reached for her hand, still holding the chopsticks. "The way I should have all those years ago, when I was too busy being an idiot."

She bit down on her lip. He had seen the marks on her skin and didn't seem to care, did he? And yes, he'd been an idiot, but she could easily pin some of that blame on her brothers. "Listen, Stephen and William made you promise. And I decided to show you what you were missing. There is enough blame about that night to go around."

"It is what it is," he agreed. "But it doesn't have to stay that way. I want to spend today with you. I want to spend the night with you. Be with you in the morning and take you to the hospital to get your mum. To sit with you when you drink your morning tea."

Is this what being wooed was like? She liked it. And he remembered that she drank tea, not coffee, in the mornings.

Still, it seemed too soon to make any promises. She needed time to think if this was really what she wanted. If she was ready. Odd question, considering her age. And if she were going to trust anyone, it would be Burke. She'd forgiven the boy he'd been that first night at the Baresi villa. Since then he'd done nothing to make her think she couldn't trust him.

"Can I think about it?" she asked, and butterflies went winging through her belly as soon as she said it, opening the door to the possibility.

"Of course you can. Just remember that I care about you. I'm crazy attracted to you. That's not going to change if you say no."

At the moment she was thinking he was rather too good to be true. He had to have a flaw somewhere, but she'd yet to find it. And that made her uncomfortable.

"You have the salmon roll anyway," he said, sitting back and smiling. "I'm getting full."

He'd eaten most of the sashimi, and there were only a few rolls left. Bella swiped some wasabi onto the salmon roll and popped it in her mouth, savoring the spicy heat. When it was gone, they were too full for any sort of dessert. Burke paid the bill, and they made the walk back to the hospital.

"Aurora should be awake now," he said. "And definitely more alert. Do you want to go see her?"

"Very much." She wanted to see for herself that her mother was all right. To make sure she wasn't having any pain. Burke would be there, too, and would know what to look for.

They went back in the hospital, making their way to Aurora's room. Burke's invitation still rang in Bella's ears. Could she do it? Was Burke the man she would finally sleep with?

She had to stop thinking so much, or the significance of it was going to grow to gigantic proportions. He cared about her, but he was still only offering one night, not a marriage proposal. She needed to remember that. The most important thing was that no matter what she chose, he must never know she was a virgin. For both their sakes.

CHAPTER SEVEN

AURORA WAS SITTING up in bed, still wearing the hospital gown, but looking none the worse for wear. Bella had stopped and picked up a bottle of orange juice and a small sandwich in case Aurora hadn't eaten yet. She'd fasted before the procedure, and now it was midafternoon.

"Maman," Bella said, happy to see healthy color in her mother's cheeks. "You did great. Dr. Mallick said you did brilliantly."

"I'm supposed to go slowly for a while, and I might be crazy, but I think I already feel better."

Burke smiled and leaned over and kissed her cheek. "The stent keeps the artery open. The increased blood flow makes a big difference in how you feel. Are you hungry? Bella picked up a snack for you."

"I wasn't for a while. The sedative made me a bit nauseated. But I might be able to eat."

"It's just juice and a sandwich. But I can get you something else—"

"Nonsense, darling, this is fine." For all Aurora's wealth and status, deep down she was not a diva. Bella had always liked that about her. When they'd been kids, they'd never been allowed to throw tantrums about not liking a gift or wanting something better. They'd had to at least try everything that was put on the table. Bella had always credited it to her mother's very humble beginnings. She'd married into her wealth; she hadn't been born into it.

Bella uncapped the juice and poured it into a cup. "Here. It's cold."

Aurora took a long drink and let out a happy sigh. "That's lovely. Just missing champagne."

Burke and Bella laughed. "No mimosas for you for a day or two," Burke warned.

"Did you two eat? You've been here all day." She looked up from her juice, her gaze shifting between them.

"Burke took me for sushi nearby, once we'd spoken to your doctor. We thought it would give you time to wake up."

"Good."

"Is there anything we can get you, Maman? The evening is bound to be a long one." Bella almost wished there'd be something. It would give her an excuse…a way to not have to make a decision about going to Burke's.

"No, thank you, Bella. I actually brought a book and some magazines. I'm going to take the opportunity to just rest. With work and the commotion with the wedding, a night to not do anything sounds like a treat." She cast a sideways glance at Burke. "Even if I do have to wear this awful gown."

"You can change out of it if you like," he said. "If you brought something comfortable."

"I can help you," Bella offered.

"Bella, I can dress myself. You don't need to hover."

Bella sat on the bed and looked into Aurora's face. "Indulge me. I've been horribly worried about you."

"I know." Aurora softened her voice. "And I'm so thankful you've been with me the past few days. You've been a real calm support, which is just what I needed. But today? I'm just going to read some magazines and get some extra rest. Tomorrow, when we go home, you can fuss all you want."

"Promise?"

Aurora chuckled. "I'll regret this, but I promise. Please, go enjoy an evening out. When was the last time you really had one? And don't say Italy. William's wedding doesn't count."

So much for having an excuse.

"Only if you're sure. And if you want anything at all, I have my mobile. I'll be back in the morning and then we'll get you out of here and back to the manor. Mrs. Flanagan and the cook are ready to spoil you rotten with healthy meals. I hear they've been scouring books and websites to find heart-healthy recipes with your favorite foods."

Burke looked over at Bella. "Mrs. Flanagan is still with you?"

She nodded. "You remember her?"

"I do. Red hair, right? Daughter about our age, maybe a bit younger?"

Bella nodded. "You've got a good memory."

"You two should catch up," Aurora said. "Go on. I'm going to eat my sandwich and then maybe nap again. I won't have this much solitude for a while."

Bella kissed her mother on her head and Burke gave Aurora's hand a squeeze. "Any pain, anything that doesn't feel right, you hit that call bell for the nurse, all right? They already have instructions to call Dr. Mallick and me."

"Thank you, dear. I will. I promise."

They left her room and Bella started to giggle. "Oh, my. My mother just called you 'dear.' You're about to bump Stephen from the Golden Boy pedestal."

Burke laughed. "I doubt it. But if being here gave your mother peace of mind, I was happy to do it."

She hesitated when they got to the elevator. "Burke, about your offer…"

He looked over at her, and his eyes took on an intensity that both frightened and exhilarated her. The thing was, she wanted to. And after all this time, she was starting to think it would be better to get it over with. Her virginity was becoming an albatross she couldn't shake.

But she'd told him that she couldn't be casual, and that was the deep-down truth. She wanted him. The kiss on the plane had been a mere taster. What if it had been just the surprise of it that had caused such a reaction? What if this was all blown out of proportion? On impulse, she took a step toward him and pressed her mouth to his.

After a flicker of surprise, he relaxed and kissed her back, his lips warm and tempting. A delicious shiver ran over her body as his tongue slipped into her mouth. She nearly lifted her hand to slide into his hair when the elevator chimed and the doors started to open.

She jumped back as if the contact burned her, and moved to make space for the people getting on the elevator.

But the truth was his kiss was hot fire and not just "pleasant." The heat of it raced through her veins, making her want things she usually could resist. And yet she didn't want to promise something she couldn't necessarily follow through on. If she said yes, and then froze…she'd feel like an idiot. The humiliation would be awful.

They reached the ground floor and the doors opened. The other passengers got out first, then Bella, with Burke's wide hand resting lightly on the hollow of her back. "Bella?" he asked.

She turned and faced him, aware they were in a busy public area, but knowing this was the moment she had to decide. She looked into his face and took a deep breath. "Here's the thing," she said, trying to keep her voice down. "If I say yes to spending the night, I still want… I need… oh, damn. I need to know that it doesn't have to mean sex if…" Heat rushed to her face and neck and she slid her gaze away from him.

But he put his hand under her chin and cupped it gently,

turning it so that she faced him again. "You always, always have the right to say no. I want you, Bella. I'll be honest about that. I want you to stay with me tonight. But if we get there and you decide you need to sleep in the spare room… then that's where you'll sleep."

"And you…"

He gave her a sideways smile. "I can take care of myself."

She caught the double meaning in his words and tried not to laugh. He made her feel so beautiful, so desirable. No man had ever done that for her before. Honestly, she tended to deliberately put herself in the background. Charlotte had been the Pemberton sister to get all the attention. It felt nice to be wooed, if she was being truthful with herself.

And she wanted to spend more time with him. After tomorrow she'd be going back to Chatsworth Manor until the beginning of the week, and then to Paris next week to work in the office full-time. Her mother was taking an entire month off, which meant that Bella would be in charge for a minimum of three weeks. She wasn't sure she was ready. Tonight could be her last hurrah for a while. Why not spend it with someone whose company she truly enjoyed? And who seemed to enjoy hers, not out of professional obligation but just because?

"What did you have in mind?" she asked. It was still afternoon. The idea that he'd been thinking they'd rush off to his place and fall in bed for the rest of the day made her incredibly anxious. If she were going to be with him she had to work up to it gradually.

He checked his watch and frowned. "It's just after three. But I have an idea. Something I think you'd really enjoy." He took her hand. "Come on."

He pulled her forward, and once they were outside in the summer heat again, he hailed a taxi. She half heard him give instructions to the driver as she climbed in, and then he made a quick phone call as they sped away, leaving the hospital and her mother behind.

"Where are we going?"

He tucked his phone back in his pants pocket and grinned. "It's a surprise. One of my favorite places in London, actually. And we should be there in maybe ten minutes."

She was intrigued and sat back in her seat, determined to enjoy the spontaneity. There'd been so little of that in her adult life that it was a strange but not unwelcome sensation. There'd been no "whisking away" on mystery dates. No propositions over sushi. This was turning out to be a day of many firsts, it seemed.

The taxi zipped into South London and it seemed like in no time at all that they were at the Horniman Museum. She tilted her head a bit, wondering what about this made it his favorite place in the city. He paid the driver, they popped out, and he took her hand. "Ready?"

The Horniman Museum and Gardens covered over sixteen acres, featuring a number of gardens, a meadow, the main museum, and various other buildings. They entered at the north end, and Burke took her hand again and headed straight to the entrance of the butterfly house.

Butterflies. Her fascination intensified.

There was a family waiting to gain entrance, and Burke looked at his watch. "We made it. Last entrance is at three thirty. This family will go in and then we've got the last slot of the day."

She squinted as she looked up at him. "You are full of surprises."

"I'm glad to hear it." He smiled down at her. "It's going to be warm in there. You might be a bit toasty."

She'd chosen bone-colored linen trousers and sandals for the day; cool enough, she supposed, and certainly cooler than Burke's khakis. But while he wore short sleeves, she had on a peasant top in sage green, the sleeves dropping to past her elbows, and her hair was pulled back in a partial braid from the sides, before trailing halfway down her back.

"I'll be fine." She smiled faintly. Making accommodations due to her injuries had become such a long-standing habit that it surprised her to realize she felt a bit resentful of it in this moment. What would she give to simply coil her hair up in a messy topknot and let the air at her nape? Small things to anyone else. And yet the thought of it made her stomach twist just a bit.

The family entered and then they advanced in line. "Burke Phillips," he stated.

"Oh, Mr. Phillips, hello." The young girl working admission looked to be a summer student, perhaps, and her cheeks pinkened at the sight of Burke. Why not, after all? He was ridiculously handsome. "You're our last entrance of the day. It'll just be a few minutes."

"Thanks," he replied, and they waited silently.

It wasn't long and she checked her watch. "Oh, you might as well go ahead. It's only five minutes. Just a reminder that we close in half an hour."

"Perfect. Thank you so much."

They entered and Bella looked behind her at the girl, then at Burke. "She didn't charge you!" Her mouth had dropped open. "Did you just get in here for free because you batted your handsome eyelashes?"

He laughed. "No, I got in for free because I'm a benefactor. I told you, it's one of my favorite places. I make a donation every year."

Well, that was a relief. "Oh."

"I love that your mind went that way, though." He chuckled again. "Jealous, darling?"

She didn't want to answer that. Instead she asked the obvious question as they moved into the house and the heat and humidity hit. "So why is this on your list?"

Burke's feet stopped and he faced her. "I spent a lot of weekend mornings here. My mother used to bring us several times a year. We'd visit the butterfly house, the museum, the aquarium, walk the gardens. Then we'd go to the café and she'd let us order whatever we liked, no matter what time of day it was. Those are good childhood memories."

And he was sharing it with her. He was so open. So comfortable with himself, and that was something she couldn't relate to at all. She was really beginning to understand how high and thick the walls were that she'd built around herself. They were invisible and innocuous until someone like Burke came along and made her realize how big they really were. Did she even know who the real Bella was? Or was she someone constructed after one dreadful, life-altering mistake?

"Are you all right?" He was peering down at her with concern. "You look upset. Should I not have brought you here?"

She shook her head quickly. "No, this is lovely. I'm just…in awe of you. You share so easily. I don't know how to do that."

"It takes a while to learn," he admitted. "I was pretty withdrawn for a while. Honestly, your brother helped me a lot. He knew what had happened, and when we met again at university, his friendship…it meant a lot. He was the one guy who knew my secret and liked me anyway. But before then… I didn't share at all."

"I haven't, either. Only surface stuff," she admitted.

"Don't worry, Bella. I still have a few secrets."

They walked along slowly. Bella found her breath slowing as she relaxed, despite the moist heat. The quiet, the tropical plants, the soft flitting of butterflies…it all soothed. She smiled as a butterfly landed on Burke's shoulder, the colors striking with black and white spots and a stunning shade of orange in toward the body. "Don't move," she said, and she reached for her phone to take a picture.

To her surprise, the butterfly stayed perched there, so light and fragile, and she snapped the photo. "It's so gorgeous. I wish I knew what kind it was."

"A leopard lacewing," he stated softly.

Of course he would know.

"What do we do now?"

"Leave it be and carry on. It'll move on when it's ready."

Her smile grew. This was such a lovely way to spend the afternoon, even if she was sweating from the humidity. She lifted her hair and fanned her neck a bit, and Burke looked over, his eyes wide with what she now considered his "soulful" look, one that must inspire so much trust in his patients. "What?"

"You should just put it up if it bothers you. We're the last ones in here. No one will see."

He was right. They were alone and she was sweltering in the heat between the pants, the long sleeves, and the weight of her hair. "Give me a moment," she said, and then with quick fingers she slid the elastic out of her braid, shook out the plait, and then gathered up the whole mass and twisted it up into a coil. She used the elastic to anchor it, though the band didn't feel quite up to the task. "It won't hold forever, but it does feel better."

"I'm glad."

And if anything more happened tonight, he'd see her scars again. The one on the back of her neck was probably her angriest one, though.

They meandered through the butterfly house. In some spots, plates were set out with sweet fruit, and clusters of butterflies could be found congregating, eating their fill. There were plaques throughout explaining life stages and signage marking the tropical foliage, but she most enjoyed it when Burke pointed out the ones he knew: the large owl butterflies, gray and brown, with large spots that looked like owl eyes on their wings; stunning black-and-green emerald butterflies, the vibrant green matching the leaves on which they sat. Dozens of them flitted through the air, and one settled on the top of Bella's topknot. Burke used her phone to take a picture and told her she should call it "hair accessories." That led her to talking about Charlotte and Jacob, and how he'd given her a butterfly pendant to show how she'd grown and changed.

"Charlotte was so good at what she did. And she was Aurora Inc. from top to toe. Always wore black and white, the signature colors. But she was hiding herself behind what she thought were expectations. Since she met Jacob, she's really blossomed into someone even more spectacular."

"We're all hiding behind something. Expectations is a good one."

"What are you hiding behind, Burke?"

"Guilt."

She stopped as the light tone of the conversation turned to something weightier. "I'm sorry. That's a tough one. Self-forgiveness... I don't know. It's easier to forgive someone else than yourself."

"Nailed it," he answered. "And what do you hide behind, Bella?"

She thought for a moment. She didn't hide behind her scars—she hid because of them. "Fear," she finally said, her throat tight.

"Of what?"

Another butterfly perched on her finger. She could barely breathe; she didn't want to disturb the beautiful creatures who felt safe enough to alight on her body. "Of people knowing I'm not perfect. My family isn't perfect but outwardly? We don't show our flaws. I don't want to be..." She hesitated.

"The only one?"

"Yes," she breathed. "I don't want to be the only one, the focus of curiosity and pity and speculation. I have never wanted that kind of attention, not even in positive ways."

"But in doing that, you haven't let you be you, either," he reasoned. "Bella."

She looked up, shocked to see tears in his eyes.

He swallowed, his throat bobbing with the effort. "If I had stopped Royce that night, if I hadn't listened to your brothers, you would have been spared all this. He'd still be alive. I failed everyone that night, and I'm so sorry. You're stuck in this prison you've made around yourself all because I was a jackass."

She ignored the butterfly on her hand and reached out to him. The butterfly flew off with a delicate flap of its wings. "It was not your fault! I was so determined to show you what you were missing I went along with Royce even though I knew it was stupid! You came along...why did you do that?"

"Because I wanted to make sure you were all right. Instead, when everything happened, I couldn't even help you."

The truth of that settled around her as she put herself in his shoes. He'd gone along to keep an eye on her, and instead he'd ended up unconscious and unable to assist at all. For someone like him—who was driven to help people—that must have been a tough pill to swallow.

She bit down on her lip. "We can't change what happened. And if I've built a prison around myself, well, that's on me. My decision to make. When I was younger my family tried to tell me I was isolating myself too much. I buried myself in the cosmetics side of the business, trying new things, learning new techniques, all so I could better hide. That is not on you, Burke. And if you spend your entire life trying to redeem yourself because of one mistake, you're going to end up dissatisfied. Like me. Let go. If it's forgiveness you need, you have it. Though there's nothing to forgive."

It was the most she'd ever said to anyone about the emotions associated with her scars. It was understood to be a nonstarter for discussion in the Pemberton household. But it felt good to say it all now. And the fact that she trusted Burke with it was both astounding and frightening.

She stepped away from him, moving to the next curve in the path through the display, needing the space. She turned around and faced him, but he didn't move. He just waited, staring at her, while everything they'd just admitted settled around them, the weight of it fragile and even beautiful.

She lifted her arms a little and realized half a dozen little butterflies had gravitated to her blouse. They were everywhere, and she caught her breath as one perched precariously on the tip of her nose. She looked past it to Burke, who was smiling widely, his phone out, snapping pictures. And then she couldn't help it either. She smiled back, a wondrous feeling made up of so many emotions she couldn't list them all. It was just a beautiful, expansive feeling that was somehow calming and grounding and perfect.

He came to her then, but didn't touch her. "They're too fragile," he said softly. "I don't want to damage one. We'll keep going and staff will inspect us for any random travelers before we leave."

"We're okay?" she asked, needing to be sure. They'd covered some heavy ground.

"We're more than okay," he replied. "What you said… I'm still not sure I believe you. But it means more than you know." His gaze delved into hers, so intense she was afraid she might lose herself in it. "I wish I could kiss you right now. But the lacewing on your nose has moved to your hairline and I'm afraid of smushing it."

"You can kiss me later," she replied, surprising herself with her boldness.

"I'm counting on it."

When they reached the exit, one of the staff had to remove the hangers-on. There was no time for Bella to put her hair down, but to her relief the young man assisting her never even blinked at the sight of the ugly white line across her neck. He just did his job, smiling and chatting the whole time, and then she was outside again with Burke, where the air was still summery but not nearly as humid and hot.

"Let's take a walk in the gardens," he suggested, and held out his hand.

She left her hair in the floppy knot and twined her fingers with his.

CHAPTER EIGHT

BURKE HELD HER hand as they walked through the gardens in the waning afternoon. The entrances wouldn't close for hours, and they had the luxury of meandering to enjoy the fresh, fragranced air.

What she'd said inside, about forgiveness—both about how hard it was to forgive himself, and also offering hers—he'd had to hold himself together and it had been tough. He'd tried to do the right thing that night all around and had failed miserably at it all. He hadn't responded to her flirting because of her brothers. But he'd watched over her just the same, and made the wrong decision to keep her safe. To keep all of them safe. Royce had died. Fiona had sustained minor injuries, but a person didn't walk away from that sort of accident without lingering emotions. And Bella…she'd paid a high price as well. She was marked for life.

But she didn't blame him. She took responsibility for her own actions. Did she know how strong she was? How rare? Who was he to judge her for wanting to keep her scars hidden in an industry that demanded perfection? Who was he to judge at all when he carried his own secrets around, hidden away from the world? All this talk about forgiveness…and he still hadn't found a way to forgive his father. And now his dad was gone and forgiveness was moot anyway. Still, what kind of a man was he who wanted to be forgiven but couldn't find it within himself to do the same?

She'd left her hair up this afternoon. He glanced over and saw the jagged lines just below her hairline. Other than in the pool, he had never seen her with her hair up. In the butterfly house they'd been alone. Now there were lots of other people milling about.

He got the feeling this was a big step for her.

They wandered past the prehistoric garden, their pace slow and lazy. Conversation, too, was light, which he appreciated as he absorbed what had happened inside. They read about different plants and environments, remarking on items of interest. The sunken garden was glorious, a riot of color but all set so precisely in the center. Bella surprised him by taking a selfie of them together. She seemed so... free. It was a marked change from the woman he'd been drawn to in Italy and the worried daughter from this morning. He liked the change. A lot.

They carried on to the bandstand, which he knew had the most amazing view of the city. Bella stopped and took a deep breath when they reached the top of the hill. "Oh. This is stunning! I wish I had a different camera. My phone just doesn't quite cut it."

The city lay below them, peaks and spires and high rises, with the Shard dominating them all. A haze had settled over the buildings there, creating a dreamlike quality.

"Good choice for the afternoon?" he asked.

"The best!" She turned to him, her smile wide. "I didn't realize how much I needed something like this. It's been wedding and work and worry about Maman for days. Thank you, Burke. This has been perfect. Even the weather has cooperated."

"No summer showers...yet," he added.

"It could rain for all I care." She reached out and put her hand on his arm. "You've made what might have been a very stressful day into something I'll remember for a long time."

He wanted to say that there could be many more afternoons like this, but could there be, really? He'd asked her to spend the night with him. He wanted that. Wanted her. But was it fair? His work was here, and yes, Chatsworth was not that long a drive, but it wasn't her permanent home. That was Paris.

Maybe he should withdraw his invitation, but how would she take that? As a rejection? It certainly wasn't. And it seemed presumptive to have a "relationship" talk at this early stage. It wasn't casual, but it wasn't not casual. It was…complicated.

"What's wrong?" she asked.

"Nothing." He smiled at her again. "Absolutely nothing."

"Good. Because I think you need to stop thinking and just enjoy the day." Her smile was wide, her eyes bright.

It was good advice, and he decided to take it. They could just let things play out organically tonight, couldn't they?

After their long walk, they were both hungry. It was Bella who suggested dinner. "Let's eat at my hotel," she said. "The restaurant there is amazing and I'd like to treat you, Burke. You've done so much for me, and for Maman."

The hotel. She'd said she was going to stay with him, but the hotel gave her a reason to go either way. Either she'd grab her bag and leave with him, or he'd leave after dinner—alone. Still, he couldn't refuse her. He rather suspected he couldn't refuse her anything if she asked, and that was a bit worrying.

They took a cab back to her hotel in Westminster. They hadn't made reservations, but a word from Bella and they were escorted to a table by the window. She'd taken her hair out of the elastic in the cab, and had run her fingers through it, creating a waterfall of dark waves that he longed to sink his hands into. They were dressed a bit casually for the setting, but that didn't affect their service at all. Within moments they were given menus and Bella ordered them a bottle of fine red.

When they were alone again, Bella asked, "Do you mind if I text Maman to check in with her?"

"Of course not. Why would I?"

She laughed. "We have a family rule about tech at the table. Started when we got our first phones and it's stuck."

"I give you permission." He grinned at her. "You know, sometimes the Pembertons really seem like a normal family."

She lifted a shoulder in a shrug. "You mean, other than the money, the properties, the titles, the servants?"

"That's exactly what I mean." He grinned as she tapped in a quick message. "It's one of the reasons I liked William so much. Everyone did, actually."

"He's a lovable guy."

"It runs in the family." He was gratified when she blushed yet again. He was trying to be subtle with his flirting, easing their way into the rest of the evening, no matter what choice she made.

"I think I'm going to start with the baked camembert and then have the quail," she said, putting her menu aside. "Newsflash: I love cheese."

He scanned the menu. "And I think I'll have the duck croquette and then the sea bass." He also put his menu aside. "I haven't been here in ages. Even if it is close to work."

"No bringing your hot dates out for some fine French cuisine?"

"I don't really date. To be honest, I don't want to date anyone where I work, because that can get messy. And I work a lot, so…"

She lifted an eyebrow. Their wine arrived and once it was poured he watched Bella take a long sip. "Oh, that's lovely," she said, closing her eyes. How had he not noticed how sensual she was before?

The wine was delicious, and so was their food, though to Burke's surprise he was so wrapped up in talking that he was surprised when his plate was empty and they were offered dessert.

Bella looked up at the server and smiled. "Opera cake, *s'il vous plaît*."

He loved that she didn't refuse dessert but instead went for something rich and decadent. "I'll have the *tarte tatin*," he said. And when the server was gone, he poured the rest of the wine from the bottle into their glasses.

"This was really nice," Bella said, sitting back in her chair. She looked utterly relaxed, for the first time since he'd seen her in the Baresi kitchen. Did that mean she was comfortable with him? He let his gaze cling to hers as he lifted his glass, slowly sipping the rich wine. They'd spent the entire day together, and it wasn't over yet. At least he hoped.

"You have bedroom eyes," she said, toying with her glass. "When you look at me that way."

There were things he might have said had they not been in a public restaurant, so instead he let a smile tease the corners of his lips. "Only when I look at you, Bella."

Appreciation lighted her eyes. "And you're a smooth talker."

"I only tell the truth."

"That's a very dangerous statement to make. It really locks you in, you know."

"Ask me anything." His breath held after he said it.

"Your favorite color."

"Green."

"Guilty pleasure for food."

Easy. "Fish and chips. In paper, with lots of vinegar."

"Mmm...yummy. Theme song?"

He considered his glass. "Hmm, that's a tough one. Pass, while I think about it."

"Thing you're most proud of."

Another easy one. "Graduating from medical school."

"The one thing you'd never want people to know about you."

He halted, brought up short by that question. The lightning round quality to the first questions had been light and somewhat predictable. This, though…he lifted his glass and drained what was left in it. He thought of his father and the wine burned down his throat and into his stomach. But that…he didn't own his father's guilt. He reminded himself of that often. "The accident," he said hoarsely. "So maybe we're more alike than you thought after all. I don't want people to look at me differently because of what happened. As they surely would. I've worked so hard at building my reputation. Of trying to outlive what happened. But it feels very much like a house of cards that could come tumbling down. So you see, Bella, I can't criticize you for hiding your scars. Because I'm hiding mine, too."

As quiet fell between them, their desserts came. It gave Burke time to reset the mood, take it from something so heavy to something more fun and intimate. "Okay. Enough about me. Your turn. Favorite color."

"Blue."

"Guilty pleasure in the food department."

"Chocolate. And ice cream."

He filed that one away for future reference. He decided against the theme song and instead asked, "What do you consider the perfect date?"

Her smile blossomed. "Today."

Now he was getting somewhere.

"The one thing you wish people knew about you."

Her eyes darkened, just a little, as her gaze met his and held. "I'm not always as practical as I seem."

"Ah." He nodded, his body tensing in a delicious way. "Hidden passions."

"You could say that."

"Arabella Pemberton, always in control."

"Appearances can be misleading."

He had a premonition of her being out of control and had to take a long, slow breath. "I think we should eat our dessert," he said roughly.

Her eyes held a spark of challenge. "Chicken," she said, and then her smile lifted on one side, mocking him, and he realized he loved her subtle but sharp sense of humor.

He hoped beyond hope that she was leaving the hotel with him tonight.

Bella had already made her choice, but their conversation over dinner had sealed it. She dipped her fork into the luscious cake and fought back the nerves about what was to come. Today Burke had been very open with her, sharing his own insecurities. It was clear that the physical attraction was a real thing and she liked him…a lot. Moreover, she trusted him as much as she'd ever trusted anyone. Today had been the perfect date. She hadn't lied about that. The butterfly house and the gardens and a romantic dinner…there wasn't a single part of it that hadn't been absolutely lovely.

"Your cake looks amazing."

"Here, try some." She put some on her fork and held it out, and he leaned forward and closed his lips around it. She was mesmerized by the sight of them touching the tines, taking the cake into his mouth. She wanted to kiss him again, badly. To be held in his arms and to have the time to kiss him properly, without sneaking it in an airplane galley or a briefly empty elevator.

"Mmm…delicious."

"It is. And rich. But every now and then you have to treat yourself."

The rest of dessert seemed to take too long. When they were finally finished, and Bella signaled for the bill, a slight awkwardness fell over them. Burke was waiting, she knew. Waiting for her to confirm what she'd said earlier. She'd chosen the hotel restaurant deliberately, because if she got cold feet it would be easy to go upstairs and spend the evening alone, as planned. But she wasn't going to do that. She was going to grab her overnight bag, drop her key and go with him. To his place.

Burke reached over and took her hand when she signed the slip to charge the meal to the room. "Bella," he said, his voice hesitant.

"Let me go upstairs and get my things," she replied quietly. "I'll drop my key in the express checkout for the morning."

His eyes widened.

"I wasn't sure, either," she said. "But I am now."

They got up from the table and she put a hand on his arm. "Wait for me in the lobby. I'll be back soon."

She took the elevator upstairs, her heart pounding the whole time. She was mostly sure of what she was doing, and the little bit that wasn't sure, she understood was nerves because this was a Big Deal. Inside the room, she took a few minutes to tuck her things into her small bag and clear her toiletries out of the bathroom. Her throat tightened as she thought of the hours ahead. Would it be wonderful? Awkward? Disappointing? Her hand paused on the door handle. Burke. Of all the men over the years, she'd chosen Burke. He was the only one who knew what happened to her, who had seen how badly she'd been marked, and he wanted her anyway.

It was time to go.

She closed the hotel room door behind her and made her

way down in the elevator again. Burke hadn't moved from his spot in the lobby, and she took a hidden moment to study him. He was such a gentleman. And sexy and smart and… there wasn't much to not like about him, really. Eventually she knew she'd have to discover his flaws, but right now she was enjoying him being rather perfect.

He turned when she approached, a smile lighting his face, warming her from the inside out. "Ready?" he asked.

At Burke's suggestion, they took the tube to Piccadilly Circus and then switched and got off at Green Park. It was his usual route to work, he said, unless he needed the fresh air and brisk walk. His flat was only a five-minute walk from the station, and he solicitously carried Bella's bag over his shoulder as they entered his building.

"When did you move out of the family home?" she asked as they climbed the stairs to his flat.

"When I got the job at the hospital. I was hardly ever there anyway, what with being away at school. It hadn't really been home for some time."

"I feel the same," she admitted. "We have the manor house and the château in Provence. But those are places to visit. We all have our own flats or houses."

"And yours is in Paris."

"It is. Stephen has one there, and William, too. Charlotte has moved out of hers and is living with Jacob in Richmond. Though if she comes over, she stays with either Maman or me. It's been nice, having sisterly sleepovers."

He opened his door and let her in first.

The space was very Burke. Welcoming and comfortable, but also modern and somehow light. His furniture was simple, a gray sofa and chair with a glass-topped coffee table on a printed rug. To the left Bella saw the kitchen and caught a glimpse of the brushed steel finish on the appliances and fixtures. "I like it," she said, turning around and smiling at him. "It's like walking into an Ikea showroom."

He laughed. "Would it be wrong to say 'busted'? There might just be a few items from that store in this flat." He took her bag. "Let me show you the rest."

The rest consisted of a lovely bathroom with a claw-foot tub and hexagonal shower, a bedroom decorated in blues and pale yellows, looking fresh and appealing, and then his bedroom, which went back to the gray color scheme again, with dove-gray on the walls and a gray-and-black duvet on the king-sized bed. The bed took up half the room, while a dresser and nightstand rounded out the furniture.

"Again, very you," she said, trying to keep her voice light. But ever since they'd entered his room, that awkward pall had fallen over them again. She knew it was just nerves. What surprised her was that they seemed to be coming from him as well as her.

One of them being nervous was bad enough.

He put her bag down by the dresser, then met her eyes. Let out a breath. When the silence drew out for three or four seconds, he asked, "Would you like a drink?"

She would. Desperately. Her nerves were coiled tighter than a spring.

He led her out of the bedroom, but grasped her hand in his and kept it there, forming a connection that felt sweet but also very intentional. In the kitchen, he took a bottle of cabernet off the counter and reached for two glasses in a cabinet.

"You seem to prefer red."

"I do." She took the glass from his fingers and added, "It's supposed to be good for your heart."

A slow smile graced his lips as his eyes warmed to dark, chocolaty pools. She could lose herself in them, she realized, and with that came the knowledge that she wanted to. And yet…she was horribly afraid that she'd do something wrong, something silly that would give away her inexperience. She had no idea what to do right now. Anything that happened would be the beginning of something, and she was walking into totally new territory.

She would not think about how she was going through this at thirty when most women had conquered this mountain in their teens, or at least early twenties.

Instead she drank the wine, holding his gaze, wanting him to make the first move so she didn't have to. He took a drink as well, then put his glass on the counter to her right before moving closer. So close that his body was almost touching hers, and she could easily reach out and touch him.

Her glass shook in her hand.

He took it from her and placed it beside his, then turned his attention back to her, his smile gone. His clear, knowing eyes, the set of his mouth…so serious. As if he somehow understood the gravity of this moment though he couldn't possibly.

He put his hand along her face, just like he had in Italy, and then leaned forward to kiss her. It was soft and slow, giving her time to be sure, to respond and to give back rather than just take. She did, kissing him, sliding her hands around his ribs to rest on his back as his lips and tongue did delicious things, stoking her desire.

She did desire him. The need rising up in her was new and demanding, but she promised herself she wouldn't let her body get ahead of her head or her heart. So she let the sensation wash over her, taking her time. He was, after all, an excellent kisser, and there was no need to rush past this delightful introduction.

Burke nudged against her and her hips bumped the countertop, so that she was braced between it and his hard, strong body. She let her hands run on instinct and they pulled his shirt out of his pants and then slid beneath the fabric to the warm skin beneath. He caught his breath—were her hands cold? His skin was smooth and warm, and she wanted to feel herself pressed against it.

But to do that she'd have to remove her top, and she wasn't ready for that stage yet. Just the thought cooled her actions a little, and she paused the motion of her fingers.

"Don't stop," he murmured against her lips. "Your hands feel so good."

"You feel good," she said in reply, the sound muffled against his cheek as his lips slid from hers and skated along her jawline, creating shivers down her arms. Her whole body was now on full alert.

"You taste good," he added, and he pulled her earlobe into his mouth. A strangled sound passed her lips, and she was mortified, until he started kissing her again, with more urgency. So he'd liked it...

He slid his hand under her loose top and rested his palm on the curve of her waist. Nothing serious, nothing pushy... and yet her body strained forward, urging him to cup her breast. They were aching for his touch now, and when he didn't move his hand, she reached down and did it for him, sliding it up until it covered her breast and the hard tip pressed into his palm.

These sensations were not entirely foreign. She'd been seventeen when the accident had happened, after all, and had dated and fooled around as any teenager would. Even since then, she'd dated some, kissed, enjoyed some harmless touching. But she'd always stopped short, right around this point, unwilling to go any further and make herself vulnerable. This was the moment, then, where she either moved forward or halted what was happening between them.

Stopping was the last thing she wanted to do, both in her body and in her mind, and despite the fears and insecurities battling inside her.

His thumb flicked over her nipple and she inhaled sharply, felt herself tremble. Burke leaned close and murmured in her ear, "I'll take care of you, Bella."

He couldn't know. There was no way. Her sister didn't even know. But he'd said exactly the right thing because she knew he was the one she could trust. He'd already seen and hadn't run away. Not even close.

She reached for the buttons on his shirt and started undoing them, ignoring how badly her fingers were shaking. She pushed the shirt off his shoulders and admired his flat abs and broad chest. She'd gotten a good look at his upper body in the pool at the Baresi villa but now she could touch it and she did so, finding it smooth and warm. His eyes fluttered shut at her light touch and she marveled that she had the power to evoke that kind of a response. When his lids lifted, there was a heat in his eyes that was new.

"I like it when you touch me."

She hadn't expected him to be vocal, either. She'd always kind of pictured this happening in silence, but his voice brought an extra layer of participation that increased the intimacy between them. "I like it when you touch me, too," she whispered.

"I haven't even started." His hand grazed her breast again. "I'm trying to take it slow for you."

"I won't break," she replied, and hoped it was true.

He smiled then, and reached back under her top. With one hand he flicked the clasp of her bra, setting her breasts free. They felt heavy and needy for his touch, and when he slid his hands beneath the freed bra and filled his palms, she sighed with pleasure.

A few moments later, he reached for the hem of her shirt. "Okay?" he asked, seeking consent for every move. Damn, it was sexy of him to do that. She blocked out the sight of her scars in her mind and nodded her head. She wanted him so much, and wanted to be brave. She didn't want to demand darkness so he wouldn't see, so she could hide. If he was going to be with her, he would have to be with all of her.

The shirt slid easily over her shoulders, and her hair fell down her back as he pulled the fabric—and her bra—away.

There was no going back now. He could see everything.

Burke closed the space between them until his chest brushed against her sensitive breasts, and he dipped his head to kiss her. "You are so beautiful," he whispered, and then he did the most amazing thing. He abandoned her lips and instead bent his head and kissed her shoulder and the puckered skin there.

She'd been telling the truth when she said there was numbness with many of her scars. But numbness didn't mean she couldn't feel at all. She could feel the heat of his lips, the wetness of his tongue as he traced the angry lines. Somehow he was making the thing she hated about herself the most into something erotic and beautiful. Tears pricked behind her eyes as she realized she was in real danger here. A woman could fall in love with a man like Burke Phillips. And that was scary as hell.

His mouth drifted south, away from her scars to her breasts, and desire shot to her core. "Burke," she said hoarsely. "I'm not going to be able to stand up much longer."

His answer was to lift her up and plunk her on the counter, which was very much to his advantage as he stepped into the vee of her legs. His head was now at the perfect height to continue what he'd been doing, and Bella braced her hands on the counter and tried not to rush anything. Except now she was getting anxious, and her body was demanding more even as it was overwhelmed with sensation.

"Come here," he said, and he slid her off the counter so she was straddling his hips. He carried her that way to his bedroom, kicking the door shut with his foot and then taking her to the bed.

Once she was on the covers he reached for the button on his pants and slid them off, standing in front of her now in blue boxer briefs. She wasn't the only one ready for the next step, and Bella undid her trousers and shimmied out of them, with only a tiny scrap of lingerie now between them.

This was going to happen. She was ready. It was the right time, and the right person. It was okay if it hurt for a minute. She told herself all of these things as Burke reached for her panties and gave them a gentle tug.

She'd thought it would happen now, but Burke apparently had different ideas and she could not fault him for his attention to foreplay. He touched, kissed and stroked until she was so wired she wasn't sure what to do with herself. When she was sure she couldn't take another moment, he got a condom out of the nightstand. He peeled off his shorts and put it on before joining her again on the bed.

"Okay?" he asked.

She was terrified. This was the moment. And if he put it off any longer she might actually explode, so she answered, "Mm-hmm."

There was a brief pain, but nothing like she'd expected, and when she looked up Burke was watching her with that intense heat in his eyes that made her feel both powerful and possessed. He didn't look away, either, as he moved, and her heart lurched as she realized that this wasn't just having sex. It was making love. Burke was making love to her and it felt so good and so scary and so right she thought she might die from it.

She moved her hips and his lashes fluttered slightly. She tried it again and he made a sound in his throat that sounded—she hoped—like pleasure. Together they found a rhythm, twined together, and Bella forgot about everything she'd been afraid of, simply getting lost in the sublime sensations taking over her body. She ground against him, seeking some sort of release from the tension coiling in her, and he picked up the pace, until Bella threw her head back on the pillow and called out. She had absolutely no control over the contractions happening, and apparently Burke liked it because he said her name roughly before climaxing.

She'd done it. She was no longer a virgin, and she didn't think Burke had been able to tell. And yet the milestone paled in comparison to the feelings inside her right now for the man holding her in his arms.

She'd gone and done the most predictably teenage thing possible.

She'd fallen in love with the first man she'd slept with.

CHAPTER NINE

BURKE WASN'T SURE he'd ever be the same again.

Bella lay on his bed, head on his pillow, dark hair every which way. She was delightfully naked, which was a treat for his eyes. His gaze slid briefly over her scars. He didn't give a damn about them and wished she didn't, either. And yet he understood, and he also understood that this was her body and she was the one who got to decide what she did with it.

That she'd chosen to share it with him tonight had been a gift. A gift so great he wasn't sure he could feel his legs yet.

"Hey, Bel?" He looked at her and smiled, his body so blissed out he was sure he looked utterly goofy. "I figured out my theme song."

"Oh?" She looked supremely satisfied.

"Yep. 'Feels Like the First Time' by Foreigner."

Her face blanked and she sat up. "You could tell? Dammit!"

He slid to the side of the bed, alarmed by her quick shift of mood. "Wait, what?"

They stared at each other.

"Never mind," she said.

But her reaction had been so sudden and severe that the seed of an idea was planted in his mind. "What did you mean, I could tell?"

Her cheeks flushed a deep red. "It's nothing. Forget I said anything."

Had this…was it possible that this had been her very first time? He didn't want to be obvious and look for blood, and besides, that didn't always happen anyway. He was more shaken by the emotional consequences of it. Had Bella hidden away all this time? Had she been a virgin…and then she'd finally chosen him?

It was a massive thing, a first time, and he tried not to panic. He kept his voice deliberately and carefully soft as he looked at her. "Bel, if I'd known, I would have been… I don't know. Gentler." Her eyes filled with tears and he felt awful. "I'm sorry," he added.

"No, it's not that. I'm just…humiliated. I didn't want you to know. I hoped you couldn't tell."

Oh, hell. He got up and went to the bathroom briefly, then returned and put his briefs back on. Then he curled up beside her and gathered her into his arms. "The song… that was for me, sweetheart," he said. "Being with you was amazing for me. I honestly didn't know. Did I hurt you?"

She shook her head quickly. "No. And you didn't need to be gentler, Burke. It was…" She swallowed, and her voice lowered. "It was perfect."

"You're sure? I wish you had told me."

She snorted. "Yeah, right. Thirty years old. And then you would have been worried the whole time. I never wanted you to know. I'm an idiot for reacting as I did."

"No, you're not an idiot. Never." But he had to admit she was right. If he'd known beforehand, it probably would have changed things. He would have worried about whether he was going too fast, about hurting her, about any number of things. "I meant it when I said I couldn't tell. I was just caught up in being with you."

"I'm glad."

"Bella, look at me."

She turned her face up to his and he grazed her cheek-bone with his thumb. "I don't want you to have any regrets about tonight. So if there's something you need, please tell me."

"Just hold me for a little while."

That was easy enough to do. He'd asked her to spend the night and they had until dawn. If it was reassurance she needed, he'd give it. It was the least he could do.

And he'd ignore the tinny sound of alarm bells ringing in his head. It shouldn't make a difference, her being a virgin before tonight. He still couldn't believe it. He liked her a lot. Cared for her, certainly. But this was a Big Deal. And he was deathly afraid she was going to experience a level of attachment he wasn't prepared for and certainly hadn't anticipated. Or worse—that he'd start feeling that attachment. That he'd fall for her. Completely and utterly. After tonight, it was a distinct possibility. What had been getting to know each other and fooling around was suddenly very serious. After all his attempts to keep his personal relationships at arm's length, somehow Bella had sneaked past all his defenses in one single day.

He pulled down the covers and invited her to slide beneath the sheets, then opened his arm so she could lie close beside him. She snuggled in, and felt so right with her warm body next to his. She sighed and her muscles relaxed, and his jaw tightened. The protective feelings running through him right now sat uncomfortably in his bones.

"Better?" he asked. He wanted to make sure she was all right but although he'd never been the kind of man to get up and leave after sex, tonight he felt that urge for the first time. Not because he didn't care, but because he found himself caring too much and a sense of self-preservation had kicked in. What was he going to do?

"You didn't mind about my scars?" she asked, her voice small.

He put his own scrambled feelings aside and turned his full attention to her. "I've never cared, beyond caring that you were hurt so badly. I'm not repulsed. If anything, they show how strong you are."

"Burke..."

He closed his eyes. This was so unexpected, the feelings of tenderness running through him. How he could feel them and still want to flee was troubling. Baffling. The only thing he could come up with was that Bella was different somehow.

God, he didn't need this.

She shifted her head and looked up at him. "Are you all right?" she asked.

"Fine, I'm fine," he answered, smiling down at her.

But he wasn't fine. He was always in control. Always knew exactly what he was doing and what the next step was. He thought he'd known with Bella but then everything had changed. Not because of her scars or because he was her first, though that did hold its own bit of gravity. It was because making love to her had been...profound. It hadn't just felt good, hadn't just filled a physical need, but it had reached into his soul and touched something.

Great. Now he was becoming a poet.

"It's all good, I promise," he said, wanting to reassure her. She deserved that. So he held her closer, wondering what he was going to do in the morning, in the light of day. He didn't want to hurt her. He'd thought they'd been two mature people accepting a night together, acknowledging a connection and acting on it, then going back to their previously scheduled lives with a nice memory. Instead he was in way deeper than he'd ever thought possible. He didn't see a way out of this that didn't involve hurting her.

Hurting someone he cared about.

He was no better than his father.

* * *

Bella closed her eyes and let the warm, firm wall that was Burke surround her.

She might not get the chance again, after all. Once he'd discovered she'd been a virgin, he'd definitely tensed up. If only she'd kept her mouth shut when he'd named that stupid song. She sighed, trying to commit every sensation to memory. She wouldn't let what had happened after ruin what had been so amazing before. Sex was definitely not overrated. And sex with Burke…she'd had no idea she could feel that way.

Perhaps she should be embarrassed by how her body had taken over, how she'd sounded—had she really called out his name?—how she'd let herself lose control. But she wasn't. It had been amazing. Nothing could take that away from her.

His fingers traced small circles on her arms in the quiet darkness. Maybe he wanted to sleep, but she wanted to stay awake so she didn't miss a single minute of being in his bed. She let her fingers glide over his chest, touching the warm skin and the sparse, coarse hair at the top of his chest. It rose and fell with his even breathing, and she didn't want to look up to see if he was looking at her or not. She was shy now that the passion had cooled, and she'd never taken the lead with a man before. Even now, she wasn't sure she was ready to start something. Burke's subtle withdrawal had been disappointing, but he'd still pulled her close. It didn't mean he wanted this to happen again. He was too much of a gentleman to turn her away now, wasn't he?

She closed her eyes and told herself to stop putting herself down. What he'd said was that it had been amazing. That he'd been caught up in her. Burke was a lot of things, but she didn't think he was a liar.

Maybe it had taken him by surprise.

Her fingers trailed over a pebbled nipple and his breath

caught…he was awake. Bella bit on her lip and kept moving her hand, touching the taut skin over his ribs, the flatness of his stomach, up his strong forearm to his elbow.

"Bella," he murmured.

"Is this okay? I mean, if you'd rather I didn't…"

He let out a sigh. "It feels good. You feel good."

Her heart leaped. Her arm brushed over the covers and discovered that it did indeed feel good when her hand bumped up against his erection. "Oh," she murmured.

"Bella, wait. I need to say something."

She hesitated and looked up. He was gazing down at her with dark, serious eyes, just visible in the light coming through the curtains. Dread spiraled in her. He didn't look like a man ready to ravish her again. He looked like someone about to impart bad news.

Well, she'd handle it. She always did. And thank God she hadn't blurted out her feelings earlier.

"Go ahead," she encouraged.

He sat up a bit, and she nudged herself into a semi-reclining position with the sheets tucked under her armpits. "I think we need to talk about expectations. I love being with you, I do. Today was wonderful. I had such a good time, and I care about you a lot—"

Ugh. *Care.* She was about to be friend-zoned, wasn't she?

"Being with you…it was so good. And I want to again." His gaze was so magnetic, looking down at her with such seriousness. "But you also deserve to know that I'm not ready for a serious relationship. My life isn't cut out for it, really. I work a million hours and I have ambitions. There are opportunities coming up that I don't want to miss. It doesn't leave a lot of time for nurturing a meaningful relationship."

"I know about a busy job, Burke. I work fifty- or sixty-hour weeks most weeks." Still, she wouldn't have let it keep her from pursuing something she'd considered worthy.

"Right. And I live here in London, and you're in Paris most of the time."

Bella thought of her brother and sister, both of whom had faced the same argument and overcome it. Because they'd loved their partners. Bella thought she felt that way about Burke, too. But if he didn't feel the same, he was right. It wouldn't work.

Her heart threatened to break into pieces. This was the first time she'd allowed herself to be so vulnerable and open with anyone, and now she was starting to feel pushed aside.

"Is this because I…" Oh, it sounded ridiculous to even say it. "Because I'm so inexperienced?"

He shifted and cupped her chin in his hand. "No. I promise you, no. This is my fault, Bella. I've never done serious relationships. I've always been so focused on my career path. And I thought I could do that here, too. That we were similar people of a similar age and that we had a lot in common but it wouldn't get…" His voice trailed away, as his brow wrinkled.

"Messy."

"Right."

"And you think it could."

"I just want to be clear and honest with you. I don't want to hurt you for the world."

She shook her head slightly, removing her chin from his touch. "And this would also manage my expectations."

The conversation had been a complete desire killer. Bella hoped she wasn't showing her emotions on her face, because she was disappointed and feeling like what had started as the most perfect night of her life was now very not. Much like a balloon after the party, when all the air started to leak out and it became a sad, limp version of itself.

"That's not how I'd have chosen to put it," he admitted. "It sounds manipulative and I don't want that. Maybe we should have talked about this beforehand."

"Maybe we should have."

"Would you have changed your mind about staying?"

She stopped and thought. Looked into his face and saw the same man who'd walked through the butterfly house with her today, the same man who'd made sure she'd eaten when her mom was having her procedure, the one who'd held her hand in the park and said nothing for long minutes, the silence comfortable. He'd wanted her, but he didn't want a relationship. Even if she'd known it then, she would have made the same decision. He was being honest now, so how could she fault him? He was a good man, she knew that. And she wouldn't trade what had been between them for anything.

"No," she answered, her voice surprisingly firm. "No, I wouldn't have changed my mind."

"I didn't expect that kind of answer."

"Let me ask you, then. If you had known I was a virgin, would you have changed your mind about asking me?"

He shook his head. "No."

"I might be inexperienced, Burke, but I'm worldly enough to know that a night together doesn't automatically end up as a committed relationship."

It stung to say it, only because she'd fallen for him, big-time. Not just because of the sex, but because of who he was and how he'd treated her over the past weeks. Today she'd imagined, for the first time, what it would be like to have someone in her corner. To have him beside her. How foolish was she?

"I feel like the world's biggest idiot," he admitted.

"Don't. You shouldn't feel stupid for sharing your feelings and your expectations," she said, and meant it. "Fewer misunderstandings that way. Too bad we can't rewind a few hours and have this talk then, you know?"

He chuckled. "I thought about it. I didn't want to kill the vibe. You're very sexy, Arabella."

And there it was. That flicker that brought the flame of her desire to life again. As long as she understood that this night was probably their only night, as long as she managed her own expectations and didn't let her heart get overly involved, tonight didn't need to be over.

"Likewise," she replied, pushing the misgivings aside and embracing the opportunity before her. "And you're a devilishly good kisser."

His lips curved in a smile, though shadows seemed to still lurk behind his eyes. "We're okay?"

She nodded, still disappointed but letting her logical brain take over. Nothing he'd said was incorrect or illogical. "We're okay." Bravado had her adding, "We could be more than okay, if you wanted." She wasn't ready for the night to be over yet.

He reached for her and pulled her close. It was a gorgeous feeling, having only the sheets and his skin against hers. No barriers. No shyness, not anymore. There wasn't room for it.

"You're beautiful," he murmured, burying his face in her hair.

She didn't need his compliments, but it touched her just the same. His hand ran under her hair, sliding along the jagged scar on her neck, but she didn't mind. Not with Burke. And she'd parse all those feelings tomorrow, or the next day. But not now. Now she just wanted to feel this way for as long as she could.

And this time she wanted to play a more active part, explore a little and see if she could make him as weak and pliant as he'd made her. So she reached under the sheets for him, and smiled a wicked little smile as his eyes closed and he groaned.

If they only had one night, it would be one to remember.

CHAPTER TEN

AURORA WAS IN good spirits when they arrived shortly before eleven. She was waiting for Dr. Mallick to sign her release papers, and then she and Bella would head back to the manor house for a few days of rest before Bella left for Paris.

Bella kissed her mother's cheek and asked about her night, while constantly aware that probably within the next hour she'd be leaving the hospital and Burke would be staying and that would be the end of that. No wedding to bring them together or medical emergency to keep them that way. They were going back to their previously scheduled lives. Without each other. The hope that had spiraled through her yesterday was absent today, leaving a dull ache in its wake. She couldn't fault him one bit for his logic. They did have demanding jobs in different countries. But she also got the feeling there was something else holding him back. It had been behind his eyes last night. And perhaps that was what bothered her the most. She'd shared so much with him, made herself vulnerable, trusted him. That he was keeping something from her hurt. So maybe this was for the best, as much as it stung.

Burke had checked in with the nurses' desk and now he entered the room, his smile relaxed and warm. Bella figured all his patients probably swooned a little when he turned that smile on them, and his warm, magnetic eyes. A stab of pain seemed to center just below her ribs. She wouldn't see that smile again for a very long time.

"Burke. You didn't have to check on me, too." Aurora beamed at him.

"Of course I did. Everything looks great. You make sure you attend your follow-up appointments, too. Dr. Mallick will want to monitor your medications."

"Don't worry. We'll make sure she follows instructions to the letter." Bella said it firmly, while pinning her mother with a stare. Aurora scowled. She was used to giving orders, not taking them, but Bella knew how to bully her into it. "You did promise me yesterday, Maman."

"I knew I'd regret that," Aurora said, but she smiled a little anyway.

"I should leave you to it, then," Burke said. He went to Aurora and gave her a hug. "Glad you're looking and feeling better," he said.

"Thanks to you."

"Not even a little," he replied.

"I'll walk you out," Bella said, keeping her voice light. The last thing Bella needed was her mother asking intrusive questions that she didn't want to answer.

The corridor wasn't much more private, and Bella's stomach churned as she prepared herself for Burke to walk away. Everything he had said last night made perfect sense—to her head. To her heart, not so much. His honesty was hard to fault. They could have this crazy attraction and he was still allowed to not be in a place for a serious relationship. The truth was far better than leading her on, making her believe in possibilities that didn't exist. Deep down, she appreciated his candor.

But her feelings were her own, and real, and to say she wouldn't feel massive disappointment when he left would be a total lie.

"Thank you for everything," she said quietly, squaring her shoulders and forcing herself to meet his gaze. She wouldn't cower. And she wouldn't let him know how hurt she was, either. She and her pride were good friends and had been for many years.

"Bella…"

"No, Burke." She inhaled and let it out again. She was tempted to ask him what else was bothering him. What was keeping him from sharing his heart with her, because she couldn't escape the feeling he was hiding something. But this was neither the time nor the place. "Not here, and not when it won't make any difference. We had an amazing time. Now we need to go back to our regular lives, that's all."

"I hurt you. When you get all practical like this, I can tell. God, Bella, I'm sorry."

She didn't want to make herself more vulnerable, so she shrugged. It took all of her energy to make that one simple movement nonchalant. "If my feelings got a little hurt, so what? I'll get over it. For God's sake, we only spent one night together. I'm stronger than that."

Now *he* looked hurt, which made no sense at all since he'd been the one to state in no uncertain terms that a relationship was off the table.

"You're the strongest woman I know," he said, his damnable dark eyes searching hers.

"See?" She smiled. "Look, you made last night better than I could have hoped or imagined, so let's just leave it at that." That much was at least true.

"As long as you're all right."

A lump formed in her throat and she ignored it. "I'm always all right," she answered. Then, because standing there with him was torture, she rose on tiptoe and kissed his cheek, breathing in his cologne for the last time. "I should get Maman ready to go. Goodbye, Burke."

He nodded, looked as if he might say something, and then reconsidered. Finally he managed, "Bye, Bella."

She turned around and walked back into the hospital room, schooling her features. She was good at that, after years of practice. And it was far better for her to do the walking away than to watch him leave.

Aurora was sitting up in bed, sipping on the cup of juice left from her breakfast. One look at Bella and she put the cup down on her tray and frowned. She swore in French—something Bella hadn't heard in quite some time—and sighed.

"I am grateful to Burke for helping me, but I could kill him for hurting you."

Bella stopped short and gaped at her mother. "What?"

"I've seen that look many times, *ma petite*. That look right there, on your face, pretending nothing is wrong and that you don't care. I saw it nearly thirteen years ago when you were dying for his attention and he acted as if you didn't exist."

Bella sank down on the end of the bed and let out a massive breath. "How did you…" After a pause, she met her mother's gaze. "I never told anyone about my crush on him."

"Mothers see things. And understand. And you are stubborn like me, my darling. I knew long ago that you got into that car that night because you wanted to show Burke you didn't care about him. Or at least I suspected. In the years since, you have avoided him completely, until the wedding. It all made sense to me. But when I saw you together, I hoped he'd finally realize what a treasure you are. And now he's gone and hurt you."

Bella absorbed all of that information—apparently she wasn't as good at hiding her feelings as she thought—and took a moment to think about how to respond. Aurora waited. Bella had the thought that maybe her mother understood more than she had ever given her credit for. Bella had been missing her dad so much that maybe she'd lost sight of how amazing her remaining parent really was.

"You could tell all that from me walking in the room." It was a statement, not a question.

"You are a master at pretending everything is fine. So am I. Like recognizes like, you know."

Bella was determined not to cry. Her mother was right—they were both strong women who had been through significant challenges in their lives. "In Italy, I got to know him better. He's a good man, Maman. And he has been so good to you. Yesterday was the most amazing day. And yes, I got my hopes up. But Burke is not interested in anything serious. He's married to his job. This morning he told me about an opportunity coming up at the Royal Brompton & Harefield that would make his entire career. He has ambitions. And a love life is not top of his list."

"Perhaps you can change his mind."

Bella dug in her heels. "Maman. I do not want to have to make anyone 'change their mind' or be convinced. Call me naive, or a foolish romantic, but if someone wants to be with me badly enough they will. I'm not prepared to compete with a career for snippets of attention."

"Your father had to compete with my career."

"For your time, maybe. But not for love. And that's a big difference."

"*Oui, ma petite*. It is. I'm glad you realize it, but sorry that you are in that position." She reached out and took Bella's hand. "It is a shame. It's so obvious he cares for you."

"It is." Bella fought back the stinging in her eyes and the tightening in her throat. "But we are adults who know what we want. Truthfully, I wouldn't trade the last few weeks even though I ended up being vulnerable. I learned some valuable lessons."

Aurora lifted a perfectly shaped eyebrow. "Such as?"

"Such as my scars maybe aren't as repulsive as I think they are. That at least one person saw them and didn't care at all. Still told me I was beautiful. That counts for something, right?"

Aurora frowned. "Now I do want to kill him."

Bella laughed. "No, it's not his fault. He's worked so hard to get where he is. I understand. And I have no regrets."

She really didn't. They hadn't argued or said things they would want to take back. She'd spent a wonderful day with a lovely man and felt as beautiful in his arms as she ever had on any red carpet or in any magazine. There had been nothing casual or flippant about it. He hadn't lied to her, not once.

"So what next?"

"Next we get you out of here and back home. We cater to your every whim. You answer any questions I have as I take over the reins for a while, and when I'm sure you're doing all right, I head back to Paris and the office. Everything just as we planned."

Aurora leaned forward and kissed Bella's forehead. "You stand at the back of the Pemberton line too often, Arabella. But I think you might just be the strongest of all of us."

It didn't feel that way, but she absorbed the compliment as it was intended. She was strong. She was resilient. And the only way to go on was forward. Even if her heart was, if not broken, cracked a little.

The doctor came in for one last check and then finally Aurora was released to go home. Their driver was waiting when they exited the hospital into the brisk summer air, and stowed their small bags in the back. It seemed no time at all and they were weaving through the city, heading toward home.

"Are you tired?" Bella asked.

"Actually, no. I feel surprisingly well. A little sore perhaps." She looked down at her lap. "A bit around the site where they put the catheter in. And a little tenderness here." She put her hand on her chest.

"But the doctor said those are normal."

"And should go away in another day or so." Aurora smiled. "I know I said I'd let you baby me, so I won't tell you not to fuss. But I do feel better."

Bella had to admit that before the procedure there'd been a strained look around her mother's eyes. She hadn't really noticed until now, when it was gone. She would always have Burke to thank for that. Aurora might have not sought medical help otherwise.

When they arrived at Chatsworth Manor, Mrs. Flanagan greeted them at the door and ushered them in. She'd been absent when they'd first arrived after the wedding, off sick for a few days. The house had felt strange in her absence.

"Maggie," Aurora said, squeezing her arm. "It's so good to see you. You're feeling better?"

"Much, thank you. And it's good to see you, too, looking so well. The procedure was clearly a success?" She formed it as a question.

"Very," Bella said, leaning forward and kissing their housekeeper's cheek. In reality, the woman was very much like a second mother to her. "How's Esme?"

"Well, thanks. Working at the inn still." Mrs. Flanagan's daughter was the same age as Stephen. She'd married once, but after a few years they'd divorced. Bella had never understood. Esme was a beautiful, warm, funny woman. "Anyway," Mrs. Flanagan added, "enough about my family. We've got everything ready for you, madame."

As familiar as the family was with the longtime servants, Mrs. Flanagan always called Aurora "madame."

"Would you like tea, Maman? I can put our things upstairs and we can have tea in the library. You didn't eat lunch and only had hospital food last night and this morning."

"I could eat," Aurora admitted.

"I'll have tea and sandwiches in twenty minutes," Mrs. Flanagan promised, and whisked away.

Bella saw her mother to the library and then took both their bags upstairs to their rooms. She dropped Aurora's bag inside and left it for Aurora to unpack…not that she wouldn't help, but she did respect her mother's right to privacy and unpacking a few items wouldn't tax her unnecessarily.

Then she went to her room, stood inside the door, and let the feelings of the past three hours wash over her.

This was what her family never understood and never saw.

She leaned against her door and dropped her head, letting out a long, shaky breath. Her heart ached. Her body ached in places she had ignored until just this moment, when she was alone and felt free enough to acknowledge the discomfort.

What she had felt for Burke—what she still felt for him—wasn't because he'd been the first and only man she'd ever had sex with. It certainly cemented her feelings in her heart, but it went far deeper than that, to compassion and acceptance. She'd waited long enough. Last night she'd wanted him to say different words. Wanted him to say "let's give this a go" and maybe, just maybe, fall in love. She was already there; all he had to do was catch up.

To have that gift sitting right in front of her and then snatched away again was devastating. She could pretend all she wanted in front of Burke, her mother, her family… but inside, she was so very hurt. He cared about her, but not enough. He trusted her, but not completely. His answers had been too pat, too perfect, too logical. And he'd avoided her eyes several times this morning. It was unlike him, so why?

And did it matter? Thinking about it didn't change a thing.

She dropped her bag on the floor and left it rather than unpacking. She gave herself five minutes to feel and wallow and let down her guard. Then she went to her bathroom and splashed water on her face, and redid her makeup in the way that covered her blemishes and still made her look fresh and dewy—well, as dewy as a thirty-year-old could look, she supposed. Then she gave her head a shake and set her lips. Women could be dewy at thirty! Just because she was feeling old right now didn't mean she was.

And if Burke could find her attractive, someone else could, too. Maybe it was time she stopped hiding away. The idea felt revolutionary. And not something she should rush into, but it was something worth exploring. Maybe talking with Maman. Or Charlotte. Whatever she did would ripple down into the company, as well. She would never make a big decision without considering the family and Aurora Inc.

"Time," she murmured to her reflection in the mirror. "Take your time, Bella." She knew herself well enough to know she was being a bit reactive to Burke's rejection. Honestly, the whole thing about someone else finding her attractive was a bit moot anyway. She didn't want anyone else. At least not now.

But the feeling of needing to stop hiding persisted as she made her way back downstairs to the library.

She arrived just after the tea had been delivered and poured a cup for Aurora and herself. Aurora took a splash of milk; Bella left hers black and took a chair at an angle to her mother. The tea was hot and revivifying, and she let out a happy sigh. Almost every problem she could remember had been tackled by ordering tea first.

Mrs. Flanagan had brought an assortment of sandwiches as well, and Bella's stomach growled in response to the sight and smell of them. "Sandwich, Maman?" she asked.

"I could nibble. Especially if that's Marjorie's bread. No one makes bread like her."

The cook had been with the family for well over a decade. Her bread was soft and fragrant, and she'd made one of Maman's favorites: turkey with cranberry and provolone. Bella bit into it and the flavors melted on her tongue. This—the sandwiches and tea—was the taste of home.

"Maman, may I talk to you about something? It affects the company in a roundabout way, and I want to get your feedback on it."

Aurora put down the tea. "Of course, darling. What is it?"

"I've been thinking a lot about how I've, well, hidden since my accident. Some of that has been personal. A lot of it has been personal." She sighed. "Oh, hell. Most of it has been. But I do realize that anything I do trickles down into the company, and by extension the rest of the family."

"And as the person who holds it all together, the last thing you want to do is be the cause of a problem."

As usual, her mother nailed it. "Well, yes. I mean, our personal lives are always fodder for the press. When Dad died…" Her throat tightened. "And then Stephen's engagement, and Gabi leaving him at the altar, and her falling for William…and then the sabotage in New York and Charlotte's very quick wedding. I do not want to be the cause of more—I guess salacious is the word I'm looking for—speculation in the tabloids."

Aurora lifted her teacup again. "This is about your scars, yes?"

Bella nodded, feeling somewhat miserable. Once she'd listed off everything that had happened, she realized that if she went public with her scars, she'd be contributing to a lot of stress the family had felt over the past few years.

"They are your scars. Whether you hide them or show them is your personal decision. Don't worry about the company. What's important is you. This has always been your decision to make."

Resentment flickered through Bella's chest for a moment. At eighteen, once she'd healed, she'd been left with the decision to how to deal with her disfigurement. She knew her parents had wanted to respect her wishes, but looking back she wondered if it wouldn't have been better if they'd told her she couldn't hide them or pretend they didn't exist. If they'd guided—parented—a little more rather than letting her make that choice all alone at a time when she was trying to come to grips with it herself.

But she wouldn't say that to Maman. One, she'd just had a heart procedure, and two, it wouldn't change anything now. Deep down she knew that her mother and father had done what they thought was the right, caring thing. She could never fault them for that.

"I don't know what I want," she admitted. "I'm just starting to feel like I've been living… I don't know. Not a lie, exactly, but not the truth, either. And certainly not living fully."

"Has being with Burke brought this on? This reexamination of what you want your life to look like?"

"Maybe. And we're not together. We're not going to be together. But the times we were…they were so lovely, and different, and he'd already seen my scars before the wedding and it didn't make a difference to him. But Maman, I don't want to be plastered all over the media, either."

"Unless you do it on your terms." Aurora finished her tea and got up to pour more. "Even the hardest things in the world are made easier when we take ownership of them."

"I don't want to negatively affect the business. We've

promoted a message of 'everyone is beautiful' but this whole time I've been wearing long sleeves and my hair down and keeping this big ugly secret. I feel like a massive hypocrite."

"Why don't you talk to Charlotte? She's still managing PR and she loves you. If you're ready, she can help you craft something that respects you and is a positive for the company as well. It's not about avoiding the fallout, Bella. It's about managing it. And our family is strong and resilient. The past months have shown that."

"But for how long?" Bella asked.

Aurora was silent for a long moment, and then she looked at Bella straight in the eye. "I understand that your concern is genuine, but I think you need to ask yourself if this worry over the business is an excuse to hold you back so you don't have to do the hard thing."

That stung. Not because it was a baseless accusation but because it was entirely possible that Bella had done exactly that. How many times had she envied her sister her strapless and backless gowns, her sweeping updos, but told herself it was for the good of the company? Really she had been protecting herself so long it had become her only way of life. In every part of her life.

"I'm sorry, *ma petite*. I don't mean to hurt you. But if you're considering this, I think it needs to be said. Aurora Inc. will survive. You can't hide behind it anymore."

Nerves tangled in Bella's stomach, mixing with fear. And yet she was tired of not being herself. She thought back to a mere twenty-four hours ago, when she'd been enjoying the afternoon with Burke, just being Bella. She'd put her hair up, not caring if he saw the scar. She'd had dinner with him. She'd made love to him, with all of her scars on display, and they'd meant nothing. He'd kissed them as if they were cherished. He'd seen her pain and honored it.

And she'd felt seen and heard and beautiful. Maybe they

didn't have a future together, but he'd given her that wonderful gift just the same.

"I need to think about it more. But thank you, Maman, for the hard truths. I needed to hear them."

"Finish your sandwich," Aurora commanded. "You need to look after yourself. And so do I. We're stronger than most give us credit for, Bella. Remember that."

Bella picked up the sandwich and ate despite the unease and anxiety centered in her belly. This week she'd work with Maman here at the house, and then she'd be back in Paris. Once there, maybe she would talk to Charlotte.

CHAPTER ELEVEN

AFTER NEARLY THREE weeks away from her flat, Bella was glad to be home again. Her apartment was in the Seventh Arrondissement, with a view of the lush building courtyard rather than the Eiffel Tower. With several windows and lovely light wood floors throughout, the space felt more airy and spacious than it was. But it was more than enough for her. Three bedrooms, two baths and a spacious living room was more than enough for a single person. Sometimes it was too much, when she was here alone, but she loved it just the same.

Charlotte was staying over for a few days before heading back to London. It gave the team a chance to have a full in-person attendance meeting, and it meant Bella could talk to her about her thoughts. Though she missed having Charlotte in the city all the time, the benefit to having her live with Jacob in Richmond was having her here to stay when she was in town.

Bella was in the kitchen cooking, making one of her personal favorites for dinner, salmon *en croûte*. Charlotte would be along soon, and the salmon with salad would make a lovely dinner for them both. She hummed tunelessly as she wrapped the salmon in the whisper-thin pastry, then brushed the top with egg wash. Cooking was also something she'd missed. Gabi's mother had done most of the cooking during the visit to the Baresis, and since then the staff at the manor house had kept her well-fed.

Charlotte knocked on the door and Bella wiped her hands on a towel before going to answer. When she opened it, Charlotte stepped inside carrying a stylish overnight bag and a paper sack from her favorite bakery.

"You brought dessert."

"I did. You're going to feed me something healthy. Which is great. My obstetrician will be pleased. But sometimes I need sugar."

Bella grinned sheepishly. It was also true that she was glad to be back as she had been on the treadmill the last two mornings, bright and early. She'd missed her morning exercise.

"Not too healthy. Salmon wrapped in pastry."

"Oh, yum. The kind you make with the lemon-butter sauce?"

"That's the one. Come in and have a drink."

Bella poured wine for herself and sparkling water for Charlotte, then added a slice each of lemon and lime to liven it up a bit. Charlotte was looking radiant, with her rounded tummy and the glow in her cheeks. Pregnancy suited her.

"You look wonderful," Bella said, admiring her sister's flair for style as her body made room for the new life she was carrying. Today she wore a sleeveless maxi dress in blue with pink flowers, with the pleated bust forming a fashionable knot in the center. Yesterday she'd worn a T-shirt dress that had conformed to her figure, and the sky-high heels she adored. Charlotte wasn't interested in hiding her baby bump at all.

"I feel wonderful. The second trimester is much better than the first," she admitted, taking a drink of her water. "Honestly, the hormones work in Jacob's favor." She winked at Bella, and Bella laughed.

"Ew! TMI, Charlotte."

"Whatever. I figured if I led with that, you'd tell me what happened with you and Burke."

Heat rushed into Bella's cheeks, and not because she opened the oven to slip the salmon inside. "Hmm. Nosy, nosy."

"You're my sister. I saw how it was in Italy. And on the flight back. What happened in London? Anything juicy?"

Bella couldn't look at her sister. Instead she went to work making the sauce for the fish. As she put ingredients in her blender, she affected a shrug. "Oh, you know."

"Bella!"

In response Bella turned on the blender, drowning out any potential conversation. She was going to tell Charlotte. She was going to tell her sister a lot of things, but she was still going to make Charlotte work for it. After all, that was what siblings did.

When the blender shut off, Charlotte pinned her with a glare. "Funny," she said, pointing at Bella. "Something did happen. Out with it."

"You're very bossy."

"This is not news."

Bella laughed despite herself. Then she sobered. It was hard, letting herself be vulnerable, even with those who loved her best. "I spent the night at his flat while Maman was in the hospital."

Charlotte's eyes got huge and she smiled triumphantly. "I knew it! Oh, Bella, he's so hunky."

Bella rolled her eyes. "Well, he's also not interested in a relationship, so there's that."

The triumphant smile turned to a frown of disgust. "Then he is a horrible man who foolishly let the best thing to happen to him get away."

It was said partly in jest, but Bella hadn't realized how desperately she'd needed to hear the unconditional support. She put the blender aside and went to sit next to Charlotte on a barstool. "I needed that," she admitted, taking a drink of her wine. "He is hunky, Charlotte. And so wonderful in every other way."

Charlotte put down her glass and turned on the stool so she was facing Bella. "Are you in love with him?"

If Aurora had asked, she would have denied it. But to her sister, she couldn't. "I think I am. It's ridiculous. There was Italy and then London. It was literally two weeks."

Charlotte lifted her hand where the diamond ring sparkled. "Reader, I married him."

Bella burst out laughing. Charlotte always had this dry, funny way of putting things that got right to the heart of the matter. She and Jacob had known each other for nine days and at the end of that time Charlotte was head over heels. If anyone understood what it was like, it was Charlotte. Or even William, for that matter. But Bella wasn't up to discussing this with her brother.

"Did you two…sleep together?"

The coil of anxiety wound tighter in Bella's stomach, but she had to talk to someone. "Yeah. We did." She hesitated and met Charlotte's eyes. Her sister was watching her soberly. Thank God she wasn't making fun or light of anything right now. Bella took a breath and said, "He was my first."

Charlotte's mouth dropped open. Then she sighed and said, "Oh, Bella. I'm sorry."

"Don't be sorry. It was wonderful." Now she wanted to cry, but she wouldn't. "He didn't know. But even so, he did everything exactly right." Her face was flaming, she was sure of it. "But it made walking away from him a lot harder than it might have been otherwise."

She took another drink of wine. Charlotte reached for the bottle and refilled the glass. "So you regret it?"

"Not a bit. I just wanted more."

"And you're sure he doesn't?"

"He made it very clear. His career is more important right now."

Charlotte scowled and made a sound in the back of her throat. "Chicken," she muttered. "Look," she said louder, "my husband runs a business in London and Aurora is in Paris, but we found a way."

"I know. And so did William and Gabi. But when I think about that, I try to remember that I shouldn't judge Burke by the same yardstick. He was honest with me, Charlotte. Although..."

"Although what?"

Bella frowned. "It's probably stupid, but that morning I just got the feeling that there was more to it than just logistics. But Burke...he's only let me see what he wants me to see. It took me a while to realize it. We all have secrets, I suppose. I can't fault him for that."

"Well, I can." Charlotte got up and went to get the bottle of Perrier. "If he doesn't see how amazing you are, sod him."

A smile crept up Bella's cheek. "I love you for that."

"Of course you do. Bella, you've spent so much time in the background, being the all-round manager of both the family and business. You're the peacemaker when the rest of us stir up trouble. You stepped up for Will when Stephen was being a jerk. You're filling in for Maman. We count on you far too much, but you deserve things for yourself, too." She looked at Bella with a keen expression. "Are you ready to take them?"

This was the opening Bella had been waiting for. "I might be. I wanted to talk to you tonight about doing things differently. One of the reasons I'm not mad at Burke is that he made me see that I don't always have to hide. My scars didn't matter to him. And I got a taste of what that's like... being free of them. What if I stopped hiding behind my hair and long sleeves? What would happen in the publicity department? I don't want to hurt the company."

"The company will survive. We had our new line sabo-taged in New York and came out stronger than ever. We had the Will-and-Stephen drama and nothing happened sales-wise. Don't worry about the company. Do what's right for you. And the company—and family—will support you through it."

God bless Charlotte.

The oven dinged, and Bella got up to take the golden-brown salmon out. She took the salad and vinaigrette out of the fridge and served them both dinner, and then they brainstormed ideas and worked through contingencies until Bella was comfortable with a route forward. Now the only thing to do was bring in the rest of the family—which would happen tomorrow, at the morning meeting.

Later, Charlotte's soft snores came from the guest room, but Bella lay awake late into the night, hoping she was doing the right thing, exhilarated and terrified by turns.

It was going to take a lot of courage on her part, but it was time she stepped into her own.

Burke decided to walk home from work. It was a gorgeous summer evening, which was a change from the fog and drizzle of the morning. He could use the exercise and fresh air to clear his head. It had been a jumbled mess since Bella had turned away from him outside Aurora's room.

He was waiting for his interview at the Royal Brompton and sweating about it. Working there was the opportunity of a lifetime, and came around just about as often. So why was he not focused on that and instead kept thinking about Bella and the night they'd spent together?

He didn't want marriage. He didn't want that battle be-tween his career and family. On the outside, the Phillips family had seemed so wonderful and…cohesive. But Burke knew better. His father had been gone a lot. The days of aristos not having to work for a living were gone. And then

Burke had also learned a horrible secret that he'd never shared with his mother. His father had a mistress.

The term sounded so antiquated. Burke had seen them once when he was sixteen. He'd gone to Norwich for a school break with a mate and he'd spied his father in a pub, cozied up with another woman. The shock had been complete. And he'd never told a living soul. Not even his dad. When the family had gone to such trouble to keep Burke's name out of the accident, he'd felt he hadn't the right to drop any sort of bombshell. He'd had his own shame to bear, so how could he fault someone else? After that, every time his father had been away, Burke had wondered if it was actually business or if he was seeing *her*.

But it explained why his mother had spent so much time with them as children, especially the girls. Father had been gone a lot. And she'd done her best to provide a stable, loving upbringing for her kids.

Burke crossed the bridge and the breeze from the Thames lifted his hair and cooled his face. While he couldn't imagine ever cheating on Bella, he had no desire to be caught in between a woman and his work. One or both would suffer because of it. He'd made peace with his single status long ago. So why was it so hard now?

He was nearly home when he stopped at a tiny market for something quick for dinner. He was standing at the checkout waiting to go through when a headline on the cover of a tabloid caught his eye.

The Not-So-Perfect Pemberton!

That part was in big font, with smaller print underneath.

Arabella Germain-Pemberton steps out strapless... and scarred!

The photo had captured Bella in a strapless black-and-white gown, her hair up, diamonds sparkling at her neck. Burke's heart lurched as he absorbed the sucker punch. She'd done it. She'd gone out in public without hiding. Why? When? He grabbed the cheap paper rag and put it on top of his tikka masala entrée on the checkout belt.

He waited to read until he got home and put the dinner in the microwave to heat. Then he flipped to the page and read it standing at the kitchen counter. Seeing her there, in full color, did something to his insides he didn't quite understand. The photog had captured her from the thighs up, so that the zigzags marking her pale skin were on full display. She was at least smiling, and not scowling or caught in one of those moments where people were speaking and looked awful on tabloid covers. She looked beautiful. Considering how protective she'd been only weeks ago, he couldn't help but be astounded by her bravery.

Without him. Regret slammed into him, not for the first time. Walking away might be for the best, for both of them, but nothing about it had been easy.

According to the article, she'd been out at a charity event for a children's hospital. She'd worn a strapless Aurora design and Aurora diamonds, but the big news was the slashes on her arms, shoulders and neck that had caught everyone's attention. There was great speculation on their origin—how long ago, what had happened. Had she been attacked? Had she been a cutter? The delight that was taken by the journos made him sick to his stomach. They made money off someone else's pain.

He couldn't believe she'd done it. He was in awe of her strength and fortitude, for she'd surely known there'd be a reaction. For a woman who'd never let anyone see her be vulnerable, had never even been with a man before… before… She was extraordinarily brave.

The microwave beeped and he opened the door and

then shut it again, so it wouldn't beep constantly. Instead of eating, he retrieved his laptop from his room and put it on the counter, then did an internet search. He was gratified to see that a statement from Aurora was near the top of the results, and that it came from Bella herself.

Society has this concept of beauty that is impossible to live up to. It would be hypocritical of me to hide away any longer, not embodying the principles that Aurora holds dear—that every person is beautiful, has their own story, and deserves happiness and acceptance.

I have scars. My history may be personal, but it is no reason to hide or try to live a lie of perfection. It's not bodies that make us beautiful, but souls.

The social media statement ended with a hashtag: *#showyourbeautiful.*

A quick glance at the results showed several hundred results in the past twenty-four hours.

In another twenty-four, he guessed Arabella would go totally viral.

He poured a drink and sat on the sofa. What had possessed her to do such a thing? He was proud of her, so very proud. But also a little bit afraid. He doubted the press would let this go. If they went digging, they'd find out about the accident. And then his name would be brought into it.

The whiskey burned in his throat as he tossed it back and went for another. To say he felt like a hypocrite was an understatement, because he was glad for her but wished she hadn't gone public for his own self-preservation. To criticize her for this would be unconscionable. He'd walked away from the wreckage with a broken arm that had long since healed. He had a blossoming career because he'd tried to use his experience to do good in the world. But if the press went digging, how would a potential employer look at his involvement that night? What if he ended up in the news as well? It wasn't a stretch; he was Viscount Downham. The title alone made him newsworthy. How much fallout would he suffer? Would it affect his future at the Royal Brompton?

He looked at the photo again and felt a longing so intense it frightened him. She hadn't called or texted or anything. Hadn't shared with him, and that was his fault, wasn't it? He was the one who'd sent her away.

He downed the drink and went to eat his dinner, though it took him a while as he mostly picked at it until it was not quite gone. He paced a while in his living room, fixed himself one more drink, let the liquor ease his conscience and bolster his bravery. Dammit, he was calling her.

She didn't answer the phone for several rings, and he was just about to hang up when she finally picked up. "Hello?"

At the sound of her voice he nearly lost his. After three seconds he finally managed, "It's Burke."

There was another three seconds of telling silence. "What can I do for you, Burke?"

"Bella," he chided softly, hurt that she took such a businesslike tone with him. "I just saw the tabloids. I wanted to make sure you're okay."

"I'm fine. It was planned, you know." At least she didn't pretend not to know what he was talking about.

"I figured it was. But…how has the reaction been?"

She sighed. "It's been a lot, sometimes. Some is a lot of support. But that doesn't sell magazines, does it? So there's speculation. I'll weather it. My family is one hundred percent behind me."

"I am, too, Bella. You must know that."

She was silent, and he got the feeling she was measuring her words. When she finally spoke again, she said, "I know you mean well, Burke, and I don't have any hard feelings. But you were clear in what you wanted, which means you don't really have a part in this." Her voice was cool but not unfriendly. Just matter-of-fact. And it cut him to the bone.

"I don't mean to be unkind," she continued. "The time we had together gave me the courage to step forward, and it will always be a good memory for me. But if we aren't going to be a thing, we can't do this."

"What, talk?" he asked, incredulous.

"Yes, talk. I accept everything you said. But that doesn't mean it didn't hurt. It's just best if we leave it at that, okay?"

He leaned back in his chair and swiped his hand over his face. Was she saying that he'd had the power to really, really hurt her? Yes, it had been her first time, but Bella didn't strike him as the type to go starry-eyed just because of that. She was too pragmatic.

And yet he supposed it was possible, because he'd been moping around here, too, missing her like crazy. He hated the thought of hurting anyone, but most of all Bella. This was why he'd fallen back on charm and stayed away from commitment. He didn't trust himself not to hurt people. If you kept people on the surface, everything was safe. He'd tried to protect her and instead he'd hurt her anyway.

"Have you been asked a lot of questions about what happened, and when?" He changed the subject, wanting to abide by her wishes. No more talk about the two of them.

"Yes. I haven't answered much. I want to focus on the future and not the past. And to be honest, I've been quite busy filling in for Maman. I was just about to leave my office when you called."

"But it's nearly eight."

"Oh, good. An early night for me, then."

She was being so cold, so different from the Bella he knew, and then it finally hit him, made sense. Bella put up walls when she felt too much, didn't she? And she'd said he'd hurt her. He was sorry for that, but glad that she hadn't forgotten him or that he was at least hard to get over. He had no right to want it but it was a tiny bit of comfort just the same.

Truth was, he didn't know what he wanted. To protect himself. To see her again. To stay untethered and free. To love her. Of course, he couldn't say any of those things. "How much longer are you filling in for her?"

"Another few weeks for sure. Then she's going to head to the château for a while. Honestly, I think Maman might semi-retire. Which means lots of changes at Aurora Inc. At least Will is back, but later this fall Charlotte will be on maternity leave."

So she was feeling the pressure of being in the driver's seat. "Please take time for yourself, too," he said softly. "You should take a weekend at the château as well. All work and no play."

"Said the pot to the kettle." Finally her voice warmed. "The hospital is good?"

"Yeah. My meeting at the Royal Brompton is next week. I've been working and prepping."

"Good luck. I know how much it means to you."

It did, really. It was his chance to really move up, to make a name for himself. One that…well, one that hadn't already belonged to someone else. He pinched the top of his nose and let out a breath. Hell. Why had he been thinking about his father so much lately?

"Thanks. I should probably go so you can go home. I'm glad you're okay. I'm glad you did what you did, too. The world deserves to know the real you, Bella."

"Thanks," she replied, her voice soft. "I'll see you."

He said goodbye and then sat there for twenty minutes,

wondering if her "I'll see you" was meant to be some sort of code or invitation or if it was simply an alternate way of saying bye.

Either way, saying goodbye hadn't been nearly as easy as he'd wanted it to be. And that bothered him more than a little. He didn't know what to do with it or how to proceed.

The fact remained—she was dedicated to her life at Aurora and he was equally dedicated to his career. And if his parents' marriage had taught him anything, it was that when people weren't dedicated to each other, nothing was worth a damn.

CHAPTER TWELVE

"That was him, wasn't it?" Charlotte asked Bella.

They were currently in Bella's office, and Charlotte was sitting with her feet up because she was having some swelling in her ankles. Charlotte was now staring at Bella with open curiosity and Bella was trying to sort out her emotions from hearing Burke's voice again.

"It was, yes. He saw a photo. Called to check in."

"Nice of him."

Bella snorted. "That is not what you really want to say."

Charlotte pondered for a moment. "Honestly, I don't know what I want to say. It's clear you care about him. It's also clear that you're standing your ground, which I very much admire."

Standing her ground, huh. She didn't want to admit how miserable she was. Work was fine. A bit overwhelming, but nothing she couldn't handle. Even the charity event and the dress…they'd planned for that and it had been more empowering than she'd imagined. When the gossip started to get to her, she channeled her energies into remembering that feeling, standing on the steps, in the kind of gown she'd always dreamed of wearing.

She'd stepped out of the shadows and into the light. It should have been glorious. Instead she just kept hearing Burke's voice saying he didn't want to be involved. As much as she told herself to be pragmatic and that it was fine, it still hurt. Because her feelings had escalated very quickly, and a man like Burke wasn't easy to forget.

"I'm fine," she insisted, and Charlotte nodded in confirmation.

"Of course you're fine. But fine isn't happy or contented or delirious with love and basking in afterglow."

Bella rolled her eyes. "No one says afterglow anymore."

"They should. Boneless, delicious illumination after mind-blowing sex."

Bella burst out laughing. It was impossible not to love Charlotte. "I'm sorry you're heading back to London tomorrow. I'm going to miss you."

"Me, too, but Jacob is already back and I'm sorry, but…"

"I get it. Spare me the details."

Charlotte got up, curving a hand around her belly as she did so. "Are you sure you don't want to fight for him, Bel? He might be worth it."

"I don't want to have to convince a man to be with me. Then I'd always wonder if he really wanted to be there or if he'd been coerced or cajoled."

"You put on some of the new lingerie line and he could be cajoled, all right. And PS, no one says cajoled anymore, either."

Bella shared a smile with her sister. Charlotte had been the bright spot over the last few weeks, working together, hanging out in the evenings, such as they were. But Bella was going to be alone soon, and she wouldn't be able to pretend or hide from herself.

"His interview is coming up. Charlotte, unless we move the company across the Channel, we can't all just uproot and move to London."

"I know. Especially you. It's easier for me to work remotely."

"Why me?"

"Because you really are the new Aurora. Haven't you figured that out yet? You've stepped in like you were born to it, which you probably were. Ask Stephen if you don't believe me. I mean, your hashtag is going to start a whole new marketing campaign."

It was true. When they'd crafted her statement, and she'd come up with *#showyourbeautiful*, it was like everything fell into place. But the new Aurora? "Maman isn't retiring. So no, I'm not her."

"Don't be so sure. I'm guessing she'd like to be more of a figurehead now. And I think the health scare affected her a lot. Are you prepared to step in?"

She was. Despite the nerves and reservations and long hours, she'd enjoyed the past few weeks a lot. William was back and they'd worked as a collective, but her siblings had all deferred to her judgment. It had given her a confidence that had been missing until now. After years of being steadfastly behind the scenes and working hard, she felt…prepared.

It was the weirdest thing.

They were heading for the elevator when Charlotte asked a bombshell question. "But if Burke came to you right now and asked you to drop everything to be with him, would you?"

She knew she had fallen in love with Burke in London. Knew it without a doubt, deep in her bones. And yet the answer came to her instantly and definitively. "No."

She expected her sister to say something like, "See? If you really loved him, nothing would stand in your way." Charlotte surprised her instead. "Good. Because although I might be pretty new at this—you know, love, marriage— it's a compromise. It's realizing what's important to the other person and coming up with ways to make that happen."

The elevator doors opened and they stepped inside.

"I'm going to miss you, Charlotte."

"I'll be on a video call with you tomorrow."

"It's not the same. Thank you. For the past few weeks, for your love and support and advice. I appreciate it more than you know."

Charlotte smiled and patted her tummy. "I swear it's Jacob. He's made me a big marshmallow."

Bella laughed, but as the elevator doors closed, she realized that Burke had never been further from her. If he wasn't willing to take a step toward compromise, what chance would they ever have? It would be better to put him out of her mind completely.

The next week passed in a blur of meetings, consultations and two very visible social engagements. For the first one, Bella didn't look to make as bold a statement as she had at the children's charity. When she attended a private and lavish fundraiser at the Louvre, where a weekend at the château was an auction item, she chose an Aurora cocktail dress with a sleeveless white silk bodice—plunging to the waist—and an ecru skirt beaded with clear and black crystals. Her shoulders were covered but not her arms, and her hair was done in an elaborate twist and anchored with more crystals.

The second engagement was an album launch by a popular rock band at Le Cabaret Sauvage, and it was an occasion for the more dramatic and daring. For that one she chose something unlike anything she'd worn before. She didn't want to be a carbon copy of her mother, who always dressed with class and elegance. Bella was only thirty, after all. She wore a long gold-sequined gown with thin spaghetti straps that crossed in the back and a deep slit that ran from hip to ankle.

The magazines went crazy, their covers shouting *Who Is Bella Pemberton?* and *Aurora's Best-Kept Secret*. She

tried to ignore them all and focused on what was good—
including the very personal benefit of wearing lighter
clothing and having her hair up, so she wasn't unbearably
warm all the time. At the office she stayed with short-
sleeved dresses and blouses with pencil skirts, sometimes
taming her hair into a low ponytail or chignon.

And when the weekend came and she was utterly shattered by her work schedule, she headed to Provence and
the château for a few days of rest and unplugging. She'd
never worked so hard...or been so invigorated.

Summer was hot in Provence, and now, in early August,
the lavender was in bloom. She'd left work early to catch
the train to Aix-en-Provence, and was picked up by a car
service for the journey to the house. They drove through the
countryside in a sea of purply blue, and the tension seeped
out of her the closer she got to the château. It was already
nearly nine, and she was ready for a glass of wine and perhaps some time looking at the stars. She'd be alone this
weekend. Maman had gone back to London for a checkup
with Dr. Mallick, and Bella was ready to enjoy the peace
and quiet.

Kitchen staff had prepared a light supper for her, and so
she first ventured to the wine cellar and then the kitchen,
sipping and munching to quell her hunger and thirst. Then
she poured a second glass of the very nice chenin blanc
that she'd picked and headed to the garden. It was dark
now, and the stars peeked out in the blanket of black sky.
The nearby lavender fields perfumed the air, and she could
pick up notes of thyme, rosemary, tarragon from the herb
pots nearby. There was a rich sweetness, too, which made
her believe the nectarines and apples in the grove were
ripe for picking.

She settled into one of the loungers, tipped it back a bit
more, and gazed up at the constellations.

She hadn't been able to forget Charlotte's words about

her stepping into the main office. Maman still hadn't said anything about a return date, but she hadn't not said anything, either. It was all up in the air.

It was a punishing pace, but Bella was still learning so of course there was a lot of adjustment. She also had the ability to reconfigure some duties and responsibilities, if need be. Taking time like this—to decompress, to be quiet—was crucial.

When the wine was gone and she'd watched a satellite arc across the night sky, she got up and went inside. She ran a bath with relaxing salts, and then crawled into her bed, sighing with pleasure as the soft sheets encompassed her body.

Her heart ached a little at being alone, but it was okay. Maybe this…maybe it was enough.

Maybe.

Burke had only been to the Pemberton château once in his life, back in his university days, when he'd gone for a bank holiday weekend with William. Late Saturday morning he skipped the last session at his conference in Avignon, rented a car, and made the forty-five-minute drive to see Bella.

It had been quite by chance that he'd known Bella was even there. He'd been talking to William, trying to convince him to pop down for a day or two, and William had said Bella was planning on spending the weekend and that he didn't want to interrupt her as she had been putting in long hours. He'd also mentioned enjoying wedded bliss and seemed reluctant to leave his wife. Burke had laughed; Will was just back from his honeymoon, of course. But the information that Bella was at the château had made her stick in his thoughts, all through the past two and a half days of meetings, lectures and workshops.

The gates to the château were open and he drove through, his guts churning. He had no idea how she'd react to his arrival. With pleasure? He hoped so. With annoyance, at interrupting her peace? Maybe. He wasn't even sure what he expected from her, what he wanted. But he wanted to see her. The whole "move on" thing wasn't working so well.

At just past noon, the heat was starting to climb. The forecast predicted a hot one today, peaking at ninety degrees. He knocked on the door and waited, then knocked again. What if she'd gone out? He should have called first. Should have—

His thoughts were cut off by the opening of the door by a young woman in plain black trousers and a white tailored shirt.

He took out his French, which was rusty though he'd gotten in some practice during the conference. *"Bonjour. Arabella est ici?"*

"Oui, monsieur. Un instant, s'il vous plaît."

She was here. Thank God. The maid ushered him inside and he waited in the foyer. The house was just as grand as he remembered, with high, soaring ceilings and beautiful finish work. The manor house was beautiful, but this…the château was stunning.

And then Bella was walking toward him, a slightly confused smile on her face. "Burke? What are you doing here?"

"I was at a conference in Avignon. Will said you were here, and I thought…well, I thought I'd drop by."

It was nearly an hour from his hotel to her château. Not exactly in the neighborhood. He felt like a fool.

Worse, he felt like the situation was totally out of his control. He'd been the one to say he didn't want a relationship, and at the first opportunity, here he was. He understood her being confused. *He* was confused.

When he looked at her, though, it seemed as if everything from the last three weeks clicked into place. All the anxiety, all the edginess, all the questioning, just fell away. It felt as if this was exactly where he was meant to be.

And that was scary as hell.

She was looking at him curiously. "Drop by?"

He nodded. Where had his cool charm gone? His control in every situation? Maybe this was a huge mistake.

"I hope it's all right. If it's not, I can leave."

There was a moment of hesitation. He couldn't tell by her expression what she was feeling. Her face looked exactly like it had when they'd first encountered each other in Italy—guarded.

But then her tense facial muscles relaxed and her eyes warmed the slightest bit. "It's okay. To be honest, it's good to see you."

"I've missed you," he admitted.

She looked around, as if suddenly realizing they were still in the foyer. "We don't need to stand here all day," she said. "Let's go to the garden. There's nice shade."

He followed her through, with no time to gawk at the open doors and the opulent rooms beyond. Bella's hips swayed gently as she walked, her posture straight and elegant. Her hair was up, too, and her small collar only partially concealed the scar there. There were so many things he wanted to ask her, but they could wait. Right now he wanted to take the temperature of the situation. Get his emotional feet beneath him.

The garden was a wonder. Stone steps, myriad planters of fragrant herbs and flowers, and Aleppo pines created an oasis of relaxation. "Wow. I'd forgotten how beautiful this is."

"Do you want to walk? There are some great views from the grove."

"If you like."

She continued on, leading him outside the garden to the lemon and nectarine grove on the property. The trees provided slight shade from the sun, and the scent of the ripening fruit was nothing short of delicious. But it was Bella he was entranced with. There was a confidence in her now that hadn't been there even a month ago. She was stronger. Tougher. Happier? He wondered. Because he'd been mostly miserable since she'd turned his life upside down.

They crested the knoll in the grove and Burke caught his breath. Fields of lavender waved below them, a carpet of purple against the robin's-egg blue of the sky. "Wow," he breathed, taking a deep breath of the perfumed air. "I can understand why you came for a weekend. It's peace and quiet and aromatherapy all in one."

She finally smiled, and his heart gave a little bump.

"It's been a month of changes," she admitted. "First the wedding, and Maman being ill, and us, and filling in for her, and then the big reveal." She looked up at him with a sheepish smile and shrugged. "For someone used to being in the background, I really outdid myself. I didn't realize until I got here last night what a toll it's taken."

That admission concerned him. "You have to be careful not to burn yourself out."

"The work is fine. Hard, but fine. Emotionally…different story."

"I'm sorry if I contributed to that."

She was looking over the lavender field again. "Not contributed, exactly. More like…the catalyst. It needed to happen. I'm glad it happened, and I have no regrets. But it's been a lot."

He wanted to touch her and knew he didn't have the right. "I have regrets. One of them being how I treated you in London."

She turned to face him again but said nothing. Waiting for him to elaborate, he supposed.

"Can we…maybe sit on that bench over there?" He gestured at an old stone bench at the edge of the grove, overlooking the valley below. It looked exactly like a place where lovers would go for a rendezvous or someone would visit to be alone with their thoughts. Made for intimacy, he realized. And while that scared him, he knew he'd bungled his earlier conversations with her and needed to make her understand better.

"Sure, if you want."

The bench was warm from the sun. She sat and then he sat after, and then, on impulse, reached over to take her hand.

"Bella, that night after we…" His throat caught and he cleared it. "After we made love, I told you I had to be honest with you about what I wanted. That I was focused on my career. That was true…but what I didn't say, what I should have said, was that I care about you. That you matter. That walking away from you was going to be the hardest thing I'd ever done. If I made you feel…disposable, I'm so very sorry."

He cringed as he said the word *disposable*.

She sighed. "I'm not going to lie. It stung that you found it so easy, after everything I'd shared with you."

"It wasn't as easy as you think." A million thoughts raced through his head, ones that he didn't want to face or deal with right now. "I know I seemed like I had it all together. I fooled myself into thinking that no one would get hurt or it would be no big deal."

"So you kissed me on the plane."

"And in the elevator. And a lot of other places."

Places being both geographical and intimate. Awareness buzzed between them again, like a bee searching for nectar in the garden blossoms. He could feel it, the longing, the need. Being with her now made him reconsider everything he thought was true.

She leaned back and tipped her face to the sun, closing her eyes. "Last night I wished you were here, and now you are. And now I don't know what to do about it. Nothing has changed."

"No, nothing has changed," he murmured, and he slid closer and leaned over to touch his lips to the corner of her mouth.

Her breath fluttered out, a delicate release that fueled his desire even further. What if they could make it work? What if they didn't give up quite yet? He didn't know how, but in this particular moment it didn't seem to matter. What mattered was he was here with her again and everything that had been wrong for the past weeks was suddenly right again.

He shifted, deepened the kiss just a little, keeping it soft and tentative but removing the question that had been un-spoken in the first kiss. She responded by lifting a hand and curving it gently around his neck, a subtle pressure holding him in place, close to her.

He nibbled on her lower lip, made himself break the contact. "Bella. I can't seem to shake you and I don't know what to do about it."

"Me either. But I want this. I wanted it the first time and I haven't yet had my fill. I know where things stand with you. I respect that. But you're here and…"

"Shh…" He put his finger over her lips. "Yes. And as much as making love to you in the lemon grove would be hot as hell, I want to be able to take my time. Not be some hurried thing in the grass."

"Then we should go back to the château."

"You're sure?"

"Very sure. I never wanted you to walk away in the first place." She put her hand on his face. "Burke, I've waited so long to start living. If I can't have you forever, let me at least have what you can give me now. With no promises and no regrets."

It should have been music to his ears, but instead it sent

a rush of remorse through his heart. "You deserve better," he whispered.

"Let me decide what I deserve."

There was no arguing with her. She was as stubborn as they came and it was foolish to disagree when he wanted the exact same thing she did. He got up from the bench and held out his hand, and she took it.

Then they raced through the grove to the gardens and into the house.

CHAPTER THIRTEEN

BELLA WAS NEARLY breathless when she reached her room on the third floor of the château. She and Burke had dashed through the heat of the afternoon to get to the house, then up the stairs. He'd stopped her twice to steal panty-melting kisses, and only the thought of an errant staff member popping around a corner kept Bella from hauling him down on top of her right then and there.

She opened the door to her room, pulled him inside by the hand and shut the door. Firmly.

In the space of a heartbeat he had her pressed against the hard wood of the door. The first night had been gentle and tender, and careful. *Careful* was not a word to describe the fire running through her veins now, or the way Burke kissed his way from collarbone to navel as he undid her blouse with rough fingers and dropped it to the floor.

It was a hurried dash to rid themselves of the rest of their clothes and then they were naked on her bed, touching and tasting and desperate to get closer, closer.

Burke got up for a moment and went for his jeans, grabbing a condom from the front pocket. "Sure of yourself, were you?" She rose up on her elbows, her hair cascading down her back as she watched him tear open the package. God, he was beautiful, all dark hair and smooth skin and strength.

"Not at all, but if there was a remote chance this was going to happen, I wasn't going to get caught without protection."

"I admire your foresight."

He got back on the bed with her and looped an arm around her hips, pulling her down several inches. "I hope in a moment you'll admire something else."

She let out a cry of delight.

This was different. So different and free and equal and oh-so-satisfying. It was need and want and giving and taking all at once. Her skin grew slick with sweat in the afternoon heat. Burke, too, had a sheen of sweat on his shoulders and she leaned forward to lick at it. He didn't hold back this time, and she lost herself in it. Their first time had been perfect, but this time it was primal and she loved it even more. Loved knowing she had the power to make Burke lose control.

When they finally slid, boneless, back onto the covers, panting with exertion and glowing with perspiration, Bella started to laugh. It rose up from her belly to her chest, up her throat and out her mouth in a rich, replete sound that was disbelief and satisfaction wrapped up in one.

She couldn't move and couldn't care less.

Burke swore lightly, and she laughed.

"Thank you," she said, her voice deliberately soft.

"For what?" he asked.

"For losing control a little bit. For being a little wild and less restrained and…calculated. I don't mean that the way it sounds," she amended. "It was just the first time you seemed focused on doing things step by step, I guess. This time…it was like you couldn't help yourself."

"I could have if you'd asked. But I'm awfully glad you didn't."

"Oh, me, too."

Finally she rolled over to face him. She no longer worried about him seeing the scars on her arms and shoulders, and it was lovely to know she could be this way—totally naked with him—and his gaze wasn't going to drop in shock or dismay or disgust.

"I think we need to talk about the fact that we can't seem to keep our hands off each other. I mean, we went from barely talking to in my bed in less than thirty minutes."

"I'm sorry. I didn't intend—"

She cut him off. "It wasn't a complaint. But we can't keep doing this, Burke. Desperate to be together in one way and pushing each other away in another. Nothing has changed. At least nothing that I can see."

The shadowed look came into his eyes again, and he started to move away but she grabbed his arm and kept him on the bed. "No, don't run away. I know there's more you're not saying. I wish you'd be honest with me."

When he was quiet, she let out a huff of frustration. "I shared so much with you. It hurts me that you don't trust me with the same. This has to do with more than just your job, doesn't it?"

This time when he went to get up, she let him, and he reached for his boxers and pulled them on. She understood the action more than he might think. He was feeling naked, both physically and emotionally. Even underwear added to a sense of protection.

She, on the other hand, made no move to get dressed. She had nothing to hide. Not now.

He sat on the edge of the bed and rested his elbows on his knees. Bella scooted over a bit, wondering what could possibly be bothering him. "Hey," she said softly. "If there's something you need to talk about, I hope you know by now that you're safe with me."

He turned his head and met her eyes. "I know that. Honestly, Bella, I don't know what I'm doing. I've had such a clear path until a few weeks ago. I knew what I wanted and I didn't stray from that trajectory. And then you came along and everything changed. And yeah, it was from the moment we slept together. Not because of you, but because of me. Because…" He hesitated and took a shuddering breath. "Because my mind and heart are at complete odds. What I feel for you is something I never really wanted to feel for anyone, and it comes down to my parents, really."

Nothing he might have said surprised her more. "You told me it was because of your career."

"It was. It is! But deep down it's more than that. My career—I love it, but I've used it, too, as an excuse to keep myself distanced from people. Damn. This is hard."

"Most conversations of this type are," she agreed.

She slid over and wrapped her arms around him. "Burke, you helped me so much. You were right from the start—I had to start talking about the accident, facing what had happened and not hiding away. Being with you was like someone lit a candle inside me. I stopped being so afraid. I feel…liberated. If I can help you in some way, with whatever you're struggling with, I want to. Because I know it's something. I can see it behind your eyes."

He sighed. "It is something."

She waited, because she sensed he needed her to be patient.

"When I was a kid, I thought our life was pretty happy. I mean, my father was gone a lot. I thought he was so important. The viscount, you know? And he had business. All of his business interests—and he'd invested in a lot of different schemes—got his attention. Mum always seemed happy and there was me and my sisters, and we did stuff together. It was, I thought, a good childhood."

She sensed a "but" coming and held her tongue.

"But when I was sixteen, and away at school, I went to a friend's for a long weekend. We went into a pub for food and I saw my father in there with a woman. Before you say anything, I didn't misinterpret what I saw. It was plainly obvious. He wasn't even trying to hide it."

Burke turned his head and looked at her. "My dad, my hero, was having an affair. And everything I'd known as stable and secure was now tainted."

Her heart melted for the boy he'd been. Her own parents had been so devoted to each other. She would have been crushed if she'd discovered they'd ever been unfaithful. "Oh, Burke, I'm so sorry."

"I know. I'm thirty and should be over it. But I watched my dad for years, wondering with each trip he went on if he were really going on business or if he was seeing her. Or worse, someone else. Wondering if my mother knew, and how long it had been that way. I somehow think she must have, but she put on such a happy face. Everything was a lie. I never, ever want to hurt someone like that, Bella."

"But you wouldn't. You're not your father."

"No? I've buried myself at work so that I don't have to have any relationships of consequence. And the one time I do find someone who makes me care, shows me what it might be like, I send her away. Because I'm afraid of hurting her. And worse—because I'm afraid of my own feelings."

She kissed his shoulder. "You don't want to become him. I get it. But I think there's more. Burke, it's clear to me that this hurt you very deeply. If you keep your relationships 'on the surface' and without any real depth, then no one else can hurt *you* like he did, either."

His back shuddered as he took in a breath. "I don't know how to love you, Bella. I never learned. But maybe it's time. If you can share your scars with the world, maybe I can share mine with you. But it's a scary thing, giving someone else this much of myself. You need to know that."

She hadn't expected something like this. What she remembered of his father, the previous Viscount Downham, was a handsome, charismatic man who looked like an older version of Burke, with crinkly brown eyes and a warm smile. He'd been charming. And he'd been friends with her father, too. "Your dad was well-liked. That must have been hard for you, knowing his flaws."

He nodded. "Especially in the earlier years. He could charm all my friends, and I wanted to shout at them, 'You don't know!' Ugh. It's been hard the last few weeks. I've tried all my life to not be like him, and it turns out I'm more like him than I thought."

She moved to sit beside him, tucking her ankle beneath her so she was facing his profile. "Nonsense. What you did is nothing like a man cheating on his wife. You were trying to protect yourself, and I think protect me as well. From being hurt. But what hurt was being without you."

"Bella. You don't know what you're saying."

"I do. I know how I feel right now. I feel honored that you shared this with me. I feel amazed and beautiful, knowing you couldn't wait to take me to bed. I feel like the moment you hugged me beside the Baresis' pool, something inside me started to heal. You did that, Burke. You did."

He swallowed tightly. "I don't know what to do next."

"Nor do I. But come back to bed and hold me, and at some point it'll become clear for us. I can't believe that this is the end, not after everything we've shared. Let's just be for a while. Whenever we have a pressing problem at work, Maman always says to let it rest for a while and the answer will come. So let's be patient and see what happens."

He reached out and pulled her close. "You are one in a million, Arabella Pemberton. It's no wonder I love you."

The words hit her like a jolt to the chest, an explosion of fireworks that sent sparks outward until she was filled with light, body and soul. "You love me?"

He nodded, his eyes solemn. "I do. I don't know what

comes next, but if I'm determined to be honest, you should know how I feel. It's too big a gift to keep to myself."

She bit down on her lip to keep from crying, and then Burke snuggled her in his arms as they nestled beneath the sheets of her bed. It was midafternoon and she didn't care. There was nowhere else in the entire world she would rather be. He loved her and she loved him. Surely there was some way they could work out a way to be together.

Burke slid out of bed a few hours later, refreshed from his postcoital nap. He was trying to think of possibilities. Ways to make their relationship work. Maybe they didn't have to rush any big decisions. Maybe they could do the long-distance thing for a little while. After all, London to Paris was easily navigated and they both had the means. Besides, Bella would only be filling in for Aurora for a little while longer, and then surely her schedule would become slightly more flexible.

He was feeling optimistic and lighter than he had in ages as he slipped into his jeans and shirt. He wanted to let her sleep; William had said she'd been putting in a ton of hours and she looked so peaceful, so beautiful beneath the pale sheet, her soft skin glowing and her lips full and slightly opened as she breathed deeply. He'd just go downstairs and maybe sit in the garden again, get some relaxation himself.

He was just crossing the cobblestones toward the grouping of chairs when his phone vibrated in his pocket, signaling a text message. He ignored it. There wasn't anything so important he needed to answer right now. But when his ringtone sounded a few moments later, he frowned and took it out, swiping the lock screen.

Will's number popped up.

"Hey, what's up?" he asked, pressing the phone to his ear.

"Go check the link I just sent you. I'm sorry, Burke. Hate being the bearer of bad news."

Dread settled in Burke's gut as he looked down at the phone and swiped over to his direct messages. Will had sent him a link to an online story from a well-known news outlet. The dread intensified, making his blood run cold.

He scanned the first three paragraphs, and there it was, his name. The story of how the accident had caused Bella's disfigurement and that he and Bella had been in the car with Royce. The credibility of the source could not be disputed: it was Fiona, the girl he'd taken along with him, and only contacted once since—the day after the accident, asking if she was okay.

She hadn't wanted her name in the news, either. She'd looked older but he'd later discovered she was only fifteen. All of them drinking underage. It had suited them all to have their names left out as minors.

Until now. Because tabloids paid good money to sources.

He thought he was going to be sick to his stomach.

He sank into a chair, cold despite the bright sun shining down on him. He put the phone back to his ear. "Dammit, Will."

"I know. Though I suppose once Bella stopped hiding, it was bound to come out."

"Has Charlotte seen it yet?"

"I sent it to her first, and told her I was calling you. If I know Charlotte, she's going to come up with a plan for damage control and present it as a fait accompli before calling Bella. Where are you?"

Burke put his forehead in his hand. "I'm at the château. Bella's inside." Sleeping. After making love to him. Dammit all.

"You went to see her."

"We have stuff to work out." He didn't say more than

that. He wasn't the kind to bring other people into his personal life, although Will was his best friend. But Will was also Bella's brother. "We care about each other a lot, Will. But it's not simple."

There was a pause. Then Will spoke, his voice firm in Burke's ear. "It's never simple. But you're the best man I know, Burke. I could see this coming in Italy and thought it might be something wonderful. That being said, if you hurt my sister, I'm going to have to mess you up a bit."

Burke choked out a laugh. He was still reeling from being called a good man. Will might not say so if he knew Burke's thoughts right now. News like this—about a drunk driving accident being hidden away—could affect his professional life. He was so close to getting a dream job. What if this messed it up?

"Will, I need to go. But I appreciate the heads-up."

"Phone if you need anything."

They hung up and Burke let out a deep sigh.

Just when things started to come together. Why did life always have to be so…complicated?

CHAPTER FOURTEEN

BELLA WOKE ALONE and looked around her. Burke was gone, and for a moment she had a flash of fear that it hadn't been real, or that he'd dressed and left her, gone back to Avignon or London or...

But then she let out her breath and told herself that was ridiculous. Burke would not run out on her like that. He wasn't that kind of man. So she slipped out of bed, put on a cool sundress, and went searching.

She found him in the garden, sitting with his head in his hands. Worry spiraled through her. Something was wrong. Something more than deep thought. Was he regretting what he'd told her? Being with her? She desperately hoped not, but she'd face this head-on. She was used to it by now.

"Hi," she said softly.

He lifted his head. His eyes were shadowed with tension and his lips were set. "Hi. Sorry. I woke up and needed some air."

He was having second thoughts, wasn't he?

"What's going on?"

He held out his phone. "Call your sister."

She froze, hand outstretched. "Oh God. Is it Maman?"

"No! No. I'm so sorry. I never even thought of that. No, your mother is fine. But you need to call Charlotte. Then we can talk."

This was not helping to dispel her fears. She punched in Charlotte's number and wasn't even greeted with a hello. "Burke. I take it you've heard?"

"It's Bella on Burke's phone. What's going on? He hasn't told me anything."

There was a big sigh, and then Charlotte cleared her throat. "Fiona came forward with the story of the crash. It's all over the media now. I'm guessing she got a good payout for all the details."

Bella closed her eyes. They'd hoped this wouldn't happen, but it had always been a possibility. "She named names?"

"Yes. Burke's and yours. Royce was already a matter of record. He wasn't a minor."

"So what do we do?"

"You do nothing for now. You stay at the château. In an hour or so I'll send over a document with talking points we can use to respond, but I don't think this is worth an actual Aurora press release. We're also getting interview requests. I've denied them all."

"Thank you, Charlotte. I'd like for us to not be reactionary and to take a measured response to this. Basically, not overreact in general."

"Exactly. Thank you for that, because I didn't want to have to talk you down from a panic attack or anything."

"I don't have panic attacks."

Charlotte laughed. "True. But you've been through a lot the past few weeks. Thanks for being so consistent."

"That's me." Sometimes she wished she weren't. There was a certain strain around the pressure to remain level-headed and consistent. Not that she'd have it any other way, but it was there just the same.

She looked over at Burke. He was clearly not taking this well. "Listen, I'll look for your email later. I'm going to go for now. Is that okay?"

"Of course. I'll be in touch soon."

"Thank you, Charlotte."

They hung up and Bella handed the phone back to Burke. "Well, I guess the cat's out of the bag. I rather hoped it wouldn't be."

"Me, too." He ran his hand through his hair. "I just had my meeting at the Royal Brompton. Everything was looking so good there. Now my face is going to be on some stupid magazine."

Bella sat down beside him. "My father used to call them 'scurrilous rags,'" she said, offering a small smile. "The story won't last forever, Burke. You were seventeen. And you weren't driving."

He stared at her. "At dinner, that night in London, I told you what my biggest fear was. You knew. Don't make me feel as if I shouldn't be upset, Bella. That's not fair."

She kept a lid on her own bubbling feelings. "Of course you're allowed to be upset. I'm just trying to make you see that the fallout won't be that bad." She put her hand over his. "Darling, if people didn't survive gossip and tattling, no one would ever stay in business." She had a sudden idea. "Listen, why don't you talk to Charlotte? She's used to running damage control. I know she'd walk you through some of this as well and put your mind at ease."

He stood up suddenly. "You expected this."

She frowned. "I always knew it was a possibility. Fiona was the one wild card we couldn't control."

"And yet you knew how I felt and you went ahead anyway." He turned away, paced a few steps, and turned back. "Wow."

An hour ago they'd been professing their love and now this. She wasn't prepared for this roller coaster of emotion and wanted off. "First of all, I didn't need to show my scars for Fiona to come forward. The Pembertons are high-profile enough that she could have come forward at any time and it would have been a story. And secondly, you were the one who pushed me away in London, saying we didn't have a relationship. So what, I'm supposed to hide who I am forever? Do you realize what you're saying?"

Her heart slammed in her chest as adrenaline kicked in from the anxiety and emotion running through her veins.

"No, of course not." He swore. "There are no winners in this."

"Clearly," she answered.

He stared at her for several moments, and she held his gaze, unwilling to back down.

"I wish I'd never gotten in that car that night," he finally said, his voice hoarse.

"Me, too, but I did, and you did, and a boy died, and we were all hurt. At some point you have to accept it and move on. Feeling guilty solves nothing. Hiding what it did to you—that solves nothing. I faced my biggest fear and nothing dire happened. I'm still here and alive. Maybe it's time you faced yours, too."

"But you didn't have the right to choose that for me, and now I have no choice."

He wasn't wrong. And he wasn't right, either. She softened her voice. "Burke, my choice to be open about myself has caused you pain. If I'd chosen to not be open, I would have spared you pain but harmed myself. You walked away from me. I was hurt. I was not angry. Nothing I did was out of maliciousness or trying to hurt you. Instead, it was about choosing me, for the first time in forever." She pressed her fist to her heart. "But I'm truly sorry that this has hurt you. I am. Like you said—no winners."

"You've won."

His sharp words were a knife to the heart. "Have I? An hour ago you said you loved me. Now it looks as though this changes everything. I'm not really feeling like a winner right now."

His face changed, dropped into a mask of sadness. "Bella."

"Maybe this is just too messy. I'm sorry, Burke, I can't deal with any more right now."

He nodded. "I'll go. I need to go back to London and see what's to be done, anyway. I'm sure this has gotten back to Mum as well. You're right. It's messy as hell."

Perhaps he was misunderstanding. She hadn't meant in general, she'd meant for them as a couple…or not as a couple. But as he left her there on the patio, she realized that twice now he'd put her aside to protect himself. The compromise she'd longed to work for with him was gone.

And with it, her hope for her future.

Her mother had been very lucky. She'd had the company and a husband who loved and doted on her. Maybe Bella just needed to be content with the professional success. It just cut cruelly to get a taste of love only to have it snatched away…again.

Burke waited two days after arriving in London to go see his mother. In that time, the story had made the rounds in the weekly tabloids, websites and entertainment programs on TV. Arabella was a big draw. Throw in a viscount and the gossip was that much spicier.

He'd gone back to work yesterday to whispers, which he'd ignored. Long looks of speculation which he also ignored. But he found himself snappish, which wasn't his usual style, either with coworkers or with patients. He had yet to hear from the Royal Brompton, but at this point everyone had to be aware of the scandal.

His mother still lived in the family home, a lovely dwelling in Kensington with ten bedrooms and seven baths and a surprisingly peaceful garden where she had taken up growing her own herbs and lettuces. When Burke walked in that Tuesday morning, a measure of calm came over him.

They met in the breakfast room, a sunny, welcoming space that had windows overlooking the garden. Beyond that, leafy trees provided more privacy as the property backed onto Holland Park. "Burke, darling. It's so good to see you. I've put out coffee. Have you eaten?"

He hadn't. His appetite was off, had been since leaving France. "I'm fine, Mum. Coffee is great."

"I'll send down for some cake. I know for a fact there's a fresh lemon drizzle waiting to be cut into."

Mothers. They reverted to making sure you ate enough in times of strife. He smiled a little. "Cake would be lovely."

She came forward, looked up into his face and then stood on tiptoe to give him a hug. "It's going to be all right, you know," she murmured, patting his back. "You just have to weather the storm."

Her choice of words made him wonder. Within a few minutes they were seated at the table, both with cups of hot coffee and slices of still-warm cake before them.

He drank. She drank. Then she put her cup down and looked at him evenly. "What is it you want to ask me? I can tell there's something. You might as well get it out."

Everything inside him cramped. He wasn't sure how to do this, but he did know that his life, for the first time since the accident, felt as if it were in utter shambles. "I've messed something up, and I don't know how to fix it."

Isabel waved a hand. "If it's about the accident, this will blow over in a few days. Another story will take its place."

"It's partly about that. But it's…bigger," he said, struggling to find the right words. "You see, Mum, I've gone and fallen in love with Bella Pemberton."

Isabel put down her fork, the cake still speared on the tines. "Oh. I see."

"Do you?"

"She made the news with her scars. I wondered if they were from the accident."

"They are. She's so beautiful and brave and strong. And I've messed up everything by just trying to do the right thing." He met her gaze. "My whole life I've tried to do the right thing and it hasn't always worked out so well."

Quiet fell between them for a few moments. Then he screwed up his courage and prepared to break his mother's heart.

"Dad had an affair when I was sixteen."

Isabel took a long, slow inhale, then released it. "I know."

His mouth dropped open. "You knew?"

"It wasn't his first." Sadness colored her hazel eyes. "I had you and the girls. Our marriage… I probably shouldn't have stayed. Not after the first infidelity. I agreed to stay and raise you three here, and he promised to be discreet."

"It was in the middle of a very public pub. He was there with…her."

"Did he know you saw him?"

"No, never."

"I see. And this has to do with Bella because?"

Isabel picked up her coffee now and took a long drink. Burke was so surprised by her question that he sat back, considering. "Because she deserves better than what you got. She deserves someone to dote on her, to not be married to his job. Which I am."

"Why?"

"I'm sorry?"

She let out a frustrated sigh. "Why are you married to your job?"

"The hours are heinous."

"No, not good enough." She folded her hands in her lap. "Fill in the blank. 'If I'm married to my job, then I'm not…'"

She let the end of the sentence hang. …*not married to a person, and I can't hurt them.*

"Go ahead and say it, Burke. It's all right." Her voice was soft, gentle. Understanding, even.

"I would never want to hurt her the way that Father hurt you," Burke admitted. "He was never here. He was always gone for work. Then when he was gone, he was with other women. You deserved better, Mum. And so does Bella. And the truth is, I do love my job. I'm dedicated to it. I've been sick to my stomach for three days wondering what's happening with the opportunity at the Royal Brompton. I'm so selfish."

He pushed away his coffee in disgust.

"Oh, what a bunch of codswallop."

He lifted his head. His mother's mouth was set in a firm line and she was frowning at him. "What is?"

"The selfish part. You don't have a selfish bone in your body. So what if you're worried about your career? You've spent years building it. The last thing you want is for something far in your past to come up and ruin it."

"Thank you!" he said, relieved she understood.

"That doesn't mean I think you're right. It just means I understand why you might feel that way. Do you know what I think?"

"Do I have a choice?" he grumbled.

"You came here, darling," she reminded him.

She wasn't wrong.

"I think you're using your career to run away. You're afraid. Not of your reputation. You're afraid of yourself. You've carried this secret around for too long and you're wondering if you're like your father. After all, if you could make such a poor decision the night of the party, who's to say you won't be that irresponsible later?"

He pushed away from the table, turning his back on her and walking to the window. She'd punched right through all his barriers, even the ones he hadn't realized he'd constructed. He hadn't been able to hate his father because he'd been too busy hating himself for getting in the car. For not taking the keys from Royce. For all of it.

She got up and followed him, and he didn't look down but felt the pressure of her hand on his arm.

"Burke, you are not your father. Just because you carry the same title doesn't mean you'll make the same mistakes. Just because you share the same DNA doesn't mean you're predestined to walk in his footsteps."

Tears pricked behind his eyes, burning hot. "I can't stand the idea of disappointing people."

"I know. I've watched you wrap yourself in charm and charisma and even compassion for over a decade, all to protect yourself. If Bella Pemberton has broken through that wall, then more power to her. It's about time you fell on your ass in love. Your sisters and I were starting to think it wouldn't happen."

Bella. Just the thought of her made his heart ache. "How did you do it, Mum? How did you stay here and pretend to be so happy when you had to be dying inside?" He turned his head to look down at her.

"I made my own choices, Burke. And I had you and the girls, and we had a good life. There were fun times. And I didn't hate your father. He was, in many ways, a good man. But we didn't share a deep passion. That's what I regret. I didn't love him, so how can I hate him for searching for it somewhere else?"

Burke shook his head. "Don't blame yourself for him cheating."

"He made his choices. But I also made mine. My wish for my children has always been for them to find someone they love, truly love right to the depths of their being. Is that Bella for you?"

He thought of her and her soft smile, wide eyes, strong chin. The way she made him laugh and how she felt in his arms. "I think it might be."

"And you're standing here in my breakfast room, worrying about some job so you don't have to think about all the ways you can screw this up. You're a smart man, Burke, and a talented physician. But you're being a coward."

A lump formed in his throat. "I came here for some love and support."

"My love and support comes in the form of kicking your ass."

He chuckled. This was not what he'd expected at all. First, that she knew about his father's affairs, and second, that she'd give his head a good shake instead of giving him a loving hug.

Isabel's voice gentled. "Burke, all I can say is this. Jobs and opportunities come and go. But when you find the one person who makes everything make sense, you have to latch onto that and never let it go."

He thought of his potential job, and how he'd been so afraid the truth would ruin his chances. And then he thought of Bella, touching his shoulder as he told her his deepest secret, and knew he'd already blown his biggest chance at happiness. She'd forgiven him once, but there was no guarantee she'd forgive him another time. "I think I might have messed it up for good," he murmured, his heart sore.

"Then you have to figure out what you're willing to do to get her back. And then tell her. Show her."

He looked at his mother. There were tears on her cheeks, and he put his arm around her and tucked her close. "I'm sorry, Mum. More sorry than you can know."

"Don't be. Besides, I'm only fifty-four. There's still time for a second chance for me, you know."

He smiled at that, gave her arm a squeeze. "I'm going to have to make some changes," he said, but oddly enough, the idea wasn't quite as terrifying as it had been less than an hour ago. Now what was scary was not knowing if Bella would say yes.

"Eat your cake first," she said, moving away from his embrace. "And have more coffee. I've missed you. Maybe we can talk through it together, hmm?"

As Burke returned to the table, a new calm settled over him. The one thing he had to do was make things right with Bella. If he could do that, everything else would fall into place. The only thing worse than being afraid of failure was the regret to be found in not trying.

And, damn, he was tired of regret.

CHAPTER FIFTEEN

IT TOOK NEARLY two more weeks for Burke to head to Paris. In that time he'd met with his current boss, had a meeting with the directors at the Royal Brompton, and come to Paris two days ago for more meetings. He was currently sitting on the balcony of his vacation rental overlooking the river and drinking a very strong coffee.

Today he needed to see Arabella, and he was scared to death. There was a very good chance that she was going to take one look at him and send him on his way. After all, he'd turned away from her twice now because of his own fears. She deserved so much better.

He'd been tested and he'd come up short. He didn't like that about himself at all. He just hoped it wasn't too late to fix, because he did love her. And if he could get out of his own way, they might just have a chance at some happiness.

He checked his phone for the time and noted it was nearly nine. It would take him twenty minutes or so to make his way to the Aurora Inc. offices and hope she wasn't in a meeting. Was it a mistake to go see her at work? He was afraid that if he asked her to meet with him, she'd say no. But what if she refused to see him at all? They hadn't spoken since he'd walked away from her at the château.

So he went inside, locked the door to the balcony, put his dirty cup in the sink, and went to the bathroom to brush his teeth and give himself a final once-over. His stomach was in knots, but he made sure he had his phone and his wallet and went out the door to hail a taxi.

He'd never been inside the Aurora Inc. building before. It was a gorgeous place, with marble floors and a reception area that had white-veined marble counters and "Aurora" in stylized lettering behind the desks. The admin staff were dressed in all black and white as well. It was classy as heck.

"Good morning. I'm here to see Arabella Pemberton."

"Do you have an appointment, sir?"

"No, I'm afraid I do not."

"Your name?"

"Burke Phillips."

"Let me call up to her assistant and see if she has time in her schedule today."

Of course there would be gatekeepers. Bella was effectively running the company. Just last week Aurora had surprised everyone with the announcement that she was stepping back from many of her duties and that the board of directors had approved Bella as her successor. He was hugely proud and somewhat intimidated.

"Sir? Ms. Pemberton is currently in a meeting, but her assistant says she can meet with you in forty minutes. Take the elevator to the fourth floor and give your name to the main reception." She gestured toward the elevator bank to his right.

"Thank you," he replied, wondering why his mouth was suddenly dry. Maybe because his whole future depended on how the next hour went?

He took the elevator up and gave his name at the desk, again with white marble and the stylized Aurora lettering, only on a smaller scale. The receptionist led him down a hallway to a small seating area, offered him a coffee and then left him alone to wait. He held on to the black mug, turning it in his hands but not drinking. He was jittery and didn't need another coffee to jack him up further.

He waited thirty minutes. Forty. Forty-five. Fifty. If she was trying to torture him, it was working.

And then she came around the corner, dressed in a white power suit, speaking to another woman in flawless French as she smiled and handed off a portfolio. Finally, finally, she turned to Burke. "Good morning."

"Hi."

He didn't know what else to say. She frowned a little. "Hang on a moment," she said, and disappeared around the corner to her assistant's desk, the woman he'd just seen her with. He heard her speaking, again in French, but couldn't make out quite what she was saying. In seconds she was back. "Come on into my office, where we can talk."

Her office was a huge room, with a stunning desk, chair, credenza, bookcase and art on the walls—all art that shouted Aurora Inc. to him. Gone was the black-and-white signature scheme. The photographic art provided wild bursts of color—dramatic sweeps of fabric in red and orange, a cascade of jewels in rich tones of ruby, sapphire, emerald, topaz. A model's face, dark skin with striking, powerful makeup. The entire collection was a statement of passion and power, and he marveled that it had all come from her, the woman who had barely met his gaze in Italy. He knew without a doubt that these choices were not her mother's. When his girl chose to step into the light, she did it with style. *She owned it.*

"You like these?" she asked, following his gaze.

"I do. You've had them put in? They don't seem like your mother's style."

"I did." She smiled slightly. "I don't want to come in and change everything. Maman was and is a fantastic, smart, dynamic leader. But I want to put my own stamp on things, too. This seemed a good place to start."

He nodded. Looked at her. Felt the air strangling in his throat. "Bella, I wish we could go back to Italy, or that day in London at the butterfly house, and that I could do things right instead of messing it all up."

"But we can't," she answered, and there was a note of sorrow in her voice. "Twice, Burke. Twice you let me hope and believe. And twice you walked away. I'm a strong woman but I wasn't ready for that."

"I know. God, I know." He ran his hand through his hair. They were standing there, in front of her desk, and he wanted to pull her into his arms. He wanted reassurance. Which was stupid because he was the one who should be giving it. "I handled everything wrong."

"We slept together and everything changed. Up to that point you'd been wonderful, open, caring. Perfect. Then it was like you became a stranger. When you left the last time, I realized that I probably don't know who you are. And if I don't know who you are, how can I love you?"

It did sound ominously like the end, and a desperate fear gripped him. "Bella, please. Just listen to what I have to say. Because you're right. You're so right. I've got to stop hiding and protecting myself and running way. It's the only way I might have a chance with you at all. Will you listen?"

Her throat worked as she looked at him with soft, wounded eyes. "Of course I will."

He took a breath. He could do this. It was Bella. There was no one in the world he trusted more, and he told her so.

"I have never trusted anyone with my father's secret," he began. "And you already knew about the accident. You know more about me than any other human on earth, and that includes my family."

"Your mother doesn't know about your father?"

"I didn't think so, but she always knew. We talked when I went home. We talked about a lot of things."

She smiled a wobbly smile.

"Anyway," he continued, "I've made a habit of never leaving myself open to be vulnerable. Short-term, shallow relationships, burying myself in work, trying to outrun my past mistakes and determined as hell not to carry on my father's cheating legacy. And then there was you, challenging me on both those things. It scared me to death. So what did I do? Retreat. Run away. I was a coward, Bella, and you deserved better. You deserved a man who would stand beside you and I wasn't there for you. But I want to be now."

She lifted an eyebrow.

"I know. It sounds like something you heard before." Panic started to grip him and he pushed it away.

She took a moment to glance away, then walked over to one of the windows overlooking the city. He could see the view from where he stood. Paris, the city of light. Full of romance and wonder. Boy, he could use a romance miracle right about now.

"Bella," he tried again, "I need you to know what's happened the past two weeks."

"Okay," she answered, turning back from the window. "So tell me."

She wasn't going to make it easy for him, and he loved her all the more for it. Bella lived life on her own terms, every step of the way. She owned her choices, good and bad. It was time he owned his.

"First I panicked. I'm sure you know it didn't take long for the sub-story to hit the news as well. I'm not as scandalous as the Pembertons, but I was Fiona's companion that night and the press went digging. First, I went to see my mother. I talked to my boss at the hospital about it, and then I met with people at the Royal Brompton. Both were supportive. My family, too. They pointed out that I'd taken the horror that was the accident and used it to do something great with my life. It did motivate me to go into medicine, and I love what I do."

"I know you do. And you're good at it. You're good with people, too, and putting them at ease. Those skills don't always go hand in hand."

Her praise gave him hope. "I also realized that my fear of the story being public wasn't really about my professional life. It was about my personal shame. What I wanted from you in Italy was absolution. But even if you'd given it, I hadn't really forgiven myself. If no one else knew, then it was my cross to bear privately. Private shame, not public. I know now that one is not worse than the other."

"It was not your fault, any more than it was mine. I have my own share of shame and guilt, Burke. I've often looked at my scars as penance. Something I've deserved."

"But you've moved past that in such a big and significant way. It's not just about that. They are also marks of your strength and perseverance. Not a single human on the earth hasn't done something they're ashamed of. You stepped into the light while I hid away. You humbled me more than once, Bella. With your trust and with your strength, which I both admire and also don't deserve. But I want to. So much. I want to be worthy of you. I want us to try. I'm here asking you to give me one last chance. I want to become the man I'm meant to be, and I want to do it with you."

Her lip trembled a bit. "That all sounds very pretty. But I'm a bit raw where you're concerned, Burke. I left myself open to you and you turned me away. How do I know you won't do it again?"

He went to her, reached down and gently took one of her hands in his, so glad he'd listened to his mother and had been prepared to show her and not just give her words. "Because I'm ready to prove it. I know you said I'm married to my career, and you're not entirely wrong. It's demanding and I love it. But I don't have to do it in London. There's a position waiting for me here, at St. Joseph's. You need to be here for Aurora. But I do not have to be in London."

She lifted her gaze and her lips dropped open. "You'd move to Paris? But what about the other job? The one that you've been dreaming of?"

He squeezed her fingers. "I could take it and lose you. The truth is, that's not much of a contest. If there's a chance we can make it work, then I want to try. Opportunities come and go. But you…there's only one you, Bella."

She sniffled and blinked rapidly. "Did you practice that?"

He choked on a surprised laugh. "No! I mean, I've been thinking for days what I would say to you, but the moment I saw you everything left my brain."

She pulled her fingers away. "Burke, I didn't do everything right, either."

He stared at her. "What do you mean?"

She took a step back. "I didn't fight for us, either. I knew you were scared but instead of holding your feet to the fire, I walked away. Both at the hospital and at the château. If I'd been willing to fight for us more, we might have worked through things. We might have been able to do this together. But I didn't. Maybe because I had this foolish notion that you had to be perfect. Maybe because, up to that point, you had been perfect. I told myself, and Maman, and Charlotte, that I didn't want to have to beg for affection, but I think maybe the truth was I didn't want to have to work at a relationship. I didn't accept that you could be flawed."

"No," he answered, stepping forward and cupping her face in his hands. "You were a hundred percent right. You did deserve better. So my question is, can we try once more? Because I do love you, Bella. As much as that terrifies me, I do. I'll take the job here and we can put in the work. I want to be the man you deserve so much."

Bella looked into his eyes and saw the man who'd looked back at her at the butterfly house that day, before everything had become so complicated. She understood shame and guilt. She understood trying to outrun the past. What had happened was that she'd been a few steps ahead of him in that regard. Did that mean she should walk away now?

"I want that, too," she murmured, "but I'm scared. I know I seem strong but I'm not sure I could take you bailing when things get complicated again." She had to be honest. It was the only way they had any hope at all.

"Love takes compromise," he finally said. "It took a while for me to realize that. It requires hard work, too. And putting the other person's needs ahead of your own. I wasn't doing that before. Oh, I thought I was being supportive, but only if it didn't affect me. And that was so wrong. I know it's going to take a while to earn that trust back. I don't want us to commute on weekends and weird holidays to build a relationship. I want to be here. By your side. I want to commit to that, Bella. To you."

Bella remembered Charlotte asking her if she would drop everything to move to London for Burke, and her answer had been no. And Charlotte had reminded her that love was a compromise. Charlotte was now based out of London and in return Jacob wasn't going out in the field anymore. They'd both made changes to their lives in order to be together. Burke was making a massive gesture here, willing to turn down a dream opportunity in order to make a relationship with her a priority. It was a huge compromise.

"And what do you expect or need from me?" she asked.

He shook his head. "Don't, Bella. I can't stand it when you make it sound so...transactional. Please, just tell me. Do you love me? Do you think you can love me?"

His voice was thick with emotion and she was shocked to see a sheen of moisture in his eyes. Her heart melted. She remembered all the ways he'd touched her, smiled at her, laughed. She also realized that he'd said the words at the château, but she hadn't said them back. And yet…he was still here.

There were times when she knew she needed to be strong and resolute, and times when she knew she had to be…human. She was great at giving advice but not so great at providing it to herself. So she asked herself what she would say to any of her siblings or friends who came to her in such a situation. And she knew without a doubt that she would say, "Do you love him? If you do, you should give him a chance. Otherwise you will always regret it."

"I do love you," she said softly. Her lip wobbled a bit and she tried to stop it by biting down on it for a moment. "I fell in love with you in London. Not because you were my first but because you treated me with such consideration, such gentleness. You let me be like one of the butterflies at the museum. You let me stay until I was ready to fly away. Can we have that again, do you think? Because I love that man. And I desperately want to believe that he is the real Burke Phillips."

Burke stepped forward and pulled her into his arms. "God, I've been waiting forever for you to say that." He kissed her cheek, her hair. "I want to be that man again. I want to stop being afraid and living in my father's shadow. Bella, I want to be like you."

"You don't need to be like me. You just have to realize that you are not like your father, and stop blaming yourself for what can't be changed. You're enough, can't you see that?"

He hugged her tighter. "William was right. You give the best advice."

She laughed, and then, as she put her arms around his ribs and held on, the strain and tension and pain of the last few weeks melted away. This was where things were right. In each other's arms.

"Just keep holding me," she whispered. "Everything falls into place when you're holding me."

For long moments they stood there, in a tight embrace.

"I can't hold you like this twenty-four hours a day. We'd never get any work done."

"If you can manage it in the morning and maybe again at night, I think that would be enough."

"You mean that?"

She leaned back and looked into his face. Hope glimmered in his eyes. "Yes, I mean that. Let's try again, Burke. Let's do it right, and not keep anything from each other. Let's help each other through our fears and insecurities. In the end, it'll only make us stronger."

"I love you, Bella. So much."

"And I love you."

EPILOGUE

Three months later

BELLA GLANCED AROUND the small ballroom with satisfaction at a job well executed and also with a very full heart. She'd seen to every bit of planning for the event. After all, it was their engagement party and she had wanted everything to be perfect.

Burke was beside her, looking dashing as ever in a tuxedo. She'd chosen a long dress in black velvet, reminiscent of Rosemary Clooney's in *White Christmas*. She'd always adored that style, and had even paired it with long satin gloves.

They'd invited friends and close business associates in addition to family. Right now, waitstaff was circulating with delectable nibbles and the champagne fountain was doing a brisk business. Aurora was chatting with Burke's mother; the two of them had rekindled their old friendship and had become quite inseparable. Charlotte was in attendance but moving slowly; her due date was three days past and she'd threatened to dance the jitterbug if it meant shaking the baby loose and getting things on the go. William and Gabi were gazing at each other, still in their cocoon of newlywed bliss, and Stephen…well, Bella was starting to think Stephen would be perennially single. Even Christophe wasn't immune to the romance in the air. He was currently chatting up Sophie Waltham, a gemologist whose family was a Bond Street jeweler who carried Aurora's jewelry line.

"Everyone looks so happy," she said to Burke, leaning against his arm. "It's lovely, isn't it?"

He tilted his head so that it rested briefly on hers. "It is. But no one is happier than me that you said yes."

The remainder of August had been a blur. Burke had taken the job at the hospital and moved to Paris and into her flat. Despite their earlier problems, they'd slid into living together seamlessly. When insecurities cropped up, they talked through them without walking away. It had only brought them closer together. Burke had proposed mid-October, presenting Bella with an heirloom diamond ring that had belonged to his grandmother. She was about to become Lady Downham after all.

Bella thought back to just six months ago and how everything had changed. And all because Burke had discovered her darkest secret and his acceptance had given her the push she needed to stop hiding. "You know, I didn't want to see you at Will's wedding. I certainly didn't want you to see my scars. But I'm so glad you did. You changed my life, Burke."

He kissed her temple. "And you changed mine. I love you, Bel. I always will."

And she believed him. Because she knew that sometimes the greatest risks, the biggest leaps of faith, yielded the very best rewards. In Bella's case, it was a happily-ever-after she thought she'd never have.

She turned her head and looked up at him. "Let's dance," she suggested, and when he took her in his arms on the dance floor, she knew anything was possible.

* * * * *

BEFORE SUMMER ENDS

SUSAN MALLERY

For Nissa—thanks for lending me your name

Chapter One

NISSA

"Darling, we're pregnant!"

"We are?" Nissa Lang asked, somewhat confused by the "we," as well as the news of the pregnancy.

Mimi was in her midforties and as far as Nissa knew, Mimi and her husband hadn't even been trying. Not that Nissa could be sure about that. Her relationship with Mimi was casual at best. Nissa was going to house-sit Mimi's grand mansion while the happy couple spent the summer in a different mansion in Norway. Not only would Nissa get paid a princely sum for things like flushing the many toilets and making sure the gardeners (yes, plural) did their thing, the money was going directly into her I'm-turning-thirty-and-to-prove-my-life-isn't-a-disaster, I'm-taking-myself-to-Italy-for-three-weeks-next-summer fund.

Knowing she had a place to live for July and August, Nissa had rented out her own small condo, to add even more money to her fund. Only the sinking feeling in her stomach told her that maybe she was about to get some bad news in that department.

Mimi laughed. "I know it's a shock. We're stunned. We didn't think we were ever going to be able to have children, but I'm pregnant and it's wonderful. I'm calling because the baby means a change in plans. Between my age and the previous miscarriages, I'm a high-risk pregnancy, and travel is out of the question. So we'll be staying home this summer. I hope you understand."

Yup, there it was. Disappointment on a stick, stabbing her right in her travel dreams.

"Of course," Nissa said politely, because that was how she'd been raised, but on the inside, she was pouting and stomping her feet. "Congratulations. You must be thrilled."

"Thank you. We're beyond happy. Take care. Bye."

With that, Mimi hung up and Nissa sank onto the sofa. She looked at the open boxes scattered around her small condo, the ones she was filling up with personal items so the charming young couple who had rented her place for two months would have room for their own things. She glanced at the calendar she'd tacked on the wall, with the date she was supposed to be out circled in red.

"This is bad," she breathed, letting the phone drop onto the cushion next to her. "What am I going to do?"

She didn't have a summer job lined up, the way she usually did. As a fourth-grade teacher, she had summers off and used the time to get a job to supplement her income. It was how she'd managed to scrape together the down payment for her small condo. She'd moved in nearly a year ago and loved every inch of the place.

She was going to use the Mimi house-sitting money and the rental income for her condo to pay for her Italy trip next year. Postponing it was not an option. Two years ago she and her fiancé of three years had broken up. Before that, her best friend had been diagnosed with kidney disease—the kind that would kill her if she didn't eventually get a transplant. Nissa had firsthand knowledge that life didn't always turn out how you expected or wanted, so putting things off was taking a serious chance of losing out. Something she wasn't willing to risk.

She'd been dreaming about going to Italy since she was fourteen years old. She'd devoured guidebooks, watched travel videos on YouTube and had planned and replanned her stay. Next year, she was spending her thirtieth birthday in Italy.

The problem was, she'd just lost her funding.

Oh, she was putting aside a little every month, but living in the Seattle area was expensive and it wasn't as if she had a six-figure salary. The summer money was how she was going to make the trip happen.

She leaned back against the cushions and considered her options. Obviously, she would have to get a different job. It was already late June, so she might not have a lot of options, what with competing with high school and college students for the best ones. Regardless, she would find something. The more pressing problem was where she was going to live for the next two months.

Her parents would happily welcome her for the summer, but they lived in a small town in Eastern Washington. There wouldn't be many job opportunities if she stayed with them. Plus Nissa didn't want to be that far away from Marisol and her kids. Not when a transplant could show up at any time.

Crashing at Marisol's place wasn't going to work. While her best friend would welcome her, the house was tiny and already overcrowded. Which left one option.

She grabbed her phone and scrolled through her contacts. Shane picked up on the second ring.

"Hey, kid."

She smiled. "You think you're such a big brother, don't you?"

"It's kind of my thing."

"I'm surprised I caught you. Why aren't you slicing and dicing?"

"I just got out of surgery. Knee replacement. The patient is going to be very happy with the outcome."

Shane was an orthopedic surgeon in a busy sports medicine practice. Four years older and definitely the smarter of the two children in the family, he'd always been driven to be the best. Nissa knew she was much more in the "average" category and was comfortable there. She didn't need to change the world, just improve her small part of it.

"I'm glad for your patient," she said. "I need to come live with you for the next two months. And don't you dare say no. You have that extra bedroom. I know you do—I helped you decorate it."

She explained how her house-sitting job had fallen through.

"I'd love to help, but I can't." Shane's voice dropped nearly an octave. "I've met someone."

She resisted rolling her eyes, mostly because he couldn't see her doing it. "Shane, I refuse to accept that as an excuse. You've always met someone. You spend your life 'meeting someone.' It's the sticking with them for longer than three weeks that doesn't work for you."

"This is different. No can do, kid. I can't have you hanging around when I'm trying to…you know."

"Seduce a perfectly nice woman who doesn't know you're going to be a hit-and-run lover? While that sounds great, I'm in trouble. It's serious and I need your help. I have people showing up in three days to move into my place. I need somewhere to go."

"Stay with Desmond."

"What?" she asked, her voice more of a yelp than she would have liked. "No. I can't."

What a ridiculous suggestion. Desmond? As if.

"He has a giant house and he's practically family."

The key word being *practically*. He was, in fact, her brother's best friend from boarding school. Because Shane had gotten a scholarship to the fancy place when he'd been thirteen, and he and Desmond had been close ever since.

Desmond was great. Nissa liked him just fine. He'd taken her to her senior prom when her boyfriend had dumped her at the last minute. She'd warned him not to marry his now ex-wife and she'd been right.

"It's a perfect solution," Shane said cheerfully. "I'm going to text him right now."

"What? No. You can't. I'm not—"

The rapid *beep, beep, beep* told her she was talking to herself. Shane had already hung up.

"I'm not comfortable staying with him," she muttered to no one in particular.

Not that she could explain exactly why to her brother. Or herself. In truth, the thought of living with Desmond made her insides get all twisty. It would be too strange.

Besides, what were the odds of him agreeing? He wouldn't. Why would he? People didn't generally enjoy having unannounced roommates for months on end. He would say no. She was sure of it. Practically sure. Mostly sure.

For the second time in less than ten minutes, she dropped her phone onto the sofa cushion and knew she was totally and completely screwed.

DESMOND

Stilling Holdings, Inc., or SHI as everyone called the company, was a multinational conglomerate with interests in everything from rare element mining to biofuels to construction to infrastructure. The different divisions were managed as separate companies, each division president reporting directly to CEO Desmond Stilling.

Three years ago, Desmond had moved the company headquarters from San Francisco to just north

of Seattle. A new ten-story building had been constructed, SHI had adopted six elementary schools,
two middle schools and a high school as their local
charity projects, and on most days Desmond managed to stay on top of everything work related. Every
now and then circumstances bested him. An airport strike in South America had delayed shipment
of needed parts to a plant in Germany, leaving road
crews in Eastern Europe without crucial equipment.
Every day of delay was a problem in a part of the
world where there was a season for construction.

In the end, he'd had his people charter two planes
out of a private airfield forty kilometers away. By
Tuesday of next week, the completed machinery
would be on its way and the road work could continue. The cost of the chartered planes would chew
up any profit, but he knew the road was more important. He would make up the money elsewhere.
He always did.

Shortly after eleven, his personal cell phone
buzzed. He pulled it out and smiled when he saw the
name and picture displayed.

"No, I can't take off the rest of the day and go hiking with you," he said by way of greeting. "Some of
us have to work for a living."

"I work," Shane protested with a laugh. "I save
lives, my friend."

"You replace joints, not hearts."

"I improve quality of life. What do you do?"

"I build roads and feed the world. This is me, winning."

The familiar banter was a welcome relief from the fast-paced, business-only rhythm of his day. Much to the chagrin of his staff, Desmond got to the office early and stayed late. When he'd been married, he'd had something to go home to, but these days, there wasn't much waiting for him in his big house, so he stayed at work later and later.

He knew he would have to make a change at some point—just not today.

"You think you're such a powerful CEO," Shane said.

"I *am* a powerful CEO."

"You're talking but all I hear is a buzzing sound." Shane chuckled. "Okay, enough of that. I need a favor."

"Done."

"You don't know what I want."

Desmond knew it didn't matter. Shane was his best friend and he would do anything for him or a member of his family. Desmond had grown up the classically clichéd lonely, rich child. The first ten years of his life, he'd been homeschooled with excellent tutors. When he'd finally been sent off to boarding school, he'd had the education of a college freshman but the social skills of a pencil. The transition had been difficult.

Two years later, he'd been sent to a college prep school where Shane had been his roommate. They'd quickly become friends. That first Christmas, Shane had dragged him home for the holiday. Inside his friend's modest house, Desmond had experienced what a family was supposed to be. For the first time in his life, he'd seen parents hugging their children and had felt warmth and affection. The presents had been chosen with care and love rather than ordered by staff. For those two weeks, he'd been just like everyone else and it had been glorious.

Ever since then, the Langs had been a part of his life. He would do anything for any of them, regardless of what they needed. His parents were still alive, but the Langs were his real family.

"Nissa needs a place to stay for a couple of months. She had a gig house-sitting but that fell through. She's rented out her condo. I'm guessing backing out on that contract could be a problem. Plus she wants the money for her trip to Italy next summer."

Technically Nissa wanted to go to Rome and Florence, rather than generically visit Italy, but Desmond didn't correct his friend. Nor did he mention he was the one who had introduced Nissa to Mimi and her husband when Mimi had said they were looking for a dependable house sitter. Of course Mimi's unexpected pregnancy would have changed their plans. He should have realized that himself.

"She can stay with me," he said. "There's plenty of room."

"That's what I said. You have what? Twelve bedrooms?"

"Eight."

At least he thought there were eight. Maybe it was ten. After his initial tour of the house before he'd bought it, he'd never much gone exploring. He used his bedroom, his home office and the media room. The rest of the house didn't interest him.

"So that's a yes?" Shane asked.

"It is. I'll get in touch with her today and find out when she wants to move in, then I'll let my housekeeper know and she'll get a room put together."

"Thanks, bro. I appreciate it. You're doing us both a big favor. So let's go out on your boat sometime soon."

"I'd like that."

"I'm on call for the next two weekends, but after that."

"Let me know what days work for you. We'll have fun."

"Thanks for helping with Nissa."

"Anytime."

They talked for a few more minutes, then hung up. Desmond glanced at his computer. But instead of rows of numbers, he saw Nissa in her prom dress, earnestly thanking him for offering to take her to the dance at her high school. He'd been in the first year of his MBA program then, having finished his undergraduate degree in three years. He'd flown up from Stanford to be her date.

At the time, he'd been doing a favor for a friend, but the second he saw her, everything changed. Gone was the preteen who had tagged along whenever he'd visited. In her place was a beautiful woman with big eyes and a mouth he couldn't stop staring at, and later kissing.

But nothing more. No matter how much he'd wanted to take things to the next level, he'd known he couldn't. She was the only daughter of his surrogate family. He loved and respected the Langs too much to betray their trust in him. So he'd done the right thing and had firmly put Nissa in the friend column, where she had stayed. And would stay.

He shook off the memories and quickly sent a text.

Shane says you need a place to stay. I have plenty of room. Just tell me when you want to be there and I'll get a room ready.

There was a pause, then he saw three dots, followed by her reply.

Really? You will? I seriously doubt you know where the spare sheets are kept.

He chuckled. You're right, but I'll have it done. Hilde will be thrilled to have someone else to care for. I disappoint her with my boring lifestyle.

Desmond, you're nice to offer, but I couldn't possibly impose.

I insist. There's plenty of room. He hesitated, then added, It's not your parents' house. Whoever you're seeing is welcome to stay over.

As in a boy? LOL That part of my life is a disaster. Kind of like yours. Can I LOL twice in a text without seeming like I'm getting weird?

You can if you'd like. When do you want to move in?

Gulp. Is Friday too soon?

It's not. I'll let Hilde know. Text me when you have an approximate time so I can make sure I'm home to give you a tour and a key.

Thanks, Desmond. You're the best. I promise to be the perfect guest. You won't even know I'm there.

He studied her words, thinking that he very much wanted to know she was there. He would have offered his place, regardless, but he'd always liked Nissa. She was easy to be around, and he felt comfortable in her presence. With her, he didn't feel as much the heartless bastard the women he dated always ended up claiming he was. Plus she'd been right about Rosemary and he'd been the fool who hadn't listened.

See you Friday, he texted.

Thanks again.

He sent a quick text to Hilde, telling her about Nissa's stay. When his housekeeper sent back questions about the types of foods Nissa liked and which bedroom would be best, he gave Hilde Nissa's number so the two of them could work it out. Once that was done, he returned his attention to his computer, because work was the one place where he had all the answers.

NISSA

Friday morning Nissa got up early to finish getting ready for her move-out. She'd packed her personal things, along with a few breakables she didn't want to leave out. All that was left was her grandmother's china and her clothes. She would take care of the clothes first thing, then wait for Shane to arrive to help her with the china. Once that was done, she would give her place a final clean, then head over to Desmond's house.

So far she'd done a good job of ignoring her upcoming living situation. If she didn't think about moving into the big house on the Sound and, you know, living with *him*, she didn't get nervous. But if she allowed herself to dwell on the reality of sharing a roof with a guy she'd had a crush on for over a decade, she got a little queasy.

Not that her crush meant anything, she reminded herself as she got dressed before heading for the bathroom. It was just a funny quirk, left over from when she'd been a teenager. Desmond had been older, fantastically good-looking and sweet to her. Of course she'd liked him. Now, as a grown-up, she knew those feelings were just remnants of happy memories. These days they were friends. Good friends. He'd been married, for heaven's sake, and she'd been engaged. They'd both moved on. Or at least she had— she doubted he had anything to move on from. So there was nothing to worry about or any reason to be nervous. Really.

That somewhat decided, she finished getting ready, then put together several boxes and got out packing paper. She set everything on her dining room table. Shortly after eight, her doorbell rang.

She let in her brother, smiling when she saw the to-go tray he carried.

"Morning," he said, giving her a quick kiss on the cheek. "I brought breakfast."

"I see that. Thank you."

She took the coffee and breakfast sandwich he offered, then led the way to the sofa in her living room. They set their food on the coffee table. Shane glanced around at the bare side tables and nearly empty floating shelves.

"You were robbed."

She sipped her coffee before smiling at him. "You know how I am. I have stuff everywhere. No one wants to live with that. So I put it all away. It's very clean looking, don't you think?"

"I don't know. It makes me feel as if you've been taken over by aliens." He nodded at the small hutch in the dining alcove. "We're just wrapping up the china?"

She nodded. "It's a full set for twelve. I don't want anything to get broken. I made space in my storage unit, so we can take the boxes down there."

"Sounds like a plan. You're moving in with Desmond after that?"

"This afternoon." She wanted to protest that she wasn't moving in with him—not in the traditional sense. But saying that would cause her brother to start asking questions and there was no way she wanted to explain about her crush-slash-fluttery stomach.

"So what's with the new girlfriend?" she asked, hoping to distract him. "Who is she and what makes her 'the one'?" She made air quotes with her free hand.

"Her name is Coreen and she's an ER pediatrician."

"A doctor," she teased. "Mom and Dad will be so proud."

He grinned. "I know. I'm the favorite for a reason, kid."

"Oh, please. They so love me more."

The joking was familiar. Shane might be more brilliant but she was no less adored by her parents. They hadn't had a lot of money for fancy things when she'd been growing up but there had been plenty of attention and affection.

"You didn't answer my question," she pointed out as she picked up her breakfast sandwich. "Why is she special?"

"I don't know. She's smart and pretty and I like her a lot." He took a bite of his sandwich. "There's something about her. We'll see how it goes. I'm optimistic and I don't want to mess up anything."

"Why would you think you mess up your relationships?"

"I'm not like you," he said. "I've never made being in love work."

That surprised her. "Not with any of the women you've dated?"

He shook his head. "There's always an issue." One corner of his mouth turned up. "Unlike you and Desmond." He made kissing noises. "You've always had a thing for him."

She willed herself not to blush, then socked him in the arm. "I had a crush on him when I was a kid. So what?"

"You followed him around like a puppy."

"He was dreamy."

Shane scowled. "Please don't say dreamy before I've finished my breakfast."

"Deal with it, brother of mine. So when do I get to meet the magical Coreen?"

"Not for a while. I want to make sure it lasts. What about you? Who's the new guy?"

"There is no new guy." Her love life was sadly lacking.

"You haven't been involved since you broke up with James. Come on, Nissa. That's been what? Two years? It's time to move on."

"I know and I want to. But it's hard to meet people. My luck with online dating is nonexistent and all the guys I meet through work are married."

"There have to be a few single dads with kids in your class."

She looked at him pityingly. "I don't date students' fathers. It's tacky and against policy."

"That makes sense. What about when you go to Italy? You can meet someone there. A handsome Italian with a nice accent."

She laughed. "Technically if we're in Italy, I'll be the one with the accent." She was less sure about a vacation romance. Not that she would object to being swept off her feet for a week or two but she doubted the affair would last past her time there.

"Want me to ask around at my practice? See if any of my work friends know of a single guy."

"No. Absolutely not. I shudder at the thought." The last thing she needed was her brother finding her guys to date.

"Hey, I have good taste."

"You've never set me up, so we don't actually know that." She tempered her words with a smile. "But thank you for thinking about me."

"I always think about you. You're my baby sister and I want you to be happy." He grinned. "And safe. Why else would I have told Desmond to walk away after your prom date?"

She'd been about to take the last bite of her sandwich. Instead she stared at her brother, her mouth hanging open.

"What?" she managed, trying to make sense of his words.

Shane winked. "I know. You're impressed, right? Like I said, I look after you."

She put down the sandwich. "Wait a second. Are you saying Desmond wanted to go out with me after prom?"

"Sure. He had a great time and was all into you, but I pointed out that he was too old and too experienced. He was in grad school and you were a senior in high school. No way that was happening on my watch."

The adult side of her brain could appreciate what her brother had done. He was right about both the age and experience difference between them. But the teenaged girl that would be with her always nearly shrieked in protest. She'd liked Desmond—she'd liked him a lot. When he'd disappeared after their one date, she'd been devastated.

"Besides," Shane added, obviously unaware of what she was thinking, "he's a part of the family. I reminded him that he owed my folks for taking him in and stuff, and he shouldn't repay them by going after you."

"You're pretty proud of yourself, aren't you?" she asked, reaching for her coffee.

"I am and you should thank me."

She held in a sigh. He'd done what he thought was right, and at the time, it had been. Her broken heart was her own business. But the information did leave her with some interesting questions, such as if he'd liked her, why hadn't he tried dating her later, when she'd been all grown up? And most important of all—what did he think of her now?

Chapter Two

DESMOND

Desmond had brought home work but couldn't seem to focus on it. Normally he enjoyed getting lost in whatever business project he was involved in. Even the things that most people considered boring—reading contracts or reviewing financial statements—were pleasurable for him. The business was rational—at any given moment he knew exactly where things were and how to improve them. He might not like the answers he came up with, but he knew he could count on them. His business was a place where he excelled. Relationships, particularly the romantic kind, had never been one of his strengths.

Oh, he could get a woman into his bed in a couple of hours. Sex was easy, but anything involving the heart was nearly impossible for him. Probably because he was too much like his parents, he thought, admitting defeat and closing his spreadsheet program. They had raised him to use his head and ignore his emotions, telling him that feelings weren't to be trusted and caring too much made a person weak. They'd certainly demonstrated their philosophy time and time again with him and with each other. There had been no hugs in his family, no displays of affection. Being told he'd done well at something was about as personal as it got when he'd been growing up.

Given the choice between reaching out and holding back, he learned to always hold back. It was what he knew and it was safer. The only place he was different was with Shane and his family. They were the people he trusted.

He remembered when his marriage had ended. Rosemary, who it turned out, hadn't married for much more than a lifestyle, had told him he was the coldest and most heartless man she'd ever known. When he'd protested that he'd been a good and kind husband, she'd laughed at him, telling him he had a chunk of ice in the space where his heart should be.

The end of his marriage had been disappointing—not so much because he missed her but because he didn't. He was supposed to have wanted to spend the rest of his life with her. Shouldn't he have mourned the loss? The fact that he hadn't reinforced her supposition. He was a man without a heart.

He tried to shake off those thoughts and return his attention to his work, but quickly realized that wasn't happening. He obviously wasn't going to get anything done until Nissa arrived and got settled. For some reason, he was more focused on that than the Asian sales report.

He got up and crossed to the large window in his study. The late-June days were long and sunny, and the garden flourished. The grass was dark green, flowers provided plenty of color in the planting beds, the trees looked healthy. The gardeners did a good job, regardless of the seasons, but in the summer, their hard work paid off.

He turned at the sound of the vacuum cleaner being turned on somewhere upstairs. Hilde had been in a state since he'd told her Nissa was coming to stay. There had been cleaning and washing and other tasks he couldn't begin to imagine. The refrigerator overflowed with food and there were fresh flowers everywhere in the house.

Her burst of happy activity made him feel guilty. His housekeeper obviously didn't have enough to do in a day. The house was large, but there wasn't anyone to make a mess. He rarely ate dinner at home, so she wasn't spending much time cooking. He would guess she was bored working for him—a problem he didn't know how to solve. If he'd stayed married to Rosemary, they would have had kids by now. That would have increased the workload. Of course if they'd stayed together, he and Rosemary would have been living in different wings of the house, barely seeing each other, except when they passed in the hallway.

His phone buzzed. He pulled it out, then smiled when he read the text.

I'm here. Just giving you a heads-up because the house is so big, I thought you'd need an extra minute or five to walk to the door and I really don't want to be kept waiting.

He was still chuckling when he heard the doorbell ring a few seconds later.

He walked through the entryway and pulled open the large front door. Nissa stood on the wide, covered porch, her long red hair pulled back in a ponytail. She had on cropped jeans and a T-shirt. Her lack of makeup meant he could see all her freckles—the freckles he'd always liked and that she claimed to hate every time they were mentioned. Her big blue eyes crinkled as she smiled at him.

"Are you out of breath from the long trek? Should I pause until you're able to speak?"

"I can manage a sentence or two," he said as he held open his arms.

She stepped into his embrace easily, as she always had. He hugged her, telling himself not to notice the feel of her body against his. Nissa was his friend, nothing more. And if a part of him wanted to breathe in the scent of her hair or enjoy the way her breasts felt nestling into his chest, he only had to play the "she's Shane's sister" card to make it all go away.

She stepped back. "Again, thank you for taking me in. I'm really happy for Mimi. Of course I am, but wow did it upset my summer plans." She smiled. "Which makes me a horrible person, so don't think about that too much. As I bring in my stuff, I'll work on repairing my character."

"There's nothing wrong with your character, and I'm happy to have you here for as long as you want to stay." He looked past her to the very full car. "Why didn't you ask me to help you move?"

"I was fine." She waved a hand in dismissal. "Shane carted boxes into my storage unit. Those were heavy. This is nothing. I'll just take a few trips to get it all inside."

"*We'll* take a few trips," he told her. "Let me show you to your room, then we'll bring in your things."

She tilted her head. "You didn't have to say yes, you know. Are you sure you're comfortable with me invading your space? I can be messy and I'm not sure we like the same music."

"Stop," he told her, stepping back to wave her inside. "I'm glad you'll be here. I'll enjoy the company and Hilde needs someone to fuss over."

"Hilde was so nice when we texted." Nissa leaned close and lowered her voice. "She asked me what kind of cheese I like. No one's ever asked me that before. I honestly didn't know what to say. I was afraid I would disappoint her if I didn't ask for something fancy, but all I could think of was cheddar."

He thought about the contents of the refrigerator. "She bought more than that. You can try them all and tell her which ones you like best."

"I can't wait." She paused in the foyer and looked up.

He followed her gaze, taking in the two-story entry, the large windows and elegant chandelier. Desmond had lived in the house long enough that he no longer saw any one part of it, but he knew it wouldn't be the same for Nissa. While she'd been to the house a few times for parties and barbecues, she'd never lived here.

She looked at the wide staircase and the long hall-way, then back at him.

"Is there a map?" she asked, her eyes bright with humor.

"It's an app."

"I almost believe you."

Hilde, his housekeeper from the day he'd moved in, appeared. She was in her mid- to late-forties, with short dark hair and a warm smile.

"Miss Nissa," she said, her hand outstretched. "Welcome to Mr. Desmond's home. Please let me know if I can do anything to make your stay more pleasant."

"I'm thinking you've already done so much," Nissa told her. "It's nice to meet you in person. I hope you didn't go to too much trouble."

"No trouble." Hilde glanced at him. "Did you want to take her on a tour, Mr. Desmond, or should I do it?"

"Go ahead," he murmured, thinking she knew the house better than he did. But instead of retreating to his office, he joined the two women as Hilde led the way.

"The formal dining room," Hilde said, pausing inside the doorway. "The table expands to seat twenty." She glanced at him. "Mr. Desmond doesn't have any dinner parties. Maybe while you're here you could talk to him about that."

A dinner party? Why would he want to do that?

Nissa glanced at him, her mouth curving into a smile. "I will happily talk to Mr. Desmond about a dinner party. Who should we invite? Ex-girlfriends?"

"Only if your ex-boyfriends come, too," he told her.

"Hmm, I'm less excited about that."

They followed Hilde into the large kitchen. She showed Nissa all the appliances and the pantry. Nissa seemed taken with the six-burner stove and the contents of the refrigerator, especially the cheese drawer.

"Does Mr. Desmond ever come in here?" she asked.

"He does," Desmond told her. "I make my own breakfast every morning and if I'm eating at home, I eat in the kitchen."

There was a very nice table by the window. Or he took his meal back to his office. He was by himself—it made no sense to go sit in the big dining room.

"You can cook?" She pressed a hand to her chest. "I'm genuinely impressed."

He smiled at her. "Gee, thanks."

They toured the rest of the downstairs. The family room and formal living room both had views of the Sound. Nissa stuck her head into his office, and gasped at the size of the laundry room. Upstairs, Hilde showed her the large, well-appointed media room. Nissa stared at the drawer full of remotes, then looked at the giant TV on the wall.

"I could never manage this," she said, shaking her head. "It's too much equipment."

"You can never have too much equipment," Desmond told her. "It's easier than it looks. There's a notebook with instructions in with the remotes."

"Uh-huh. Good luck with that. I'll just livestream on my tablet."

Their last stop was her room. Hilde had prepared one of the suites, with a small living area attached to the bedroom. Both had a Sound view. His housekeeper had done a great job with everything. There were plenty of plush towels in the oversize bathroom and fresh flowers sat on the desk.

Nissa looked around. "This is really nice and much bigger than my condo." She hugged Hilde. "You did far too much work for me, and I want you to know how much I appreciate all of it." She turned to him. "You're being really nice. Thank you."

"Happy to help."

Hilde showed her the laundry chute tucked in the closet. "Just send your clothes down and I'll take care of them."

Nissa shook her head. "I'm going to do my own laundry. You don't have to do extra for me."

Hilde's expression turned stern. "I'll do your laundry."

Nissa raised her eyebrows. "If it's that important to you."

"It is."

She moved next to him. "She's determined."

"Best not to mess with her."

They all went downstairs and outside to Nissa's car. With the three of them working together, it didn't take long to get everything unloaded and delivered to her suite. On the last trip up the stairs, Desmond carried an armful of her hanging clothes. The action felt oddly intimate, as if he were seeing into something private. Silly, really, he told himself. So what if a few of her dresses were draped over his arm?

Once they'd dropped off everything, Hilde excused herself to go start dinner. Desmond hesitated.

"You have the Wi-Fi code," he said, pulling a house key out of his pocket. "Here's this."

She took it. "What about an alarm code or something?"

"It's only set at night. I'll get you the instructions to deactivate it. Or you can ask me."

"But what if you're out on a hot date?"

"I'll probably be home."

"Not seeing anyone these days?"

"No."

She sighed. "Me, either. I'm focused on growing my Italy fund." She waved her hand. "Which you are contributing to by helping me out. Did I say thank you already?"

"Fifteen times."

She grinned. "You'd better get used to it, then. I plan to thank you a lot more."

"You're family, Nissa. And always welcome here."

He chose his words as much for himself as for her. That was what he had to remember. That while she was a beautiful, sexy, smart woman and there was just something about her that got to him, he was not to go down that path. She was someone he needed to look out for and protect, even from himself.

"Thank you." Her gaze met his. "So how does the whole dinner thing work? Is there a bell? Or does a butler show up and escort me?"

"Dinner's at seven. In your honor, we'll be eating in the dining room. After tonight, just let Hilde know if you're going to be home or not. She'll plan meals accordingly."

"You have a great life, Desmond. Next time, I'm going to remember to be rich."

He thought about telling her that his life wasn't what she thought and there were times when he felt isolated and alone. That she was the one with the warm, loving family and to him, that was priceless. But he knew saying the words would be to admit something he wasn't ready to face.

"I'll see you tonight," he told her instead.

NISSA

Nissa got settled quickly. Putting away everything she'd brought with her turned out to be easy, what with the giant closet with built-in drawers, actual shoe shelves and more hanging space than any three closets in a normal house. The bathroom was equally spacious. There were two sinks, drawers between the sinks and a floor-to-ceiling cabinet for whatever items she might have left over. Oh, and the toilet not only had a remote control, it lifted the lid when she walked into the room, as if giving her a weird toilet greeting.

"I am so out of my element," she murmured as she plugged in her tablet to charge while she was at dinner. She wasn't totally sure she could find her way back to her room after she left, but she was determined to make the effort. Hilde had promised a special dinner. Given the luxuriousness of the house, Nissa had no idea what that meant, but she knew it was going to be good.

By six, she was starving, what with having missed lunch. She showered and changed into a dress because it seemed that she should. She debated curling her hair, but that felt like too much, so she settled on a little makeup, then used up the time until seven by flipping channels on the TV in her bedroom. Fortunately for her, there was only a single remote and no fancy equipment to worry about.

At six fifty-eight, she left her room and only took two wrong turns before finally making it to the stairs. Once on the main floor, she found her way to the family room where she saw Desmond standing by a built-in bar that had previously been hidden behind concealed doors in the wall.

In the second before he saw her, she used the opportunity to take in his tall, lean body and broad shoulders. Desmond had always been good-looking. Quiet in a confident kind of way, with a thoughtful expression that had made her feel he was really listening when she spoke. A heady occurrence for the younger sister used to being dismissed by her older brother.

Later, as a teenager, she'd thought of Desmond as her brother's cute friend. Interesting and nice, but not, you know, swoon-worthy. That hadn't happened until he'd taken her to prom. A topic she planned to discuss with him, as soon as she found a casual opening.

He saw her and smiled. "You made it."

"I did."

"All settled?"

"Yes, with closet space to spare." She held up a hand. "Before you ask, I have everything I need.

Hilde was very thorough in her preparations. I'm telling you so you can put it in her employee evaluation."

"Good to know." He motioned to the bar. "May I fix you a cocktail?"

"Yes, you may."

She moved closer to the bar and looked at all the bottles on the shelves. "I don't know what most of those are."

"You probably don't want to try them at once. Do you have a favorite drink or may I make a suggestion?"

"Suggest away."

When she went out with her friends, she usually just had a glass of wine or a margarita. Nothing fancy. At her place, she had the obligatory bottle of red wine in her tiny pantry and a bottle of white in her refrigerator and that was it.

As she watched, Desmond pulled out a bottle of rum, along with cranberry juice, a small, unlabeled glass container and a bottle of champagne.

"What's in there?" she asked, pointing at the container.

"Vanilla simple syrup. Hilde made it earlier today." He expertly opened the bottle of champagne.

"So you planned the cocktail you're serving me?"

"I gave it some thought."

"That's so nice. Thank you." She smiled at him.

"You're making me feel special. What if I never want to leave?"

"You're always welcome here, Nissa."

The man had a very nice voice, she thought, his words wrapping around her like a hug. She'd always enjoyed listening to him speak. There was a formality to how he put his sentences together—no doubt the result of a very expensive prep school education.

He mixed the first three ingredients in a shaker, then strained them into a glass and poured champagne on top. After handing her the glass, he waited while she took a sip.

"It's nice. Thank you." She liked the combination of flavors and the fizz from the champagne.

He poured himself a scotch, then they sat across from each other, each on a large, comfy sofa.

She tasted her drink again. "How did you happen to choose this particular drink?"

"I thought you'd like it."

"You have an entire cocktail menu selection handy in your brain?"

"Something like that. Just one of my many skills."

"Because your parents made sure you were prepared for any social situation?"

He nodded.

"So a formal dinner? Meeting the queen?"

He smiled. "Easy."

She raised her eyebrows. "You've met the queen?

And we're talking the actual Queen of England, here. Not Bert, who does a drag show on the weekends?"

He chuckled. "Who's Bert?"

"Don't avoid the question."

He leaned back in his seat and rested one ankle on the opposite knee. "I have met the Queen of England. Twice."

"OMG! And you didn't think to mention me to Prince Harry before he met Meghan?"

"No, I didn't. Did you want me to?"

"Not now! He's married. But before would have been nice. I could have been a princess."

"Technically she's a duchess."

She waved her hand. "One and the same. You disappoint me."

"I apologize for not making your duchess fantasies come true." He studied her, a lazy smile tugging at his mouth. "I wouldn't have taken you for the princess type."

"Nearly every girl is, and let's face it. I'm pretty ordinary."

"I wouldn't say that."

"You're always so nice to me. Thank you. Even when I was an annoying teenager, you made me feel special."

Before she could say anything else, Hilde came into the family room with food on a tray. She set fried zucchini and a luscious-looking dip on the cof-fee table between them.

"Thank you," Nissa said, eyeing the appetizer. "That looks delicious."

"I hope you enjoy," Hilde said before returning to the kitchen.

Nissa set down her drink and reached for a nap-kin and a piece of zucchini. "Does she always stay this late?"

"No. Tonight is special. She wanted to be around for your first dinner. She's excited to have someone to fuss over."

Nissa appreciated the sentiment, but felt badly that Desmond's housekeeper was staying late on her account.

"Can you tell her to go home and that we'll serve ourselves?"

"I can try, but it won't work. I've already men-tioned that to her. She's not listening."

"If I'm the highlight, you must be a really bor-ing client."

"I think I am. She would be much happier with a family who had a couple of kids and a dog."

"But she doesn't leave you?"

"No. She's loyal."

She took a bite of the zucchini and had to hold in a moan. It was crisp and tender at the same time. The breading flavors were perfectly savory, but when combined with the slightly spicy dip, they were even better.

"This is amazing," she said, reaching for a second slice. "Can we have this every day?"

"If you'd like."

"You're very accommodating. So I'm going to thank you again for letting me stay."

"Will you stop after that?"

"Is it important?"

"Yes. I'm happy to contribute to your Italy fund in this small way."

She laughed. "All right. Thank you and now I'm done. At least for today."

"Good. Have you planned out your trip?"

"A little. I'm hoping to take three weeks. One in Rome, one in Florence and one in Tuscany." She picked up her drink. "And yes, I know Florence is the capital of Tuscany, but it seems as if it's the kind of place that deserves its own week."

"I agree. You should take the trip you want. You've been dreaming about it since you were fourteen."

She had been. A school report on Italy had sparked her interest. Her mother liked to tease her that for an entire year, she'd talked about nothing else.

"How could you possibly remember that?" she asked.

"You found out I'd been there and asked me questions. A lot of questions."

"Was I obnoxious?"

"No. Even then you were charming." He studied her. "You know I could—"

"No," she said firmly. "Just no."

"You don't know what I was going to say."

"I do. You were going to offer to pay for my vacation and while that's very sweet, the answer is no. I want to earn this myself, because that way it's meaningful."

"All right. Too bad you lost the income from Mimi's house-sitting job."

"I know. I'm sad about the money, but happy for her about the baby." At least she tried to be, because it was the right thing to do. But the cash would have been nice, too. "I'll find another job. There's a temp agency I've worked for before. They have very eclectic clients, so that should be interesting."

"You're comfortable having people renting your condo?"

"I wouldn't say comfortable, but they're paying me a lot. I put away everything that's personal, so I'm not freaked about that."

She thought about Shane helping her, which caused her to think about what her brother had said about Desmond and being warned away. Only half a cocktail hadn't given her enough courage to bring up that particular topic.

"What blood type are you?" she asked, reminding herself it was always good to know.

He looked startled by the question. "Ah, A positive."

"Oh, that's not super common. I'm O negative, but I have weird antibodies or something. I can't remember. I'm not a good donor candidate but my blood is very sought after."

"Do I want to know why you know that?"

She grinned. "You forget, I'm a teacher. At my grade level, I teach everything, including science."

Not the reason she'd asked about his blood type, but he would probably accept the explanation. Regardless, she was saved from having to deal with the problem when Hilde appeared and said dinner was ready.

Nissa led the way into the formal dining room where two place settings had been arranged at one end of the table. Desmond poured wine while she admired the beautiful china plates and the fresh flowers. Once they were seated, Hilde brought out tomato gazpacho soup and a basket full of crusty, warm rolls.

"Bread," Nissa breathed, eyeing the temptation. "I love bread." She smiled at the housekeeper. "This all looks wonderful. Thank you so much."

"You're welcome."

Hilde shot Desmond a look that Nissa couldn't interpret. She waited until they were alone to ask, "What was that glance about?"

"I'm sure she was trying to tell me to eat dinner at home more often."

"You don't?"

"Many nights I grab something to-go."

"When you could eat like this?" She took a roll and placed it on her side plate, then tasted the soup. It was the perfect blend of fresh and seasoned with a touch of creaminess.

"I get busy. It's easier than having a set time to be home."

"If you didn't have an empire, you could enjoy your life more."

He smiled at her. "If I didn't have my empire, I couldn't afford Hilde."

"Oh, right. I guess everything's a trade-off. I love my work, but no one gets rich being a teacher."

"Did you want to be rich?"

She laughed and waved her hand at the dining room. "There are obvious perks. But if you're asking if I wish I'd chosen a different profession, no. I love what I do. The kids are great and I really enjoy my days. Do I wish the school district budgeted more money? Of course. But otherwise, I'm a happy camper."

"You're an upbeat person."

"I am. Some of it is my personality and some of it is the joy of annoying others."

He grinned. "Attitude. I like it."

"It's easy to be brave when there's nothing on the line," she told him, only to remember there was a topic she needed to discuss and that waiting for the false courage of alcohol was a flawed plan. If she wanted the information, she was simply going to have to ask the question.

She cleared her throat. "So Shane helped me pack up my grandmother's china."

"You mentioned that."

"Right. While we were doing that, he teased me about living with you and during that discussion he mentioned that back when I was in high school and you took me to prom, that he warned you about me. I mean he warned you to not plan on going out with me. Later. After prom. Obviously we went to prom. Together."

She pressed her lips together, wondering how much of a mess she'd made of that.

Desmond studied her for a second before saying, "He's right."

Was he being difficult on purpose? "About what part?"

"All of it. I enjoyed our evening together and when I mentioned that to him, he reminded me you were a lot younger and less experienced than I was."

"So you should leave me alone?"

"Exactly."

"Which you did."

His dark gaze met hers. "Yes."

"I'm perfectly capable of making my own decisions about who I date," she reminded him.

"Now. Back then you were barely eighteen and I was in grad school. We were in different places."

True, but still. "You had a good time with me, didn't you?" she asked.

One corner of his mouth turned up. "I did. Very much."

"Me, too." She thought about how attentive he'd been, and the slow dancing. And the kissing. The kissing had been spectacular. "You were a great date."

"You, too."

They stared at each other, then his gaze lowered to her mouth. She wondered what he was thinking and if he had any regrets about listening to her brother. If they'd started dating back then they would be… She wasn't sure exactly what, but something. Maybe they would have stayed together all this time.

Desmond looked away. "They say we're in for a warm summer," he said.

Was it just her or was the man the tiniest bit flustered? "Do they?" she asked, hoping she was right and not indulging in a little too much wishful thinking.

Chapter Three

NISSA

After a dinner of pan-grilled chicken with fresh plum salsa and green beans, followed by coconut layer cake for dessert, Nissa and Desmond lingered over decaf coffee. She'd always found him easy to talk to, and tonight was no exception.

"When will you find out about your first temp job?" he asked.

"They'll text me tomorrow, telling me where to be and when. If there's a uniform, I'll swing by the offices and pick it up."

One eyebrow rose. "Uniform? Like at a fast-food place?"

"I don't work in food service. I've tried, but I'm not good at it. A lot of businesses have a shirt they want employees to wear. Even temporary ones. Oh, a few years ago I sold hot dogs down by the aquarium, so that's food. I did okay. There weren't a lot of choices, so that helped." She smiled. "To be honest, I have no idea how servers keep the orders straight. Or carry so many plates at once. Or those big trays. If it were me, everything would go tumbling."

"Then we'll clear the table one plate at a time."

"Probably a good idea."

Hilde had left after she served the main course, telling Desmond she would take care of cleanup in the morning. But Nissa and he had already put everything in the dishwasher and wiped down the counters. All that was left were their dessert plates, forks and the coffee mugs.

He glanced at his watch. "It's getting late. I should let you turn in."

They finished up the last of the dishes, then started up the stairs. She had to admit, it felt strange to be in Desmond's house, going to their bedrooms. She'd only been here a few times for parties and those had all ended with her going home.

"Thanks for dinner," she said when they reached the landing. "It was amazing."

"That's all Hilde," he told her.

"I'll thank her in the morning."

They stared at each other. He had a nice face—all strong lines and chiseled features. She thought about moving closer and, um, what? Kissing him? That could be awkward. If he kissed her back, then what? They went to his room and had sex? She didn't do casual relationships and it wasn't as if Desmond had been secretly pining for her.

When she thought about it, she realized it had been over a decade since their prom date. She'd graduated from college and everything. If he'd been so interested, he could have easily asked her out a thousand different times. Before he met Rosemary, after the divorce. She'd been right here—there'd been plenty of opportunity. But he hadn't. Not even once, which was a pretty clear indication that the man wasn't interested at all. So making a move would be stupid. He would be way too nice in his refusal and she would feel like an idiot. Worse, he might ask her to leave and it wasn't as if she had a bunch of places where she could go.

And just like that, whatever vague fantasy she'd been harboring disappeared with a nearly audible poof.

"All right then," she said with a forced smile. "Good night."

She turned and walked determinedly toward her

bedroom. Lucky for her, she'd picked the right direction and managed to find her way to the familiar space. She closed her door behind her, then leaned against it.

No more Desmond-is-handsome-and-sexy thoughts, she told herself. No more anything, where he was concerned. She was going to live here for two months and she needed to remember that and act like a polite but disinterested roommate. Anything else was a slick, steep road to disaster and no one wanted that.

NISSA

Saturday morning Nissa drove to North Seattle. She stopped for donuts on the way and arrived at her friend's house a little after ten.

The neighborhood had seen a revitalization over the past few years. Rather than tear down and start over rebuilding, most residents were sprucing up their older homes with new windows and roofs, and the occasional second story over the garage. Nissa found parking right in front of the house and looked at the unmown lawn. Before leaving today, she would make a point to run the push mower over the grass.

She hesitated before getting out of her car. She loved her friend, but sometimes the visits were emotionally challenging. A few years before, Marisol had been diagnosed with kidney failure. Everyone had been shocked, Marisol and her daughters most of all.

SUSAN MALLERY 55

Nissa had known the family since Marisol had been assigned to be her mentor when she'd first started teaching. They'd become close quickly. Nissa had been there when Marisol's husband and the girls' father had been killed in a car accident. Marisol had helped Nissa when she'd decided to end her engagement. They were best friends who depended on each other.

Nissa got out of her car and walked onto the front porch. She knocked once, then waited. Seconds later the door was flung open as Rylan and Lisandra, ten-year-old twins, greeted her enthusiastically.

"Nissa! You're here."

"Are those donuts? Did you get the maple ones?"

"And chocolate. They're my favorite."

"Yes, yes and yes," Nissa said with a laugh, hugging both girls with her free hand. She stepped inside and saw Marisol on the sofa.

Despite the fact that it was already in the low seventies, her friend had a blanket draped across her lap. Her face was pale, and there were dark shadows under her eyes. The toll of her kidney disease was becoming more and more visible.

"Hey, you," Nissa said, handing the donuts to the girls and crossing to the sofa. She hugged her friend. "How are you feeling?"

"Today's a good day," Marisol said. "Thanks for coming by."

"I haven't seen you in a couple of weeks. I want to

catch up." She looked at the empty mug on the coffee table. "Let me get you some more tea. I'll make myself a cup, as well. Two donuts each for the girls?"

Marisol nodded, then leaned back against the sofa and closed her eyes.

Nissa went into the small kitchen. The house was clean and bright, but on the small side. It could do with a spruce-up of its own, but she knew that wasn't in the budget. So far the insurance was covering all of Marisol's medical bills, but she'd had to stop working at the end of the semester and unless there was a kidney transplant, she wouldn't be returning to work in the fall.

Nissa helped the girls choose their donuts, then put a couple more on a plate and carried them and Marisol's tea back to the living room. She got her own drink and joined her friend on the sofa. The girls finished their donuts and retreated to their room.

"How are you really feeling?" Nissa asked when she had taken a seat.

Marisol shook her head. "It's not bad today. I'm tired, but that's to be expected." Exhaustion was just one of many symptoms she endured.

Marisol reached out and squeezed Nissa's hand. "I don't want to talk about being sick. What's happening with you?"

Nissa smiled at her. "I will accept the change in

topic, but only because it's what you want. I'd rather talk about you."

"I'm boring. Tell me about living with Desmond. You've had a thing for him for years. How is that working out? Are you plagued by illicit thoughts?"

Nissa laughed. "Illicit thoughts? Have you been reading Jane Austen again? His house is wonderful and he's the perfect host. I'm doing fine."

Marisol leaned close. "And the illicit thoughts?"

"Fine. One or two. I can't help it. He's very appealing."

"Maybe you living with him is a sign."

"Or God having a sense of humor," Nissa pointed out. "I was just thinking about this last night and if the man had wanted to date me, he would have done something about it before now. So he doesn't and I'm fine with that."

"If you're sure."

"I am. We're friends. That's all."

Marisol sighed. "But I need to live vicariously through you. It's hard when you're not dating. Do you know what your first temp job is going to be? Maybe you'll meet someone there."

"I'm going to be at a doggie day care for a couple of weeks. I'm not sure about that being a hotbed of dating activity."

Marisol wrinkled her nose. "I'm afraid you're right. Oh, unless one of the dogs has a cute dad.

You could date him. It wouldn't be like at school where dating a parent is against policy."

The girls came into the room. Lisandra had a board game in her hand.

"We decided on Monopoly," Rylan announced.

Nissa smiled. "One of my favorites. I'm in. We'll do that, then I'll take you two to Kidd Valley for lunch."

Marisol was on a special diet that was designed to not stress her body. Nissa would fix that before she took the girls out. After lunch they would go to the park to run off some energy while Marisol rested.

As they set out the game and Marisol counted out the money, Nissa asked, "How's day camp?"

"Good," Lisandra told her. "The other kids are nice. We've been doing a lot of craft projects. In a couple of weeks, we're going to learn how to make movies."

"That sounds like fun."

"It is."

They were good girls, Nissa thought, and they'd already been through so much. First losing their dad, then having their mom get sick. She knew they were scared for her. Without a kidney transplant, she wasn't going to survive a year. When she was gone, Nissa would step in. She'd already agreed to be the girls' guardian.

But that wasn't going to happen, Nissa told herself. Marisol would get her kidney and everything would be fine. It had to be. And if it wasn't, she would be there for the twins, partly because she'd given her word, but mostly because she loved them.

DESMOND

Four days after Nissa moved into the house, Desmond found her presence everywhere. Several pairs of athletic shoes and sandals clustered by the door to the garage. A sweater, a hoodie and a light jacket hung on the coat rack. Magazines and books were scattered throughout the family room. Instead of turning on the television in the kitchen and finding it was tuned to his favorite financial channel, he instead saw *House Hunters International* on HGTV.

She had invaded and while she lived with him, nothing would be the same. A truth that he found strangely appealing. His life was too predictable and boring. While he liked the quiet, he also enjoyed knowing there was someone else under the same roof. And if that someone was as lively and appealing as Nissa, then he was a lucky man.

He walked into the kitchen and found her sitting at the kitchen table, a bowl of cereal in front of her. She had on jeans and a T-shirt from the doggie day care center where she was working. She'd pulled her long hair back into a braid and she wasn't wearing any makeup.

For a second, he remembered her at seventeen—

fresh-faced and beautiful enough to make him ache. He'd enjoyed how she always had something funny to say and that her first instinct was to be kind and thoughtful. Even now, when she saw him, she picked up the remote and hit several buttons.

But instead of landing on the financial channel, the TV changed to a cooking show.

"That's not right," she murmured, before looking at him. "I can't remember the number."

"Or where you put your keys."

She winced. "You heard that yesterday morning?"

"They heard you in New York."

She laughed and handed him the remote. "I was panicked. I didn't want to be late on my first day. I can keep track of my phone and my purse and everything else in my life. Just not my keys. It's a curse." She flashed him a smile. "Good morning."

"Morning. How did you sleep?"

"Great. The bed is super comfortable and it's much quieter here than at my place. It's all the land you have. No noisy neighbors getting in at three in the morning."

He walked to one of the cupboards and pulled out a bowl. "There's a shelf in the mudroom. I'm going to put this right there. When you walk in the house, put your keys in the bowl. That way you'll know where they are."

"Isn't it early to be that sensible?"

"It's a solution. Unless you enjoy the drama of nearly being late every morning."

She took the bowl from him and set it next to her place setting. "I really don't. I've always thought it's because I have three bubbles and the keys push me into four."

He poured himself coffee. "Three bubbles?"

"You know, above my head. Like thought bubbles. I can keep track of three things or follow three instructions. But the fourth one pushes out the first one. There's only three spaces. So the work I brought home, my purse, my phone, my keys." She shrugged. "One bubble too many."

"Use the dish. Then the keys don't need a bubble."

"That is really smart. Thank you."

He glanced at her breakfast. "What are you eating? The liquid is gray."

She wrinkled her nose. "It's a protein-enriched cereal with almond milk. Want some?"

"Based on the look on your face when you describe it? No, thank you."

"I'm trying to eat healthy."

"There are better ways to do that."

She put down her spoon. "What are you having?"

"Greek yogurt with fresh berries and granola. Toast with almond butter."

She immediately pushed away her bowl. "Is there enough for two?"

He grinned. "There is. Drink your coffee. I'll make you breakfast."

"I can help."

"Not necessary."

He got out the ingredients and put four slices of bread into the toaster.

"What do you do about lunch?" he asked.

"Hilde made me something to take. I feel guilty, but I'm not going to say no. The woman's an amazing cook."

"She is." He scooped the plain Greek yogurt into two bowls. "How's the job going?"

"I like it. The dogs are great. They each have a different personality. The weather's been nice, so they're outside a lot."

He rinsed fresh blueberries and raspberries. "What about cleanup?"

She laughed. "Okay, yes, that's a part of it, but you forget. I work with kids—I'm used to smelly messes. It's not that big a deal. We run around and play ball. I was with the big dogs yesterday and they get along great. When there's a new dog, the day care has a whole process of getting acquainted. There's a group of dogs that are more shy, so the new ones start there and get to know everyone before moving into their size group."

She sighed happily. "In the afternoon, after a rousing play session, we all relaxed in the shade and took a nap for a couple of hours."

"Even you?"

"I didn't sleep, but I did get to cuddle. It's fun. Makes me think about getting a dog." She shook her head. "Don't say it. I know I can't. I work all day. The poor thing would be trapped in my condo and that's no life. But it's fun to play with everyone else's. I wish I could bring Rylan and Lisandra with me. They would love it."

He set her yogurt in front of her and returned to finish the toast. "Who are they?"

"Oh, my friend Marisol's kids. Ten-year-old twins. They're turning eleven in a few weeks and going into middle school in the fall. I can't believe how fast they're growing. Marisol was my mentor when I first started teaching. We became friends and now we hang out all the time. That's where I went on Saturday."

He'd wondered where she'd gone, but had known he had no right to ask. Funny how quickly he was getting used to having her around.

"They're so strong," she added, dipping her spoon into the yogurt. "Marisol lost her husband a few years ago. She was devastated, as were the girls. It was a hard time."

"How are they doing now?"

Nissa hesitated. "They're dealing. It's always something, isn't it?"

There was something she wasn't telling him, he realized, setting the toast in front of her and taking a seat at the table. Not that he would ask. Her friends were her business.

"They're in summer camp, which they really enjoy. But I was thinking I'd like to plan a couple of activities with them this summer. Something more fun than just lunch and going to the movies."

He could see her freckles and the various colors of blue that made up her eyes. Her mouth was full and soft and there wasn't any part of him that didn't want to kiss her. No, not just kiss. In a perfect world, he would slide her onto his lap. She would wrap her arms around him, maybe straddle him while they kissed. He could already feel the weight of her body and the feel of her mouth as she—

He slammed the door on that line of thought. No and no. But heat had already begun to burn, starting a chain reaction that would end with him hard and unable to stand without revealing his serious lack of control. He needed a distraction.

"Let's take them out on my boat," he said.

Nissa took a bite of her toast. "You have a boat?"

"Yes. On Lake Washington. We can spend the day going around here, or head out through the locks and explore the Sound."

"When did you get a boat? I love boats. Why

haven't you invited me out on it? I thought we were friends!"

He held in a smile. "My apologies. I thought you knew. You are welcome out on my boat anytime you would like. Bring your friends. We'll make a day of it."

"Is it a nice boat?"

He raised one eyebrow. "Have you met me?"

She laughed. "Right. Let me rephrase that. How nice is it?"

"It's about fifty feet long with three guest cabins, a good-sized salon. The area up by the flying bridge is covered, so you don't have to worry about too much sun."

"Fifty feet? I have no idea how big that is, but I'm going to assume I couldn't drive it."

"No. There's a captain."

"Other than you?"

"It's big enough that it requires a skill set I don't have time to develop."

"What about getting a smaller boat you could drive yourself?"

"I've thought about it."

But the larger boat was better for parties. Something smaller would mean just him and a couple of friends and somehow that never seemed to happen. He'd thought when he and Rosemary moved up here, they would have a boat for the two of them, but then they'd split up and he'd relocated by himself.

He paused, telling himself he wasn't as pathetic as that all sounded. He couldn't be.

"So you'd have two boats?" she asked.

He smiled. "There's a dock right here on the property. I could keep the smaller boat close."

"Because the big one is too, um, big to be here?"

"Exactly."

She looked at him. "I keep forgetting about the rich thing. I mean I know it in my head, but I don't think about it when we're talking and hanging out."

"That's a good thing."

"Because you know I'm not in it for the money? Is that a real problem?"

"What do you think?"

"I guess it must be, but even without the money, you're still dreamy." She nibbled on her toast. "If you're serious about the boat, I'd love to ask Marisol if she and the girls would want to come out. But you have to be sure."

He would rather talk about her thinking he was dreamy. What did that mean and did being dreamy mean he could nudge her toward his bedroom?

"I'm sure."

"Thank you. That's very nice. And while you're in a giving mood, may I please have a bit of the garden to play with?"

"I have no idea what you're asking." His garden? For what?

"I miss gardening. My mom and I used to garden all summer long, but she and Dad have moved and I live in a condo, so I never get to dig around in the dirt anymore. I thought while I'm here I could plant some flowers, do a little weeding. You know, play."

"You're welcome to dig away," he told her, not sure why she felt the need to ask.

She didn't look convinced. "One of us should probably talk to your gardener. The landscaping is very beautiful, but formal, and I'm not sure anyone will be happy with me claiming space for random flowers and a tomato plant."

"I'll speak to Hilde," he told her. "She oversees the gardeners."

"Thank you. I love Hilde. She's so good at her job."

"She is. I'd like more Hildes in my life, especially at the office. The person who usually coordinates the company summer party is out on maternity leave and her second-in-command is having trouble handling everything." More than once, he'd thought about bringing Hilde in to manage the project.

"Do you need help?" Nissa asked. "I'm available. I don't know anything about a big corporate party, but I could run errands or help with setup."

Which was exactly like Nissa, he thought. "Thank you. I'll let you know if things spiral out of control."

"If that happens, ask Hilde and I'll be her assistant."

She smiled as she spoke, looking impossibly beautiful, sitting there at his kitchen table. James had been a fool to let her go, he thought.

"Would you like to go to the party?" he asked, surprising himself and, based on her wide eyes, her, as well.

"Sure, if it's okay." She smiled. "I guess if you're the boss, you get to say."

"You might want to recall your acceptance when I tell you my parents will be there."

She brushed away the warning. "I've only met them a couple of times, but they seem perfectly nice. Besides, I've never been to a real office party before. Are there rules? A dress code? Can I wear a hat?"

"Did you want to wear a hat?"

"I don't know. Is it a thing? Like the Kentucky Derby, where all the women wear hats?"

"Your mind is a confusing place. You may wear a hat if you'd like. I'll text you the particulars. In the meantime, I'll let Hilde know about the garden and speak with the captain about some dates to take out the boat." He smiled. "I'm leaving breakfast with a to-do list."

She fluttered her eyelashes. "Then my work here is done."

Chapter Four

NISSA

Nissa drove out onto the street. Despite the heat, she had the windows rolled down, mostly because even she could smell the dog on herself. She loved her doggie day care job, but wow, did she get stinky. She desperately wanted a shower and a change of clothes, but she had a more pressing problem to deal with.

Thirty minutes later, she parked in front of the large building that housed Desmond's company. Right now she needed someone to talk some sense into her and he was the most sensible person she could think of.

She walked inside and was immediately aware of the fact that she was dressed completely wrong. While everyone else had on business attire, she was wearing jeans and a purple T-shirt with a dog logo on the front. Her athletic shoes were grass-stained, her face had smudges, plus the whole smell thing. But she'd come too far to turn back now.

She walked up to the security desk and gave her name. "I'd like to see Desmond Stilling please."

The uniformed man looked doubtful. "Do you have an appointment?"

"No."

She thought briefly about explaining how she and Desmond had been friends forever and that she was currently living with him, but decided against it. The "living together" comment might be misunderstood.

"Maybe you could get in touch with his assistant and give her my name," Nissa suggested.

The security guard did as she requested. Seconds later, his eyes wide with surprise, he allowed her through the security gate and led her to an elevator that whisked her to the top floor.

When the doors opened, an attractive forty-something woman in an elegant suit greeted her.

"Mr. Stilling is in his office. If you'll follow me, Ms. Lang."

"I can do that."

The floors were hardwood, the walls a neutral

color. There were a lot of plants, big windows and a general air of business. Everyone was hurrying or talking or busy on a computer. A few glanced up at her, then turned away before making eye contact. She wasn't sure if that was good or bad.

She and her escort walked through a series of open doors before finally passing an anteroom and a final set of double doors. Nissa stepped inside and saw Desmond behind a large desk. All that was really impressive, but what totally got her attention were the floor-to-ceiling windows. Desmond had an incredible west-facing view of the water and Blackberry Island and the Sound beyond.

He came to his feet. "Nissa. I wasn't expecting you. Everything all right?"

She pointed to the windows. "Did you know you had this? How do you work? It's so beautiful. In the winter, you'll be able to watch the storms blowing in. Wow. Just wow."

Desmond nodded at the woman waiting next to Nissa.

"Thanks, Kathy. I'll take it from here."

Kathy left, closing the door behind her. Nissa shook her head. "This is great. I love it. I'm not really an office kind of person, but if I could work here, it wouldn't be so bad."

"Sadly, most of my employees don't get this kind

of view. But the break room is on the floor below mine and it faces the same direction."

"It was very nice of you to give everyone that space." She rubbed her hands up and down her jeans, then exhaled. "I want a dog."

She took a step toward him. "It's been four days and they're so fun and sweet and affectionate. Dogs are the best. They love with their whole heart and they're so happy to see you and I want one. Or all of them. I need you to talk me down. I keep telling myself what we talked about before. I'm gone too much and my condo is small and this isn't a good time, but it's hard. Just one fluffy dog. Is that too much to ask for?"

He smiled at her. "You don't need me here for this conversation, do you?"

"Yes, I do. That's why I came here. So you could be sensible. It's just I think about going hiking with a dog, or camping, and it would be fun."

"You could take it out on my boat."

Her eyes widened. "Could I? Oh, we could buy one of those doggie life jackets." She shook her head. "No. Stop it. You're not helping."

He sat on the corner of his desk. "You're not getting a dog. Once you move on to another temp job, the need won't be so intense."

"You're killing my dream."

"Your dreams are too big to kill and you know

I'm right. You will probably get a dog eventually, but this isn't a good time."

"I know. But I want one."

"Deep breaths. It's just a couple more weeks."

"I feel pouty."

"What can I do to help? Would you like a hug?"

She would. A nice, squeezy, Desmond hug with her body pressing against his. Of course he was offering comfort and she was hoping to get a little hug action, which wasn't fair of her. Plus, you know, the smell.

She took a step back. "Don't get close to me. I have doggie stink on me. I need to go home and shower. Thank you for reminding me to be sensible. It's just they're so sweet. We never had pets when I was growing up. I should ask my mom about that. Did you?"

"Have pets? No. My parents wouldn't have allowed them in the house. Too much mess. They barely tolerated me."

She smiled as if she got the joke, but she knew in some ways, he wasn't kidding.

"Want me to scold them when I see them at the office party?" she asked. "I will. I have a great scolding voice. It comes from years of being stern when the situation requires it at work."

One corner of his mouth turned up. "While I would pay money to see that, I would never ask you to do that. Besides, that was a long time ago. These days they're far more interested in getting me married."

"Why?"

"They want an heir."

"Because of the empire, right? That makes sense. My parents want me to get married and have grandchildren for them. So it's kind of the same thing."

They looked at each other. She knew he was thinking it wasn't the same thing at all, but he was too nice to say that.

An unexpected and unpleasant thought occurred to her.

"Is me living with you getting in the way of a relationship?"

"I'm between women right now."

Whew. "Is there a waiting list? Or an application process?" she asked, her voice teasing.

"There's a form they fill out online."

She laughed, knowing she liked him a lot. She always had.

"I'm going to go while I'm feeling strong about not getting a dog," she said. "Thank you for your help."

"Anytime. I'm always here for you, Nissa."

She nodded and let herself out of his office. On her way back to her car, she told herself while the words were nice, he only meant them as a friend and not anything remotely more than that.

DESMOND

Unless he had plans to do something with Shane, Desmond usually worked on the weekends. He did so in his home office, but still, there was work. Without interruptions from phone calls and meetings, he could get through a pile of paperwork, review reports and generally get caught up. Not the healthiest decision for himself personally, he acknowledged, but excellent for the company.

But on this particular Saturday, he had trouble concentrating. The cause was obvious—Nissa. Despite the fact that he could neither see nor hear her, he knew she was around. Out in the yard, to be exact, doing whatever it was she planned to do in what she referred to as her "temporary plot of earth."

As he'd suggested, Hilde had talked to the gardeners, who had given Nissa a section of the garden to do whatever it was she wanted to do. Her interest in planting flowers wasn't anything he could relate to, but it was obviously important to her, which meant it was something he would make sure got done.

As long as she was happy, he told himself. While she was living here, she was his responsibility.

He turned his attention back to the spreadsheet on his computer. Three minutes later, he swore softly, saved his work, then closed the program. He wasn't making any progress on the work he'd brought home.

Better to admit defeat and let it go than to keep staring unseeingly at the screen.

He got up and walked through the house to the back door and stepped outside. Typical to the Pacific Northwest, the warm weather had given way to several days of cool temperatures and lots of rain. Today it would barely reach seventy degrees, as they transitioned back to something more summerlike.

The backyard was about an acre of manicured lawn and tidy plant beds. There was a huge pool off the rear deck and beyond that, a stone path led the way down to the dock and Lake Washington. Tall, thick hedges provided privacy on either side of his property.

He glanced around but didn't see Nissa anywhere. He started to circle around the house and found her on the south side, on her knees, using a spade to dig out roots.

She had on jeans and a T-shirt. Her long hair was pulled back in a braid and a big hat covered her head and shaded her face. Gardening gloves protected her hands. Nothing about her was the least bit provocative, but he still found himself moving more quickly as he approached—as if he couldn't get there fast enough.

Just the sight of her made him feel better about the day. He waited for her to look up and smile when she saw him—as she always did—looking forward to the sense of anticipation her smiles always produced.

Before she saw him, she rose gracefully to her feet, then reached for a shovel. He hurried over and took it from her.

She looked up at him and grinned. "Checking up on me? I'm in demolition mode, so don't judge. Later, when the new plants are in, you'll see a riot of color."

"Why didn't you ask for my help?"

She frowned. "For what?"

He waved the shovel. "The heavy work."

"Desmond, I can dig out a few plants. I'm stronger than I look."

"I have no doubt about that, but I'm stronger than you. Tell me what you want dug out."

She shook her head slowly. "I don't know. Are you capable of manual labor?"

"Very funny. Which ones?"

She pointed to a couple of bushes and a few flowers. "Those, please. I don't want to dig out too much. Come September, everything I plant will be taken out and the garden returned to its former glory. I kind of feel bad for your gardening team. There were actual tears when I told them what I wanted to do."

"I doubt any of them cried."

"It was pretty close to that. They weren't amused by my request to have some yard."

He stepped on the shovel, pushing it under the

first bush. With the recent rains, the soil was damp and he dug in easily.

"Do you want me to talk to them?" he asked, lifting the bush out of the ground.

"What? No. I was sharing, not hinting. Come on, Desmond. Look at your yard. It's beautifully designed and maintained. These guys take pride in their efforts and here I am, messing with it. I'm being incredibly self-indulgent. But I can't help it. Digging in the dirt makes me happy." She paused, then laughed. "Actually watching you dig in the dirt isn't bad, either."

"Glad to help."

He made quick work of the plants she wanted removed. Once he was done, they tossed them into the composting bin.

"What's the next step?" he asked, helping her sweep up the path.

"I go buy plants. I talked to my mom earlier this morning and she gave me some good ideas. Because it's already July, I'm not going to be able to grow anything like vegetables, so I'm sticking with pretty flowers that make me happy."

"How is your mom?"

"She's good. She and Dad are going to come over to this side of the mountains in a few weeks to hang out with me and Shane."

"They're welcome to stay here," he said, thinking

it would be nice to spend time with Shane and Nissa's parents. They had always been kind to him, drawing him into the family and including him in their traditions. Around her family, he'd always felt...normal.

"They were going to stay with Shane, but I'll make the offer," she said. "I'm sure he'll be excited." She gave him an impish smile. "Apparently he's still dating his new lady friend. We're talking about four weeks' worth of relationship. You know how rare that is for him. Having my parents bunking in his place will cramp his style."

Desmond chuckled. "I'm happy to help the cause."

She looked at him. "Do you think he's going to get serious about her?"

Desmond hesitated before saying, "Shane hasn't said much to me about her," which was the truth. What he didn't say was that Shane had his reasons for not wanting to commit to anyone. Reasons Nissa didn't know about and that Desmond wasn't going to mention. Shane was his best friend and Desmond would never betray a confidence.

"When are you going to buy plants?" he asked, hoping she didn't notice his attempt to change the subject.

"Right now. Fred Meyer is having a sale," she said, naming a popular local superstore chain.

"Or you could tell the gardener what you want and he could get them from the nursery he uses."

She sighed. "Wow, you really have led a sheltered life. I don't know exactly what I want. I'll wait to see what looks good and appeals to me. Plus, buying the plants is part of the fun. It's satisfying to bring them home and then plant them myself."

"If you say so."

She pulled off her gloves. "You sound doubtful and that makes me feel challenged. All right, you're coming with me to the store. You obviously need to experience the thrill of plant buying." She paused. "Unless you have plans or something."

"No plans." And if he'd had any, he would have canceled them. He would much rather spend the rest of the morning with Nissa.

"Great." She glanced at the tools scattered around. "Let's leave these here. We'll need them for planting later."

Five minutes later they were in her car, heading to Fred Meyer. There had been a brief discussion about which car to take, but she'd insisted on hers, claiming putting plants in the back of his expensive Mercedes would make him weep and she didn't want to be responsible for that. Which was how he found himself in the passenger seat of her Honda CRV.

She chatted as she drove, mentioning the change in the weather and how she was still trying to be strong about not getting a dog. He tried to pay attention to her words but kept getting caught up in his awareness of her. They were sitting close in her car. It would be easy to slide his arm across the console and settle his hand on her thigh.

Or not, he told himself firmly. Nissa was a friend. She was too important for him to mess with that way. Besides, he owed her family. The last thing they would want was her hooking up with some heartless guy.

They pulled into the crowded parking lot. Desmond was surprised at the number of people at the large store. Nissa had to circle a couple of times to find a spot near the nursery.

"Why so many people?" he asked as they got out.

She looked at him over the vehicle. "It's Saturday. People do their shopping on Saturday. Fred Meyer sells food and clothes and home goods, as well as plants. It's a popular and convenient one-stop shopping spot."

He glanced around. "I didn't know that."

"Have you ever been?"

"I don't shop much."

"Or ever. Do you at least buy your own clothes?"

"My suits are custom-made, and my tailor has my measurements." At her look of incredulity, he quickly added, "I have a shopper at Nordstrom who takes care of the rest."

She stared at him. "I forget who you are. To me you're just Desmond whom I've known forever."

Something flashed in her eyes that he couldn't name, but then it was gone. "You're a friend and a part of my life. But there's so much more to you, isn't there?"

He walked around the car until he was standing in front of her. "No. I'm exactly who you think I am."

"With a billion-dollar fortune and a multinational company."

"It's not a billion dollars."

She smiled. "But you're closer to a billion than to a million, right?"

"Maybe." He brushed a bit of dirt off her cheek. "It doesn't change anything."

"Except if you weren't rich, you'd be shopping at Fred Meyer, like the rest of us."

"I'm shopping here today."

She leaned in for a hug. Desmond pulled her close, wrapping his arms around her. She felt good, leaning against him. Warm and feminine. He wanted to do more than hug. He wanted to have her look up at him so he could kiss her. A long, lingering kiss, totally inappropriate for a store parking lot. But she didn't and he knew better than to go anywhere near that sort of thing.

"All right you," she said stepping back. "Let's go buy plants."

She went in through the nursery entrance, pointing at a flatbed cart. "You get to push that, but be careful. No bumping into people. It's not nice."

"Yes, ma'am."

Once they were in the fenced area, she started walking along the aisles of plants, choosing pots of flowers as she went. While he didn't know any of the names, he recognized a lot of them from her mother's garden.

He put the plants on the cart and was mindful of the other customers. But when he saw a small display on the other side of the nursery, he excused himself and went over to study the beautiful plants.

Long, elegant stems supported creamy flowers with purple centers. Nissa joined him.

"Do you like orchids?" she asked.

"Yes. Because of your mom."

"My mom didn't grow them. She loved getting them, but they seemed to be the one plant she couldn't keep alive."

He looked at her. "Your dad brought one home for her the first time I came to visit. Shane and I had just arrived when he walked in with the orchid. Your mom was surprised, but happy, even as she told him it was too expensive and he shouldn't have."

Nissa stared at him. "How do you remember that?"

"I remember everything about my visits to your old house."

He could walk it blindfolded. He knew which stairs creaked and how to jiggle the handle when the toilet got fussy. On Christmas, stockings were opened first thing, followed by breakfast, then the real presents.

"I'd never been in a house like that," he added.

"Small?" she asked with a laugh.

He shook his head. "Normal. You all loved each other. I could see that. Your parents made me feel welcome, maybe for the first time ever. Your mom made me a stocking. I'd never had a Christmas stocking before. Those were the best Christmases of my life."

He hadn't meant to admit all that, but it was too late to call the words back. Besides, he didn't mind Nissa knowing how he felt. Being with her family had always been the best part of his year. He was accepted as just another kid in the house. Her mother had looked out for him and her father had talked to him about life in a way his own father never had.

She reached past him and picked up one of the orchids. "We'll put this in the kitchen and see what happens."

"I'd like that."

Their gazes locked. He felt something pass between them. A connection, he supposed. Shared memories of good times.

She looked away first. "This Christmas you need

to hang your stocking. Otherwise, how is Santa going to fill it?"

He chuckled. "Is that what I've been doing wrong? Thanks for the tip."

"Anytime."

Chapter Five

NISSA

By late afternoon the plants were in the ground and watered. Nissa and Desmond put away the last of the tools. She'd expected him to simply drop off the plants by the path and disappear back into the house, but he'd stuck with her through all the hard work.

"I couldn't have gotten through all this today," she told him. "I would have had a bunch more to put in the ground tomorrow. You were great."

He flashed her a smile that made her insides a little quivery. "I had a good time."

They picked up the last of the tools and put them

in the shed before heading into the house. She was hot and sticky, but satisfied. She was on her way to having fun flowers for summer—temporarily, but that was good enough for now. One day she might be able to buy a house and then she'd have a real garden with vegetables and maybe a cherry tree or two, and all the flowers she wanted.

When they reached the kitchen, Desmond glanced at her. "Hilde left chicken marinating and a few salads. I was going to barbecue. You're welcome to join me if you'd like. Unless you have plans. It's Saturday, after all."

Plans as in a date? Yeah, not so much these days. In fact she hadn't been in a serious relationship since she and James had broken up over two years ago.

"I don't date," she blurted before she could stop herself. "I mean I can, but I don't. Or I haven't been. Um, lately."

She consciously pressed her lips together to stop herself from babbling like an idiot, despite the fact that the damage was done.

"So dinner?" Desmond asked, rescuing her without commenting on her babbling.

"I'd like that. After I shower. Meet back down here in half an hour?"

"Perfect."

There was an awkward moment when they both tried to go through the kitchen door at the same time.

Desmond stepped back and waved her in front of him. She hurried out, then raced up the stairs and practically ran for her bedroom. Once there, she closed the door and leaned against it.

"Talking isn't hard," she whispered to herself. "You've been doing it since you were two. You know how to do this."

But when it came to being around Desmond, knowing and doing were two different things.

She headed for the bathroom, trying to decide what to wear as she went. It was a casual dinner at home. She shouldn't worry about dressing up. But hanging out with her host was anything but casual, which left her in a quandary.

After a quick shower, she discovered that her wardrobe had not become sophisticated or elegant since the last time she'd checked. She'd packed away her work clothes, leaving her with an assortment of jeans, cropped pants, shorts and tops. Oh, and two summer dresses, one of which he'd already seen.

Shorts were way too casual, she thought. Plus, she wasn't as confident about her thighs as she would like. So she settled on cute cropped pants and a co-ordinating tank top, both in bright apple green. She gave her hair a cursory blowout and put on mascara, then decided to call it a win.

She made her way downstairs and found Desmond already in the family room, opening the secret bar.

"What are you in the mood for tonight?" he asked.

"Did you have a suggestion?"

"I thought we'd go old school tonight and have gimlets."

She'd heard of the drink but had never tasted one. "I'm in."

She watched him while he collected botanical gin, limes, a few basil leaves and what she'd come to recognize as simple syrup.

He worked quickly and with a confidence that she envied. No matter the situation, Desmond always seemed to fit in. She did well with friends and in her classroom, but in new situations, she was awkward.

He added ice to a shaker, then measured and poured in ingredients. He'd showered, as well. He had on jeans and a polo shirt. Both showed off his muscled body. The man obviously worked out. She would guess there was a gym in the house—probably in the basement.

He capped the shaker and shook it, then put a strainer on top of each of their glasses and poured. After handing her a glass, he led the way to the sofa.

She kicked off her sandals before sitting down and tucking her feet under her. She sipped her drink. "This is nice," she said. "Very refreshing." She liked the lime with the botanical gin and the hint of basil was unexpected.

"I'm glad you like it." He leaned back against the

sofa. "I texted with your mother. She and your dad are going to stay here when they visit."

She grinned. "And you're okay with that?"

"Of course. I enjoy their company and I'm happy to repay their hospitality."

"Will your parents also be staying here when they come to Seattle?"

A muscle in his jaw jumped. "No. They prefer to stay at a hotel. Separate hotels."

She stared at him. "They're not at the same hotel?"

"No. They haven't been together for a few years now. They were never close but recently they've stopped pretending. My mother spends most of her time in Paris while Dad lives in New York."

"Are you all right with that?"

"My opinion isn't relevant. If you're asking if I'm worried they'll get a divorce, the answer is no. They won't. There's too much at stake. Besides, they each have their lives."

"But not with each other."

"You're thinking they were once in love and now they're not. It wasn't like that with them. They had a merger. It was a sensible decision that grew both businesses. Romance wasn't part of the package."

"That's sad."

"Why? It's what they expected and it's what they got. Even when I was little, they rarely saw each other. They took separate vacations, sometimes bringing me along, sometimes leaving me with my nanny."

She'd known the basics of his past, but not any details. Certainly not that his parents had been so estranged. Or maybe that was the wrong word, because it implied that at one time there'd been a connection.

"I can't understand how anyone would do that," she admitted. "Marry for business reasons."

He looked at her. "Marrying for love is a relatively new idea. For hundreds of years marriages were arranged with economics in mind."

"I wouldn't have liked that. I'm not sure I could go through with an arranged marriage simply for the sake of the family fortune."

"Back then, you wouldn't have had a choice."

"Did your mom?"

"I don't know. She doesn't talk about it. When I've tried to ask questions, she'd always told me she's perfectly content with her life. She also pointed out that her way was far more sensible. Emotions were messy and unnecessary." He raised one shoulder. "Neither of my parents has much interest in feelings. They don't see the point of love and affection. It comes with not having a heart. It's sort of a family trait."

"They have hearts."

"They're not mean or cruel, but they don't believe in love. Duty, yes. That makes sense to them.

But to do something just out of love isn't their way. Or mine."

She finished her drink and put the glass on the table. "I don't accept that, Desmond."

"You should. I've been told I'm quite the heartless bastard more than once."

"Whoever said that was wrong. You care. You love me and my family. I know you do."

His gaze locked with her, making her aware that using the *L* word might have sent the conversation in a direction she didn't want to go.

She cleared her throat. "What I mean is you love us the way you love family. Regular families, not your family. I didn't mean romantically. You're not in love with me or anything. You love us the way we love you."

His mouth twitched as if he were trying not to smile. "Would you like me to change the subject?"

"Yes, please."

"And pretend this never happened?"

"That would be great."

"The Mariners are doing well."

Baseball, she thought with gratitude. There was a safe topic.

"They are. I wonder if they'll make the playoffs this year."

Later, as she put together a green salad and Desmond cooked the chicken, she thought about his comment about not having a heart. He couldn't really believe that, could he? Desmond was kind and generous—of course he cared about people. But she understood why he might want to hold back. His marriage to Rosemary hadn't ended how he'd wanted, and that sort of thing left a mark. She knew she was still dealing with James scars and they'd never even been married. That kind of pain could change a person.

That had to be it, she told herself. Because if Desmond thought he was heartless like his parents, he was the wrongest of wrong.

NISSA

Wednesday after work, Nissa walked into the kitchen to find Hilde at the island, several cabinet doors spread out in front of her.

"What are those?" she asked.

Hilde waved her closer. "We're remodeling the kitchen. Mr. Desmond approved the budget and hired a decorator, but he won't help me make decisions about what to order."

Nissa turned in a slow circle, studying the huge kitchen. She was pretty sure her entire condo would fit in here with plenty of room for a deck or two. The mid-tone cabinets went up to the ceiling and the island was in a good location, but the stove seemed old and the hardware on the cabinets was dated.

"Was anything done to the kitchen when Desmond moved in?" she asked.

Hilde shook her head. "No. Mr. Desmond had his bathroom remodeled and the house painted. New carpet was put upstairs but nothing else. This kitchen is about twenty years old."

"Then it's time. What do you have so far?"

Hilde opened a cabinet and pulled out several appliance brochures, along with paint swatches and three different floor plans.

"I have all this, but it's not my kitchen," Hilde said, sounding stressed. "Mr. Desmond needs to decide and he won't."

Nissa grinned. "Then I'm going to have to explain to him how that's totally unacceptable. Is he in his study?"

"Yes, Miss Nissa. He's been home about half an hour."

Nissa walked down the long hallway that led to Desmond's private study. The door was open and he was sitting at his manly desk, his attention on his computer.

His gaze was intense, she thought as she paused in the doorway. Desmond was the kind of guy who focused on one thing at a time. She allowed herself a few seconds of wondering what it would be like to have all that attention focused on her, then softly cleared her throat.

He looked up and smiled when he saw her.

It was a good smile, the kind that welcomed and told her he was pleased to see her. As if she were important to him. Telling herself not to read too much into his reaction, she leaned against the doorway and folded her arms across her chest.

"You are needed in the kitchen," she said.

"Am I?"

"Yes. You need to make some decisions on the remodel and today is the perfect time."

The smile disappeared. "It's not my thing. Hilde's handling it."

"It's your house and you get the final say. Whether or not it's your thing, it's your responsibility. Come on, Desmond. Look at a few samples. Wave imperially at one of them and we will all rush to do your bidding. You'll like that part of it."

His mouth stayed straight but she saw humor flash in his eyes.

"People do my bidding all day long," he told her. "I don't need it at home."

"Then indulge me." She dropped one arm to her side and raised the other as she pointed down the hall. "Kitchen. Now."

"You're so bossy."

"I can be and that should frighten you."

He got up and followed her back to the kitchen. Nissa held up both hands.

"Ta-da! I bring you Mr. Desmond."

Hilde motioned to the cabinet samples on the island. "We have to pick which one. They're going to be custom-made, so the trim can be changed to how you like."

Desmond studied them. "Any of them is fine."

Nissa moved close. "Don't say that. You have an opinion. Door style. Simple? Ornate? Something in between?" She pointed to a Shaker style. "I think that's too plain, but you don't want anything really fussy. This is a big kitchen and there are going to be a lot of cabinets."

Desmond looked at the doors, then out the big windows toward the backyard.

"This part of the house faces more north than east, so there isn't as much natural light. So nothing too dark."

He moved closer to the cabinets and studied them.

"This detail," he said, pointing at quarter-round trim. "No inlay."

They discussed other possibilities before Desmond chose the ones he liked best. From there the discussion moved on to appliances. Hilde made a case for a warming drawer.

"I've always wanted one," she admitted. "They're so nice for entertaining, and in the winter. It's no fun to put hot food on a cold plate. My mom bought me a silly plug-in plate warmer. It's like a folded heating pad. While it works, a warming drawer would be pretty amazing."

Desmond nodded at Hilde. "A warming drawer it is. What else?"

"The stove." Hilde fanned out several brochures. "I like this one best. It's big and a little more expensive but it has two ovens and a grill."

Desmond nodded. "I like the grill. I can barbecue in the winter."

"Yes, and it changes out to a griddle. I would use that a lot."

He refused to weigh in on which refrigerator, so Hilde and Nissa discussed options. When it came to the layout, all three plans worked, but one involved a lot more construction, basically turning the kitchen ninety degrees.

"I don't think it's worth it," Nissa said. "It's a lot more work and money, and for what? To me, everything is where it belongs right now." She smiled at Hilde. "But your opinion is more important than mine. You're the one who works in this kitchen."

Hilde tapped one of the other designs. "Yes, I agree. Why make so many changes? I like how things are now. It just has to be refreshed."

Hilde and Desmond studied the other options before picking one. After that they moved on to paint colors and made their choices very quickly. When they were done, Hilde made a final list of their choices.

"Thank you, Mr. Desmond. I'll call the decorator in the morning."

"You're welcome, Hilde. I shouldn't have waited so long to get involved."

Nissa walked him back to his office. "That was fun. I love spending other people's money."

"I appreciate your help." He walked into his office, then turned back to her. "I was wrong to push that all on Hilde. She wasn't comfortable making the decisions herself."

"Plus you're her boss, and she has to think about that. I, on the other hand, am free to annoy you whenever I want."

"You're never annoying."

"Really? Because sometimes I try to be."

He smiled. "No, you don't. You're easy to be around. I like that."

Was that the same as liking her? Like as in like-like? Because she knew Desmond liked her as a friend, but was there anything else she should know about?

He started for his desk, then paused. "Are you still up for the company party?" he asked. "My planner was asking about my plus-one."

"I'll be there. I'm looking forward to meeting

your staff and telling them what you were like as a teenager."

He chuckled. "I'm not worried. There are no secrets in my past. Besides, if there were, I would trust you to keep them."

"I totally would. Except for the embarrassing ones." She paused, not sure what to say next. It seemed like they were almost going somewhere, but maybe that was wishful thinking on her part.

"Dinner at seven?" she asked instead.

"I'll be there."

Two weeks into living with Desmond, Nissa had settled into a routine. She went to work—she was still at the doggie day care—came home, showered, had dinner with Desmond and then retreated to her spacious room where she relaxed with an audiobook or watched something on one of the streaming services he made available to her.

She'd gone over to see Marisol and the girls every weekend and kept in close touch with her friend. Shane kept talking about getting together, but so far he claimed to be too busy with work, which she took as code that he was still involved with his mystery woman. If the relationship went on much longer, she was going to have to do some serious investigating. In the meantime, she had a party to get ready for.

Mid-July meant summer sales, so she'd indulged

in a mini shopping trip. She'd bought a new summer dress for the event—a pretty black fit-and-flare
style that fitted perfectly. She already had fancy sandals and a cute evening bag she'd bought years ago.

She took the time to curl her long hair. Actual
curls didn't last, but she ended up with waves that
looked great. Exactly at six, she went downstairs to
meet Desmond.

His summer office party didn't start until seven,
but he'd said he wanted to get there early and she'd
been fine with that. They would drive there and back
together—something that made sense, given their
living arrangement. It wasn't a date, she told herself
as she reached the main floor. It was convenience.
Kind of like carpooling. There weren't any—

"You look beautiful."

She turned toward the voice and saw Desmond
in the archway by the dining room. He had on dark
pants and a dark gray shirt—nothing special and
yet the sight of him made her heart beat just a little
faster than usual.

"Thank you," she said, her gaze locking with his.
"I wanted to look nice for your work friends."

"Mission accomplished." He motioned to the door.
"Shall we go?"

Her nerves continued to be on edge, even as she
settled next to him in his fancy Mercedes. Her throat
was dry and her skin felt hot, which didn't make

sense. This was Desmond. She *knew* him. They were friends. She would trust him with her life. More important, she would trust him with her family, so what was the big deal?

Rather than answer the question, she decided to distract herself with conversation. "Hilde's very excited about the party. You were sweet to invite her and her husband."

"I thought she would enjoy the event."

"She said last year's party was wonderful. Apparently there's dancing."

He glanced at her, his mouth curving into a smile. "I heard that."

"Do you dance with the office staff?"

He returned his attention to the road. "No. But they often dance with each other."

"You must have to balance issues like that," she murmured, watching him merge into traffic as they headed south on I-5. "Being a concerned boss, but not getting too involved. Being in charge without being a mean boss."

"Maybe I am a mean boss."

"I don't believe that. You wouldn't be. You care about people."

"I try to be fair."

She smiled. "See. You can't help it. I'm excited about seeing your parents."

He spared her another glance. "Are you sure about that?"

"Okay, excited is strong, but they've always been really nice to me. Plus, it's fun to see what your mom is wearing. Evelyn has amazing fashion sense and the jewelry is spectacular."

"I wouldn't have thought of you as the jewelry type."

She laughed. "Why would you say that? I don't have much because I can't afford it and if I have extra money I want to save it, but that doesn't mean I don't like sparkly things as much as the next girl."

She thought about the last time she'd seen Desmond's mother. It had been at his housewarming party a couple of years ago.

"That diamond necklace she wore," she said, thinking about how it had glittered. "I doubt I could afford the insurance on it."

"It's probably heavy and uncomfortable to wear," he teased.

"I would be willing to suffer. See how much character I have?"

They talked easily for the rest of the drive. As they approached Seattle, the traffic got heavier. Desmond drove into the city and made his way to the Chihuly Garden and Glass, where the party would be held. He pulled up to the valet parking he'd arranged, then helped her out of the car.

"I've never been here," she admitted, looking at the building in front of them. "I should have come. I always meant to. I'm a huge fan of his work. Did you know there's a massive Chihuly installation in Montreal? It's made of all these individual pieces and every year they have to take it apart and bring it in for the winter."

"I didn't know that, but I'm not surprised. His work is all around the world."

They walked toward the entrance.

"I'm going to stay up front so I can greet everyone as they arrive," he told her. "You're welcome to explore the museum, if you'd like. It's closed to the public for the party, so you'll pretty much have it to yourself."

"I'd love to look around. Thanks for the suggestion."

She really did want to explore and she knew standing with him while he welcomed his guests would only invite a lot of questions. It wasn't as if she and Desmond were a couple. She was just a family friend.

They went inside. He excused himself to go talk to his staff while she collected a brochure on the museum and prepared to be dazzled. But just before she stepped into the first room, she glanced back at Desmond. He'd gone out of his way to make the evening special for those who worked for him. Not exactly the actions of a man who had no heart.

Chapter Six

NISSA

Nissa spent over an hour admiring the various installations. While she'd started out as the only admirer, by the time she entered the outdoor garden the party was in full swing and there were people everywhere. Several smiled at her, but no one came over to talk to her, making her realize that except for Hilde, she didn't know anyone who worked for Desmond. Not that it mattered, she told herself. She was capable of starting a conversation herself.

She took a glass of champagne from a server and looked around, searching for a likely prospect.

Her gaze settled on a familiar older couple. Evelyn and Charles Stilling looked like what they were—wealthy, cultured and well traveled. She knew that each of them had inherited a part of what had become Stilling Holdings, forming the bigger company when they'd married. What she hadn't known until recently was that marriage had been about business rather than affection.

Now she studied them, wondering how they could survive so many years in a loveless marriage. She wouldn't like that at all. For her, marriage was about giving her heart to one man for the rest of her life. She wanted a traditional family with kids and pets and camping.

Evelyn turned toward her and the light caught the spectacular sapphire necklace she wore. Nissa smiled. Okay, maybe she would add a few jewels to her wish list.

She was still smiling when Evelyn glanced in her direction. The older woman studied her for a second before heading in her direction. Nissa moved toward her, as well.

"I don't know if you remember me," she said, holding out her hand. "We've met a few times. I'm Nissa Lang, Shane's sister."

"Yes, of course."

Evelyn had dark hair and eyes. She was tall, slim and moved with a grace that Nissa envied. Maybe she'd studied ballet or maybe she was blessed with natural grace. Nissa wasn't exactly clumsy, but she didn't have anything close to Desmond's mother's style.

"How was your trip to Seattle?" Nissa asked.

"It was commercial travel. One does the best one can, under the circumstances." Evelyn sipped her champagne. "Are you here with Desmond?"

"You mean as a date?" Nissa tried to ignore the sudden surge of nervousness. "No. I came with him because it was easier. I'm staying with him for a few weeks while my condo is rented out." She held in a groan. Really? She'd had to say *that*? "It's not anything romantic. We're friends. Just friends. We have been forever. Desmond would spend Christmas with my family, which, um, I guess you knew because he wasn't with you."

She forced herself to stop talking and offered a tight smile.

Evelyn's expression sharpened. "You're living with him."

"I'm staying at the house. In my own room. Not, you know, *with* him." She made little air quotes, then wished she hadn't.

"So, have you seen the exhibit?" she asked brightly, hoping to change the subject.

"I don't need to. Dale and I are friends."

Dale? As in Dale Chihuly? Sure. She wasn't even surprised.

"Do you think you're right for him?" Evelyn asked bluntly. "You're hardly his type and you bring nothing to the table. How will you help him with business? Be an asset when he travels? What kind of a hostess will you be?"

Nissa went cold. "What are you talking about?"

"It's obvious you have feelings for him. I'm not sure what your ridiculous charade is about staying with him, but not *with* him." Evelyn copied her air quotes. "Desmond always does the right thing. He made a mistake with Rosemary, but he rectified it immediately and he never looked back. She begged for a reconciliation, but he wouldn't have any part of her, once he recognized her for what she was. The same thing would happen with you, Nissa.

"You're the kind of girl who expects love when you marry. Desmond's incapable of that. I consider that a point of pride, but I doubt you'd agree." Desmond's mother offered her a cold smile. "He knows what's expected from him and he will do as we ask. Silly girl. I almost feel sorry for you."

With that, she turned and walked away, leaving Nissa feeling embarrassed and exposed, although she couldn't begin to say why. Although she knew it was her imagination, she felt as if everyone was staring at her, judging her. She felt awkward and out of place and wished that she could be anywhere but here.

She glanced around, looking for an exit and if not that, at least somewhere to hide. She'd barely taken a step when Desmond appeared in front of her.

"Are you all right?" he asked, sounding concerned.

"I'm fine."

He stared at her. "I saw you talking to my mother. What did she say?"

"About what?"

"Nissa, you went white."

Oh no! She couldn't tell him what Evelyn had said—she couldn't talk about it with anyone. "That must be a trick of the lighting. I'm fine."

His dark gaze never wavered. "You don't usually lie to me."

Obviously he got his bluntness from his mother, she thought, wishing she could see humor in the moment, rather than feeling uncomfortable.

"Maybe just this once you could let it go," she told him.

He surprised her by nodding. "Are you hungry?"

"Not really." Her stomach was too upset for her to eat.

"Then come with me."

He took her hand in his and drew her back inside. There was a large dance floor set up under the glass roof. A band played and several couples were dancing.

He took her half-empty champagne glass from her and set it on a table, then pulled her into his arms and started moving them to the music.

At first she could barely follow his movements. She was acutely aware of everyone around them, and worried that his mother was watching. But gradually the heat of Desmond's body, the feel of him holding her, made her relax. She told herself she would deal with her conversation with his mother another time and that she should simply enjoy the rest of the evening.

One song became two and then three. Finally Desmond drew her to the side and found a couple of empty chairs. They sat down.

"That was nice," she said, smiling at him.

"It's like prom."

"Yours?"

He looked at her. "No. Yours. Everyone is dressed up. You look amazing."

"Look at you with the compliments." She tried not to think about what his mother had said—that Desmond was incapable of love and she was silly. "It was a long time ago."

"But still a good night."

"Yes, it was." She'd been so crazy about him, she thought, remembering how the evening had gotten better and better. The best part had been him kissing her at the end. Wonderful sexy kisses that had made her think a future was possible.

"And then you walked away from me," she added softly.

"You know why."

"Imagine where we would have been if you hadn't."

She hadn't meant to say the words, but somehow she had. Desmond's gaze sharpened.

"You mean if we'd kept seeing each other?"

She nodded. "I think about that sometimes."

"So what happens?"

"We'll never know."

He started to speak, then suddenly looked away and came to his feet. One of his assistants walked over.

"A few of the guests are getting ready to leave," she told him. "You wanted me to let you know when that happened so you could say goodbye."

"Thanks, Brittany."

The woman nodded and retreated the way she'd come. Nissa stood. "Go play the host. I'll be fine."

"I won't be long." He pointed to the buffet. "Eat something. You have to be hungry."

"I will."

He turned away, took a step, then spun back to her. Before she knew what was going to happen, he pulled her close and kissed her. The brief contact seared her skin and sent liquid desire pouring through her, but before she could react in any way, he was gone, following Brittany to where his guests were leaving.

Nissa stood there for a couple of seconds, not sure what had happened or how she felt about it. She smiled. Scratch that last thought, she told herself. She knew exactly how she felt about Desmond kissing her. She felt good. And if it happened again, she was going to enjoy every second of it.

DESMOND

Desmond left work nearly two hours earlier than usual. There was no reason—no pressing appointment or phone call. Instead he went home because he knew Nissa was there and he wanted to spend time with her.

He tried to tell himself she would still be there when he left at his usual time, but for some reason the words had no effect. Normally he was disciplined to the point of annoying his friends, but not today. Not with her.

He arrived home a little after four and walked into the house. Nissa was in the family room, the TV on and tuned to a local news show, although the sound was off. She was sitting on the sofa, her hair

still damp from her shower. She was reading something on her tablet, wireless headphones on her head.

She was wearing shorts and a T-shirt. Conventional clothing that shouldn't have stirred anything
inside of him, and yet did. Or maybe the problem
wasn't the bright yellow T-shirt, but the woman
wearing it.

He wanted her. Knowing it was a mistake, that
he shouldn't cross that line did nothing for the need
that lived inside of him. He wanted her and the brief
kiss the night of the party had only made that wanting increase.

He thought of crossing to her, of tugging her to
her feet and then pressing his mouth to hers until
she wrapped her arms around him and begged him
to take her to his bed. Assuming Nissa begged. He
wanted to know. Was she quiet or did she moan? Was
she shy or adventurous? He wanted to learn every
inch of her body and discover all the ways he could
pleasure her, then he wanted to do it all again, simply because he could.

And then what? He could imagine taking things
that far, but the next step always eluded him. What
if she fell in love with him? She would want roses
and a happily-ever-after. While he could give her the
former, the latter wasn't possible.

He remembered when he'd been twelve or thirteen. His parents had sat him down for what they'd

billed as "an important conversation." He'd been horrified they were going to talk about sex, but instead they'd explained about his responsibilities to the company. How he was expected to excel at business and build upon what he would inherit.

To that end, he was expected to marry appropriately. A young woman of note, perhaps with a small fortune or another firm worth acquiring. Love was for others, not for him. He could date whomever he wanted, but to take things further was unthinkable. He was to always make the sensible choice, to leave emotions for those who lived smaller lives. He remembered his mother turning to his father and smiling.

"We don't have to worry about Desmond. He doesn't feel things very strongly. He hardly has any friends and no real connections."

She'd said it with such pride. He remembered thinking the reason he didn't have friends was because he was tutored at home. He wanted to be like the other boys he saw through the mansion windows.

Then he'd been sent to boarding school where he'd discovered making friends was harder than he had thought. He'd never fit in, until he'd met Shane. Even though they'd stayed close for the past twenty years, he couldn't help wondering if his mother was right. If there really was something wrong with him. An inability to connect the way everyone else did.

He hadn't wanted that, but no matter how he tried, he couldn't seem to feel the things others did. He might put on a decent show, but the truth was, he was more like his parents than he wanted to admit and in the end, his lack of heart would destroy Nissa. And that was the one thing he refused to do.

So instead of acting on his need, he forced a smile and walked into the room, loudly calling her name. She looked up and smiled at him.

"You're home early," she said.

"I ran out of work."

"I doubt that." She put down her tablet and removed her headphones. "Why don't you go get changed and I'll make tonight's cocktail? I looked online and think I found a good one."

"I look forward to it."

Ten minutes later he was back downstairs. She was in the kitchen, muddling mint in a shaker. As he watched, she poured in simple syrup, rum, lime juice and some kind of puree. After shaking, she added club soda, then poured the drink over ice.

"A pear mojito," she said proudly. "I know it's not your usual thing, but it got great reviews."

"I'm sure I'll like it."

They touched glasses. Nissa pointed to the deck.

"Let's sit outside. The temperature is perfect. Hilde made enchiladas for dinner. We only have to heat them in the oven. There's a delicious salad, too. I'm super excited."

"About Mexican food?"

She grinned. "It's my favorite. I think I was born in Los Angeles in a previous life."

He chuckled as he followed her outside. They sat next to each other on the lounge chairs in the shade. The temperature was in the low eighties and the lake beyond was calm with only a hint of shimmer from the sunlight.

"Tell me about your day," he said, sipping the mojito. It was surprisingly refreshing.

"It was good. I miss the dogs, but delivering flowers doesn't leave me so stinky at the end of my shift. Some of the arrangements are really heavy, which I didn't expect." She flexed an arm. "I'm getting a workout."

"Are they too heavy?"

She raised her eyebrows. "Do not even think about trying to rescue me," she told him. "I'm perfectly capable."

"I know you are, but I want to make sure—"

She held up a hand to silence him. "No. I can do this."

"All right. You delivered heavy flowers. Anything else?"

She laughed. "I'm discovering I don't know the area as well as I thought. There are little streets I've never heard of. But I have GPS on my phone and that makes it easy. Siri loves telling me to make a U-turn because I've gone the wrong way."

"She does have attitude. Do you want to become a florist?"

She looked at him. "Why would you ask that? I love being a teacher."

"I know but when you were working at doggie day care, you wanted to get a dog. I wondered if the trend would continue."

"I might want to plant more flowers in the garden, but I'm going to stick with my current profession." She paused and took a sip of her drink. "What else? Oh, I talked to my friend Marisol today and mentioned the boat thing again. She said she was excited about it. Assuming you're still willing to play host."

"I am. When would you like to go?"

Nissa hesitated. "She hasn't been feeling well for the past couple of weeks, but she's better now. Still weak, but better. How about Thursday? I know it's a weekday, but I have it off and the girls don't have camp that day."

She looked so earnest, he thought, meeting her gaze. Like she was worried about asking for too much. How could she not know that he would give her anything?

"Let me text the captain and see if he's available then," he said, pulling his phone out of his pocket and typing. When he was finished, he looked up. "How old are her daughters? Do you know how much they weigh? We'll want the right size life jackets for them."

She gave him the information and he texted that, as well. Seconds later, Captain Pete wrote back saying he was available and looking forward to it. They settled on a time. When Captain Pete asked about lunch, Desmond suggested the usual picnic fare.

"We're set," he said. "Let's leave at ten and stay out until two or so. Remind everyone to wear sunscreen and bring a hat. We'll have lunch on the boat. The weather is going to be good and the winds will be calm, but if there are any upset tummies, we'll just head back."

She looked at him. "You're very good to me, so I spend all my time thanking you."

"No thanks necessary. I'm looking forward to it." Not just spending time with Nissa, but meeting her friend. He knew a person could learn a lot about someone by how they were with their friends.

NISSA

Nissa tried to relax as she drove to Marisol's house. After several really bad days, Marisol was finally feeling better, but Nissa knew that could change at any second. Happily, when she got to the house, her friend was up and dressed, looking pale but determined.

Lisandra and Rylan practically danced around her, asking questions, one after the other.

"Is it a really big boat?"

"Does it go fast?"

"Mom says the toilet is different—more like an airplane toilet, but we've never been on an airplane, so will we know how to flush?"

"Will we eat lunch on the boat? Can I have a soda?"

Nissa gathered them close and hugged them. "I'm glad you're excited. I am, too. I've never seen the boat, so I can't answer your questions, but we're on our way to the marina right now, so you can see it for yourselves."

Marisol laughed. "They've been like this for two days. I'm amazed they got any sleep last night." She looked at Nissa. "Thank you for arranging this. It's a great distraction for all of us."

"I'm excited, too. Apparently the boat is very fancy."

Marisol raised her eyebrows. "I'm more interested in meeting Desmond. I've been hearing about him for years."

Nissa tried not to flush. "Yes, well, he's a good guy and we're friends."

As Marisol knew about Nissa's ongoing crush, the post-prom debacle and pretty much everything else on the Desmond front, she wasn't likely to buy the whole "friend" thing, but the girls would and that was what mattered.

It didn't take long to collect their tote bags and confirm everyone was protected with sunscreen. They all piled into Nissa's car and she headed for the marina.

She carefully followed the instructions Desmond had given her and was soon entering a code to unlock the big gates that protected the parking lot of the fancy boat section of the marina. There was a big clubhouse, a bar with plenty of outdoor seating and dozens and dozens of boats. Maybe hundreds of them, neatly pulled into slips, bobbing slightly in the water.

She wanted to say there were big boats and small boats, but there weren't. Everywhere she looked were massive seagoing vessels that had to be multiple times bigger than her condo, or Marisol's house.

In the back seat, the girls went quiet and next to her Marisol sucked in a breath.

"He owns one of those?" her friend asked.

"I guess so."

She pulled in next to Desmond's Mercedes, then texted him that they had arrived. He replied that he would be right out. Everyone got out of her car and collected their bags as she saw a gate open and Desmond walk toward her.

She looked at the man multiple times a day—they were living together, so she shouldn't be surprised by his appearance. But there was something about his casual dress—board shorts, a Hawaiian shirt and boat shoes—that made her shiver just a little.

Marisol stepped close. "You didn't say he was so handsome."

"I did."

"You weren't specific enough. The man is hot. How do you resist him?"

Nissa sighed. "If he ever asked the question, I wouldn't, but so far, he's showing amazing self-control."

"Men can be so stupid."

Nissa smiled. "Tell me about it."

When he had joined them, she made introductions. He insisted on carrying their bags as they went inside the gate and onto the ramp that led down to the boats. Marisol went slowly, hanging on.

"Is the walk too much?" Nissa asked anxiously.

"The exercise is good for me."

They passed several boats on their way to the end of the small pier, stopping in front of the one on the end. It was big and sleek, with a dark blue hull. There was a huge covered deck up what felt like three stories, and a bigger open space out back. Large windows allowed them to see a living room and dining area. Smaller windows were darkened so she couldn't see in. Those were probably the bedrooms, she thought, unable to take in how incredibly massive and beautiful the boat was.

"Welcome aboard," Desmond said, waving toward the five stairs that led to the side of the boat. "I'll give you a tour, then we'll get everyone fitted for life jackets and have a quick safety talk before we head out."

Marisol was still hanging on to the pier railing. She looked at the narrow stairs and the gate on the side of the boat, then shook her head.

"I don't think I can do that," she said quietly. "I'm feeling better, but I'm not sure it's possible." She glanced over her shoulder. "Why don't I wait at the clubhouse?"

"Mom," Lisandra and Rylan said together, their voices thick with disappointment. "You have to come. It won't be fun without you."

"I have to agree with them," Desmond said, passing the totes to Nissa and walking over to Marisol. "Do you trust me?"

Marisol's brown eyes widened. "I'm not sure what that means."

"Do you trust me?"

Marisol's expression turned doubtful. "I guess."

Before she could say anything else, Desmond swept her up in his arms. Marisol shrieked and wrapped her arms around his neck.

"What are you doing?"

"I would have thought that was obvious."

He moved to the stairs and took them easily, then stepped over the side of the boat and set Marisol on the deck, before turning to the girls and waving them onboard.

"Come on. We don't want to leave without you."

The girls scrambled after him. Nissa followed, taking the stairs before stepping through the gate and onto the boat.

She immediately felt the movement of the boat—a physical reminder that they were on water. Excitement blended with anticipation as she wondered how great it would be when they were actually moving!

Desmond kept his attention on Marisol. "You doing all right?"

"I am." She studied him. "Now I know what Nissa was talking about."

Nissa didn't know what her friend meant, but decided to go with it. She set their totes on a padded bench as Desmond started the tour.

As she'd seen from the outside, there was a very large living area, a "salon," Desmond called it. The kitchen or galley was much bigger than she would have thought and there were three small bedrooms and two bathrooms onboard.

They returned to the rear deck and were introduced to Captain Pete, a small, wiry man in his fifties.

"Welcome aboard," he said cheerfully. "Who might these young mermaids be?"

Both girls giggled as they introduced themselves.

"Nice to meet you both." Captain Pete leaned close. "So I have some work to do before we can get underway. It would go a lot faster if the two of you would like to help me."

The twins nodded eagerly. Pete led them to the finger pier and started explaining about the lines holding the boat in place. Desmond looked at Marisol.

"I thought we'd spend the day on the upper deck. There's plenty of cover so the girls will be out of the sun. There's a nice breeze and the view can't be beat."

Marisol put her hands on her hips. "You're about to tell me you're going to carry me again, aren't you?"

"I was going to ask rather than tell, but yes."

Marisol glanced at Nissa and mouthed, "He's a keeper," before turning to Desmond. "You're a good man. Thank you."

Desmond carried her upstairs. Nissa followed and found herself on a big, covered deck with plenty of seating, and tables to hold food and drinks. There was a sink, a refrigerator and a stack of towels.

"This is really nice," she said, looking around. "I think I'm in love."

Desmond settled Marisol on one of the bench seats, making sure she had plenty of pillows.

"It's a good boat."

"It's a luxury yacht. How far can it go?" she asked. "Could we sail up to Canada?"

"Probably not today, but she's capable of making the trip."

Nissa thought about what it would be like to spend a few days on the yacht. From what she'd seen, everyone would be really comfortable. Of course the quarters might be a little tight with Captain Pete along. Assuming she and Desmond went as more than friends.

Not that he'd made any moves on her. There had been one brief but mighty kiss and nothing since. A fact that left her confused and wondering if it had simply been a friendly kiss and she'd been wrong to read more into it.

"We have to work on our communication skills," she murmured to herself.

The girls raced up the stairs to the upper deck.

"We saw the engine room and got fitted for our life jackets," Lisandra said.

"The ropes are called lines and the bathroom is called a head," Rylan added. "Captain Pete said once we're underway, we can both steer!"

Captain Pete joined them and made sure the adults knew where their life jackets were, then gave a brief safety lecture. After that, Desmond joined him on the main deck. The powerful engines roared to life and shortly after that, they were off.

The day was perfect—warm and sunny. The girls spent part of their time upstairs with their mom and the rest of it with Captain Pete who was more than patient with their endless questions.

Marisol and Desmond talked as if they'd known each other for years. Nissa listened as her friend expertly extracted information on Desmond's childhood and business. When it was time for lunch, he carried Marisol down to the dining area in the salon.

There were different kinds of sandwiches and salads, cut fruit with dip and potato salad, along with pitchers of lemonade and ice water. Marisol admitted she had an appetite, something that didn't happen much these days.

"It must be the fresh air," Marisol said with a laugh. "I haven't felt this good in a long time."

Rylan put down her sandwich and pulled her hair back in a ponytail. "Look how long it is," she said to Nissa. "Fourteen inches from my fingers." She turned to Desmond. "I need to get to sixteen inches before it can be cut off."

"Me, too," Lisandra added. "My hair's that long, too."

Nissa leaned toward him. "They're growing out their hair so they can donate it. There's an organization called Wigs for Kids. Fourteen inches is good, but sixteen is better."

"That's a big commitment," he told the girls.

"Donations are important," Rylan said. "We want to help."

Nissa wondered if she would say more and confess how Marisol was waiting for a kidney. Nissa still hadn't explained why she was sick—it wasn't her secret to tell—and so far Desmond hadn't asked.

"I know you're doing a good thing," Marisol said, fingering her daughter's hair. "But I'm probably going to cry when they cut it off."

"I'm not," Lisandra said proudly. "I'm going to be brave."

"You already are."

NISSA

After lunch they continued their journey around Lake Washington, then went through the Montlake Cut to Lake Union in the center of Seattle. They dodged paddleboarders and saw a seaplane take off. By two, the girls were sleepy and Marisol looked ready to go back. Captain Pete turned the boat so they were headed for the dock.

Nissa moved next to Desmond on the benches.

"This was wonderful," she said. "We've all had a great time."

"Me, too," he said, gazing into her eyes. "I don't get out on the water enough."

"You should do it more. It's fun."

"That could be the company as much as the boat," he told her.

Which sounded great but made her wonder if there was one person's company he meant in particular, and if so, hopefully that person was her.

Chapter Seven

NISSA

Nissa couldn't remember the last time she'd had such a busy social life. Normally she was a stay-at-home kind of person. Once she'd finished at work, she tended to like going to her condo and settling in for the evening. Oh, there were the occasional drinks out with girlfriends or dinner at Marisol's place, but for the most part, she lived a pretty quiet life.

Lately, though, she was going and doing. Just in the past week there had been Desmond's work party, then a day out on the water, and now she was once again curling her hair and pulling out her new party dress for dinner with Desmond, Shane and his girl-friend.

Maybe she wasn't as much of a homebody as she'd assumed. Maybe her quiet lifestyle was more about a lack of things to do. Something she should consider. Maybe when the summer was over and she moved back into her condo, she should think about expanding her social horizons. Maybe start taking a class or join a volunteer group. She'd been considering getting one of those foreign language apps to brush up on what she would guess was her very rusty college Italian. Instead of that, she could take a class at the community college and be with people.

After she finished applying her makeup, she added "check out Italian classes" to her calendar so she wouldn't forget, and then stepped into her dress.

It was the same one she'd worn to the Chihuly event, but it wasn't as if she had two "nice dinner" dresses. Her social events tended to be more casual. But when Shane had suggested dinner and named a restaurant, she knew that casual wasn't going to cut it.

As she pulled the hot rollers out of her hair, she wondered about the mystery date her brother would be bringing. He hadn't said much about her, beyond that he liked her. As she rarely met anyone he was dating, tonight was going to be fun.

She fluffed her hair, put in the pair of pearl earrings her parents had given her for her twenty-first birthday, then went downstairs.

Even though she was braced, she still had to consciously keep her mouth from falling open when she saw Desmond. The man could wear clothes. Once again he had on dark trousers and a dark shirt. Nothing overly special, yet he looked sexy and strong and more than a little tempting.

He smiled at her. "You look beautiful."

She waved away the compliment. "I know this is the dress I wore last weekend, but I wasn't prepared for all the fancy dinners and parties. My teacher's wardrobe isn't up to your level."

"You always look perfect."

She raised her eyebrows. "Perfect? Really? Don't you think that's pushing it just a little?"

"Not at all."

She sighed. "You are a great date. Do you know that, because you are." She shifted her wrap to her other arm. "I can't wait to meet Shane's girlfriend. He's been going out with her at least five weeks. Mom and I don't have the original start date of their relationship, so we can't be sure. Even if it's just five weeks, that's like a personal best for him. She's given me a list of questions to ask. I hope I can remember them all."

Desmond shook his head. "Does it occur to you

that conversations like this are one of the reasons your brother keeps his private life to himself?"

She grinned. "Of course, but who cares about him being uncomfortable? We need information!"

"You'll have a whole dinner to ask your questions."

"Oh, because you don't want to know anything? You have to be just as curious as I am."

Desmond glanced away, as if hiding something from her.

"What?" she demanded. "You know something. What is it? Tell me!"

He returned his attention to her. "Shane is my friend and anything he and I have discussed will stay between the two of us."

"That's so unfair. Not even a hint? Tell me something. You have to!"

He took her hand in his, brought it to his mouth and lightly kissed her knuckles. "As I said before, you look beautiful and I'm looking forward to spending the evening with you."

While she appreciated the compliment and the feel of his mouth on her skin, she knew he was trying to distract her from her interest in her brother's personal life.

"You're very loyal," she grumbled, snatching back her hand. "It's disappointing."

"I would be just as loyal to you."

An interesting concept, she thought. She suspected he was telling the truth. From what she'd observed, Desmond would be an excellent boyfriend. Attentive, kind, funny, charming.

"Rosemary was never good enough for you," she told him. "You should have listened to me."

"Yes, I should have. Shall we go?"

They drove to the restaurant where he handed off his car to the valet. Nissa looked around at the waterfront setting. Despite the fact that they were meeting at seven, it was plenty light. Sunset in this part of the country was still after eight thirty.

As they walked toward the entrance, Desmond put his hand on the small of her back. She instinctively moved closer to him, trying not to get too caught up in the heat from his touch. He was being polite, nothing more.

Once inside, he gave Shane's name and they were immediately shown back to a table by the water. Her brother was already there, and next to him was a petite, dark-haired woman. She was pretty, with an air of quiet elegance Nissa immediately liked.

They both came to their feet when she and Desmond approached the table. Shane engulfed her in a big bear hug before kissing her cheek.

"Hey, munchkin."

"Hey, yourself." She gazed into his eyes. "You good?"

His smile was happy. "I am." He turned. "Nissa, this is Coreen. Coreen, my baby sister, Nissa."

They shook hands, then Shane introduced Desmond. The four of them took seats across from each other. Nissa told herself not to stare but it was hard not to be interested in her brother's date. She couldn't remember the last one he'd introduced to anyone in the family. There had been Becky back in high school, but they'd known her for years before she and Shane had started going out.

"It's wonderful to finally meet you," Coreen told Nissa. "I've heard so much about you."

Nissa glanced suspiciously at her brother. "Is that good or bad?"

He grinned. "I only told her the good stuff. It didn't take long."

"Ha!" She pointedly turned away from him and looked at Coreen. "Shane said you're a doctor?"

"I am." Coreen smiled. "I'm an emergency room pediatrician at the hospital."

Nissa smiled at her brother. "Like I said before, Mom will be so proud."

"That's the least of it. I know she's going to grill you later."

"She won't have to grill me. I'm giving up everything I know for free." She smiled at Coreen. "Shane has been pretty quiet about you, so we're all curious. I'm here representing the entire family, but don't worry. We're a friendly bunch."

"That's what I've heard. Shane told me you're a teacher. That's a wonderful profession. You must have a lot of patience."

"So speaks the pediatrician."

"I like kids."

"Me, too."

Shane leaned toward Desmond. "They don't need us here for the conversation."

"Apparently not."

Nissa ignored them both. "I usually get a summer job but this year, for an assortment of reasons, I've been doing temp work. It's been interesting. I spent a couple of weeks at a doggie day care. That was fun, but made me want to have a dog. Then I delivered flowers for a few days. Now I'm working for some big international company that is doing a very large mailing. They've brought in people to stuff envelopes and apply postage. I keep reminding my boss about the existence of email, but so far she's not listening."

Their server appeared and they all ordered drinks, then discussed the menu. Coreen was pleasant and obviously crazy about Shane, which made Nissa like her more.

Coreen talked about how long she'd been at the hospital and how she'd moved up from Los Angeles where she'd done her residency at the UCLA Medical Center.

Nissa listened attentively, enjoying the information and how approachable Coreen seemed, only to be distracted by Desmond and Shane having some kind of silent communication. It wasn't anything overt—more subtle eye contact and a quick head shake on Desmond's part, as if he didn't want to do whatever Shane expected.

"I've only ever lived in the Pacific Northwest," Nissa admitted. "Born and raised. Our dad was a ferryboat captain for years. In the summer we would tag along on his trips." She looked at Desmond. "So his boat is way bigger than yours."

"Thank you for putting me in my place."

The server appeared with their drinks. Shane raised his glass.

"To finally getting together," he said.

"And meeting Coreen," Nissa added.

"Desmond and I met at boarding school," Shane said. "I was there on scholarship, but he got in the old-fashioned way. His parents paid the bill."

Nissa looked at her brother, trying to figure out why he would say such an odd thing.

"I was nervous about having him as my roommate," Shane continued. "But we got along right away. I used to drag him home with me every holiday so he didn't have to rattle around alone in his massive estate."

"I came willingly," Desmond said mildly enough, but there was something in his tone.

Nissa couldn't place it. Not annoyance or even resignation. Concern, maybe? Exasperation?

"We liked having him around," Nissa said, still confused about what was happening between the two men. "I had a huge crush on him when I was a teenager."

"I didn't notice," Desmond murmured.

Nissa laughed. "You knew about it, but of course you didn't do anything about it. Such a gentleman."

"How long have you two been going out?" Coreen asked.

"They're not dating," Shane said, his voice a little loud. "You thought they were together?" He laughed. "They're just friends. Have been for years. The crush thing is long over."

Okay, this was too strange, Nissa thought, unsure of what to do or say. She glanced at Desmond, but he was too busy watching Shane to notice her.

Not sure if she should say something or ask to speak to her brother alone, she decided to try changing the subject.

"Anyone know what's good here?" she asked, picking up her menu. "I would guess the seafood is delicious."

They each studied their menus. The server came by and told them about the specials, then took their orders. Conversation took a more conventional turn and Nissa started to relax enough to enjoy herself. But between the salads and the entrees, Shane surprised her by asking to speak with her outside.

"Family business," he said to Coreen and Desmond. "We won't be long."

Family business? What family business? Nissa followed him out onto the deck and turned on him.

"What has gotten into you? You're acting strange, even for you, and it's freaking me out. If you're this weird on your dates, it's no wonder you've never gotten married."

Instead of laughing at her or getting annoyed, Shane surprised her by apologizing.

"I should have warned you," he said. "About what was happening."

"I have no idea what you're talking about. You'd better tell me or I'm calling Mom."

Shane grinned. "That's your best threat? You'll call Mom?"

"You don't think she and Dad will get in the car and drive over the mountains to check on you?"

His humor faded. "Oh, right. They will. Okay, so none of this is about you. I'm testing Coreen."

"Testing her how? And why?"

He shuffled his feet, as if buying time. "Look, I like her."

"Yes, I can see that. For what it's worth, I like her, too. In a totally different way," Nissa added. "So what does that have to do with anything?"

He looked at her. "I don't like women."

Nissa laughed. "Since when?"

He groaned. "I mean, I don't get involved. I don't do serious. But with Coreen, I'm tempted to take things further and I want to make sure she's interested in the right things."

She poked him in the chest. "You're not making any sense."

"Desmond is a rich, good-looking guy. Coreen knows who he is and that he's single. Will she hit on him while we're gone? That's what he's going to let me know."

She felt her mouth drop open and had to consciously close it. "You're setting a trap for your date?"

"It's not a trap if nothing happens."

"And Desmond agreed?"

"He wasn't happy. He told me I was a jerk for doing this to her, but he said he would help me out."

Nissa had no idea what to say to that.

"But I like Coreen," she complained. "I don't want to find out she's icky and I don't want you to lose her because you're a moron."

"Better I find out now than in a year."

"Or you could just talk to her and ask the question."

"If she's who I hope she is, the question will break her heart. If she's not, she won't tell me the truth." He glanced at his watch. "They've had enough time. We can go back in."

"And say what? If she asks what we've been talking about, what should I say?"

"Tell her we were discussing Mom's birthday present."

"I'm not a good liar."

He put his arm around her. "One of your best qualities, Sis."

DESMOND

"You're quiet," Desmond said, thinking that it was better to simply state the obvious than to try to talk around it. "Are you angry?"

"About what Shane did to Coreen?" She looked at him. "No, but I am confused about why he felt he had to test her that way. I asked him why he didn't just ask what was going on with her and he pointed out that someone who would go after you wouldn't be honest with him, which I guess is right... But the whole situation makes me sad. Why isn't my brother more trusting of women?"

"You'll have to ask him that."

"Oh, like he'll tell me anything." She sighed. "Someone, somewhere really broke his heart."

"Yes."

She understood that was a big admission for him. As for the details, she would work on getting them from Shane.

"You weren't happy playing along," she said. "He told me you thought he was being a jerk."

"I was just hoping he was wrong to worry about Coreen. I don't want to have to tell my best friend that the woman he's dating just tried to pick me up."

"Is that an ongoing problem?"

He thought of the women who had been thrilled to be alone with him, regardless of who they were with. How they'd moved closer, running their hands along his arm or his thigh, offering their number and anything else he might want. They knew he was rich and for some people, money mattered more than anything.

"Sometimes. Not with your brother's dates."

"But Coreen was good, wasn't she? Tell me she didn't do anything, because I really like her."

"She wasn't the least bit interested in me. She talked about how great Shane is and how much she had wanted to meet you. I think she's the real deal."

"That makes me happy."

He smiled. "I thought it might."

"I'm just surprised. I just thought Shane had it all together, but he doesn't. Sure, he's a gifted surgeon and he has a great house and stuff, but inside, he's just as broken as everyone else."

She looked at him. "I know you didn't want to help him, but you did anyway. You're a good friend."

"I'd do anything for him."

"I know. You love each other." She smiled. "In a very manly, friendship kind of way."

Some of his tension faded. "We do."

He pulled into the garage and they both got out. When they walked into the kitchen, Nissa came to a stop and faced him.

"Do you miss Rosemary?" she asked.

Her eyes were the most perfect shade of blue, he thought, meeting her gaze. Clear and deep, with long lashes.

"No."

She smiled. "You don't want to elaborate?"

"She married me for my money and when I told her the marriage was over, she walked away. There wasn't much to miss."

"I told you not to marry her."

"Yes, you did, and next time you give me that kind of advice, I'm going to listen."

"Do you think it's going to work out with Coreen and Shane?"

"I hope so. She seems crazy about him. Any other questions?"

Like did she want him to come upstairs with her and make love all night? Because if she did, he was more than willing.

But instead of asking that, or teasing him or mentioning a snack, she simply said, "I'm tired and I'm going to bed. Good night, Desmond."

And with that, she was gone, leaving him alone with the sense of having blown something important. Not that he could, in any way, say what it was.

NISSA

Nissa kept to herself for the next few days. The dinner with her brother had unsettled her—no, not the dinner. The testing of a perfectly nice woman because Shane didn't want to trust her.

His need to do that surprised her, and made her wonder what else she didn't know about him and about Desmond. She felt foolish—like the country mouse seeing the big city for the first time, and it wasn't a happy view. She felt sad that Shane felt the need to go so far to protect himself, which meant something really bad had happened to him and she had no idea what.

The evening had also opened her eyes about what

Desmond's dating life must be like. How could he know if someone was in it for him or for the money?

Monday after work she drove back to his big house, determined to shake off her mood. If Shane wanted her to know the details of his personal life, he would have told her, so she was going to have to let that one go. As for Desmond, she could only be herself around him and draw comfort from the fact that he knew she liked him for him. The rest of it was just a part of who he was, but not important to her.

After showering and changing her clothes, she went downstairs and talked with Hilde about the progress being made on the decisions for the remodel. Construction was due to start in mid-September and would take about four weeks. She would be long gone by then, but promised to come back and view the finished kitchen.

She checked her email and social media, texted with Marisol, all the while listening for Desmond's car. When she finally heard him pull into the garage, she got up and walked through the kitchen to wait for him.

He stepped into the house and saw her. His immediate warm, welcoming smile made her feel all tingly down to her toes.

"I'm ready to talk," she told him. "Because I know you've been missing my sparkling conversation."

"I have. Let me put my things away and I'll join you in the family room."

She went to wait for him. He returned in about ten minutes. He'd changed out of his suit and looked casual and relaxed in jeans and a T-shirt.

"The young executive at home," she teased. "It's a good look."

"Thanks." He crossed to the bar and started pulling out ingredients. "Why are we speaking again? I ask the question out of curiosity and not to annoy you. I missed having you to talk to."

"I needed to work things out," she admitted. "The money thing is so strange to me. Although in Shane's case, it's not about money. I suppose that's what upset me as much as anything. Someone damaged him and I don't know who it was or when it happened."

"He was gone a lot," Desmond reminded her. "He went off to boarding school when he was thirteen, and then to college."

"Meaning there are many parts of my brother's life I don't know about?" She nodded. "I figured that part out. I was just surprised by all of it. And sad for both of you. It must be hard to be so afraid to trust someone you want to care about. I don't think I could do that." She smiled. "I do tend to just put it all out there."

"That's part of your charm."

"It's a different view of the world."

He held out a lemon drop for her and picked up his scotch.

"Don't stop trusting people," he said. "I've always admired how you embrace the world, flaws and all."

They took their usual seats on the facing sofas.

"You make me sound foolish."

"No." He looked at her, his gaze intense. "I said I admire you, Nissa, and I mean that."

He did? "You do?"

"Yes. You have the purest heart of anyone I know. I only want good things for you."

There was something in the way he spoke the words, as if there was a secret message in them. One she couldn't decipher.

He smiled. "I want you to marry for love."

"Why else would I get married? Giving someone your heart, accepting theirs in return, that's the point of marriage. Knowing that for the rest of your life, this is the one person you can count on to care about you, no matter what."

His dark gaze was steady. "Did you have that with James?"

"No, and that's why I didn't marry him. Something was missing. It took me a few months to figure that out, though. He kept pressing me to set a wedding date and I kept resisting. Then one day I knew what was wrong. I didn't love him enough to want to marry him."

"I'm sorry you had to go through that."

"Me, too. It was hard on both of us." She thought about how angry James had been when she'd ended things, but the fury had quickly turned to hurt. He'd told her he would love her forever. She hoped that wasn't true.

"Do you ever hear from him?" Desmond asked.

"No. I gave him back his ring and that was the end." She looked at him. "Do you hear from Rosemary?"

"No." He smiled. "Let us remember, she wasn't in the marriage for me. Once she realized she wasn't getting any money, she was ready to move on."

"That makes me sad."

"Why? Marrying her was a mistake, but a recoverable one."

"Yes, but she reinforced all your ideas about women only being after you for money. That's not right and it's not true. Not everyone is like that."

He surprised her by smiling. "That's true. Some of them are after me for the sex."

Despite the emotions churning inside of her, she laughed. "You are such a guy."

"Women like sex, too."

"They do," she admitted, thinking that she found him very sexy and that she'd enjoyed every fantasy she'd ever had about him. Based on what she knew about him as a man, it wasn't a giant leap to think about how he would be as a lover. He liked to see a job through—an excellent quality for a sexual partner. Not that they were going there.

"Life is complicated," she said, picking up her drink.

"It can be."

"I remind myself that a year from now, I'll be in Italy. That helps."

She caught a slight tightening around his mouth.

"What?" she demanded. "You were thinking something."

"I wish you didn't have to work at a job you don't like to pay for it."

She stared at him. "What are you talking about?"

"You hate stuffing envelopes."

"Of course I do. It's not the sort of thing anyone likes, but it's no big deal and totally worth it."

"If you'd just let me give you the money," he began.

She set down her glass and glared at him. "Stop, Desmond. We've talked about this. No and no. This is *my* trip and I'm happy earning the money. This is my dream and I want to make it happen. I want the satisfaction of having earned it. Why can't you understand that?"

"I do understand that you're being stubborn. We're friends. I care about you. Why won't you let me do this for you? Then you could take off the rest of the summer and enjoy yourself."

"Life doesn't work that way."

"Sometimes it does. Sometimes good things happen. If you let them. It makes me feel good to help you. Why is that bad? Why can't you accept that? Why do you always have to be so stubborn about everything?"

"What?" she said, her voice rising slightly. She wasn't mad—not yet—but she was on the road. "You're the one who totally expects to get his way. Why does it annoy you that I want to do the work? Most people have to."

"I agree and I wish I could change that, but I can't. However, I can give you a trip to Europe." He leaned toward her. "You're being ridiculous. If we were married, you'd have no trouble letting me pay for the trip or anything else. Why is this different?"

The absurdity of the statement propelled her to her feet. "You didn't just ask that. If we were married, we would have agreed to spend the rest of our lives together. It's totally different from being friends." She put her hands on her hips. "Not that it matters because we're never going to *be* married, or anything other than what we are, mostly because you're never going to ask me out. Heaven knows we're certainly never sleeping together. What if my brother disapproves? What if he tells you not to? So don't talk to me about—"

The reality of what she'd just said sank in slowly, but when it was fully absorbed, she stopped talking midsentence.

No, she thought in horror. *No. No. No.* She hadn't just said that. About them being married or more than they were or the sex thing. She couldn't have because if she had, Desmond would assume some or all of it was what she wanted. He would think she'd been hoping for more all this time, and then he would, well, she didn't know what, but it would be bad.

His dark gaze locked with hers. She saw questions in his eyes and tension in his body. She didn't know which was worse—the comment about marriage or the hint about sex. Were they equally bad or should she rank them somehow?

The silence between them lengthened. Nissa wasn't sure what to do. Running away seemed the most logical next step, but to where? Her room upstairs? Once she closed the door behind her, she was going to have to stay there forever, slowly starving to death. Once she was dead, she wouldn't care about facing him.

"Did you want me to ask you out?" he asked, coming to his feet.

She held in a high-pitched keening sound she

could feel building up inside of her chest. "Um, back in high school? After prom? Yes, I did. I called you and you never called me back."

"I meant now."

Crap. Double crap. Did he really expect her to answer that? To bluntly say what she thought of him and hoped would happen? Not that she'd ever put her hopes into words, but she was fairly clear on the fact that she—

"Nissa?"

She cleared her throat, careful to keep her gaze fixed on a point just over his shoulder. "You're very attractive and we have fun together. Going out would be, you know. Nice."

"So you like me."

She groaned as she returned her gaze to his. "Of course I like you. We've been friends for years. Why are you doing this? Why all the questions? Why don't you tell me how *you* feel? I get why you didn't ask me out back in high school. Shane was right. I was too young for you. But it hasn't been that way for a while and it seems to me if you were the least bit interested, you would have done something, so I don't get why you feel the need to drag all this information out of me when you have no intention of—"

He circled the coffee table and reached for her. One second she was feeling confused and embarrassed and the next she was in his arms and his mouth was on hers and she was remembering how glorious his kisses had been so many years ago and discovering they were just as delicious now.

Chapter Eight

NISSA

Desmond gave as much as he took, kissing Nissa
with a need that fed her own desire. No matter how
tightly he held her, she wanted to be closer. His hands
stroked up and down her back, then dropped lower
to cup her rear. She instinctively arched toward him
and was both surprised and happy to feel the hard
ridge of his erection against her stomach.

She pulled back and stared at him. "You want me!"

One corner of his mouth turned up. "Why are you
surprised?"

"You're always so controlled. I believed you about

just being friends and you were lying the whole time."

"I wasn't lying. I was doing the right thing."

"And now?"

"You seem willing to go in another direction."

This conversation had more twists and turns than a round of Candyland, she thought. "So you want to sleep with me."

"That's more blunt than I would have put it, but yes. I would very much like to take you to my bed and make love with you."

The words sent heat pouring through every part of her. A faint tingling began to radiate out from her midsection. She felt her breasts getting heavy and a telltale ache settling low in her belly.

"That's very clear," she said quietly.

"Nothing has to happen," he told her. "I mean that. You're too important to me to want this relationship messed up. We can go back to what we've always been. I won't ever push you."

She believed him. Not only did she know his character, Desmond had never lied to her.

She thought about how much she liked him and how good they were together in every other way, then she put her hands on his chest.

"I'm on the pill but I don't have condoms with me. I'm hoping you do."

His eyes dilated. "Upstairs."

She smiled. "I've never seen your bedroom."

"Would you like to?"

"Very much."

They stared at each other for another two heart-beats, then he took her hand and led her toward the stairs. They went up faster and faster, until they were racing to the top.

Laughing together, they ran down the hall and into his bedroom. Nissa had a brief impression of high ceilings, a large fireplace and a view of the Sound before she saw the massive bed against the far wall. Then Desmond was kissing her and noth-ing else mattered.

While his lips claimed hers, his hands were ev-erywhere. She understood his desire to touch all of her because she felt the same way about him. She stroked his back, his shoulders and his chest. He tried to pull off her T-shirt while she attempted to work the buttons on his shirt.

They bumped hands and arms and nothing was accomplished. Finally they stepped away from each other and quickly stripped off their clothes. Then they were holding each other, skin against skin. He retreated again, just long enough to fling back the covers from the bed, before lowering her down and joining her.

He explored every inch of her, with his hands and his tongue, teasing her into an arousal that had her panting as she strained toward her release. Kissing her deeply, his skilled fingers between her legs, he eased her over the edge, then drew out her orgasm until she was boneless.

Only then did he enter her, his dark eyes locked with hers. He filled her over and over again, exciting her until she had no choice but to soar a second time, with him only seconds behind.

NISSA

Satisfaction and happiness battled for dominance. Nissa, still naked and wrapped in Desmond's arms, her head on his shoulder, was willing to let them decide on the winner. She would be content with either or both emotions. Her breathing had returned to normal and her mind was starting to clear, but none of that changed the fact that she and Desmond had just made love.

She shifted so she could look at him. When his gaze met hers, he gave her a slow, sexy, "I'm the man" kind of look that told her he had zero regrets.

"That was nice," she murmured, her tone teasing.

"Very pleasant," he agreed.

They smiled at each other. He propped himself up on one elbow and stroked her bare shoulder.

"You're really all right?" he asked.

"Very."

"Good."

He moved his finger from her shoulder to her breast. Sparks immediately began to light inside of her. They got more intense when he reached her nipple and lightly stroked the tight peak.

"So next time, I was thinking you could be on top," he said, looking at her. "If that's all right."

"I can do that." Straddling him, arching into his thrusts. Yup, she was a firm yes.

He used his thumb and forefinger to gently pinch her nipple, before leaning close and taking it in his mouth and sucking. Pleasure shot through her, making a bee line for her core.

"That's really good," she breathed, her eyes sinking closed.

He got to his knees and shifted to her other breast, drawing it in and—

Somewhere in the distance she heard a high-pitched ringtone. At first she didn't recognize the insistent clanging noise, but then the meaning of it sank in and she pushed him away before scrambling out of his bed and diving for her shorts.

It took her two tries to answer, then she gasped. "It's happening?"

On the other end of the call, Marisol's voice was thick with tears. "They just called. They found a donor. Everything checks out and I'm scheduled for surgery tonight."

"I'm on my way." Nissa felt her throat tighten as she fought tears of her own. "I'm so happy for you. Tell the girls to hang tight. I know they're scared, but I'll be there for them and for you. Don't you worry."

"Thank you. I love you so much."

"I love you, too."

She hung up the phone and reached for the rest of her clothes. Desmond had gotten out of bed and crossed to her. She gave herself a second to admire his strong body before pulling on panties and picking up her bra.

"What's going on? Who was that?"

Because he didn't know. She'd told him Marisol was sick, but not the particulars.

She fastened her bra and pulled on her shorts. "Marisol has terminal kidney disease. We've been waiting for a donor kidney so she can have a transplant. One just came through." She pulled on her T-shirt. "I'm sorry the timing isn't the greatest, but I have to go be with the girls. Marisol is having surgery tonight so they need me. I hope you understand."

DESMOND

Desmond had no idea what Nissa was talking about. He'd known Marisol was ill, but it had been obvious that Nissa hadn't wanted to go into detail, so he'd never asked. A kidney transplant? Wasn't that a dangerous surgery? Of course if her disease was terminal, then not having the procedure wasn't an option.

All those thoughts were pushed aside when he realized Nissa was going to be leaving. He quickly pulled on his own clothes and followed her down the hall to her room. She darted into her closet and pulled out a small suitcase.

"My to-go bag," she said with a shrug. "Because I'll need to stay with the girls."

"I'll go with you."

She was already starting for the stairs. "You don't have to. I know this is sudden, but I have to get to her house and drive her to the hospital. I'll call. I promise."

He was on her heels. "I know you will, but that's not the point. You're dealing with a lot. I'll drive. My car will be more comfortable for Marisol and the girls. We can recline the front seat for her."

They'd reached the main floor. Nissa hesitated only a second before nodding.

"Thank you for the offer. I'll admit, my head is spinning."

They got into his car and he backed out of the garage. Once they were on the street, she gave him Marisol's address and told him the quickest way to get there.

"Tell me about Marisol's disease," he said quietly. "There's no other treatment?"

"No. Her doctors tried everything before deciding a transplant was her only hope of survival. Until then, she's kept alive by dialysis. I volunteered to be a living donor, but while our blood types would work—I'm considered a universal donor—we didn't pass the cross-matching test. Basically she has antibodies against my cells. You can only donate to other A or AB positive people."

"That's why you asked my blood type."

"I ask everyone," she said. "Just in case. I wanted to talk to her about doing a paired exchange. That's when you have a donor who is willing, but can't give to you. So you find someone else in the same position, but who can give to you. So far we haven't found anyone."

"You would have given her a kidney?"

A stupid question. It was obvious she would. Nissa loved her friend and she was simply that kind of person.

"Of course. She needs to live. She's got the twins and they've already lost their dad." Tears filled her eyes. She shook her head and inhaled. "I'm not crying. I'm not going to cry. I have to be strong for the girls."

"You'll be taking care of them," he said, starting

to understand what was happening. "You're going to what? Move into their house?"

"Yes." She turned to him. "I'm sorry, Desmond. I wanted to tell you all this before, but Marisol didn't want people to know. Things got weird when some of her friends realized she might die. Plus, she's protective of the girls."

"Are you their guardian?"

"If something happens to Marisol?" She nodded. "Yes. If she dies, I'll step in and raise them."

She spoke so calmly, he thought. As if she was simply going to water houseplants for a few weeks. But it wasn't that.

"What about your trip to Italy?"

He realized it was a ridiculous question as soon as he asked it, but couldn't call it back.

She smiled. "Marisol is going to be fine. That's what I believe. But if she's not, I guess I'll save a little longer and the three of us will go together in a few years. It's not like my dream trip is going away. Italy will still be there."

She was willing to turn her life upside down, he thought, stunned by her acceptance of such massive responsibility. He didn't know anyone else who would be willing to take on two children the way she was.

"Rylan and Lisandra must be terrified," he said.

"This is a lot for anyone to deal with but they're only ten."

"They've been very brave, but it is a burden. They don't like seeing their mom sick and I know they're scared about the possibility of losing her. They've both been in counseling, which helped." She shook her head. "I wish I could take her disease from her. I don't have the responsibilities she does. It would be easier for me."

His gut clenched at the thought of her facing death or transplant surgery, but he didn't say anything. Instead he focused on getting to Marisol's house as quickly and safely as he could.

When they arrived, Marisol was sitting on the sofa. She looked more pale than she had, but there was hope in her eyes. Her daughters were on either side of her, clinging to her. They had both been crying.

Nissa rushed over and knelt in front of the three of them, holding out her arms. "We're going to get through this," she said firmly, hugging them. "We're going to be strong and pray and come out the other side."

"You're a blessing," Marisol said.

Desmond felt out of place, and moved toward the small dining room to give them more privacy. He still couldn't completely absorb what was happening. Marisol was facing a terrifying procedure and there was nothing he could do to help. For once, his ability to write a check was meaningless. Not a feeling he enjoyed.

He circled the small table, part of him listening to the low rumble of voices in the other room, and part of him noting the battered table and rickety chairs. He moved into the kitchen and saw it was a decent size, but the cabinets needed replacing and the appliances were practically antiques.

"Desmond?" Nissa called.

He hurried back to the living room.

"We need to go," she said, standing.

The girls each picked up a tote bag, then Marisol struggled to get to her feet.

He immediately moved close and helped her up. "I can carry you to the car."

Marisol gave him a smile. "While that's the most action I've seen in years, how about you just help me walk there?"

"Whatever you want."

When they arrived at the hospital, someone was waiting with a wheelchair. Marisol had already pre-registered so only had to sign a few forms before they took her upstairs. Nissa and the girls led the way to where they would wait out the surgery.

The waiting area was filled with comfortable sofas, a table and chairs and lots of books and board games. Nissa had brought blankets and pillows for when the twins were ready to try to sleep.

"They'll get to see Marisol before she goes into surgery," she said. "Just for a few minutes."

To say goodbye, he thought grimly. In case something went wrong. Because if Marisol died, Nissa would suddenly be both mother and father to two ten-year-old girls.

How had he not known that? Why hadn't she been talking about it, worrying and making plans? But she hadn't. She'd simply agreed to a life-changing possibility. Who did that?

A few minutes later, a nurse came and got them. Desmond stayed behind, wishing there was something he could do to help. The surgery was beyond him and Marisol already had a donor, but maybe something with the girls.

When the three of them returned, Rylan and Lisandra were both crying. Instinctively, he held out his arms and they surprised him by rushing to him and throwing themselves against him. He hung on tight.

"I know you're scared," he said. "But we need to think positive thoughts. Why don't we pray together, then decide what we want to do next? It's going to be a few hours until we hear anything."

"We're supposed to get an update every two

hours," Lisandra told him. "That's what the doctor said."

"Good to know."

Nissa sat next to him and the girls knelt on the carpet. They all joined hands and prayed for Marisol's safe recovery, then asked for blessings for the family of the person who had passed away, thereby donating the kidney for the transplant.

When they were done, Desmond watched while tears filled the girls' eyes and knew they were seconds from a very understandable meltdown. What they needed was a distraction.

"Is the plan for you to go live in Marisol's house?" he asked Nissa.

She nodded, looking a little shattered herself. "Yes."

"I have a suggestion. Why don't the twins come stay at my place while their mom is in the hospital?"

Both girls stared at him.

He smiled at them. "I have a very big house that might be fun for the two of you. You could each have your own room, but with a bathroom in between, so you're close."

Nissa brightened. "He's right. It's called a Jack and Jill bathroom. I'm not sure why. But it's very cool. Oh, and Desmond has a pool. And the house is right on the Sound."

The twins looked at each other, then at her. "You'll be there?" Rylan asked, her lower lip quivering.

"Of course. I've been staying there while my condo is rented out. It's very nice there. Hilde, the housekeeper, would love to spoil you both. She's a fabulous cook and she makes cookies and brownies."

He was glad Nissa was onboard with the idea. Everything had happened so quickly. Two hours ago, they'd been in his bed and now they were at the hospital, dealing with Marisol's surgery and her children.

The twins looked at each other and slowly nodded.

"That sounds nice," Lisandra said, wiping away tears. "But not until we know about Mom."

"Of course not," Desmond said quickly. "We're going to stay right here and wait to hear the good news."

Nissa shot him a grateful look, before pulling tablets out of the tote bags. "Okay, let's get comfortable and find something to entertain ourselves."

Time passed slowly. Two hours in, a nurse came and said the surgery was going as well as could be expected. Eventually the girls fell asleep on one of the sofas. Nissa rescued their tablets before they slid off onto the floor, then pulled him into a far corner of the room.

"Are you sure about all of us staying with you?"

she asked, searching his face as she spoke. "It's going to be a lot to take on."

He gave her a gentle smile. "Have you seen my house? There's plenty of room. Hilde will love it, and I think being somewhere else will be a distraction for the girls when they need one."

He waved his phone. "I've been doing some research on kidney transplants. After Marisol is out of the hospital, she's going to need to take it easy for a couple more weeks."

Nissa bit her lower lip. "She's going into a skilled nursing facility until she can come home."

"Or she could move into the house. There's a guest room downstairs and we can get a nurse in."

Her eyes widened. "Desmond, you can't do all that."

"Why not? I like Marisol and her kids. They've been through enough. You know the money doesn't matter to me." He chuckled. "I do like to write a check to solve problems."

"Don't say that. You're being so nice." She blinked several times as if holding back tears. "Having her come to your house would be wonderful, but it's a lot to take on."

He waved away the comment. "We'll have a nurse in to help. It will be easy. And she'll feel better knowing her daughters are right upstairs."

What he didn't say was that part of his motivation

was that he didn't want Nissa to move out. Not now. After last night, things were different between them. He wasn't sure what was happening, but he liked it. He wanted to keep her close for as long as possible.

"I'll talk to her in a few days, when she's feeling better," Nissa told him. "I'm sure she'll agree, but I can't say yes for her."

"Understood."

She shifted her weight. "About what happened earlier."

"You mean getting the call from Marisol?" he asked, pretending he didn't know what she was talking about.

"No, before-before. Us."

"Oh, that. Regrets?"

"No! Of course not." She blushed. "It was wonderful."

"Good. Me, too."

Her gaze locked with his. "I want to be with you again, but with the girls around, I can't. At least not at first. Because they're going to need me."

"I know. I thought that for the first couple of nights, they'd share a bed and you could sleep in the other room, so they could easily get to you if they need you."

"That's a great idea. I'll do that. Should I go back to the house and get the rooms ready?"

"I've already texted Hilde. She's taking care of it right now."

"You've thought of everything."

"I hope so." He drew her close and wrapped his arms around her. "We're going to get through this. Whatever happens, the girls have you and you have me."

"Thank you for understanding how important this is to me."

"Anytime."

He kissed the top of her head and released her. She returned to the sofa closest to where the girls slept. He would guess she was going to watch over them all night, if necessary. And he would watch over her.

NISSA

Marisol's surgery took four hours. The surgeon was pleased with the outcome and told them there hadn't been any complications. Now the real waiting game began. They had to get through the first twenty-four hours, then the second, and so on. With each passing day, she would get stronger.

The girls cried when they heard the news and fought leaving the hospital. Nissa knew they had been through so much—they had to be exhausted. She convinced them to get a little sleep at Desmond's house before they returned in the early afternoon.

They wouldn't be able to see their mom until after lunch sometime.

Despite the late hour, Hilde was there to greet them when they arrived at the house. She showed the girls their room and the adjoining bathroom. Nissa took Desmond's advice and suggested they share a bed, with her right next door. The twins were relieved by that idea and quickly got ready for bed.

Nissa stayed with them until they were asleep, then went into her own room where she found Desmond reading in the chair in the corner. He put down his book as she entered, then crossed to her and pulled her close.

As he held her tight, all her emotions seemed to crash in on her at once and she started to cry. Tears quickly changed to sobs that shook her body and made it impossible to get control. But he seemed unfazed, continuing to stroke her back and murmur quietly that she would be fine.

After several minutes, she managed to calm down enough to catch her breath and slow the flow of tears.

"I don't know what that was," she admitted. "I think I scared myself."

He smiled at her as he wiped her cheeks. "You've been dealing with a lot. It's good to get it out." He leaned in and lightly kissed her mouth. "I finally got Hilde to go home. She'll be back first thing to make breakfast. She can't decide between pancakes and waffles, so be prepared to have all the food on your plate."

Nissa managed a shaky smile. "She's been so wonderful."

"Having kids in the house is her dream. She's thrilled to have people to take care of."

He kissed her again, lingering just long enough to make her aware of the fact that about eight hours ago, she'd been naked in his bed. A situation she'd like to repeat—just not tonight.

As if reading her mind, he said, "Go to bed. You're exhausted. I'm right down the hall if you need me."

She looked into his dark eyes. "Thank you for everything. You've been amazing."

"I was happy to help."

With that, he walked out of the room.

She watched him go. She'd always known that Desmond was a great guy, but she hadn't known how dependable he was in a crisis. He'd calmly taken charge of the situation and had made everyone feel safe.

Funny how everything she learned about him only made her like him more and wonder what would have happened if he hadn't listened to her brother, all those years ago.

Chapter Nine

DESMOND

Desmond didn't get a lot of sleep that first night. He'd called to check on Marisol every hour. Her condition was unchanged, but the ICU nurse had said she was resting comfortably and her vitals were good. Now it was just a waiting game.

He got up early and showered, then headed downstairs. Hopefully the girls would sleep late. Getting some rest would make the stress easier to deal with. He'd told Hilde not to come until after eight, but of course his housekeeper was already at work in the kitchen.

When she saw him, she started to pour him coffee.

"So you don't listen to me anymore?" he asked, his voice friendly.

She smiled. "I want to be here when the girls wake up. To make breakfast and show them around the house. They need to feel safe here."

"Thank you."

"You're welcome."

He drank his coffee and chugged the protein drink Hilde made for him as he tried to decide if he should wait for Nissa to get up before heading to the office or instead write her a note. She made the decision for him by walking into the kitchen.

She looked pale, and there were shadows under her eyes. When she saw him, she crossed to him and wrapped her arms around his waist.

"I didn't sleep," she admitted, leaning against him. "I kept worrying and checking on the girls. But everything is good at the hospital and the girls slept through the night."

"I'm glad on both accounts."

She straightened and greeted Hilde, then walked over to the coffee. His housekeeper stared at him, her eyebrows raised. He stared back, not saying anything. Finally Hilde simply smiled and went back to work prepping for breakfast.

"What's the plan for today?" he asked. "Don't the girls have camp?"

"Yes, but they're going to stay home with me. We'll go to the hospital this afternoon. Seeing their mom is the best thing for them. She's already explained that she's going to look terrible, but that she'll be on the mend, so they're prepared."

Nissa grimaced. "As prepared as you can be, considering what's happening. I've already called in to work and told them I quit."

He stared at her. "Your job?"

"Uh-huh. I'm sure eventually the girls will want to go back to camp, but I'm not going to push them. I'll stay close. It's better for them."

"What about your Italy fund?"

She smiled. "It's doing okay, and if I have to put off my trip for a year, then I will. This is more important."

He knew enough not to (once again) offer to pay for everything. Although that argument had had a fairly stellar outcome. Still, the trip was important to her.

She took the cup of coffee Hilde handed her. "I thought it might be fun for the girls and me to go to their house and paint their bedroom. They're a little older now and the bright pink is getting to be a bit much."

He thought about the worn furniture in the living room and dining room and how the kitchen needed updating. The girls' room was probably in the same shape.

"Marisol's going to be in the hospital for ten or twelve days, then staying here for another couple of weeks. That's almost a month. Let's redo her house."

Nissa stared at him. "What are you talking about? Redo what?"

"All of it. Paint, refinish the floors, put new carpet in the bedrooms, fix up the kitchen."

"You can't do that."

"Why not?" He leaned against the island. "I give tens of thousands of dollars away every year to charities because I think it's important to help out where I can. Marisol has been to hell and back. Why can't I help her? I know her and I like her. Unless you think she'd be upset."

"I don't know what to think." She looked at him. "Just like that?"

"Wouldn't you do it if you could?"

"Sure. In a heartbeat." She sipped her coffee. "It would be a great project for the girls, but we'd have to come up with a kitchen design and what about contractors?"

"Desmond has people," Hilde said quickly. "I could help, too."

"You're outnumbered," Desmond said with a grin. "I'd like to do this for Marisol and her daughters. Let's give them their dream house."

"You're going to make me cry again," she said, turning away.

"Happy tears?"

She nodded. "Thank you, Desmond. I'm overwhelmed by your generosity. Yes, let's do it. Let's fix up Marisol's house."

NISSA

Three days after Marisol's surgery, Nissa stood in the middle of her friend's small house and stared at the petite woman with glasses. Erica was the architect Desmond had hired to take on the remodel. Nissa had told him they were just doing a remodel and no architect was required, but he'd only smiled at her and now she knew why.

"You want to what?" Nissa asked, trying to keep her voice from rising to a shriek. Lisandra and Rylan were staring at her with identical expressions of confusion, which made her feel better. At least she wasn't the only one wondering what on earth they were talking about.

"It's being done all over the neighborhood," Erica said with quiet confidence. "Adding a second story onto the house is time-consuming and expensive, but adding a second story to the garage is much easier. Many of these older houses are well constructed, with strong foundations that can take the weight. I've already confirmed that."

She unrolled large sheets of paper and put them on the kitchen table.

"This is only a two-bedroom house," Erica said, pointing to the drawing of the original floor plan. "With a single bathroom. The master is a decent size, which gives us a lot to work with."

She flipped to a second drawing. "We take the current full bath and make it an en suite with the master and take a little from the second bedroom to give Marisol a walk-in closet. The new staircase goes here, and we put a powder room under the stairs. A toilet and sink will fit just fine."

She smiled at the twins. "For you two, we take the whole space over the garage. You each get a large bedroom with a Jack and Jill bathroom. The toilet and tub-shower combo are shared, but you'll each have a sink with a long counter and plenty of storage. The closets are about the size you have now, but you'll each have one so that doubles what you're used to." She flipped to yet another page to show the upstairs.

"As for the kitchen," Erica continued, pointing to the room next to them. "The layout works great. I suggest we just do a quick update. New cabinets that go to the ceiling to provide more storage. New flooring and new appliances. Quartz countertops." She looked around. "Fresh paint throughout the house, and that's pretty much everything."

Nissa told herself fainting would cast a pall on an otherwise happy day, so she rested her hand on the back of a chair and did her best to keep breathing.

"How long would all this take?" she asked.

"Four weeks." Erica's voice was firm.

"That's not possible. Won't we need a permit, and won't that take a while?"

Desmond smiled. "I know a guy."

"Of course you do." Nissa turned to the girls. "This is a lot to take in. You'll want to think about it, but do you have any initial thoughts?"

The girls exchanged a look.

"We want to do this," Lisandra said firmly. "Mom's been talking about wanting to update the kitchen. She was saving for it before she got sick."

The girls disappeared into their mother's bedroom, then reappeared with a folder. Inside were pictures from magazines showing different kitchens.

"Excellent," Erica said. "This will give us a sense of her style. Oh, that's a beautiful farm sink." She pointed to a picture. "And I like these cabinets very much. They'll go perfectly."

Erica began rolling up her drawings. "I'll have a preliminary design to you by this afternoon. We'll meet tomorrow to choose finishes and the work will start the day after."

"So fast?" Nissa asked, barely able to breathe.

"Why wait?" Desmond looked at the girls. "We want to get this done, don't we?"

The twins nodded.

"It's like a TV show," Rylan added. "Where they do the work and later the family gets to see their new house!"

Erica smiled at the twins. "You two are going to have to think about paint color. We'll be putting in nice durable carpeting, so I'll have samples for you to look at tomorrow, along with fixtures for your bathroom. So you have homework."

Nissa's head was spinning. "We have to pick out bedroom sets."

"I'll have ideas for those, as well," Erica told her. "Not to worry. My office is going to be one-stop shopping."

The rich really did live different lives, Nissa thought. Not that she was going to complain. The house was going to be amazing and something that Marisol would have forever. But it was a lot to take in.

"All right," she said, going for cheerful, rather than panicked. "We're going to leave Erica to work her magic and go visit your mom. How does that sound?"

"Excellent," Lisandra said. Rylan nodded.

They thanked Erica for her help. Desmond said

he was going to stay with the architect to go over a few details and would meet her at home. As she and the girls walked to the car, the twins couldn't stop talking about the house remodel.

"I hope we can get storage under the bed," Lisandra said. "And lots of shelves."

"I want one of those bunk beds where the bottom bed is a full size and the top one is a twin bed so we can have sleepovers."

"Oh, that's a good idea. And we need desks." Lisandra waited while Nissa unlocked her car. "Mom needs a little desk in her room, too. Or maybe the cabinet kind so it can be closed up and look nice when she's not using it."

"We'll have to email Erica when we get back from the hospital." Nissa smiled at them. "Are you both going to be able to keep a secret?"

The girls nodded.

"Mom deserves a good surprise," Rylan said. "And so do we."

Later that night, Nissa read to the girls until they fell asleep. At first they'd complained they were too old to hear a bedtime story, but the ritual allowed them to relax and doze off.

Nissa made sure the bathroom night-light was on, then quietly left the room. As long as they were sharing a bed, she was in the room next door. She was sure that once Marisol was released from the hospital, the twins would feel better about everything.

She went downstairs and walked into Desmond's study. He was behind his desk, typing on his computer. As always, the sight of him made her heart beat a little faster. His appeal was more than how good-looking he was. She liked that he was strong, and being around him made her feel safe.

He looked up and saw her. His intimate smile did nothing to calm the fluttering.

"Are they asleep?" he asked.

She nodded. "They're exhausted. Between staying up most of the night of their mom's surgery and dealing with everything else, not to mention the excitement of the remodel, they were ready to crash."

"What about you?" he asked, coming to his feet.

"I'm a little tired."

"I bet."

He walked to the sofa in his office, grabbing her hand on the way. He sat and pulled her down next to him, then put his arm around her so she could rest her head on his shoulder.

He was warm and just the right height to be the perfect pillow, she thought, breathing in the scent of him.

"You smell good," she said, snuggling closer.

"So do you. How was your visit with Marisol?"

"Good. She's alert and feeling better every day.

The doctors are thrilled with her progress. She should be released right on time." She raised her head to look at him. "Is it still okay for her to come here?"

"Of course. I have a hospital bed and table being delivered on Monday. Marisol will have twenty-four-hour-a-day nursing care for the first few days, then a night nurse until she goes home. A physical therapist will be here to help her recover the muscle tone she will have lost by being in bed so much and Hilde has already consulted with the hospital's dietitian to get meal ideas."

"I'm impressed." She smiled. "I shouldn't be—this is how you roll—but I'm still impressed."

"How I roll?" His voice was teasing.

"You know what I mean."

He kissed the top of her head. "I do."

"The twins said they're ready to go back to camp," Nissa told him. "Tomorrow we have our meeting with Erica, but the day after, they'll return to camp."

"You sure they're ready?"

"I think they're the best judge of when that happens. I'm going to stay home so if they start to get upset and want to leave, I can go get them."

"You're a good friend."

"I love them."

"That's very clear," he said.

"You're being incredibly generous. Thank you for that."

"I'm happy to help, and you can stop thanking me. Helping Marisol and her family makes me happy."

"So you have a selfish motive," she teased.

"Very."

She laughed. "I know that's not true. You're a good guy, letting the girls stay here, and then taking care of Marisol when she gets out of the hospital."

"There's plenty of room in the house."

She sat up and slid back a little so she could see his face. "Why this house? It's huge and while it's beautiful, you buying it isn't intuitive."

"I wanted a home for a family."

"Sure, if you're going to have seventeen kids."

He chuckled. "I was thinking two or three, but I've always had a big house. I like the location and the size of the lot. The view. I felt comfortable here."

"You're right about that," she said. "The place is huge, but also homey." She cleared her throat. "Did Rosemary like it?"

One eyebrow rose. "Asking about the ex-wife?"

"Apparently."

He shook his head. "She didn't like anything about it. She didn't want me to relocate the company headquarters. She was happy there." He paused. "Some of it was Shane, I think."

"My brother? What does he have to do with anything?"

"She and Shane didn't get along. Neither of us

could figure out why, but his theory is that Rosemary was afraid Shane could see through to the real her."

"If he had been able to, he could have saved you a disastrous marriage. Or maybe not. Maybe you were determined to marry her. I warned you off her and you didn't listen."

"Something I still regret."

"Was the divorce difficult?"

"Not legally, but I felt as if I'd failed. My parents weren't happy, more because they wanted an heir than they cared about Rosemary."

Nissa remembered what Desmond's mother had said to her at the party and wondered if the other woman would be happy with anyone he chose.

"Rosemary tried to convince me not to give up on the marriage," he added. "When she figured out I was done, she stopped trying. She accused me of never loving her."

"That's not true. You married her. Of course you loved her."

"I didn't," he admitted. "I married her because she was what was expected. Love never entered into it."

Given what she knew about his parents and how his life was different from hers, she shouldn't be surprised, but she was.

"I'm sorry," she told him. "That makes me sad."

He touched her cheek. "I never want to make you sad."

"You're not responsible for how I feel." She deliberately lightened her tone to lighten the mood. "I hope you've learned your lesson, young man. Next time marry for love."

"Yes, ma'am."

Nissa studied him. "You gave her a generous settlement, even though you didn't have to, didn't you?"

"Why do you ask that?"

She smiled. "You so did. It's your style."

"I didn't want her to end up with nothing. The money didn't matter to me."

She again thought about what his mother had said at the party.

"I don't get marrying for money," she admitted. "Marriage is about love and connection and being together always. That's what I want—solid, steady love. I want kids and a dog and maybe a couple of cats and a regular life."

"Did you think you'd find that with James?"

The unexpected question made her wince. "No."

He stared at her. "I don't understand. You were engaged to him."

"I know." She shifted so she was sitting cross-legged, facing him. "Okay, I'll tell you but you have to swear to keep it to yourself."

"Who would I tell?"

"Shane. My mother."

"Ah, good point. You have my word."

She thought about the day James had proposed. "He and I were fighting. I had been complaining about your engagement to Rosemary because you wouldn't listen to me. James was frustrated. He said I talked about you all the time and if he didn't know better, he would think that I…"

Was in love with you. That was what James had claimed but Nissa wasn't comfortable blurting that out, so she searched for a slightly less embarrassing description.

"He felt I was too involved in your engagement," she amended. "He wanted to know if he mattered at all. I said of course he did. He wanted me to prove it. Then he asked me to marry him."

Desmond frowned. "That's not exactly romantic."

"It wasn't and now, looking back, I can see that even then I wasn't sure if I loved him the right way. I mean I loved him, but not enough to want to spend the rest of my life with him."

At Desmond's look of confusion, she added, "My mom walked in right then. She'd heard him propose and had assumed I said yes. She was thrilled and immediately told my dad and then it was kind of a done deal."

"You never said yes."

"Technically, I didn't. The next day he showed up with a ring and we were engaged."

"But you didn't get married."

"I kept putting off setting a date." For an entire two years, she thought, feeling guilty about how she'd handled the situation. "I told him I wanted to save the down payment for my condo first. He wanted to know why I was so determined to buy a place on my own instead of saving for a place for the two of us."

His dark eyes gave nothing away. "What did you tell him?"

"I didn't have a very good explanation. Eventually he got tired of waiting for me. He said I either had to pick a date for the wedding or the engagement was off. I gave him back the ring."

"He was a fool," Desmond told her. "He should never have let you go."

"I'm not sure keeping me was an option."

"I'm sorry for my part in it."

She touched his arm. "Don't be. If we hadn't been fighting over you, we would have been fighting over something else. We weren't right for each other. I just wish he'd understood that. I'm afraid I hurt him."

"You're too softhearted."

"That's not possible."

She was going to say more, but just then he leaned over and kissed her. The feel of his mouth on hers had her shifting toward him. He pulled her onto his lap and deepened the kiss. Heat immediately burst to life, making her tingly all over. She wrapped her arms around his neck and kissed him back, enjoying the feel of his tongue against hers and his strong hands moving up and down her back.

When he drew back, she was breathless and hungry.

"I know you can't stay the night," he began. "But maybe you could spare an hour."

Anticipation made her smile. "An hour is very doable."

Chapter Ten

DESMOND

The remodel of Marisol's house moved forward relatively smoothly. Desmond received daily updates
from Erica, letting him know that the team was sticking to the aggressive schedule. He'd been forced to
pay a premium for some of the work to be done so
quickly, but the extra money was worth it. He wanted
the house done on time.

Late Saturday morning, he took the girls out to
see the progress. Nissa was working with Erica, picking out light fixtures and door pulls. While the twins
were excited to talk about paint colors and bedding,

they lost interest when it came to the details. He'd offered to keep them busy for a few hours. Nissa had looked doubtful but had agreed.

They arrived at the house to find workmen swarming all over the place. The second story was already framed and the new roof was nearly finished.

"Good thing it's not raining," Lisandra said as she scrambled out of his car.

"Summer's the best time to replace a roof," he agreed, making sure Rylan made it safely to the sidewalk. They walked in through the open front door and found themselves in the middle of a huge open space.

The kitchen had been gutted and the flooring had been pulled up. All the draperies were gone and shiny new windows replaced the old ones. Several patches covered the walls.

They made their way to the rear of the house. The master was empty, the windows were new and the carpet had been torn up. They could see the framing for the new closet and half bath under the stairs.

"It looks so different," Rylan breathed. "Mom's gonna love it."

They admired the kitchen cabinets stacked together in the center of the garage. Behind them were the new appliances. While the front yard was untouched, the backyard had been torn up. New sprinklers were being installed and most of the old, tired plants had been ripped out. Desmond knew that next week a new covered deck would be installed.

"This is really nice," Lisandra told him. "Thank you for being our fairy godfather."

He chuckled. "You're welcome."

"Can we get our hair cut?" Rylan asked. "It's long enough. We measured."

Desmond held up both hands. "No way. I'm not allowing you to cut your hair while your mom's in the hospital."

"Can we go to the mall?" Lisandra asked. "And then out to lunch?"

He eyed them suspiciously. "You're playing me, aren't you?"

The twins grinned at him, then each took one of his hands.

"It will be fun," Lisandra promised. "We can go to the Lego store. Boys like that."

"I haven't been to the Lego store before," he admitted. "I would like that."

An hour later, they were at the mall. The place was crowded with Saturday shoppers, but the girls stayed close. As promised, they took him to the Lego store where each of them chose something to put together. He promised to help with any of the tough parts, but suspected they would do fine on their own.

They went to the Cheesecake Factory for lunch. The twins sat across from him in their booth, each of them studying the very impressive menu. Once their orders were placed, they turned their attention back to him.

"When are we going to tell Mom about the house?" Rylan asked.

"I don't know. When do you think we should?"

The girls considered the question.

"We should wait until the very end," Lisandra said firmly. "So it's a super big surprise. Like on TV. So we shouldn't say anything now."

He looked at Rylan. "Do you agree?"

"Yes, but it's hard not to tell her when she asks what we've been doing. Plus I know the house is going to make her really happy."

"I hope it makes you happy, too."

The girls looked at each other.

"It will," Lisandra said. "We love our new rooms. They're so big and they're going to be beautiful and we can have friends over and everything. Plus the new kitchen. We can make cookies and help with dinner."

He didn't mention that Erica was replacing their mismatched cookware and dishes with new.

"I'm ready to go home," Rylan said quietly, then looked at him. "Does that make you mad? Your house is nice, but we miss our mom."

"It doesn't make me mad, at all. You've been

through a lot. First waiting for her to get a transplant, then the surgery itself. That's a lot to deal with."

Their server came and took their orders. When she'd left, Desmond smiled at them.

"I have liked getting to know you both. You've been really brave and strong."

"Mom told us we had to be," Lisandra admitted. "Sometimes it's hard. But Nissa's always there and now you're part of the family, too."

Rylan nodded. "It's like having a dad, only different." She brightened. "Like a stepdad."

The unexpected turn in the conversation made him uncomfortable. He'd never been good with people thanking him and hearing he was a part of the family was so much worse. Not that he didn't want to be—he liked the twins and enjoyed having them around. It was more that he wasn't sure he was up to the responsibility. What if he let them down?

"Are you Nissa's boyfriend?" Rylan asked.

"I, ah…"

Lisandra leaned toward him, her long hair swinging across the table. "Mom needs a boyfriend, so if you know any good ones, you should tell her."

Desmond did his best not to bolt for the exit. "You want your mom to start dating?"

The twins nodded. "It's time," Rylan told him. "We still miss our dad and we'll always love him, but our mom needs someone in her life. Someone who will love her and bring her flowers and make us all feel safe."

He was in over his head, he thought grimly, not sure what to say. Asking for a moment to text Nissa for help seemed inappropriate.

"You don't feel safe now?" he asked instead.

The twins exchanged a glance.

"We do," Lisandra told him. "Most of the time. Not while Mommy was sick, though. That was hard. We cried a lot. Now she's getting better so we can think about other stuff, like a stepdad."

Why him? Why couldn't they talk to Nissa about this? Or their camp counselor?

"Your mom might not be ready to start dating," he said with a shrug. "Hearts are tricky things. With being sick and then having the surgery, she's probably not ready to think about getting a boyfriend right this second."

"That makes sense," Rylan said. "But if you see a good one, you'll tell us?"

"I will."

He would also be letting Nissa know about the conversation so she could tell him if he'd screwed up anywhere and she had to step in and repair the damage. He liked the girls a lot—they were brave and smart and funny. But taking them on full-time? He couldn't imagine it. Yet Nissa had been willing to do just that. If Marisol hadn't pulled through the surgery, Nissa would be their legal guardian. He had no idea how she was so brave. He couldn't have done it, not for anyone. Kids needed so much, including someone who could love them back. And that person wasn't him.

NISSA

Nissa tried not to bounce in the front seat of Desmond's car, despite her growing excitement.

"I can't believe they're releasing her today," she said. "I knew it was going to be this week, but it's a day earlier than we'd thought. She's got to be so happy to be taking the next step of getting out of the hospital."

She looked at him. "Thank you again for letting her stay with you and arranging everything."

"Happy to help."

They'd gotten a call the previous evening from one of the nurses on Marisol's team. She was progressing so well, they were ready to release her, assuming things were ready at home. Nissa knew that the hospital bed and table were in place, along with a comfortable recliner.

She'd confirmed that he was good with the earlier date, then had let the nurse know they were ready to welcome Marisol home.

"Did we do the right thing with the girls?" she

asked anxiously. They'd made the decision not to tell them what was happening. Just in case something went wrong and Marisol had to go back to the hospital.

"They'll find out when they get home," he said easily. "Let them have the fun day at camp. There will be plenty of happiness to go around tonight."

"You're right." She leaned back against the seat. "My stomach is fluttering."

"You're a good friend."

"So are you. This isn't what you signed up for when you agreed to let me stay with you for a couple of months. Desmond, are you all right with the invasion? First me, then the twins, now Marisol and her nurses. There will be a physical therapist in and out, and my parents are planning to show up in a couple of weeks. It's too much."

He glanced at her. "Do you hear me complaining?"

"No, but—"

"Let it go. The house is happy with everyone running around and so am I."

"I want to believe you."

"Then you should."

He parked in the hospital lot.

"Once we know she's ready, I'll pull around front," he said.

Nissa nodded and got out.

"Let's go get Marisol so she can get started on the rest of her life."

Most of her transplant team showed up to say goodbye. Marisol hugged everyone, then waved as she was wheeled to the elevator. Nissa stayed close.

"Both your nurses have been in touch with the team," Nissa told her. "They understand where you are in your recovery and what the medication regimen is going to be. Once you're feeling better, we'll cut back on the nursing hours, but there's no rush on that."

Marisol grabbed her hand. "You're a good friend and I love you."

"I love you, too."

They left the elevator and moved toward the wide glass doors. Nissa could see Desmond was already in place, the car parked and the doors open.

As they went outside, Marisol raised her face toward the sun and took a deep breath. "This feels good," she said with a smile. "I'm a blessed woman."

Despite the recent surgery and her time in the hospital, she looked good. Her color was coming back and the faint gray cast to her skin had faded, along with the dark circles under her eyes. She was starting to look healthy again.

The drive home was uneventful. Marisol couldn't believe her beautiful room with the view of the Sound and a private patio. There were comfy chairs for her to rest in and the stone deck was smooth enough that she could use her wheelchair if she wanted.

"My goal is to get up and around as quickly as possible," she said. "I'm looking forward to my physical therapy. It's the only way to get strong again. I need to be in fighting shape to start my life!"

"We'll get you there."

Nissa and Marisol's nurse got her settled in bed. Nissa unpacked all her things, then sat in the chair next to her bed.

"The girls are going to totally freak when they find out you're here."

Marisol grabbed her hand. "Thank you so much for taking care of them."

"Of course. I was happy to step in while you had your little miracle."

Marisol yawned. "Sadly a car ride is too much excitement for me, but later, I want to talk to you. How are things with you and Desmond? Was he okay having the girls around? Anything going on that I should know about?"

Nissa thought about how she and Desmond were now much more intimate than they had been and the giant remodel waiting for Marisol, but kept quiet about it all. Her friend needed to rest.

"There's really not that much to share, but we'll definitely talk later." She kissed her cheek. "I promise."

"Good." Marisol released her hand and closed her

eyes, then immediately opened them again. "Go back to work. I know you quit to take care of the girls. I'm here now, so you can go get another temporary job to help with your Italy fund."

Nissa hesitated. "I'm not sure I should."

"You absolutely need to. I already feel guilty about the time you've spent with them when you could have been earning money. Believe me, if I had any extra money, I would insist you take it."

"Marisol, no! I'd never accept it. You're my friend. I love you and the girls and I'm honored to have been able to help. You have to believe me."

"I'll believe you when you go back to work, then."

"You're kind of bossy."

"You know it."

Nissa smiled and rose to her feet. "I'll call the temp agency right now."

"Good." Marisol closed her eyes. "See you in a bit."

"Yes, you will."

NISSA

Thirty minutes into her shift, Nissa knew she'd made a horrible mistake. Sign dancing was way harder than it looked. Her arms ached and her back wasn't happy, but the worst part of her job was the unsolicited advice people yelled as they drove by.

Apparently a large percentage of drivers felt she lacked rhythm, which was kind of insulting.

She'd thought the job would be easy—it was over a four-hour shift and the pay was decent. She'd watched several videos online to get an idea of how to twirl, dip and spin the sign. Again, it looked soooo much easier than it actually was.

Part of the problem was she kind of did lack the whole rhythm thing, and she wasn't much of a dancer. The big chicken tail she had to wear didn't help, either. It kept messing with her balance.

A pickup truck slowed and the driver's window rolled down.

"You gotta work it, lady. Put some heart into it."

The driver continued through the intersection.

She supposed being told to put some heart into it was better than other, less civilized comments she'd heard. Thank goodness she only had a half hour left on her shift. Once she got home and her body stopped hurting, she was going to have to reconsider her employment options. She was starting to think she wasn't sign-dancing material.

She tried to focus on the upbeat music playing in her earbuds, but it wasn't enough to distract her from the horn honks and the searing pain in her shoulders and upper arms. No one had warned her that the sign got really heavy in hour three. Obviously she was in much worse shape than she'd realized. She should take advantage of living in Desmond's house and use the gym there. Hadn't he mentioned it was in the basement somewhere? And while she wasn't a fan of basements in general, she had a feeling his was much less creepy than most.

"Nissa?"

She turned toward the sound of her name and saw a dark blue sedan pulling up to her corner.

"Nissa, is that you?"

She lowered the sign and walked toward the car, only to come to a stop when she saw James step out onto the sidewalk.

No, she thought, fighting humiliation. No, no, no! She was not just about to come face-to-face with her former fiancé while she was sign dancing and wearing a chicken tail.

He, of course, looked perfectly normal in suit pants and a white shirt with a blue tie. The sleeves were rolled up to his elbows—always a good look on a guy.

James was tall and handsome, with soft brown hair that was forever falling onto his forehead, and glasses that made him look smart and kind.

He moved toward her, smiling. "What are you doing?"

She held up the sign. "Working one of my crazy summer jobs."

"As a sign dancer?"

"I just started today." She rotated her free arm, feeling the pain shooting into her back. "It might not have been my best decision, but I'm—"

"Saving for something," he said, finishing her sentence. "Of course you are. You're the best saver I know." He studied her. "How are you? You look good."

"So do you."

He did. Not in any way that tempted her, but he seemed...happy.

She smiled. "Of course you're lacking a chicken tail, so obviously I look better."

He grinned. "Yeah, that tail is really something. How are you doing?"

"Good. On summer break, so that's fun, although I'm missing my kids. I've started counting down to the start of school. Oh, Marisol has a new kidney. She got a donor a couple of weeks ago and came through the surgery great. She's home recovering right now."

She and James had been together when she'd found out about her friend's illness.

"That's great news. I'm glad for her. How are the girls?"

"Excellent. They've been so brave. They're ten now."

"No, really? They're growing up fast."

They stared at each other. Nissa wondered how

they'd reached the awkward part of the conversation so quickly. At one point she and James had been planning their lives together.

"What's new with you?" she asked.

His expression turned sheepish. "I'm engaged."

"What? You are? That's amazing. Who is she? When's the wedding?" She dropped the sign, flung herself at him and hugged him. "James, I'm so happy for you."

He hugged her. "I'm happy for me, too. Her name is Cami and she's an office manager for a doctor. She's beautiful and funny and sweet and I'm crazy about her." He stepped back. "You were right about us, Nissa. When you said we weren't in love enough. I fought you on that, but you were right."

He shrugged. "What happened with you and me was kind of driven by circumstances. I always felt Desmond was between us in a way. Like he had a piece of your heart that no one else could touch. I wanted all of you."

"I'm sorry you felt that way," she said, careful not to say it wasn't true. Because sometimes she thought the same thing. That Desmond had always had a piece of her heart, and if that was true, she wasn't sure what it said about her future happiness with someone else.

"I shouldn't have proposed the way I did," he continued. "And I shouldn't have just gone along with everything when your mom overheard it. You never wanted to marry me."

"I'm sorry, James."

His smile returned. "I'm not. Because of what happened, I found Cami. It's what you talked about. The rightness of it. She and I get along much better than you and I ever did. And when she walks in the room, I know I'm the luckiest man alive."

Envy collected in her belly, but she ignored it. She was determined to be the kind of person she should be rather than pouting like a spoiled brat because James had found his one true love and she hadn't.

"Good for you," she said. "I'm so happy for you."

"Me, too. You seeing anyone?"

"No," she said, thinking she wasn't sure what she and Desmond were doing but traditional dating in no way described it. "Things are kind of crazy right now."

"You'll get there," James said kindly. "I know you will."

He reached for her again, hugging her. She returned the embrace, delighted for him and the knowledge that she didn't have to feel guilty about their relationship anymore.

Still hanging on to him, she drew back enough to see his face.

"So when's the big day? Tell me everything."

DESMOND

Desmond stared at Nissa as she smiled at James. Even from across the intersection, he could feel their connection. He'd left work to come by, not liking the idea of her dancing on a street corner. Not that he was checking up on her so much as making sure she was all right. But instead of finding her dancing around and shaking her chicken tail, he'd discovered her talking to James, of all people. Worse, she'd been hugging James, and he didn't know what the hell that meant.

The light turned green and he drove through, trying not to watch as Nissa laughed at something James said. Desmond returned to his office, planning to get buried in work, but once he got to his desk, he found he couldn't concentrate—not the way he should. Every time he looked at his computer he saw Nissa with James.

He stood and crossed to the window, staring unseeingly at the blue water of the Sound. In the distance were the San Juan islands, with Whidbey and Blackberry Islands the closest. Normally the view got his attention, but not today. All he could see was Nissa smiling up at James.

What had happened? Was it a chance encounter or were they really seeing each other? And if it was the latter, when had they gotten involved in the first place?

His phone buzzed. He walked over to his desk and saw the text was from Shane.

Sorry, man. Should have warned you earlier, but I didn't know things had changed until this morning. Hope you can handle it.

He swore silently. Shane knew? Things were serious enough that Shane knew? How had that happened? She'd told her brother about getting back together with James.

No, Desmond told himself. She wouldn't do that, not without saying something. He and Nissa were sleeping together. Okay, they'd never discussed their relationship or any expectations. Their transition from friends to lovers had been unexpected, and then Marisol's surgery and the arrival of the twins had kept them from talking, but he knew Nissa. She wasn't the kind of person who was involved in more than one relationship at a time.

Except he'd seen her with James himself. He knew that part of it was real. And Shane knew about it, so it was more than his imagination.

He dropped the phone onto his desk and collapsed in his chair. There was only one solution. When he got home, he was going to insist he and Nissa talk.

There was no way he was going to waste time speculating on the situation when he didn't have all the facts. It was the logical solution. Until then he would get his mind back on his job.

Which, as it turned out, was much easier said than done.

Chapter Eleven

NISSA

Nissa didn't consider herself a quitter, but when she returned to the office, she turned in her sign and chicken tail for good. She simply wasn't sign-dancer material. As she made her way to her car, she wondered how long her back and shoulders were going to ache. She'd always assumed her active lifestyle was good enough in the exercise department, but obviously not. She was going to have to start some kind of regular workout. Maybe a little jogging and certainly lifting weights. Her upper body strength was pathetic. And while she was at it, maybe she should look for a dance class. The world at large had not appreciated her moves.

She drove to Desmond's house, working on her plan, but as she pulled into the driveway, all thoughts of exercise and everything else fled when she saw a familiar silver Ford Explorer parked by the garage. She barely turned off her engine before grabbing her purse and flying into the house.

"Mom? Dad? You're here?"

"In the family room," her mother called.

Nissa raced into the large room and saw her parents sitting on a sofa, Marisol across from them looking happy, with good color and an easy smile.

"Look who turned up this morning," Marisol said with a laugh.

Roberta, Nissa's mother, stood and held open her arms. "I know, I know. We weren't supposed to be here for two weeks, but when you told me Marisol was out of the hospital, I said to your father that I just couldn't wait that long to see her and know she was healing."

Her mother hugged her and kissed her cheek. "Plus, we miss you, little girl."

Nissa laughed. "I think Marisol is the real draw, but I'm glad to have you here." She hugged her father. "Does Desmond know you've arrived?"

"Shane said he would text him." Roberta smiled. "That poor man is going to feel invaded."

"There are plenty of bedrooms," Nissa said, squeezing Marisol's shoulder. "The girls are going to be thrilled."

"They are," Marisol agreed. "They should be home from camp any second."

"I'm going to run upstairs and shower," Nissa said. "Don't go anywhere. I want to hear everything that's been going on."

Barry, her father, gave a mock sigh. "You two talk almost every day. How much could you have to share that the other doesn't know?"

"You know it doesn't work that way, Dad," Nissa told him with a grin.

She walked into the kitchen and found Hilde prepping for dinner.

"Your parents are so nice," the housekeeper said when she saw Nissa. "I knew they would be. Your mother said Shane and his girlfriend will be joining everyone for dinner."

Nissa winced. "That's a lot for you to get ready. Let me go take my shower, then I'll come back and help."

Hilde shook her head. "It's an easy menu and I'm happy to do the work. Desmond is alone too much. It's good to have the house full of love."

"I agree," Nissa said, before heading upstairs.

She made quick work of her shower, then blew out her hair and put on crop pants and a sleeveless shirt.

Her shoulders and back were still sore, but hopefully that would get better in the next couple of days.

She went back downstairs, hoping Desmond would be home soon. She wanted to see him. Not that there would be any sneaking around tonight, what with her parents just down the hall. Still, she always felt better when he was nearby.

She could hear conversation from the family room. The happy squeals told her the twins were back from camp. They'd always loved Nissa's parents, who acted as surrogate grandparents to the girls.

She'd just started for the family room when she heard the garage door open. She hurried to the mudroom where she waited until Desmond walked into the house. She rushed to him.

"Shane told you, right? You're not totally shocked my parents are here, right? They came early because of Marisol. They wanted to know she was all right. But this really makes for a houseful. Is that okay?"

Instead of smiling at her and reassuring her, he gave her a quizzical expression. "I saw the Explorer so I knew they'd arrived, but Shane didn't tell..." He frowned. "He texted me earlier."

"That's what my mom said. He warned you they were here."

Desmond's mouth tightened. "That wasn't exactly

what he said. I thought he was talking about something else."

She studied him, aware of a tension in his body. "What's wrong?" she asked. "There's something. Did you have a bad day at work?"

Before he could answer, her mother joined them.

"Desmond, there you are. I hope you're not too upset that Barry and I have rudely shown up with no warning."

He smiled at her as he hugged her. "Roberta, you're always welcome here. You know that."

"Thank you for saying that, even if you don't mean it." Her mother laughed. "We just couldn't stand to wait to see Marisol. She looks amazing. So much better than anytime in the past couple of years. The surgery was a blessing. I'm praying for the other family, who lost their loved one. Praying they'll find comfort in the organ donation."

She linked arms with him. "Now come join us, Desmond. We've taken over your family room. The twins are telling us about their day and Barry is going on about the Mariners. You know how that man loves his sports."

"I do."

Nissa trailed after them, hoping she was wrong about Desmond. But even as he chuckled and joined in the conversation, she couldn't help thinking there was something lurking in his eyes. Something she couldn't quite define, but knew in her gut the source wasn't anything happy.

DESMOND

Desmond escaped from the group in the family room long enough to go upstairs and change his clothes. In the few minutes he had to himself, he tried to figure out what was going on. Obviously Shane's text hadn't been about James at all, but had instead been a heads-up about Roberta and Barry showing up a couple of weeks early.

Based on his brief conversation with Hilde, he knew that Shane had also warned her, so another guest room was ready and his housekeeper was hard at work on dinner.

More pressing for him was the question about James and Nissa. Obviously Shane didn't know about them, assuming there was a them. Once again he knew he had to talk to her to get clarity on the situation, but given the crowded house, he wasn't sure how that was going to happen.

He went downstairs in time to answer the doorbell. Shane and Coreen stood on the wide porch. Shane grinned, but Coreen looked a little apprehensive.

"You got my text?" Shane asked. "I wanted to let you know you were being invaded."

"I did. And having your parents here isn't a problem."

"You say that now, dude," Shane teased. "Wait until they decide they never want to leave."

"I'd be okay with that."

He liked Roberta and Barry and in the past couple of weeks, he'd discovered he liked having people in his house. Nissa, most of all, but everyone else was welcome, too. After years of solitude, he enjoyed the conversation, the shrieks of the girls playing.

He greeted Coreen, then said, "There are a lot of people. The good news is you won't be the center of attention."

Coreen shot him a grateful look. "Thanks for saying that. I hope it's true."

Shane pulled her close and kissed the top of her head. "She can be shy. What can I say? She's charming."

As they walked toward the family room, Shane released Coreen. "You'll want to stay out of the line of fire for the next few minutes," he said quickly, before raising his voice and calling, "Do I hear my best girls?"

There was a heartbeat of silence followed by yells of, "Uncle Shane? Is that you?"

The twins raced into the foyer and flung themselves at him. Shane managed to pull them both up into his arms and squeezed them tight while giving them kisses on the cheek.

"You're so big! When did you get so big? How old are you now? Five?"

"Uncle Shane, you know we're ten," Lisandra said with a laugh.

"One day we're going to be too big to pick up and then what?" Rylan asked.

"You'll always be my best girls."

They all walked into the family room. While Shane introduced Coreen to his parents, Desmond pulled one of the sofas back a little so he could drag in a few club chairs scattered around the room. Nissa helped, tugging a small side table close.

"If you keep having this much company, you're going to have to reconfigure your family room," she teased, smiling at him.

Her expression was open and affectionate. There wasn't any guilt, no hint of her keeping secrets. But the knot in his gut said he still wasn't sure about what he'd seen.

"Who wants a drink?" he asked when there was comfortable seating for everyone.

"Do we get something fun?" Rylan asked.

Nissa headed for the kitchen. "I'm sure we can find something good for you." She glanced at Desmond. "I'll have whatever you make for my mom and Coreen."

He poured scotch for Shane and got a beer for Barry, then got out vodka, cranberry juice and the lavender simple syrup Hilde had left in the small bar refrigerator.

Nissa returned with glasses of watermelon lemonade for the girls.

"Dinner is going to be spectacular," she announced, handing the girls their drinks. "Caprese skewers to start, then pulled pork tacos with guacamole, and rice."

Lisandra rubbed her stomach. "I can't wait. I'm hungry."

"Me, too," Nissa told her, moving toward the bar. "Lavender cosmopolitans. Very fancy."

"Only the best for my ladies."

As he poured ingredients into the shaker, he felt her lightly brush his arm. Just a quick touch, to connect them. Once again he looked into her eyes and saw nothing there but happy affection. So what the hell had been going on earlier?

Once everyone had their drinks, they all took their seats. Hilde brought out a couple of bowls of tortilla chips with regular salsa and pineapple salsa.

Roberta took a chip and scooped up pineapple salsa, then took a bite.

"That's delicious," she said before turning to Coreen. "So, dear, how long have you and Shane been going out? And where did you meet?" She glanced at her son. "Some people keep their personal life far too quiet for my taste."

Coreen blushed and ducked her head. "We, ah, met at the hospital where I work."

Shane put his arm around her. "I'd seen her a few times but she was always so busy. I couldn't figure out how to approach her. Then I saw her at the Starbucks, so I waited until they called her name and I reached for her coffee at the same time."

Roberta pressed a hand to her chest. "That's so romantic. Was it love at first sight?"

Coreen blushed harder. Desmond saw Nissa straighten, her expression sympathetic.

"So I had an interesting day," she said, holding up her drink. "Maybe interesting is the wrong word."

"What happened?" Shane asked quickly in what Desmond would guess was an attempt to distract his mother from grilling Coreen.

"It turns out I'm a terrible sign dancer."

"A what?" her father asked.

Nissa laughed. "Sign dancer. You know, those people who wear a costume, hold a sign and dance on street corners."

Roberta looked concerned. "Nissa, we love you so much but you don't have much rhythm. Why would you be a sign dancer?"

"Just a temporary job, Mom. But you're right. I was terrible at it, plus it's really hard to hold a sign like that for hours and hours. I kept getting all kinds of comments." She grinned. "Some of them weren't very helpful. Even though I did my best, it wasn't a good fit for me, so I quit. I'll find something else. It's just for a few weeks, until school starts."

Desmond listened intently, waiting to see if she would say what else had happened while she was sign dancing.

"I would have loved to have seen that," Shane said.

"Oh, you would have just mocked me and driven on." She picked up her drink, then put it down. "But I did get to talk to someone really unexpected. James saw me and stopped to talk for a few minutes."

Her parents looked at her. Shane's brows drew together and Marisol tensed.

"James?" Marisol asked. "What did he want?"

Her protective tone told Desmond that Nissa hadn't said anything about James to her best friend. That had to be good news.

Nissa waved. "It was fine. Don't worry. I'm glad we got to speak. He wanted to let me know that he's found someone special and they're engaged. Her name is Cami and he seems really happy."

Her mother didn't look convinced. "Anything else?"

"Nothing." Nissa smiled. "I was happy for him and relieved. I always felt guilty about not wanting to set a date for the wedding when we were engaged."

"It was a sign," Roberta said firmly. "You weren't thrilled to be getting married. I was so sad when you broke up but it's obviously been for the best."

"That's what I said," Nissa told her. "I'm glad James and I got the chance to talk about what happened. I was happy to see him and to hear about Cami. They're getting married in about six weeks and going to Tahiti for their honeymoon."

"Tahiti?" Barry shuddered. "That's a long flight."

Roberta patted his leg. "For you, dear. Some people don't mind flying."

"I don't want to go anywhere I can't get to by car or boat," Barry grumbled. "Planes fall out of the sky."

"Ignore him," Roberta told Coreen. "Barry's a retired ferry captain. Given the choice, he would always go by boat. The only way I got him to Europe was to drive to New York and take a cruise ship across." She sighed happily. "But it was the trip of a lifetime. Every day was magical."

Conversation shifted to other forms of transportation and who had been to Europe, but Desmond kept his attention on Nissa. She was listening and laughing, completely relaxed and happy. As if nothing had happened. Which it apparently had not.

He'd been an idiot, worrying about Nissa seeing James. While they had never defined their relationship, she wasn't the type to be with two men at once. He knew that because he knew her. So why had he worried? Why had he immediately thought the worst? And perhaps most important of all, if he was so sure he didn't have a heart, then why had he cared in the first place?

NISSA

Nissa enjoyed visiting with her parents and having Shane and Coreen hang out. Everyone stayed up too late, not wanting the fun evening to end. It was after midnight when they called it a night.

While Coreen was saying good-night to Barry and Roberta, Nissa pulled her brother aside.

"You seem happy," she told him, careful to keep her voice low. "Things still going well?"

"They are." He glanced over his head toward his date. "She's pretty amazing."

"She is. So no more games?"

He looked at her. "No more games," he agreed. "I kind of freaked out that night. I feel dumb about what happened."

"What did happen? Who hurt you so badly that you weren't willing to trust Coreen?"

"The who doesn't matter, but obviously someone betrayed me. It was a long time ago, Nissa. I was in medical school."

"Why didn't I know?"

He touched her cheek. "Because I was played for

a fool and I didn't want to talk about it. I promised myself I would never trust again. But that's a lonely way to live."

"You men and your absolutes. What is it with that?"

He grinned. "We're quirky."

Coreen joined them along with Nissa and Shane's parents, cutting off any further chance for conversation.

Once Shane and Coreen had left, Nissa made sure her parents were settled. When she checked on the twins, they were already in bed and asleep. She hesitated outside of Desmond's room, but then didn't knock or go inside, instead retreating to her own. Sneaking around didn't seem like a safe bet with the house so full. Getting caught with Desmond would raise a lot of questions that she wasn't prepared to answer which, sadly, meant sleeping alone.

On the bright side, whatever had been bothering him when he'd first gotten home had worked itself out. By dinner, he was his normal friendly, charming self. Plus, now she understood her brother a little better. She was grateful he was letting himself fall for Coreen.

She took off her makeup and brushed her teeth, then crawled into bed, grateful that she could sleep in if she wanted.

She drifted off instantly only to be awakened two hours later by the night nurse shaking her.

Nissa sat up and stared at her. "What's wrong?" she asked, knowing there was no good reason for Marisol's nurse to be in her room at—she glanced at the clock on her nightstand—two thirty in the morning.

"I'm sorry to bother you, but Marisol is running a fever. It came on quickly and it's still climbing. I'm worried her body is rejecting the transplant. I've called her doctor and he wants her to come to the hospital right away."

Nissa was already moving. She got out of bed and flipped on the overhead light.

"Is she responsive?" she asked, ignoring the fear that exploded inside of her. She had to stay focused. She could give in to terror later.

"She's getting less so. I'm about to call an ambulance."

"Don't. At this time of night, we can get her there faster by driving her ourselves. Go wake Desmond, please. Tell him we need to take her to the hospital. I'll be downstairs in two minutes."

Nissa bolted for the bathroom. She splashed water on her face, then quickly pulled on clothes. She grabbed her purse before hurrying to her parents' room. Her mother woke up as soon as she entered.

"What's wrong?" Roberta asked.

Nissa quickly explained about Marisol. Her

mother got up at once, pulling a robe on over her nightgown.

"Are you going to tell the girls?"

Nissa shook her head. "Let's get her to the hospital first and find out what's happening. If it's bad…" Nissa swallowed against rising dread. "If it's serious and she's in danger, I'll call and you can bring the girls. It might be nothing." She prayed it was nothing, but didn't know if that was possible.

"I'll stay in touch," she promised. "Try to go back to sleep."

"I'll sleep later," her mother said firmly. "I'll go watch TV in your room. That's where the girls will go if one of them wakes up. I don't want them to find your room empty."

Her father had slept through the entire conversation. As they moved into the hall, her mother hugged her.

"I'll be praying," Roberta promised.

Nissa hugged her before running down the stairs. Desmond was already there, carrying a nearly unconscious Marisol out to the car. Nissa followed. The nurse was on the phone, letting the hospital know they were on their way.

Desmond drove quickly, obeying the stoplights, but speeding where he could. The lack of traffic meant the trip was made in half the usual time. Nissa watched her phone, waiting for instructions from the nurse. When the screen lit up, she read the message.

"We're to drive up to the emergency entrance," she said. "Don't park. A team will be waiting."

She glanced over her shoulder. Marisol was still in the back seat. Breathing, but her eyes were closed, and she seemed unaware of what was happening.

"I'm scared," she whispered, fighting tears.

"Me, too."

She saw the hospital up ahead. Desmond followed the signs to the ER and drove directly to the entrance. As soon as he stopped the car, medical personnel swarmed the vehicle. Marisol was lifted onto a gurney and rushed into the hospital. Desmond pulled away to go park the car.

Nissa waited for him just inside the entrance. When he walked inside, she rushed to him and let him pull her close. They hung on to each other.

"We can't lose her now," she whispered against his shirt. "We just can't. She's come through the surgery. She's getting better. I don't want her to die."

"Me, either. Let's wait and see what the doctor says. Maybe it's no big deal."

She looked at him and saw the worry in his dark eyes. "You don't believe that."

"I'm trying to convince myself."

They settled in the waiting room. A few patients came and went. An ambulance pulled up with victims of a car crash. It was close to five when Marisol's doctor walked out looking exhausted but relieved. Nissa gripped Desmond's hand, telling herself not to read too much into his expression.

He sat down across from them and exhaled. "She's all right. There's no sign of rejection, which is our biggest worry. She has a virus—nothing you or I would find difficult to shake, but it's more challenging for her. She was a little dehydrated and she admitted she's been doing too much over the past few days…"

He smiled. "Something about a party going past midnight?"

Nissa winced. "That's my fault. My parents came into town and my brother and his girlfriend came over and we stayed up late."

"She can't do that right now. She needs her rest and plenty of fluids. I made that clear to her. This was a scare, but she'll be fine. She just has to be careful and take things easy for a few more weeks."

Nissa nodded, tears filling her eyes. "I'm so sorry. I didn't mean to hurt her."

Desmond put his arm around her. "It wasn't your fault."

"It's my family. I should have thought to tell her to go to bed."

Marisol's doctor shook his head. "That's on her. She needs to read her own body's signals. She was feeling good and did too much. It happens, Nissa. It's not on you. But everyone needs to keep her condition in mind."

He stood. "You can see her if you want. We're going to keep her on fluids another hour or so and then she'll be ready to go home. Where she needs to rest." His voice was kind but stern.

"We'll make sure that happens," Nissa said. "Thank you so much."

"You're welcome. We all care about Marisol. She's been through a lot. No way we're going to lose her now."

When he'd left, Marisol texted her mother to let her know what was happening. They agreed to let the girls sleep in. Hopefully by the time they were up, Marisol would be back home and asleep in her own bed. Seeing her there would make them less scared when they heard what had happened.

They made their way back to Marisol's room. An IV dripped steadily, nearly in time with the up-and-down line of her heartbeat on the monitor. As they moved close to the bed, Marisol opened her eyes and smiled at them.

"Hey, you two. Sorry if I scared you."

Nissa squeezed her hand. "You nearly gave me a heart attack. I'm glad you're feeling better."

"Me, too. I guess I got too wild last night." She grimaced. "I should have listened. My nurse came and told me I was doing too much at least three or four times, but I ignored her." She glanced around the small room. "Next time I'll do what she says. I don't want to end up here again."

"Next time she needs to force you to obey her," Nissa said firmly.

"I'm not sure dragging me across the living room is in her contract." She looked at Desmond. "You carried me to the car, didn't you?"

He nodded. "Happy to do it."

"I really do intend to start walking everywhere on my own."

Desmond moved around the bed and took her other hand. "You're fine. You have a virus and you need to rest and stay hydrated. Those are easy things to do. In a couple of days, you'll feel better. It was a cheap lesson."

"You're right. I'm lucky that's all it was." She smiled at them both. "Thank you for being my friends."

"We love you," Nissa said. "We'll always be here for you."

"I know that. It gives me strength." She cleared her throat. "All right, you two. You look terrible. I'm going to be about an hour. Why don't you get some breakfast and then come back? By then they'll be ready to release me and we can all go home and get some sleep."

"You sure you'll be all right?" Nissa asked.

Marisol waved to the door. "I'm fine. Go eat and have coffee. You'll feel better."

Nissa looked at Desmond, who nodded.

"Text me if you need anything," Nissa said. "We won't be long."

Marisol said she would and they left. In the hallway, Desmond put his arm around her.

"You doing okay?" he asked.

"Yes. She looks good and hearing from the doctor was very reassuring."

"You know what would make you feel even better? There's a fast-food place down the street. We could go get a breakfast sandwich."

She smiled at him. "You know I love a breakfast sandwich."

He chuckled. "Yes, I do."

Chapter Twelve

DESMOND

Desmond was relieved when life quickly returned to normal. Marisol got plenty of rest and fluids and within a couple of days was feeling much better. The twins had been spared the worst of the ordeal. As everyone had hoped, they slept until after their mom was back home. They'd been told what had happened, but seeing their mom right there, looking better than she had, helped them deal with the information.

Late Saturday morning, he stepped onto the deck to join Marisol. Nissa and her parents had taken the girls to the Woodland Park Zoo for the day.

He set down two glasses of lemonade and sat in the lounge chair next to her. The temperature was perfect—midseventies, with only a few clouds in the sky. They were out of the sun and Marisol had a blanket across her legs.

"You're spoiling me," she said, picking up the glass and smiling at him. "Don't stop. I really like it. I'm just pointing out the fact that I've noticed."

"You're feeling better."

"I am. I'm seeing my doctor on Monday, but I'm sure he's going to tell me the virus is gone. I'm sleeping through the night and my energy is coming back." Her humor faded. "Sorry I scared everyone. I'm being more careful."

"Screwing up is how we learn."

"I know I learned my lesson. I'm going to do everything my doctor tells me. I don't want another trip to the ER. I'm also ready to go home. Not that you haven't been a welcoming host."

"You can stay as long as you'd like, but I do understand wanting to be in your own place. Just a few more days."

Not only because she needed to recover, but there was still work to do at the house. The kitchen was finished, as was the upstairs addition, but they were waiting on a few fixtures and a couple of pieces of furniture. The plan was for Marisol and the girls to go home next Friday.

"I'm ready to be there now, but it makes sense to wait. I need to be a little stronger to manage on my own."

"You'll have a night nurse for the first couple of weeks."

She looked at him. "Desmond, no. That's ridiculous. You've already paid for too much. I don't need a nurse."

He picked up his lemonade and smiled at her. "Too bad. One's going to be there regardless."

"You're a difficult man."

"So I've been told."

"And a generous one. You've been very good to me and I don't know why."

"I'm in a position where I can help. It makes me happy to do so. Besides, we're friends."

"We are." She smiled. "Thank you. Being here rather than in a skilled nursing facility has been a blessing. And you've been so kind to the girls."

"Not being kind," he told her. "I like them. They're fun to be with. We're all going out on the water tomorrow, and Captain Pete is going to start teaching them how to drive the boat."

"That's a terrifying thought," she said with a laugh. "They are relaxed and happy. That makes my heart glad. They've been so worried about me when they should just be worried about being kids."

She frowned. "Oh, I've been meaning to ask. What's the deal with my house?"

The unexpected question surprised him. He wasn't sure what she meant or how to answer.

"I don't know what you're talking about," he said, hoping he didn't sound evasive.

"I heard the girls mention something about a new sofa and how they hoped it was comfortable. You did something, didn't you?"

He swore silently, not sure how much she knew or how to misdirect her. Perhaps some version of the truth was the easiest solution.

"I bought you a new sofa. It's a sectional with a built-in chaise. I thought you'd need something like that to help you recover. That way you don't have to go lie down every time you want to rest for a few minutes. You can sit with the twins on the sofa and be a part of things."

Tears filled her eyes. "That's so thoughtful. You're a good, good man."

"It's a sofa, Marisol. Nothing to get too excited about."

He thought she might push back on that, but she surprised him by saying, "You don't like me saying you're kind or nice, do you?"

"I, ah, it makes me uncomfortable."

"Because you're supposed to be a badass?"

He chuckled. "I have never thought of myself as a badass."

"You know what I mean. Macho and tough."

"I lean more toward contained and self-sufficient."

She sipped her drink. "Given that, how are you dealing with the house invasion? It's hard to be contained with two ten-year-old girls running around, not to mention nursing staff and Nissa's parents."

"I like having people around."

"Then why don't you make that happen on a permanent basis?"

He smiled. "Invite random strangers to move in? That would be awkward for all of us."

"Not strangers. Regular people. Why aren't you married?"

The blunt question surprised him. "I was. It didn't work out."

"Yes, I know about Rosemary the Awful." She smiled. "That's what Nissa and I call her. It's the marrying for money thing. I don't get it. There's an old saying that if you marry for money, you're going to earn every dollar. Marriage is supposed to be about loving someone."

"The way you loved your husband?" he asked, then shrugged. "Nissa mentioned you lost him a few years ago."

"Yes, like I loved him. He was a good man and we were devastated by the loss. If I hadn't had my girls, I'm not sure I would have been able to go on. But they needed me so I had to at least pretend to keep it all together. After a while, I wasn't pretending anymore, but I still miss him every day."

He believed that. Life had been hard for her— first losing her husband, then fearing for her life as she waited for a transplant. He didn't want to think about what might have happened if one hadn't come through.

"I don't miss Rosemary," he said.

"I should hope not. But that doesn't answer the question. Why haven't you fallen in love with someone else and gotten married again?"

Not a question he wanted to answer.

"I'm not the marrying kind."

She pointed at her face. "Do I look like I believe that?"

"That doesn't mean it's not true."

"What about having children? Don't you need heirs?"

He did—for the company. His parents had certainly been on him about that during their brief visit. And he wanted children in his life. Having the twins around had only confirmed that.

"I don't have a heart."

He hadn't meant to say that, but somehow the words had slipped out. He expected Marisol to roll her eyes or tease him, but she didn't. Instead she nodded slowly.

"So that's the problem?" she asked. "You don't think you're capable of love?"

"Yes. I keep people at a distance. I've done it all my life. It's what I know. Rosemary married me for the lifestyle and the money, but I've realized I married her because she checked all the boxes. I never loved her. I don't get close to anyone."

Marisol laughed. "Uh-huh. Sure. We'll ignore how you feel about Shane and his parents, but I can't not mention Nissa. You care about her. Plus, there's all that fun stuff you're doing behind closed doors. I'm guessing there's not a lot of distance there."

"How did you know?"

"I might be recovering from surgery, but I still have eyes. I've seen the way you two look at each other. There's some naked business going on for sure. So not that kind of distance?"

"I'm talking emotionally."

"You're telling me you don't let people get close and you don't want to be close to them. But you're right there with my girls and you're letting me stay here for as long as I need. Not to mention Nissa and her parents. You've opened your home to all of us, and you're taking care of everyone. Those are not the actions of a man who doesn't have a heart. Are you in love with her?"

There was no need to ask who the "her" was. "No."

"Just like that? You don't want to think about your answer first?"

"I don't love her. I can't. She needs a good man in her life, someone who can love her with his entire heart. I can't do that and I won't hurt her."

He thought Marisol might push back, but instead she simply smiled at him. "That's a whole lot of worry for a man who claims he can't care."

"I'm not a monster."

"No, you're not, but you are hiding from the truth, Desmond. You care more than you think and I can't help but wonder if that's the real problem."

She was wrong, he knew that, but saying that wouldn't convince her. The easier path was to let her believe what she would and let the rest take care of itself.

NISSA

Nissa pressed her hand to her stomach. Nerves had been growing for the past couple of days and now they were just plain acting out. For the past two days, she'd been questioning the decision to surprise Marisol with a remodeled house. They hadn't ever talked to her about it—what if she didn't want a bunch of strangers messing with her stuff? What if she hated everything they'd done? What if she blamed Nissa for all of it and stopped being her friend? And perhaps most important of all, why hadn't she thought about all this *before* the work had begun rather than after?

"It seemed like a good idea at the time," she whispered to herself as she finished getting dressed. The twins were excited and had been bursting to tell their mom what had happened. Her parents had been to the house a couple of times already and were thrilled with the changes. But none of that mattered if Marisol wasn't pleased.

Nissa went downstairs. Her parents and Desmond were sitting at the table, finishing breakfast. She took one look at the food on their plates and felt her stomach lurch. No way she was eating anything, she thought, pouring herself a cup of coffee.

"Are you all right?" her mother asked, eyeing her. "You're really pale."

"I'm fine. Just a little apprehensive about what's going to happen today."

"Second thoughts?" her father asked. "You should have considered them before you ripped off her garage roof and built a second story."

"Barry!" Roberta glared at him. "That doesn't help."

"I'm teasing." Her dad flashed her a grin. "The house is great."

Nissa glanced toward the doorway. "Where's Marisol?"

"She's already eaten," Desmond told her. "She's getting in an early therapy appointment before we load up the cars and take her home. She can't hear us."

"Good." Nissa sat at the table, doing her best to avoid looking at any of the food. "We've kept the secret this long. I don't want to ruin that now." Besides, if Marisol was going to yell at her, Nissa would prefer to put that off, as well.

"She's going to love it," Desmond told her. "The twins were very clear about what she likes and doesn't like. We didn't push back on that."

"I'm less concerned about elements of the design than the entire project." She drew in a breath. "There's no going back now. It's done." She tried to smile. "Thank you for taking the day off work."

When the time came, they would load up his car and her parents' Explorer to transport everyone to the house.

"I wouldn't miss the big reveal," he said, his voice teasing.

"I hope it goes okay," she murmured, also hoping that at the end of the day, she and Marisol were still friends.

Two hours later, everyone pitched in to carry suitcases, clothes and toys to the two vehicles.

"We've accumulated way too much stuff," Marisol said, watching the loading process from a bench in the foyer.

She'd been instructed not to carry anything heavier than a throw pillow, and Roberta was keeping an eye on her to make sure she complied. Between Nissa, Desmond, Barry and the twins, it didn't take too many trips to load the two vehicles.

"I'll bring over anything you've forgotten," Nissa told her friend.

Marisol studied her. "You feeling all right?"

Nissa faked a smile. "Never better."

"You don't look right."

"It's my stomach," Nissa admitted, thinking it was the truth. The writhing was still there, and getting more violent by the second. "Maybe something I ate."

"You sure you're up to this move?" her friend asked. "You can stay behind if you'd like. It's not as if you haven't seen my house before."

Nissa managed a slight laugh. "I want to get you settled at home." Once that happened, however the situation played out, she would feel better…or possibly worse. Either way, there would be a change.

Marisol slowly walked to Desmond's car. The twins got in the back and Nissa rode with her parents. As they'd discussed in advance, Barry left first with Desmond fake forgetting something in the house so his car arrived about five minutes later. That way Barry, Roberta and Nissa could be waiting in the driveway and not miss Marisol's reaction.

Nissa did her best not to throw herself across the back seat and beg to be put out on the side of the road. They'd done what they'd done and if Marisol was upset, she was going to have to deal with it like a grown-up.

Quicker than she would have liked, they arrived. As they got out of the SUV, she looked at the house and thought whatever happened, the place looked fantastic.

The railings had been replaced, and the front door was now a deep blue. The new windows gleamed in the perfect summer morning. The old shrubs had been replaced with bright green hedges and the grass had been fertilized and reseeded. The second story over the garage blended seamlessly with the house's roofline.

Her mother hugged her. "You did a good thing for your friend."

"It was mostly Desmond. He paid for it all and his team did the work."

"However it happened, she's going to be delighted."

Desmond's car pulled into the driveway. Nissa kept her gaze on Marisol, waiting for the moment her friend noticed all the changes. But Marisol was busy unfastening her seat belt. She climbed out of the car.

"I can't believe I'm finally home," she said with a laugh, turning around to help the girls out of the back seat. "Not that you weren't a gracious host, Desmond, but home is where—"

She stopped talking and stared at her house, first at the porch, then at the lawn and hedges.

"What did you do?"

The twins each grabbed a hand.

"Mom, you have to come see! Everything's different and it's so beautiful." Rylan practically danced in place.

Lisandra pulled her toward the porch. "It's like on TV!"

Marisol looked from the house to Nissa and Desmond. "What did you two do?"

"It wasn't just them," Lisandra told her. "It was us and Erica and everybody."

"Who's Erica?"

"Perhaps not the point," Desmond said drily, and walked to the front door. "Shall we?"

He opened the front door, then stepped back. The girls led Marisol inside the house. Nissa followed, hoping it was going to go well.

Light spilled in through the new windows, and the hardwood floors gleamed. There was a big over-stuffed sectional in a pretty blue-green fabric and lots of pillows and a few throws. A couple of club chairs provided additional seating, and on the wall above the refurbished fireplace was a new big-screen TV.

To the right was the dining room. Marisol's big table was still there, but a new hutch filled the long wall, providing tons of storage. New linens and dishes were in place on the table and on the living room side of the huge two-level island.

Marisol pressed a hand to her mouth as tears filled her eyes. "You redid my house."

Nissa bit her bottom lip, not sure if that was an informational statement, a complaint or happiness.

"It's so beautiful," Marisol added, turning to Nissa. "Everyone did this for me?"

"Who else?" Nissa asked, moving close and hugging her. "You're not mad?"

"Mad? You've made this my dream house. I can't believe you did this."

She held out her arm to Desmond, who joined them in a three-way hug. The twins danced impatiently around them.

"There's more," Rylan said eagerly. "You have to see it all."

They went into the kitchen where Marisol ran her hands along the stunning quartz countertops. The girls pointed out the new appliances and the pull-out drawers in the lower cabinets. Marisol admired the new pots and pans and agreed she liked the dishes very much.

They went out back. New outdoor furniture sat on the new covered deck. A stainless steel barbecue stood in one corner and all the plants had been replaced with hardy, regional favorites.

Returning to the house, the twins took her down the short hall that had led to the two bedrooms. Marisol came to a stop as she pointed.

"There are stairs." She spun to face Desmond. "You gave me a second story?"

He grinned. "You didn't notice it when we drove in?"

"No. I was too busy looking at the yard and my front door." She pressed a hand to her chest, as if trying to catch her breath. "No wonder my physical therapist has been pushing me to work on my thigh strength. She knew about the stairs."

Nissa opened the door to the half bath tucked under the stairs, then pointed to the door leading to the master.

"You might want to check that out."

Marisol began to cry again when she saw her refurbished bedroom. The furniture was all new, as was the area rug over the hardwood floors. The girls showed her the remodeled bathroom and the new walk-in closet.

Nissa's throat tightened a little as she watched her friend's happy reaction.

"I was terrified she would be mad," she admitted to her mother.

"You did everything with love. She knows that."

They all returned to the base of the stairs. Desmond picked up Marisol and carried her to the second story. Once on the landing, he put her down.

"I'm going to get busy building up my strength," she said firmly. "I want to be able to get up here myself."

"You will," he told her, nodding at the two doors. "Take a look."

The girls' rooms were mirror images of each other. There was a big window, one overlooking the front of the house and the other overlooking the back. A comfy chair was tucked in the corner by the window and a desk was next to it. Bookshelves stood on either side of the closet door.

Against the north wall stood the loft-style bunk bed, with a full bed on the bottom, a built-in chest of drawers at one end and a twin bed up top. Rylan had done her room in shades of blue, while Lisandra had chosen purple as her main color.

Barry looked around. "Good use of space," he said. "Quality materials."

"It's lovely," Roberta added.

Marisol nodded, wiping away tears. "I can't take

it all in." She looked at Desmond. "I don't know how to thank you."

"Be happy and healthy. That's all I need."

"This is so wonderful," Marisol murmured. "It's like a dream."

"Except it's real!" Rylan shouted.

Everyone laughed, then started downstairs. Marisol insisted on going on her own. She went slowly, but made it to the main floor.

"Let's unload the car," Nissa said.

Marisol pointed to the stairs. "I'm going to start practicing while you do that. Five stairs today, six tomorrow, until I can make it upstairs on my own." She laughed. "My physical therapist will be so proud of me."

Nissa wanted to say she didn't have to push herself, but knew that Marisol would want to be able to reach her kids in case something happened.

They brought in all the suitcases and tote bags. It didn't take long to get it all put away. By then Marisol had finished her five stairs and was exploring the kitchen. Nissa showed her where the manuals had been stashed.

"You'll need to learn how to use your fancy new appliances," Nissa teased.

"I will. And I'm having you both over for dinner, just as soon as I'm comfortable standing long enough to cook."

Desmond leaned against the island. "Don't worry about that. I set you up with a meal delivery service through the end of September." He glanced at his watch. "You should already have an email from them telling you about the program. Nissa and Roberta picked out the first two nights' choices, but after that, you can choose from a wide selection."

"So much for not having a heart," Marisol said before hugging him.

Marisol looked at Nissa. "Thank you. It's the most wonderful surprise ever."

Nissa looked around at the beautiful new house and knew her friend was right. Not because of the things that had been purchased, but because of the love that would always live here.

Chapter Thirteen

NISSA

A few days after the fantastic house reveal, Nissa found herself feeling oddly restless. She had no idea of the cause, but she couldn't shake the sense of something being not right. She liked her temp job—she was working in a small bakery where the owner's daughter had to unexpectedly go on bed rest for the last two months of her pregnancy. Nissa was learning all about decorating cakes and cookies, not to mention working the front counter. The money was good, the owners warm and friendly. So her problem wasn't the job.

And it wasn't missing Marisol. She'd already been over to the house several times. The twins were settling in to their new rooms and her friend could make it up the stairs on her own. Everyone was happy and healthy, so they weren't what was making her feel almost itchy inside her skin.

She wandered through Desmond's large house, as if she'd left the answer in one of the beautiful rooms, but there was nothing to be found. Finally, she went into her parents' room. Her father was out golfing with Shane while her mother packed them up for their trip back home.

Nissa knocked once on the open door before walking in and sitting in the chair in the corner. Her mother looked up from the pair of jeans she was folding.

"You're troubled," Roberta said, putting down the jeans and settling on the bed. "What's wrong?"

"I don't know. I can't seem to settle."

Her mother nodded. "I know the feeling. Restlessness with a vague sense of dread."

"That describes it, but I don't know the cause, so I can't fix it. Maybe I should start a regular exercise program."

Her mother laughed. "While that would be healthy, I doubt it will solve the problem."

"I know, but it might be a distraction. I just can't figure out what's wrong. I'm ready for the new school year and I'm excited about my students. The temp job is fun and interesting. I'm saving plenty of money for my trip next summer. My renters have sent a couple of emails saying what a good time they're having. Marisol's doing great, you and Dad are healthy. So what's my problem?"

"You really don't know?"

Nissa shook her head. "Do you?"

"You're in love with Desmond."

Nissa half rose out of the chair, only to collapse back on the seat. Her mind went completely blank as she momentarily forgot how to breathe. It was as if her entire being had to reboot.

"What? No. In love with him? I can't be."

Her mother watched her with that "I'm going to be patient because I love my child, but wow is she dumb" look.

"Why would you think that?" Nissa asked. "It's ridiculous. We're friends."

Friends who slept together, Nissa thought, wondering if her mother had figured out what was going on the way Marisol had. She wasn't about to ask. Discussing love was one thing, but sex wasn't a topic she wanted to share with her mother.

"Nissa, you've had feelings for Desmond since you were fourteen years old. At first I was sure it was just a crush, but they never fully went away. Now you've been living with him and spending time with him. It makes sense that what you'd had before would grow into something bigger."

"It doesn't make sense to me," she admitted, emotionally poking at her heart to try to find out what was happening in there. In love with Desmond. Could she be? Did she want to be?

"I like him a lot," she said slowly. "He's kind and funny and generous and we have fun together. He's a really great guy. I trust him. But that's not love."

She looked at her mother. "His parents hate me."

"No, they don't."

"His mother does. Evelyn told me that I wouldn't in any way be an asset to him and that he would break my heart." She frowned, trying to remember the exact words. "Okay, maybe not that, but it wasn't good."

"Desmond isn't close to his family. He's not going to care what they think."

"He might care a little. Mom, I can't be in love with him. It would ruin everything."

"How so?"

"He doesn't think he has a heart."

She expected her mother to scoff at the suggestion, but Roberta surprised her by nodding slowly.

"I can see how he would think that. Of course not having a heart isn't the problem. It's that his heart has been broken over and over again."

Nissa raised her eyebrows. "Since when? He's

never been dumped. He's the one who ended things with Rosemary."

"Yes, but why? It's not as if he suddenly decided he didn't want to be married to her. Desmond figured out why she'd married him. He saw she was only in it for the money and not for the man. How do you think that made him feel?"

She'd never thought about the situation from that perspective. "He would have been upset." Hurt, certainly. She wasn't sure that he'd ever truly loved Rosemary, but regardless, the end of the marriage would have been difficult.

"Let's go back a little in time," her mother said. "What about all those young women who tried to get his attention because he was rich and not because of who he was?"

"You know about that?"

"It doesn't take a genius to know it happened over and over again. Before them, he was dealing with his parents. They weren't exactly nurturing when it came to their son. He was raised by a series of nannies until he was sent off to boarding school. Who loved him then? It might be easier for Desmond to tell you he doesn't have a heart, but the truth is, his has been shattered and he's afraid to trust."

Nissa tried to take it all in. Her mother's words made sense, she thought. It wasn't about him loving so much as him trusting himself enough to risk caring about someone. About her.

That last thought surprised her. Was that the problem? She didn't know how he felt about her? Oh, she knew he liked her and they were good friends, but none of that would upset her. The real problem was much bigger because there was so much potential for everything to go wrong. Staying friends with Desmond would be easy but falling in love with him would change everything.

"Loving him isn't a good idea," Nissa said, still easing into acceptance.

"Oh, I don't know. You've waited for him for a long time. Don't you think you're due for a little happiness?"

"You're ignoring everything we just talked about. Desmond can't or won't love me back."

"That's what he said," her mother told her. "Let's wait and see what he does. A man's actions often have a lot more significance. He didn't help Marisol just because he's a nice guy, he helped her because he wanted to do something nice for your friend. You're at the center of everything that's happened."

Nissa wished that were true, but she was having a hard time believing Desmond saw her as more than a friend he liked in his bed. As for her feelings…

She thought about how she felt when she was around him and how he'd always been the best man she'd ever known. She thought about his kindness and thoughtfulness, how he made her laugh and how she knew, when something bad happened, that he would be there. She thought about how she wanted to take care of him and be there for him, so he would know, no matter what, that she had his back.

"Oh, no," she whispered. "I'm in love with him."

Her mother smiled. "I'm just so proud. Now what are you going to do?"

"You mean after I throw up?"

"Yes, after that."

"I'm going to tell him." She had no idea where she would get the courage, but she was going to do it. She had to. After everything that had happened to him, Desmond needed to know she loved him fully and truly, with no reservations. Not for the money or anything else, but just for himself.

NISSA

Nissa's parents left an hour later. She spent the rest of the morning trying to get her courage together, only to fail a thousand times. It was close to three when she finally got herself downstairs and heading for his office. She was going to do it, she told herself. She was going to confess her feelings. With a little luck he would sweep her into his arms and tell her

he felt exactly the same, then whip out an engagement ring and get down on one knee.

Okay, that last bit was unlikely—most men didn't
keep a diamond ring in a spare drawer, just in case
they needed to get engaged. But having him tell her
he loved her back would be great. Or if not that, then
at least maybe he could mention he liked her a lot
and wanted to go out with her and be in a serious
relationship that would lead to love. Any other option was going to be difficult to handle, but she was
determined to be mature. Or at least not beg.

She saw his office door stood open. That had to
be a good sign, she told herself, not that she could
remember a time when it had been closed, but still.
She would take all the good signs she could get. She
wiped her suddenly sweaty hands on her shorts, then
cleared her throat and walked directly into his office.

"Hey, Desmond," she began, only to come to a
stop when she saw his expression.

He didn't look happy to see her as he stared at
her from across his desk. In fact he looked kind of
scrunchy, as if he was upset about something. No,
not upset. That was the wrong word. So was mad, but
she immediately knew there was a problem.

"What happened?" she asked. "Is everything all
right?"

Emotion flashed in his eyes, but was gone before
she could figure out what he was thinking.

"I don't want you to be in love with me."

"Wh-what?"

She managed to speak that single word before all her air rushed out and the room began to spin. The only way she stayed upright was by grabbing the back of the visitor's chair and telling herself to breathe.

"I don't want you to be in love with me," he repeated, his voice firm and completely lacking in any feeling. He might as well have been telling her that quarterly taxes were due in two weeks.

"But how did you—"

"I overheard you talking to your mother earlier."

Heat rushed to her face as humiliation swept through her. "You were there?"

"In the hall. I was coming to tell your mother she had several things in the family room. I didn't want her to forget them."

He sounded so formal, she thought as her chest tightened and her eyes burned. So distant. Gone was the man who had laughed with her, kissed her with so much passion and made every day just a little bit brighter.

"I apologize for eavesdropping."

"I hardly think that part matters." She forced herself to meet his cold gaze. "I take it you don't return my feelings."

He opened a desk drawer. For a single second,

she thought he would pull out an engagement ring. Only she knew that was wrong and when she saw what he held in his hand, she felt her heart shatter into a thousand pieces.

He stood and placed a hotel room key on the desk between them.

"I've made arrangements for you to stay there for the rest of the summer. It's a suite, so you'll have plenty of room. You can check in now. Hilde will bring you your things."

He was getting rid of her, she thought, ready to go numb anytime now. Because hurting as much as she did was going to be unendurable in the long term.

"You want me gone that quickly," she said, knowing he could hear the pain in her voice.

"You're welcome to pack them yourself," he said stiffly. "I thought you'd prefer to go as soon as possible."

She looked from him to the key and back. "I'm not running from you, Desmond. I'm sorry you feel the way you do about what's happening. Regardless, I think the hotel room is a little dramatic. You could have just said you weren't interested in me that way. I would have gotten the message."

She took a step back. "I won't need the hotel room, although the offer is generous. I'll get my things together and be out of here within the hour." She looked at him, memorizing his handsome face and wondering how long it would be before she saw him smile again.

"I appreciate what a gracious host you've been. Until today, the summer has been amazing and you've been a big part of that. What we had together…" She tried to collect her thoughts. The pain was still there, but it was contained by a new confidence and a certainty that she'd done nothing wrong.

"I've been in love with you a long time," she said softly. "Probably from the night of my prom. The feelings got buried, but they were still there. James wasn't wrong when he accused me of being too involved in your life, but I couldn't see what he was talking about."

She walked to the door, then turned back. "I'm not sure what you're afraid of. I get that you'd have trouble believing someone loved you, what with your parents and learning Rosemary was only in it for the money. But what about you and Shane? You've been friends for years. You love each other." She managed a slight smile. "In a very manly way, of course."

He didn't react to her words and her smile faded.

"My parents have been devoted to you," she continued. "And even ignoring my recent declaration, I've been very consistent about being your friend. I'm sad after all this time, you still won't trust us."

She paused, only to realize that there was nothing left to say. She'd been honest and had told him everything, and none of it had changed his mind.

"Goodbye, Desmond."

DESMOND

Desmond saw the determination in Nissa's eyes and the strength in her body. She'd laid herself bare to him and she wasn't afraid. No matter what happened, she was going to be honest to the end and accept the consequences. He wasn't sure he'd known anyone that brave.

"I don't want to hurt you," he said.

"Too late."

"This is short term. If we stayed together, I would destroy you. Everything seems fine now, but eventually you'd figure out that I'm just like my parents. That I don't have a heart and that even if I wanted to love you back, I don't know how. That would eat away at you, over time. I don't want that for you."

She smiled at him. "Really? This is for my own good? It's not like you to lie, Desmond."

"I'm telling the truth. You don't know who I am. Not deep down inside."

"I know you better than you think. I'm going to tell you something that is going to make you angry and you're not going to have anywhere to put that anger, which will frustrate you. You'll want to protect me, even more than you do now, and that will only make this situation more difficult for both of us."

"I doubt it can be much more difficult," he told her.

"Want to bet?" She raised a shoulder. "Remember the Chihuly event? How your parents came?"

"Yes." Although he had no idea how they related to any of this.

"Your mother and I had a little chat. She told me that I shouldn't get my hopes up. That you wouldn't be interested in me because I didn't bring anything to the table, so to speak. I couldn't help you in business or socially and I didn't belong in your world."

Anger erupted. "She had no right to say that."

"But say it, she did."

The anger grew and bubbled, making him want— He swore quietly. He wanted to protect her, just like she'd said. He was furious and frustrated and he wanted to take on the world, only that wouldn't do any good.

"You guessing what would happen doesn't change anything," he told her.

"I didn't guess." She drew in a breath. "You're wrong about all of it, Desmond. You're missing the entire point. If you were like your parents, if you were as heartless as you claim, why would my loving you make a difference in what was happening between us? Me loving you should only enhance the lovemaking, so in theory, you should be taking advantage of me. So what if I get my heart broken? It doesn't matter to you. Heartless people aren't moved by that sort of thing. But you do care about me, perhaps more than you want to. I'm not the problem. You are."

She shook her head. "I didn't see that before now, but it's true. You find it easy to write a check because that's safe. But giving of yourself, that's the hard thing. Because when you give, you take a risk that you'll be rejected. The only way to know love is to give love, and that's what you've been unable to do. It's not about the money or having a heart. It's about being brave enough to risk it all."

She raised her head and squared her shoulders. "I love you, Desmond, but you're right. I don't belong here. Not anymore. I need to be with someone who's willing to fight for me. I want a man who loves me back, heart and soul. I want to be someone's everything and you can't give me that."

She pressed her lips together. He thought she might say more, but instead she turned and walked out of his office. He stood where he was, listening to her move around his house, then she walked to the stairs. He would guess she'd collected her things and now she was going to pack them and leave.

She was right to go and she was right to tell him

she didn't belong to him anymore. She was right about all of it.

Unable to watch her walk away, he left his office and got in his car. When he started driving, he had no destination in mind, but he knew he wouldn't go home for a long, long time.

NISSA

Nissa drove to Marisol's house. She'd texted to say she was on her way and her friend had said she would be waiting. She was strong and brave right up until Marisol opened the front door and said, "The girls are at a friend's house, so I'm hoping you're here to see me."

Nissa started to say that was fine, but burst into tears instead. Marisol pulled her close.

"It's that man, isn't it? I knew he was going to be trouble. Want me to call around and see if I can find someone to beat him up? I might know a few people."

Despite everything, Nissa managed a smile. "You don't know anyone to beat him up."

"Not personally, but you'd be amazed what you can find on the internet."

They went inside. Nissa was together enough to look around the house and admire how great it all looked before collapsing on the sofa.

"I'm such a fool."

"No," her friend said firmly sitting next to her. "It's not wrong to love someone. He's single, you're single and you were sleeping together. Love is kind of the next step."

"Not for him."

"Then he's the fool, not you. Tell me what happened."

Nissa explained about the conversation with her mother and her decision to suck it up and confess her feelings.

"Only he already knew," she said. "He'd overheard the whole thing and when I went into his office, he handed me a key for a hotel room. He expected me to stay there instead of with him."

"Like I said, a fool."

Nissa felt her eyes fill with tears. "I'm trying to be brave, but it hurts."

"Of course it does. He broke your heart. You know you belong together, but he's not willing to see that. At least not yet."

"You can't still have hope."

"Of course I do. I'm a romantic at heart."

Nissa supposed that was because she'd loved once. Marisol knew what it was like to give her heart and get someone else's in return. She knew about the ups and downs of any relationship and how good it felt to find the right person, even if that love didn't last as long as she'd hoped.

"Do you ever think about falling in love again?" she asked.

Marisol surprised her by shrugging. "Sometimes. At first I couldn't imagine it. But since the surgery, I'm ready to start imagining the possibility, if that makes sense. He'd have to be very special to step into our lives, but I'm hoping someone like that is out there."

Nissa squeezed her hand. "I hope so, too."

She said the words automatically, but what she was thinking was how incredibly brave her friend was. To have lost her husband, faced a terminal illness, then to have gone through transplant surgery and come out the other side still believing in love was amazing.

"I want to be like you when I grow up," she said.

Marisol laughed. "Aim higher. So what's the plan? Would you like to stay here? The girls could move into one room and you could take the other."

"Thank you but I'm going to head over the mountains. I've already texted my mom and she said they're fine with me staying there until my renters leave in a couple of weeks. I'll use the time to clear my head and get ready for the upcoming school year."

"A wise plan. What about Desmond?"

Nissa didn't want to think about him, but it was impossible. Between the ache in her heart and the fact that she already missed him, there was very little else on her mind.

"He knows how I feel," she said firmly. "What happens next is up to him."

Chapter Fourteen

DESMOND

The house echoed with silence. The Monday after Nissa had left him, Hilde had told him she needed to take a couple of weeks off to visit her family in Estonia. Desmond had bought her a business-class ticket and had assured her that he would survive in her absence. She'd arranged for someone to come in a couple of days a week to do basic cleaning and make sure there was food in the refrigerator. Not that he was eating. Or sleeping.

When he was at the office, he couldn't focus on what was happening and when he was home, he wandered from room to room, listening to the echoes of conversations he and Nissa had had on nearly every topic imaginable.

He stood by her small patch of the garden, filled with random plants and flowers that had been on sale the day they'd gone to Fred Meyer. He waited by the hidden bar in the family room, hoping to hear her footsteps on the stairs so he could fix her a cocktail. He searched for items she might have left behind—a book, a scarf, a pen—anything that he would have to return, as an excuse to go see her. Only he knew he couldn't barge into her life. She'd gotten away from him and wasn't that the point of all this? To let her go live her normal life with a normal man who would love her and cherish her and give her everything she could ever want?

Thursday afternoon, he traced a now-familiar route through the house. He'd yet to find anything she'd forgotten and the quiet no longer comforted him as it had before she'd moved into his house. Instead the rooms echoed with memories and laughter, with words he couldn't quite hear and conversations that seemed to mock him.

He hadn't eaten in days and he couldn't sleep. He would guess both of those conditions were making the situation worse. The solution to the problem seemed just out of reach. Every time he thought he was about to understand all of it, his mind went blank and he started walking the house again.

He'd just returned to the kitchen, more because he'd heard it called the heart of the home than because he was the least bit hungry, when his cell phone rang. He answered it without glancing at the screen, then wished he hadn't when he heard his mother's voice.

"I called the office, Desmond. They said you weren't in. Are you ill?"

"I'm fine, Mother, how are you?"

"I'm doing well. I have some excellent news. Do you remember Pedra Holder? She was such a beautiful girl. A brilliant pianist. She married far too young and of course the relationship failed. But she's divorced now, with two darling little boys. I had lunch with her mother and she said Pedra was asking about you."

"I have no idea who she is."

"Of course you do. You met her several times when you were home on holiday. She's tall and blonde. Oh, I'll text you a picture. You'll recognize her at once. My point is, she's back in San Francisco. I'll get you her contact information. You can fly down and take her to dinner."

"Are you setting me up?"

"Why are you asking that question? Isn't it obvious? I've been patient long enough, Desmond. You decided Rosemary wasn't the one, and all this time later, you're still single. We need heirs and Pedra is a proven breeder. We'll have to be extra careful on the prenup, of course. Make sure the two children she has won't inherit anything, but that's why we have lawyers."

He sat on the bottom stair, not sure which was more shocking. His mother referring to the daughter of a friend as a "breeder" or the assumption that he was single.

"I'm not going to be going out with Pedra or anyone else, so you don't have to worry about the lawyers."

"Why ever not? Don't tell me you're actually involved with that Nissa girl. You can't be. I'll admit she's pretty enough, but Desmond, do be sensible. She's simply not one of us. She would never fit into your lifestyle. She doesn't have the education or the socialization."

His mother lowered her voice. "If you're worried about giving up great sex, then keep her on the side. Marry Pedra to have children and use Nissa for sex. You won't be the first man to solve a problem that way."

He wondered if she thought she was being helpful. He knew she wouldn't be deliberately trying to provoke him. That wasn't her way. For his mother, life was all about position and power and making sure she achieved her desired outcome.

"Have you ever been in love?" he asked. "Truly, romantically, wildly in love?"

He expected her to immediately say no and tell him love was a nonsense word invented by sad people with sad lives as a way to get through the day. But instead she sighed.

"Yes. Once. Many years ago. One of my tutors. He was just out of college, so your grandfather didn't want to hire him, but he was a brilliant mathematician and it was only for a few weeks. His name was Marcus."

He was as surprised by the wistful tone to her voice as by what she was saying.

"You were lovers?"

"Why do men always ask about sex? Fine, yes, we were lovers, but for me it was about so much more than that. Marcus was a wonderful man with a brilliant mind. He went on to join NASA where he worked on the Space Station."

"But you didn't marry him."

"What?" Her voice sharpened. "Marry him? A penniless mathematician with no family, no prospects? And do what? Live in the suburbs in a tract home, popping out babies every three years?" She laughed. "That was not my dream at all."

"But you loved him."

"Yes, and I enjoyed our time together. Then I married your father."

"It was more of a merger than a marriage."

"Call it what you will. We've been together forty years and we've provided a very comfortable life for you. Now it's your turn to do your duty. Have children, Desmond. I've been very patient and it's past time. Call Pedra and set up something, then fly down to San Francisco and dazzle her. If things go as I hope, you can move the company back to where it belongs. Your father and I are getting tired of flying to Seattle. The weather is always miserable there."

He glanced out at the warm, sunny day. "You're right, Mother."

"About the weather, or about the rest of it?"

"About everything. It is time I married and had children. It's time for me to do a lot of things."

"Excellent. I'll text you her contact information right now. And a picture of her boys. They're charming, but as I said, they won't be inheriting. All right, Desmond. Good luck. I'll speak with you soon."

She hung up and seconds later, the contact information was delivered, along with a couple of pictures of two smiling little boys.

He ignored both as he tried to process the fact that his mother had once fallen in love. He wouldn't have thought her capable. But apparently it had happened, not that she'd let her feelings stop her from moving forward with her life. Marcus had touched her heart, but there was no way he was getting his hands on her life or her bank account.

So she *could* love, but she'd chosen not to. Duty came first. Duty and money. He supposed if he were to ask his father the same question, he would get a similar answer. For all he knew, there was a woman somewhere, his father's true love, kept in a lovely apartment. Cherished but never seen in public. It was like something out of a nineteenth-century novel.

He didn't want that, he thought. He didn't want to marry for duty and produce heirs. He didn't want to get in touch with Pedra and fly down to San Francisco to take her out. He wanted to be with Nissa. He wanted a house full of family and friends. He wanted kids running around and a messy garden with plants bought on sale. He wanted Nissa smiling at him, touching him, telling him she loved him. He wanted her so much, he wasn't sure how to survive without her.

But if he went to her and told her that, then what? What happened when she found out that he was— that he was—

"What?" he asked aloud.

What exactly was she supposed to find out? That he could be difficult and moody, that sometimes he got too involved in work? That he wasn't overly fond of his parents, but he tried to be dutiful? That she made everything better and that he'd never once in his life felt about anyone else the way he felt about her?

If he really didn't have a heart, how was it possible to miss her so much? If he didn't love her, why could he so easily see a future with her? If he wasn't a normal person with regular emotions, how could he feel sorry for his parents and the ridiculous choices they'd made?

He stood up and searched through his contacts. When he landed on the right one, he pushed the call button and waited.

"I wondered how long it would take to hear from you," Barry said, his voice a grumble. "You've made my baby girl cry. That's not something a father forgives easily."

"I know. Can you meet me for coffee?"

"You in the area?"

"I'm heading over now."

"It's a six-hour drive, son."

"Not if you charter a plane."

There was a pause before Barry said, "And that's what you're going to do?"

"I am."

"All right, then. After that, we'd best meet for a beer." He gave Desmond the name of a local bar. "See you in a couple of hours."

"I'll be there."

DESMOND

The bar wasn't much to look at from the outside, or the inside, but Desmond didn't care about that. He glanced around until he saw Barry sitting at a table in the back, a beer in front of him. Desmond paused by the bar and ordered a beer for himself, then walked toward Nissa's father. When the older man looked up and saw him, Barry's expression wasn't welcoming.

"You can't buy your way out of this," Barry told him. "Not with a fancy plane or your big boat. You hurt her. She's been crying since she got here. How do you think that makes us feel? We trusted you, Desmond. We let you into our life and our hearts. We welcomed you and this is how you've repaid us."

Each word was a kick in the gut with a few of them slashing at the heart he'd claimed not to have. As Barry glowered at him, Desmond realized that he'd been more wrong than he'd realized. Shane wasn't taking his calls, and now Barry was looking at him like he'd destroyed something important.

He supposed he had—he'd broken Nissa's heart.

"I'm sorry," he began.

Barry turned away. "I don't want to hear it."

Desmond knew that wasn't true. Barry had agreed to meet him, so he must want to hear something.

"My mother wants me to marry some socialite she knows. Pedra. She already has two boys from a previous marriage, so my mom is concerned about a prenup. The other kids shouldn't inherit any part of the family empire. She pointed out that not only was Pedra a proven breeder—and that's an actual quote—if Nissa was so important to me, I could keep her on the side."

Barry's gaze narrowed. "Don't make me take you down, son. Because I can and I will."

Desmond ignored that. "I asked her if she'd ever been in love. I already knew she didn't love my father. Theirs is a true marriage of convenience. She admitted she had, many years ago, but she wasn't the least bit tempted to stay with the man she loved. She didn't see the purpose."

He looked at Barry. "That's how I was raised. I don't say that as an excuse, but as an explanation. I grew up knowing I had a duty and that the family business was all that mattered. Growing it, being more powerful. I needed to fit in with society." He thought about all those wonderful evenings with Nissa. "How to make a great cocktail. I look good in a suit, I speak four languages, but no one ever bothered to teach me or even show me how to be a good person. No one ever talked about love or respect or treating people with decency. The little I know, I learned from you and Roberta."

"Apparently you forgot the most important lesson of all," Barry told him.

"I didn't forget it, I didn't think it applied to me. I didn't think I had a heart. It never occurred to me I could love anyone, not the way you love Roberta or she loves you. I thought I wasn't capable of those kinds of feelings and because of that, I wanted to protect Nissa from me. If she fell for me, then she would be saddled with a man who could never love her back."

One of the servers put a beer in front of him, then walked away. He moved the glass in a slow circle.

"I told myself I was sending her away for her own good. Better to end things quickly, let her get over me and have a chance at someone better."

"I'm still going to beat the crap out of you," Barry said conversationally. "Just so you know."

"Fair enough." He paused to gather his thoughts. "I was wrong about all of it. About letting her go and thinking it was better for her, about not having a heart, about being incapable of loving. I do have a heart and it's a pile of rubble right now."

He looked at Barry. "I hide behind my money. I write a check instead of getting involved. I keep my distance from people because it's what I know and therefore it's easier. The only place I've ever felt that I could truly be myself was when I was with you and your family. No. Wait. That's not true. I was myself with Nissa. When she was living with me, I was exactly who I was meant to be."

He picked up his beer, then put it down. "I love her. I think I have from the night I took her to her prom. She is an amazing woman and for reasons I don't understand, she loves me back. I don't deserve her or her heart, but she wants me to have both. I'm sorry I hurt her and that I betrayed your trust in me. I want to spend the rest of my life proving myself to both of you, and most importantly to Nissa. And I'd like your permission to ask her to marry me." He paused. "If she'll have me."

Barry took a long swallow of his beer and set down the glass. "No."

Desmond hadn't expected that. He'd thought the older man would lecture him, but the flat-out refusal hit him like a sucker punch.

"You did say you'd take me down," he murmured. "You were right."

"Let me tell you something, Desmond. You've always been like a son to me, but if you want my blessing, I'll only give it on the condition that you grovel before you ask. I mean take full responsibility. No piddly-ass 'I'm sorry if you're upset' crap. Being sorry she's upset doesn't own up to what got her that way in the first place. You need to grovel like you've never groveled before."

"Yes, sir."

Barry threw a few bills on the table. "All right, let's head home. Roberta took Nissa out to the movies. They should be getting back in the next half hour or so. You'll be waiting on the front steps." Barry grinned. "Like a homeless dog."

Desmond would have been happy to wait on the curb, he thought, following the man he hoped would be his future father-in-law outside. The where didn't matter. All that was important was seeing Nissa and telling her how sorry he was and how much he loved her.

NISSA

"Oh, that movie was so charming," Nissa's mother said with a sigh as they drove back home. "I loved it. Did you like it, dear?"

Nissa faked a smile. "Sure. It was funny."

Or at least the audience had laughed a lot. Nissa hadn't seen the humor in two people thrown together in unexpected circumstances and then falling in love. The romantic comedy had reminded her of what it had been like to be with Desmond, only for her, there hadn't been a happily-ever-after ending. Instead she was heartbroken and he was, well, she didn't know where he was but he wasn't with her.

The pain hadn't faded. She would have thought it would start to get better, but obviously more time needed to pass before that was going to happen. She thought about him constantly. At night, when she managed to fall asleep, she dreamed about him. Every part of her ached for him. She'd lost her appetite and could barely get through the day.

She was giving herself the rest of the week to wallow. On Saturday her tenants were moving out. When they were gone, she would return home and get ready for the upcoming school year. She was going to find a cheap yoga class and take an Italian course. She would hang out with her friends and cook healthy meals and just plain fake it because she knew that after a while, she wouldn't be faking it anymore. She would be healed. Right now that seemed impossible, but she'd seen how strong people could be and she was determined to act just like them.

Exhausted but fairly sure she wouldn't be able to sleep, Nissa leaned back in her seat and closed her eyes. The steady sound of the motor and the movement of the car relaxed her. She opened her eyes when she felt them turn into the driveway. Her mother stopped in front of the garage.

"Would you go around front, Nissa," she said as she got out. "I think I saw a package on the porch when we drove up."

"Sure, Mom."

Nissa slung her handbag over her shoulder and walked around to the front of the house, only to come to a stop when she saw Desmond sitting on the front porch steps. He rose when he saw her.

It was late, nearly ten, and dark. The porch light illuminated the shape of him, but not his expression. She had no idea why he was here or what she was supposed to say to him. The man had broken her heart into so many pieces, she wasn't sure it could ever be whole again and yet she wanted to run to him and hold him. She wanted to feel his body against hers, listen to his voice and tell him how much she loved him and had missed him, which made her the biggest idiot ever born.

"I'm sorry," he said, walking toward her. "I was a fool. Worse, I was cruel and unthinking and I apologize for that, as well."

He stopped in front of her. "Nissa, you are the most warm, giving person I know. You embrace the world and see only the good in people. You are funny and beautiful and there are a thousand reasons why I didn't see what was right in front of me, but I didn't. Until now. I love you. I love you and I'm so sorry for not recognizing that before. I'm sorry I hurt you and I'm sorry for what you've been through. I was totally in the wrong."

She blinked, not able to take it all in. He loved her? He *loved* her?

"What happened?" she asked, not quite able to believe.

"I talked to my mother."

"I know she's not a fan, so she can't be responsible for your change of heart."

He smiled. "She is. She wants me to marry for duty, like she did. I don't want that. I don't want a cold, sterile existence. I want plants on sale and your books everywhere. I want laughter and kids and dogs and a loud, crazy house. I want a life with you. Can you forgive me just enough to let me try to earn my way back into your world?"

Deep inside a tiny spark of hope ignited. It grew and grew until she felt the pain of missing him start to ease.

"Because you love me?" she asked.

"Yes. With all my heart. For always. I love you, Nissa, and I hope you still feel the same way about me."

"I'm not the kind of person to simply fall out of love."

"That's what I was hoping you'd say."

He leaned down and kissed her. At the feel of his mouth against hers, her heart filled with all the love it had been denied. She flung her arms around him and gave herself over to his kiss and everything it promised.

They stood on the front walkway, wrapped in each other, kissing and whispering their love for several minutes. Then Desmond stepped back and dropped to one knee.

"Nissa Lang, you are the most amazing woman

I've ever known. I love you and I promise to love you for the rest of my life. Will you marry me?"

As he spoke, he drew a small ring box out of his jeans front pocket and opened it. Inside was a sparking emerald-cut diamond set in an art deco design.

"I know this isn't traditional, but it reminded me of you," he said. "If you don't like it, I'll get you something else."

She pretended to consider the offer. "Because you couldn't get a diamond solitaire? I just don't know."

He smiled. "Nissa, did you want to answer the question?"

She tugged him to his feet, then stared into his beautiful dark eyes. "Yes, Desmond. I'll marry you. I love you. I want us to be together always."

"And the ring?"

"I love it exactly as it is."

He slid the ring on her finger. It fit perfectly, which she took as a sign.

"I can't believe this is happening," she admitted. "You really came all the way here and you love me."

"I can't believe I almost lost you."

They settled on the porch stairs, his arm around her. "Where do you want to live?"

She looked at him. "We can move into my condo, but you're going to find it a little small."

He smiled at her. "I meant, is the house all right? Do you want to buy something together?"

"I love your house. It's beautiful and big. We can have lots of kids." She grinned. "After we tell my parents, we need to let Hilde know we're engaged."

"And Marisol and the girls, and Shane." He kissed her. "So I was thinking we'd go to Italy for our honeymoon."

"That would be amazing. I'd love that."

His expression turned wary. "Traditionally, the husband pays for the honeymoon. Are you going to be okay with that?"

"Of course."

"Because when I offered to pay for your trip to Italy before, you got really mad at me."

"That was totally different."

He kissed her again. "I'll never understand you."

"I think in about fifty years you'll do just fine."

He grinned at her. "Even if I'm still trying to figure it all out, I know those are going to be the best fifty years of my life."

"Mine, too."

* * * * *

MILLS & BOON

Coming next month

THE PRINCESS AND THE REBEL BILLIONAIRE
Sophie Pembroke

Isabella had to admit to herself that she was just postponing the inevitable. She had the whole rest of the week here in this glorious villa, beside this beautiful lake, with Matteo. Not making the most of it would be a terrible waste.

Throwing open the doors to the shared balcony that joined their bedrooms, Isabella let the morning air rush in, and felt her own breath rush out.

Once again, Matteo was already sitting at the table on the balcony. There were shadows under his eyes that suggested his sleep might have been as disturbed as her own. But he looked up as she appeared, and a slow smile spread across his face at the sight of her, making him look instantly younger. More free.

Was he remembering that moment last night, too? The one when he'd been close enough for her to kiss, if she'd moved her head just ever-so-slightly? Was he thinking about the suggestion he'd made to her?

The smirk on his face suggested he probably was.

"Good morning," he said, his voice low and warm. "Sleep well?"

She took her seat. "Like a baby." It wasn't a lie. Babies were notoriously bad sleepers, weren't they?

"Me too." The smirk hadn't gone anywhere. "So, how are we going to spend our second day in secluded paradise? Chess? Poker?"

He was teasing her now, but she didn't rise to it. Instead, she looked out over the lake, the balcony suddenly claustrophobic, despite all the fresh air. This villa was huge, and she knew that if she asked for space Matteo would give it to her. He wasn't the kind of man to press where he wasn't wanted, she could tell that already from the way he'd backed off last night after the merest suggestion of more.

The problem was, she wasn't at all sure she wanted him to keep backing off. But she wasn't certain enough to let him in, either.

She wanted him; she wasn't lying to herself about that anymore. But it was so against The Rules. And beyond anything she'd let herself want for so long—ever since Nate. The desire she felt for Matteo…it was overwhelming, and terrifying.

And it felt amazing, all the same.

She stared out over the water and the mountains in the distance. The June air was warm and welcoming, but the breeze from the water kept things fresh in the shady trees that surrounded the villa.

She didn't want to be trapped inside today—otherwise, this villa was no better than the palace in Augusta that she'd escaped from.

Maybe she wasn't ready to take the risk of letting Matteo in quite yet. But perhaps she could take the tiny risk of letting herself out. Just a little bit.

One small first step towards where she was almost ready to admit she really wanted to go.

To bed, with Matteo.

Isabella placed her empty coffee cup down on her saucer. "I'm going for a walk, down by the lake," she said, before she could change her mind. That would give her time and space to keep figuring out what she wanted from this week. Time away from the allure of Matteo's smile, or those green eyes that pulled her in whenever she caught them.

Matteo grinned. "Great! I'll come with you."

Continue reading
THE PRINCESS AND THE REBEL BILLIONAIRE
Sophie Pembroke

Available next month
www.millsandboon.co.uk

LET'S TALK
Romance

For exclusive extracts, competitions
and special offers, find us online:

- facebook.com/millsandboon
- @MillsandBoon
- @MillsandBoonUK

Get in touch on 01413 063232

For all the latest titles coming soon, visit
millsandboon.co.uk/nextmonth

MILLS & BOON

THE HEART OF ROMANCE

A ROMANCE FOR EVERY READER

MODERN

Prepare to be swept off your feet by sophisticated, sexy and seductive heroes, in some of the world's most glamourous and romantic locations, where power and passion collide.

HISTORICAL

Escape with historical heroes from time gone by. Whether your passion is for wicked Regency Rakes, muscled Vikings or rugged Highlanders, awaken the romance of the past.

MEDICAL

Set your pulse racing with dedicated, delectable doctors in the high-pressure world of medicine, where emotions run high and passion, comfort and love are the best medicine.

True Love

Celebrate true love with tender stories of heartfelt romance, from the rush of falling in love to the joy a new baby can bring, and a focus on the emotional heart of a relationship.

Desire

Indulge in secrets and scandal, intense drama and plenty of sizzling hot action with powerful and passionate heroes who have it all: wealth, status, good looks…everything but the right woman.

HEROES

Experience all the excitement of a gripping thriller, with an intense romance at its heart. Resourceful, true-to-life women and strong, fearless men face danger and desire - a killer combination!

To see which titles are coming soon, please visit

millsandboon.co.uk/nextmonth

  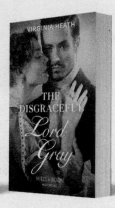

MILLS & BOON
MEDICAL
Pulse-Racing Passion

Set your pulse racing with dedicated, delectable doctors in the high-pressure world of medicine, where emotions run high and passion, comfort and love are the best medicine.

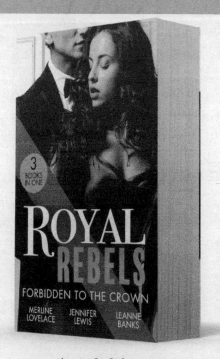